The Kingdom Of America

E. B. Alston

A Righter Book Complete and Unabridged

This is a work of fiction. All characters, events and circumstances portrayed in this story are products of the author's imagination. Any resemblance to actual people and events is purely coincidental.

Righter Publishing Company
Post Office Box 105
Timberlake, NC 27583

www.righterpublications.com

First Paperback Edition
May, 2005

Printed and bound by:
Lightning Source, Inc.
1246 Heil-Quaker Boulevard
La Vergne, TN 37076

Library of Congress Control Number: 2004097644

ISBN 0-9747735-7-3
The Kingdom of America
By E. B. Alston

Appreciation

I thank my wife, Barbara, for doing the final edit and for her support on my biggest project. I also thank all those who read the various editions of the manuscript and provided encouragement and advice about what needed to be improved. Susan Siegmann has my undying gratitude for her proofing skills and keen eye for typos. And I thank Shannon Haire for her inspired suggestions about how to improve the narrative.

Other Books by the Author

The Last Voyage of the Dan-D
The Emerald Necklace and Other Stories
Those Whom the Gods Love
And Deliver Us From Evil
The Deal of a Lifetime

Introduction

This novel began as a three part project. The first part takes place in 2020 when two brothers, one talented wife and one nephew initiated radical changes in the criminal justice system in one state. The improvement was immediate. In a highly unusual manner their process expanded beyond the original state and eventually grew to encompass a big part of the United States.

Then they tackled the education system in areas under their control and their revolutionary methods brought quick results there too.

The brothers and nephew shared one characteristic. They were autocratic in the manner of the ancient Roman emperors and they became addicted to having power.

Over a number of years their system evolved to the point that they operated a super state government within United States territory. During the period demographic changes occurred that caused the United States to have two differently focused populations. Inevitably this brought about a break up of the country.

The second part of the story is about how the nephew, Alexander, finagled himself into being head of an aristocratic government and called himself a king. He calls the new country America. He builds a militant society that holds itself as superior to other people and proves himself and his new country in their first war. He is succeeded by his cousin, George who institutionalizes the monarchy. George's son, Edward, carries it to it's apex by vigorous expansion of his territory. Edward dies in 2084 and is succeeded by his son, Henry.

The third part begins in 2084 when the United States pulls itself out of the doldrums and determines they have to fight fire with fire. They attack young King Henry's possession, the former state of Virginia in order to regain some important territory. They choose that moment because the new king is young and recently crowned. According to their intelligence he is a dilettante who loathes the military and is unfit to rule. Their intelligence proves wrong. The United States is defeated, humiliated and ends up ceding Maryland, Delaware and the District of Columbia to the Americans during peace negotiations.

The remainder of the account tells how the new territories adjust to aristocratic government and a class society. The young king is single and during a visit to Baltimore in June of 2084, he meets a young woman who is destined for greatness. Their story is told against a background of international politics and war.

Gene Alston, April 2, 2005

Appendices at the end

Appendix One	The Clark Dynasty
Appendix Two	Admissions and Annexations
Appendix Three	List Of Characters

Author's note

Every political, scientific, technological, sociological and psychological condition for the events outlined in this story exists in the United States of America in 2005.

Prologue

In the wee hours of March 24, 2084, the United States launched a surprise attack on King Henry's territory formerly known as the state of Virginia. Since 2049, Virginia had been a part of the Kingdom of America. Think about it. An absolute hereditary monarchy with a king, earls, dukes, duchesses, knights, ladies, commoners and a labor class in the US of A. Who could ever believe that lords and ladies would rule over these fair shores of freedom again?

Medieval style Catholicism is the faith of the Kingdom and the church controls education in all of His Majesty's kingdoms and empire. What happened to allow this to transpire? The seeds of change resulting in this turn of events were planted in September 2020 in North Carolina.

The Kingdom of America

Chapter One

In 2020, Graham Clark won the multi-state lottery. He used this windfall to mount a write-in campaign for the Governor of North Carolina on a draconian crime reduction platform.

Major party candidates mocked his campaign and ridiculed it as goofy. Every obstacle was put in his way. Major print and television media refused to run his paid ads. Some took his money but refused to run the ads because they objected to their content.

He was ridiculed by the "legitimate" candidates and the chattering classes. But they were not serious in their attacks because they didn't think he had a chance of winning. To them, his candidacy was a ludicrous sideshow useful only to break the monotony of the real campaign.

By 2020, the salt-of-the-earth people in the United States had no advocacy in government, the media, academia or entertainment. Nobody stood up for the man who worked hard at his job, tried to raise his family, went to church regularly and paid his taxes. The so-called silent majority was also the invisible majority because nobody paid them any attention. All media focused on criminal rights and offbeat, unproductive, lifestyles. Criminal justice had evolved to the point that hard-working honest people were labeled criminals and jailed because they defended themselves when being robbed or assaulted. In 2020 nobody spoke for them. Their only options were to vote for the least objectionable of the candidates while they were alternately ignored or ridiculed by the media.

Graham Clark was one of them and he was determined to do something about it. When the media refused to air his ads, his brother, William took leave from his job to help with the campaign. William's son, Alex, also took off to help. But the most effective campaigner was Graham's wife, Rachel. She was a natural campaigner; energetic, attractive, photogenic, witty and she had the ability to mesmerize any crowd.

After realizing that widely read newspapers and major television stations would not run their ads, Graham's team hit the old fashioned campaign trail, visiting every county in the state. This turned out to be a fortunate move because small town newspapers and radio stations didn't have the animosity toward his platform that the major media outlets had. Their constituency was the salt-of-the-earth crowd, the same as Graham's and they became his allies.

Local radio stations hosted call-in programs for the candidate and his team. It evolved into a grass-roots campaign in the fullest sense and allowed them to speak to local civic clubs, chambers of commerce and church groups.

Rachel was a good campaigner and she was in great demand. She happened to be in Charlotte the third week of October addressing the local woman's club. On Sunday morning after her address to the women, a debate was to be held on the Charlotte television station for the mainline candidates. As a joke, they invited her to participate. What they didn't know was Rachel knew how to play this game. She stole the camera the moment she walked onstage and immediately captivated the studio audience and the cameramen. From a photogenic standpoint, she didn't have a bad side. Another advantage she had was that she didn't need professional advisors, language coaches, spin experts and political consultants like the other candidates had. Her husband had done no polling, had no focus groups and no political advisors. He was running on his convictions.

The other candidates soon discovered that Rachel was an able defender of her husband's platform and rapier keen in debate. In no time, they were on the defensive as she manipulated them on camera to the point where they were an object of ridicule with the studio audience howling in derision at some of their responses. While they spent time in torturous explanations which explained nothing, Rachel was quick to respond in clear, understandable language. Everybody knew where she stood. They knew she was genuine and they instinctively understood that the man married to her had to harbor well thought out convictions and would act on them if given the chance.

The studio audience was eating out of her hand by the time the program ended. If the show hadn't been live it wouldn't have seen the light of day. But it was and Rachel made the mainline candidates look shallow, self-serving, insincere, and silly and out of touch with their constituents on statewide television. It turned out to be the most widely viewed debate of the campaign. The size of the show's audience was magnified by word-of-mouth. When she began to draw blood, those watching called their relatives, friends and neighbors who tuned in and then called their own relatives, friends and neighbors. Graham's campaign got a lot of momentum and support from that evening's debate. The joke backfired in the profoundest sense.

Prior to this election, less than a million North Carolina voters decided who would represent them. It was different this time as voters from the ignored law-abiding majority flocked to the polling booths to write in the name of the first candidate in fifty years who spoke for them.

14

Professional opinion makers were stunned. Out of three and a half million votes, Graham got over three million. There was a coattail effect as Graham's message filtered down. Some local candidates for the legislature had taken a cue from him and added a watered down version of his message to their own. This meant he would have allies in both houses of the legislature.

There were a few desultory challenges to Graham's win. But the impact of his huge majority cowed the losers and the media, who were stunned by the realization of how out-of-touch they were.

In March of 2021 both houses of the legislature passed Governor Clark's crime bill intact. To facilitate the process, the governor activated a National Guard MP battalion and kept the legislature in the legislative building until he got what he wanted.

Salient points of the bill were:

- Fleeing from a uniformed officer was made a capital crime. The act of doing so automatically convicted the person and declared him or her an outlaw to be captured dead or alive by any citizen. The bill made use of deadly force mandatory by law enforcement officers to prevent escape.
- Possession of illegal drugs with intent to sell was made a capital offense.
- Possession of illegal drugs for personal use was punished by exile from the state for a minimum of five years and a maximum of life for repeat offenders. Unauthorized return to the state was a capital offense.
- All convictions for capital crimes resulted in execution.
- The appeals process in capital cases was shortened to fourteen calendar days between conviction and execution. This appeals process was applied retroactively to all death row inmates. Twenty two days after passage of the bill there were no inmates on death row in North Carolina.

Judicial resistance followed but Governor Clark had an unexpected ally. The Chief Justice of the State Supreme Court became an early convert to the need to do something drastic to arrest society's slide into total lawlessness. Local judges who were hostile to the new regime issued injunction after injunction only to have them overturned within the hour by the State Supreme Court. Before an appeal could be advanced to a higher court, justice had already been served and there was no criminal's life to be saved. The administrative branch persuaded the judicial branch to assign capital cases to judges who agreed with the chief justice. Gradually the criminal justice system began to enforce the new laws and everywhere they did, violent criminal activity ceased.

Some local law enforcement units embraced the new system with great zeal while others refused to obey the new laws. Both county and city law enforcement officials in Durham refused to comply. The judiciary in Durham supported them. The governor set an example by putting the city and county under martial law and ordered the National Guard to disarm and abolish the Durham police and sheriff departments. They enforced the law while new law enforcement leaders and personnel were appointed who would comply. The chief justice appointed new judges. By the time responsibility was returned to local authorities, the crime rate in Durham was virtually non-existent.

Other areas adjusted differently. The sheriff and police departments in the Charlotte-Mecklenburg area embraced the opportunity to such a degree that even Governor Clark was concerned. In the Greensboro-Guilford area, the police were reluctant to enforce the new laws while the sheriff's department took immediate steps to comply. Winston-Salem-Forsyth was just the opposite. Rural counties and smaller towns adjusted promptly and had the least conflict regarding how to manage the change.

The federal judiciary was slow to react. By 2021, the federal system carried a back-breaking workload with appeal after appeal. They were unable to move expeditiously enough to counteract Governor Clark. By the time they got around to issuing a federal order, enforcement of the new laws had had the desired effect and they were powerless to force the North Carolina judiciary into line. Once the crime rate fell, the public in North Carolina was happy and all incentive to turn back the clock evaporated. Complaints from criminal rights advocates fell on deaf ears in North Carolina.

Federal Justice Officials discussed sending a team of federal marshals to arrest the governor and his staff. But the governor was warned and sent word telling them that any attempt to arrest him would result in a dangerous situation where state and federal law enforcement officers would come to battle each other. The federal government was risk adverse in the extreme because they had so many pots boiling over. Nobody on the federal side was willing to risk any kind of confrontation. They had trouble on several international fronts and over two hundred congressmen and senators were just being exposed as taking huge bribes from foreign trade lobbyists. With this going on,

Graham Clark was a very minor problem and dealing with him would have to wait.

Three months after the bill's passage, a television newswoman commented that a beauty queen dressed in a bikini with a million dollars in her purse could walk unmolested from one end of the state to the other.

In June of 2022, after much legal wrangling, the new North Carolina laws finally reached the U.S. Supreme Court. As expected, the Court ruled the North Carolina law unconstitutional. But the governor and the legislature ignored the Supreme Court. There was a precedent for this. When President Andrew Jackson was informed that Chief Justice Marshall had ruled against him in a jail custody case he refused to comply and sent word that if the Chief Justice wanted the man released he would have to do it himself. But this was an unprecedented act by a sitting governor.

Meanwhile, improvements in the quality of life in North Carolina were so dramatic that nobody in the state wanted to go back to the old days. Thoughtful observers noted that those who might yearn for the old days had left the state, or they were dead. North Carolina and its governor were reviled and ridiculed by the chattering classes all over the world.

The U.S. government remained in the midst of racking domestic and international crises and failed to take concrete action against North Carolina. As a result, North Carolina became an island of peace and safety in a lawless world. The state prospered as crime control costs plummeted.

These dramatic improvements were noticed in neighboring states and in 2024, after failing to identify a local candidate with the nerves of steel required to force the necessary change, a group in South Carolina mounted their own write-in campaign to elect Clark their governor. Resistance was more determined and more organized this time. Court orders squelched television advertisements. There wasn't enough time to counter the court action before the election was over.

Clark himself remained out of the spotlight and refused to discuss the South Carolina campaign which was being waged on his behalf except for saying that if elected, he would serve. But his very capable wife, brother, nephew and his allies in South Carolina campaigned vigorously on his behalf.

The national media had a field day over this travesty. The NAACP weighed along with opponents of the death penalty and the American Bar Association. The day before the election a federal judge issued a federal injunction forbidding anybody to write Governor Clark's name on a ballot.

Clark won anyway. And when he arrived in Columbia to be sworn in, a cadre of U.S. Marshals was there to enforce a new court order holding him in contempt if he allowed himself to be sworn in. His bodyguard of SCNG and NCNG MP's stood the marshals down.

In an unprecedented move, his tremendous margin of victory amid spectacular voter turnout made him governor of two states. There was a substantial coattail effect among local legislative candidates similar to what happened in North Carolina and the South Carolina legislature passed the governor's law in record time as criminal elements in South Carolina fled to adjoining states.

In 2025, the U.S. Supreme Court ruled that a man could not be governor of two states at the same time. North and South Carolina ignored the Supreme Court's decision. There were raging congressional speeches condemning Governor Clark. They called for military intervention but the federal government was still caught up in the influence peddling scandal. Government officials and the very congressmen who condemned Clark were too busy trying to avoid jail to take any concrete action. That is, if they could have agreed on what to do. The federal government still faced daunting new crises every day and each one brought a humbling diversity of opinions as to how to deal with them.

Meanwhile, in North and South Carolina, only one opinion mattered.

In 2026, Governor Clark appointed his brother, William, to a new post of Education Reform Chairman. William tackled the education establishment in North and South Carolina in the same draconian way his brother had tackled the criminal establishment. He methodically dismantled the existing education bureaucracy on a school by school basis and forced them to educate students by European and Japanese methods. No coddling of students, no trying to make learning "fun." The new focus was constant attention to fundamentals and a prompt weeding out of those students who were troublemakers. They were segregated from academic students, taught to do manual labor and forced to behave.

By 2030, North and South Carolina students led the nation in test scores. Graduates of colleges and universities in these two states got the pick of jobs nationwide. By 2040, sixth grade students in these two states scored higher on national tests than college graduates from other states.

In 2028, North Carolina waived the two-term maximum for a seated governor and the state of Georgia elected Clark as their governor. There was the usual media frenzy and ridicule, but the courts did not try to intervene and the governor handily beat everyone else. The feds took notice but were still preoccupied with other matters.

The governor ignored federal correspondence. This was a characteristic of the Clarks and they honed it to a very fine edge. Besides, the improved economies in North and South Carolina were noticed and the substantially increased tax revenues from those states quieted backroom complaining. After all, Governor Clark would die one day and things would become normal again. Meanwhile everybody benefited from the changes he had initiated. That is, everybody but the criminal element, the news media and lawyers who fed at the criminal rights litigation trough in those states.

In 2031, the three states under Clark enacted tort reform legislation limiting lawsuit awards to provable damage amounts. Within six weeks, civil courts were virtually idle.

Governor Clark died of cancer in May, 2032 when he was sixty five years old. His brother, William, was appointed to complete his terms in office. The new governor in turn appointed his son, Alexander, education czar for the three states.

The Clarks were autocratic in the extreme and they gathered around themselves a cadre of true believers who assisted them in every way possible. The long term effect was only those supporting the governor were allowed to obtain political office in the three states. One mind came to control all political activity. And the Clarks were very effective. By now, the three states enjoyed a level of prosperity that was the envy of the rest of the United States.

In 2034, Virginia joined the group of states that shared William Clark as governor. Its proximity to Washington, D.C. caused a great deal of alarm in the federal government. But by now what had become known as "The Group" (they consciously avoided the word "Confederation"), had a powerful lobby in Congress and a dedicated team of focused, talented, capable and honest legislators posted in influential positions. They were not shy about blocking any action they deemed unhelpful. They were virtual appointees of the governor.

Because of tax money saved by reduction of crime control costs and the favorable business climate, the group states continued to share an unprecedented prosperity. The four states provided twenty-one percent of the tax revenue collected by the federal government for the 2034 budget year.

During the period following the election of Graham Clark as governor, society within the group states slowly replaced the old sentimentality with a harder sense of reality. Their young people referred to the period after the late 1990's as the "Teddy Bear" period and ridiculed it as being excessively sentimental. In addition, subtle demographic changes occurred. People who were upset and revolted by the harder and sterner atmosphere moved to other parts of the United States, while those who craved law, order and efficiency migrated into the "Group States" as they were becoming known. They included people of high ambition and a strong desire to achieve who believed they had a better chance to realize their goals in an orderly society.

Economically, the population began to evolve away from a consumer-orientated society, towards a society focused on career, family, church and country. Ominously, "country" came to be defined as the Group States and not as the United States of America. A corroding animosity grew between the two differently focused populations. It was subtle at first but was fanned by the news media that had an early and virulent hatred of the changes wrought by the Clarks and the galling economic success these changes brought. Plus the mortifying educational reforms whose successes were evident from the onset. An additional embarrassment came when the Group's college athletic teams began to dominate national collegiate sports.

Alexander grew weary of constant vilification of his father's governorship by the mainstream media and launched a magazine called *The American Weekly*. He hired the best writers he could find and they produced a slick, high quality product without advertisements and a deliberate avoidance of negativism. Its tone was relentlessly upbeat; it never publicized or glamorized his father but instead focused on hard factual news. Commentary was always down-to-earth with a positive slant. *The American Weekly* was vilified by its competitors but their animosity and virulent attacks against it turned a lot of people off and discredited their message. The magazine never responded or referred to comments by their enemies but tended to ignore them altogether. Each week it was mailed free to every household and business in the group states. Anybody else could subscribe to it at a reasonable price and in time, it became widely read all over the United States.

In 2036, Tennessee and Kentucky joined the group. Other states attempted to enact similar reforms on their own but their leaders lacked the stubborn autocratic determination of the Clarks to force legislative support to bring them to fruition. The federal government continued to be preoccupied with wave after wave of domestic and international crises. Despite their concern over the dilution of federal authority, they feared disruption of the flow of tax dollars they could ill afford to lose. In addition, there were the ever-present focused, united, determined and influential congressmen and senators from the group states who by now dominated the national legislature.

In 2037, the Education Minister tackled physical fitness. He wanted children in his states to be physically fit. All children of school

20

age were enrolled in mandatory physical fitness programs. Boys and girls age twelve and up were required to spend summer in non-coeducational military style basic training camps where they were put through strenuous exercises and taught to be independent and resourceful. He persuaded the governor to build playgrounds and parks in urban areas, spacing them so that everyone lived within walking distance of an open play space. Sidewalks were added where there had been none and parking was not provided at the new parks. If one chose to drive, there was no place to park. Vigorous games like tag, hide and seek and dodge ball became popular again among younger children. The lack of crime allowed children and families to move freely about and relax anywhere they wanted to go.

The success of *The American Weekly* encouraged Alexander and his father so much that Alexander started a daily online and print newspaper following the same news philosophy as the magazine. They called it simply *The American News*. It was ad-free and delivered at no cost to citizens inside their territory. It enjoyed even greater success than the magazine.

In 2038, the governor, in a top-secret directive, ordered Georgia Tech to develop man-carried and vehicle-mounted nuclear powered electromagnetic weapons. In the same year he ordered NC State University to complete development of nitrogen-fueled vehicles and their support systems.

William Clark, Jr. died in 2040 at seventy-five years of age. His son, Alexander, was appointed to complete his remaining terms in office. Alexander turned out to be even more autocratic than his father and uncle had been.

In 2041, Alexander initiated a move toward internal self-sufficiency resembling a mercantilist economy where the value of exports exceeded the value of imports. He imposed stiff tariffs on foreign goods in a move to foster development of domestic industries in areas under his control. By now the consumer economy had ceased to exist within the group because there was no market for cheap, low quality goods.

The federal government threatened legal action and the world howled in protest and attempted a worldwide boycott. But it was ineffectual because of the demand for the group's products.

More new patents were issued to individuals and firms under Alexander than the rest of the Unites States combined. Businesses were well run; deliveries were always on time, prices stable and product rejects virtually non-existent. The states under Alexander's governorship were a lucrative market and his decision caused considerable economic dislocation around the world. There were many complaints and pleas for leniency but Alexander turned a deaf ear to them all. He wasn't concerned about the effect of boycotts anyway since they were striving for self-sufficiency. The U.S. Supreme Court refused to hear the case, deeming it to be of no use since their decision would not be honored or enforced.

Alexander converted to Catholicism. His wife, Celeste was already a devout Catholic. He became a zealous champion of his new faith.

Alexander also began to send agents to states adjoining his territory to lobby them for inclusion into his group. This bore early fruit. As a result he established a political organization whose purpose was to expand his territory. They recruited agents in targeted states and funded their activities on Alexander's behalf. The legality of this activity was highly questionable but by now Alexander's congressmen and women were a powerful lobby in the national legislature and it was difficult to propose anything that could conceivably handicap the Group States. The Supreme Court had long since given up trying to force Alexander do anything.

In 2044, Ohio, Indiana, Illinois, Michigan, Texas, Alabama, Mississippi and Minnesota joined the group. Alexander became more autocratic by the day. By now the group completely dominated the United States Congress.

After three years of subsidizing small startup farming enterprises, Alexander mandated a self-sufficiency rule that prevented importation of foodstuffs from outside the group which were locally available. In the same directive, restaurants were required to serve, and grocery stores required to sell locally grown fresh food items when available. Importation of frozen foodstuffs was banned if comparable fresh items were available locally. This decision caused most fast food restaurants to close.

In 2045, the Federal government admitted that sixty-seven percent of all federal tax revenues came from the group states. Governor Alexander ordered the building of a seat of government for the group in Nashville, Tennessee, including a lavish governor's mansion.

The education system began categorizing students using an old Armed Forces Qualification Test (AFQT). The scores were used to classify students for the focus of their education. Low scoring children were educated for careers as laborers, median scoring children for technical jobs and those scoring highest were trained for advanced positions in government, industry and education. One of the planned effects of this policy was to increase parental focus on their children's development.

Governor Clark was an avid history buff and expressed the opinion that an autocratic system provided the most efficient form of government. In 2046, Congress, now completely dominated by Alexander's men and women, passed legislation forbidding the posting of non-group state citizens to military bases within the group. This caused a huge alarm within the executive branch of the federal government and the Joint Chiefs of Staff but there was little they could do. The national media cried wolf about it but nobody in Governor Clark's domain paid them any attention.

In October, 2048, Governor Clark simultaneously announced successful tests of the new electromagnetic weapons and their deployment to National Guard troops within group states, the completion of the hydrogen powered vehicle project, and of the group's intention to separate from the United States at the end of 2048. The state legislatures passed strict laws to prevent the export of electromagnetic weapon technology and hydrogen vehicle fuel systems outside the group states.

Pandemonium reigned within the Federal government. They tried to negotiate, even engaging the U.N. but Alexander was way ahead of everybody and refused to consider any delay in forming a breakaway government. Indecision, disagreement, panic, other extremely challenging situations and a chronic lack of funds prevented any effective effort toward forestalling a determined Alexander.

Chapter Two

On 1 January, 2049, the group states declared themselves a free national entity separate from the United States and called it America. The United States government protested the name but since their official name was the United States of America there was little they could do. Besides, Alexander had made up his mind and once Alexander made up his mind that was it.

Alexander was an avid student of classical Greek and Roman history and one had to go back thousands of years to find a ruler who was Alexander's equal in self confidence, strong will and determination.

International recognition came promptly as much of the world rejoiced at the breakup of the United States. European diplomats predicted further disintegration of the United States and welcomed decline of its power and international influence. In all American correspondence the U.S. was to be referred to as "The United States".

The United States couldn't afford to do much about it. The breakaway deprived the U.S. government of eighty-one percent of its tax revenues.

The new nation had a population just under two hundred and eighteen million.

During internal debates about what to call their leader, Alexander suggested monarchy was his preference because of the amount of historical information available about monarchial government. Alexander was a practical man and pointed out that they wouldn't have to reinvent the wheel. As a result, in March, Alexander and Celeste were crowned King and Queen of America in an elaborate ceremony in Nashville. Alexander was to be referred to and called "His Majesty" and Celeste was to be called "Her Highness." Abbreviations in correspondence were to be HM and HH respectively. The United Nations deplored the establishment of a non-representative form of government, especially a monarchy in this modern age. But they were unable to decide what to do and didn't have any money to do anything. They could only rail at the audacity and presumption of the world's newest king.

In 2050, His Majesty's government implemented universal military service for the two highest scoring AFQT test groups. Medium scoring individuals were assigned to the ranks and those scoring highest were made officers. After graduating from military school and receiving their commissions, all officers were to be addressed as "Sir" whether in or out of uniform.

Since the American government didn't have to share tax revenues with the U.S. government, they were flush with cash. The King used part of it when he ordered the conversion of all motor vehicles to the hydrogen fuel system by 2053. He also decreed that transmission of plasma weapon technology to any foreign country was treason.

In 2051, the portion of Pennsylvania west of I-83 to Harrisburg and I-81, and the state of Maine were admitted into the Kingdom. This caused a huge uproar in the U.S. media which, for years had ignored signals expressing sentiment for the change from those areas. The U.S. government was still smarting over the successful American breakaway and was too cowed to do anything. The only comments in congress were demagogic speeches by members of Congress from New York, California and Massachusetts.

HM government ordered identification chips to be implanted in all members of the labor class to allow their locations to be tracked by satellite.

In 2052, Vermont was admitted into the Kingdom. This caused another media uproar. The U.S. government made a timid and half-hearted attempt to block it but the daunting variety of proposed solutions prevented any timely action while Alexander chalked up another success.

A Chinese agent managed to steal a plasma weapon and took it to a secret laboratory in Inner Mongolia. No one outside HM government knew that the location of every plasma weapon was tracked by satellite. The American government demanded the weapon's return. The Chinese government denied having it. With the Chinese ambassador present, the King ordered a missile attack on the site where the weapon was stored and the King refused to allow the Chinese diplomat to leave his presence until the site and the weapon were destroyed.

Twenty six hours later the Chinese launched nineteen intercontinental nuclear missiles targeting American cities. The world watched in horror as the missiles were launched and continued watching as they reversed course. Their guidance systems were reprogrammed in flight by Royal Air Force technicians to strike China's largest population centers, destroying them and killing an estimated fourteen million Chinese, including many government officials. The world was stunned. Chinese infrastructure suffered horrendous damage and with the loss of so many high government officials China was paralyzed for years.

No expression of sympathy for the Chinese government or its suffering people came from anybody in the American government.

They didn't publicly regret the millions of deaths or the destruction. Nor did they offer any humanitarian aid or rebuilding assistance to the Chinese. Alexander's every decision was setting policy for future incidents and he was not sympathetic to enemies, another characteristic of the Roman government which Alexander greatly admired. The U.S., the U.N. and other governments provided meager assistance but HM government stood aside while the Chinese suffered. The world noted the American attitude, criticized it publicly and considered this whenever they thought of doing something which might displease the Americans.

In 2054, Oklahoma, Louisiana, Arkansas, Missouri, Iowa and Kansas were admitted into the Kingdom. These defections from the U.S. caused the United States to protest to the U. N. but Alexander ignored them and refused to meet with U. N. representatives.

Algeria was annexed. In August, an American oil field engineer was kidnapped by a band of Algerian rebel tribesmen. They demanded a million-dollar ransom. Alexander refused to pay. The tribesmen threatened to torture their captive and kill him. The American ambassador relayed a message from Alexander to the Algerian dictator, Kamal Farouk, asking him to obtain the safe release of the American citizen. He pointed out that the engineer was in Algeria at Farouk's request. Farouk was either unable or unwilling to rescue him. Alexander asked for permission to send in a rescue mission consisting of a company of Royal Marines but Farouk refused to grant permission for American troops to enter his country. A British diplomat managed to visit the captive, where he witnessed him being mistreated by the Arab tribesmen. This information was passed on to the American ambassador who demanded that Farouk rescue the American. Farouk lost his temper. He told the American ambassador that foreigners were kidnapped all the time in the Middle East. The victim's government quietly paid the ransom and got their citizen back more or less the worse for wear, depending on how long it took for the funds to be delivered.

"It's the only way these tribes survive," Farouk advised the American ambassador. "They have no other way to obtain money for necessities."

The American ambassador was outraged but his ire was nothing compared to Alexander's. The French ambassador tried to caution Farouk about infuriating the Americans but he was cut off.

"America is a long way from Algeria and it's just one man," Farouk reminded him confidently.

The Algerian ambassador reported to his boss that the Americans were up in arms over the matter and the king had ordered cancellation of all military leaves, ordered mobilization of reserves, requisitioned the entire fleet of American owned cruise and cargo ships and had also requisitioned every American owned airliner.

When his foreign minister passed this information on to Farouk, his only comment was the American king was bluffing. The U.N., the French, British, German, Spanish, Italian and Russian governments all sent urgent messages to Farouk to resolve the situation before things got out of control. They also sent delegations to Alexander urging patience. Alexander heard them out but was tight-lipped about his plans. Farouk continued in his belief that Alexander was bluffing.

On the third day of the crisis, the Russians reported to Farouk that the entire Royal American Navy was steaming at top speed towards the Mediterranean. Farouk held firmly to his belief that it was all a bluff.

Meanwhile, the king ordered a clandestine rescue operation. Two companies of Royal Marines were inserted under cover of darkness and positioned on a hill above the tribal camp. At daybreak, the Royal Marines attacked the camp, killed every tribesman they could catch and rescued the American Engineer. The Americans were aware that an Algerian Army unit was located behind a low sand dune east of the rebel camp. The Algerians didn't make contact with the American force before the Marines attacked the rebel camp. Nor did they participate in the attack or make any move to protect the tribesmen. But when the American transport helicopters arrived to pick up the rescue force, the Algerians opened fire, disabling all of the transport helicopters. American escort gunships returned fire destroying all of the Algerian force's tanks and quite a number of artillery emplacements before they too were knocked down.

The Royal Marines and survivors of the pickup force put up a stiff fight and they were holding out in a ridiculously lopsided battle. The Algerian commander was in a rage. He was being humiliated by two companies of infantry. After having lost almost all of his infantry by eight a.m., the Algerian commander ordered the Americans attacked by helicopter gunships, bombed by planes and shelled relentlessly by artillery. The American's hand carried plasma weapons took a heavy toll on the Algerian gunships but were no match for the bombs and shells. After two hours of this the Americans were finally overwhelmed. Observing the devastation this tiny force had rained upon his army, the commander ordered the two wounded American survivors executed on the spot.

Farouk still assumed there would be the usual round of diplomatic protests and wrangling and now he expected some kind of censure. The U.N. was poised to intervene but they had not been contacted by the American government. The French and the German governments urged, in the strongest possible language, that Farouk offer an apology at once and to indicate a willingness to make amends for the incident. The American ambassador remained inside his compound. When Farouk demanded his presence to confer on the matter, he was told the time to confer had long passed. American news media broadcasted the events and calmly advised that the king was taking appropriate action. The Russian ambassador called on Farouk with spy satellite information about the size of the armada bearing down on his country, telling him there were no forces anywhere in the world capable of resisting the onslaught that the Americans were prepared to make. The U.N. continued to urge patience and offered to mediate.

The commander of the units who fought the Royal Marine rescue team was terrified at the prospect of taking on more Americans and urged his leader to back off.

"Your Excellency, they fought like tigers and wouldn't surrender. A thousand such men would destroy our whole army."

Farouk dismissed his worrying, "You let one little incident make you a coward. America is far away. Nobody is going to war over one man."

The Algerians had collected the surviving plasma weapons and took them to a secure location for examination and possible transfer to a country capable of reverse engineering the technology. After the Chinese incident, the American government added a remote command destruct feature. It was activated at eight a.m. Algerian time. The explosions killed another twenty-two Algerians.

On the seventh day of the crisis, Farouk publicly asked for the U.N. to intervene and offered to meet with Alexander to "iron things out." Alexander didn't acknowledge his offer.

On the eighth day the British ambassador met with Farouk to try to persuade him to surrender to the Americans before the onslaught began. Farouk dismissed the threat the Americans posed and chided the ambassador for thinking he was a quitter.

"I have a formidable military force myself," he pointed out. But after the ambassador left he put his military on heightened alert and called for a general staff meeting at nine the next morning.

Before dawn on the next day, the ninth day of the crisis, Farouk was awakened and told that American Commandos (The Tennessee 105th Royal Commando Regiment) were inside his palace compound. He was then informed that all Algerian seaports and airports were in American hands and tens of thousands of American troops were disembarking on Algerian soil. The last information he received before his capture was that the Royal American Army was on the outskirts of his capital.

Farouk was arrested along with his family, his staff, and all of his retainers. They were then unceremoniously executed. Their bodies hung from the balcony of his palace while the Royal Army and Marines overran the remainder of the country. After the fighting was over, their remains were cremated in the open and their ashes, in a televised public ceremony, were dumped into the public sewer.

The Americans completely and brutally wiped out the Algerian military. Those who fought courageously, those who tried to surrender and those who tried to hide or desert met the same fate. Heroes and cowards were brutally massacred, often cut down by the same burst. Those soldiers who somehow managed to slip away were hunted down and when found, were executed. Years after the battle, Algerian army survivors were still being hunted and executed by a vengeful American military. They lived in abject fear of discovery or betrayal by an unguarded remark made by an acquaintance or a relative. They learned that the Americans never forgot and never forgave an enemy.

While Algerian military forces were being systematically destroyed, foreign nationals were rounded up and sent out of the country. This included the diplomatic corps and that touched off a worldwide furor. After the military had been taken care of, the civilian population was methodically and ruthlessly subjugated. The slightest show of defiance was met with brutal suppression. A raised fist in a crowd was enough to bring a savage response and plasma weapons inflicted horrible wounds. Even tribesmen living in their remote mountain fastness, who had resisted being governed by outsiders since Roman times, were brought to heel or annihilated.

An Algerian colonel managed to slip into Morocco where he was given political asylum by the Moroccan government. He foolishly allowed an Italian news reporter to interview him on camera. He was still shaken by the violence of the American attack and didn't discuss anything of military value. But intelligence operatives from many countries took note and rushed to spirit him to a place where he could be interrogated and be safe from American vengeance. The Russian intelligence attaché arrived at his hotel room a few minutes after the interview was aired on television. He was too late.

The Moroccan dictator was furious that the Americans would blatantly assassinate someone to whom he had guaranteed safety. He demanded the American ambassador explain and apologize for their high handed actions. He was in a rage when the ambassador was ushered into his office.

"You had no right to come into my country and murder a citizen of my neighbor!" he shouted before the American ambassador had a chance to sit down. "I guaranteed this man safety and your government didn't even try to contact me to negotiate custody!" He was still shouting and pacing around the room, waving his arms.

The American ambassador remained calm, "It was a military necessity."

"You goddamn Americans think everything is a military necessity. You had no right to attack my neighbor."

"They failed to protect an American citizen who was in their country at their government's request."

"So," he said with heavy sarcasm, "You invaded a peaceful country, murdered its ruler and his family and massacred his military forces."

"They killed an American and the force that was sent to rescue him."

"For one man's life, you killed over two hundred thousand men?"

"Yes," the ambassador replied calmly.

The ambassador's calm demeanor angered the dictator even more. He pointed his finger at the ambassador's nose, "What would you say if I ordered all American property in Morocco seized and every American in the country arrested?"

"I would remind you that a quarter of a million American troops are less than one hour from your border and another quarter of a million can be deployed before nightfall."

He took his finger away from the ambassador's face and stared at him. He turned and walked to his desk and sat down.

Then the American ambassador coolly informed him that the 105th Royal Commando Regiment could be inside his palace in twenty-five minutes.

By month's end Algeria had a second Alexander as its ruler, one whose decisiveness and courage was at least equal to the first one. The world watched in awe as America honored a new set of heroes.

The effectiveness of American military forces in their first war shocked world leaders. The attack on Algeria happened so fast no

30

one was prepared to collect intelligence on American tactics and equipment or how the Americans fought. The only information that filtered out was that the American attack was violent and brutal and they annihilated the opposing force. But Americans were unreasonably protective of their own and most observers reasoned that the American's were angry over the kidnapping and murder of the engineer and the destruction of the rescue force. Besides, nobody liked Farouk and most of the world's leaders were glad to see him go. Still, it was unsettling how quickly the Americans mobilized, transported and deployed their forces, completely overrunning an entire country of forty-three million in a few days. The American tiger had teeth.

The effectiveness of plasma weapon technology was even more troubling and no other country had been able to develop anything like it. The Chinese incident was still too fresh in everyone's mind for anybody to consider stealing one to reverse engineer. The Russians redoubled their own efforts to develop advanced weapons as did the Chinese. More sophisticated world leaders thought of this as an isolated incident because the king and his government had never indicated a desire for an empire. American government was more interested in managing their own affairs and the prosperity of their domain. Still, the methods used by the Americans to subjugate the civilian population caused a lot of back room discussion and unfavorable media comment.

Alexander blamed himself for sending in a small, easily overwhelmed rescue force without sufficient backup. He promised himself that he or his government would never be guilty of that again. He learned a lot from the exercise. He had made his decisions more from instinct than from prior planning. He fully understood the ethical basis of the international community's reluctance to go to war as a means to settle disputes but he had been infuriated by Farouk's behavior. Once he decided to go to war, he pulled out all the stops and America went to total war footing in less than a week. This was a happy circumstance made possible by his development of the American military reserve organization and it had paid off. He learned that when faced by a determined, quick acting foe, no country was immune to transformation by an outside source. This taught the Americans two valuable lessons. One was that in order to insure their country's safety and independence, they must hone vigilance to a fine edge and always be prepared to defend American interests with fierce determination. The other was, with a trained force that could be quickly mobilized they could extend American power to any point on the globe. From that day forward, Alexander and his successors worked to develop a military capability that could be mobilized in twenty-four hours and placed in any spot on the planet. Alexander also learned that removing the upper echelons of government at the beginning of the conflict insured success.

Because of the difficulty in locating the engineer, implantation of identification and locator chips in all American citizens was ordered.

In 2055, Nebraska, South Dakota and North Dakota were admitted to the kingdom.

His Majesty also ordered the military to shift to using Latin. By 2057 all military commands would be in Latin, a language that had been in disuse for hundreds of years.

In 2057, New Mexico, Arizona, Utah, Colorado, Wyoming and Montana were admitted.

The U.S. government was losing territory at an alarming rate but couldn't agree among themselves as to what to do about it. They seethed in impotent rage at the audacious new country and its king.

The leakage continued. In 2058, Idaho was admitted and Oregon was admitted the following year. By now the United States was a shadow of its former self with only fifteen states remaining. They were California, Connecticut, Delaware, Florida, Hawaii, Maryland, Massachusetts, New Jersey, New York, Nevada, Rhode Island, West Virginia, Wisconsin, Washington and Washington, DC.

In 2060, Venezuela was annexed. Chronic unrest in this unhappy country had become intolerable to His Majesty's government. American oil and manufacturing interests were at risk due to the continuing disorder. Royal army troops occupied the country in February and a royal governor was appointed to rule the country. Alexander shrugged off the diplomatic protests and media frenzy.

In October, the king requested permission to address the United Nations on the first Monday in December. This surprised everybody. There was a lot of speculation as to why he was coming and what he wished to discuss. None of his Kingdoms were members of the U.N. and his government had historically ignored its existence.

When NBC News found out that the King and Queen would be in the city, they invited him to appear on the NBC Sunday morning panel discussion. To everyone's surprise, he agreed and arrived at the New York studio on Sunday morning, December fifth, accompanied by Queen Celeste, an aide and one bodyguard. Since most dignitaries of his status came with an entourage including bevies of advisors and security people, the studio had expected a much bigger group. Everyone was surprised to discover that the man they had been demonizing for years was quiet-spoken, down-to-earth, personable and friendly. Although he was seventy-seven years old, he was athletic, mentally alert and could have easily passed for a man in his sixties.

The carefully chosen panel of commentators included Pamela Whitehead from the *New York Times*, a virulent critic of the king and his kingdom; Paul Johnson, editor of the *Atlantic Monthly* magazine; Jason Whittemeyer, a reporter from the *Baltimore Sun* and Norman Rockefeller VI from the U.S. State Department. The discussion got off to a lively start.

The transcript of the program follows:

Whitehead: Your Majesty, you are exceedingly, some would say excessively, protective of your subjects.

HM: It is my duty to protect my people.

Whitehead: Don't you think you were overreacting when you brutally conquered Algeria because one American oil field engineer was kidnapped?

HM: No, I do not. He was in the country at the request of the Algerian government and he was murdered by the Algerian army along with the force sent to rescue him.

Whitehead: Algeria was an independent country. You violated their sovereignty when you sent in your Marines without their permission.

HM: The Algerian government engaged in treachery.

Rockefeller: But you sent your military forces in without permission.

HM: I could not stand idly by while my citizen was being mistreated and his life threatened by savages.

Whitehead: Savages? They were ignorant rubes compared to the utter brutality of your military.

HM: We do not tolerate deliberate mistreatment of Americans.

Whittemeyer: But you didn't have to subdue the civil population with such brutality.

HM: We handled it in a manner that reduced loss of life.

Johnson: American lives or Algerian lives?

HM: Both. But I must admit reducing risk to our people is always our highest priority.

Rockefeller: Don't you think your government's protective attitude toward its citizens goes a little overboard?

HM: No. We would go to the ends of the universe for any of my subjects.

Whitehead: For a kidnapped janitor?

HM: Certainly.

Rockefeller: That is remarkable, Your Majesty. And would you deal with them with the same severity as you dealt with Algeria?

HM: Yes.

Whittemeyer: Your Majesty, your devotion to the welfare of your subjects when they are abroad is well known and amply demonstrated, but what about your subjects at home?

HM: What do you mean?

Whittemeyer: It is said you are a tyrant and your Kingdom is virtually a prison.

HM (*Laughing*): Long lines of United States citizens line up at our borders every day seeking permanent entry into my country.

Johnson: I'm told that your government is very selective about whom they admit.

HM: Yes, we are.

Whitehead- Isn't that elitist?

HM: Yes, it is.

Whitehead: Then you admit that you are trying to build an elitist society?

HM: If we want to be successful, we must do exactly that.

Whittemeyer: But that's discriminatory.

HM: Definitely.

Whitehead (*Sarcastically*): So you think of such discrimination as a virtue.

HM: Absolutely.

Whitehead: What pity.

HM: Why would we want to be? Look at this great city. Is this what democracy brings?

Whittemeyer: What do you mean by that?

HM: You suffer crime, disorder and insecurity. Your infrastructure is in shambles. Your government is near bankruptcy.

Whitehead: But we are happy and free.

HM: I didn't see many happy faces on the way here this morning. I saw desperation and hopelessness.

Johnson: Living in a big city is stressful.

HM: Atlanta, Chicago and Dallas are large cities. My people in those cities are relaxed and smiling as they go unafraid about their peaceful daily lives.

They had been to those cities and knew that what the King said was true.

Rockefeller (*Changing the subject*): Your country's severity in dealing with violent criminals is well known. Do you deal with non-violent criminals as harshly as your hasty executions of violent criminals?

HM: We don't have prisons in the manner that you have in the U.S. We have secure holding areas where criminals who have committed capital crimes are kept while awaiting execution. Non-violent criminals' property is confiscated to repay the victims of their crimes and the government's expense in bringing them to justice. If that is insufficient they are placed under a kind of house arrest where they retain their jobs but they and their families live in government barracks and eat in government mess halls. They are allowed no personal property beyond the clothes on their back. They remain in this reduced state until their debt is completely repaid.

Whittemeyer: That is very harsh, Your Majesty. Suppose they cannot repay their debt during their lifetimes?

HM: The perpetrators remain in the program until they die. Surviving family members are allowed to return to normal society and their normal duties.

Whitehead: Duties! Every time an American opens their mouth they talk about 'duties'. You are punishing innocent family members.

HM: The family unit benefited from the crime whether they knew about it or not. Also, we believe this approach is an effective deterrent for crimes of this kind.

Johnson: How many are receiving this kind of punishment today?

The King looked to his aid: Aide: "A few over two-hundred in all of your territories, Your Majesty."

Johnson: That's not many considering the populations in your countries.

Rockefeller: We understand that you punish pornographers and molesters by exile.

HM: Yes, we do.

Whitehead: Why exile?

Whittemeyer: Yes, why exile for sex crimes?

HM: Because it works. There have been no repeat offenders since we started the program.

Rockefeller: Amazing! Where do you exile them to?

HM: Iran.

Whittemeyer: That is cruel! Do they have your government's protection when they're in Iran?

HM: No. They are subject to Iranian law.

Johnson: Suppose they get into trouble with the Iranians?

HM: It's their problem.

Whitehead: But they may never get back home.

HM: That is not a problem as far as my government is concerned.

Whittemeyer: That is a very hard policy, Your Majesty.

HM: So be it.

Johnson: What does the Iranian government get out of this?

HM: They are amply reimbursed for their services.

Whitehead: Nineteen years ago you embraced Catholicism. Since then the Catholic Church has played an increasingly visible and active role in education in your kingdom. Is Catholicism the official religion of your country?

HM: We respect all Christian faiths. The Catholic faith is predominant but the Church receives no public money.

Whitehead: Who funds the education system?

HM: The government.

Whitehead: So their schooling guarantees that American children will grow up as Catholics.

HM: Family guidance plays a significant part in matters such as this.

Whittemeyer: Only Christian Faiths? No other faiths are tolerated?

HM: We are a Christian nation. To be an American is to be a Christian.

Rockefeller: Yours is an intolerably narrow viewpoint.

HM: Are you a Christian?

Rockefeller: Yes, and I am also a Catholic.

HM: Don't you believe it is the true faith?

Rockefeller: Why yes, I do.

HM: Then, sir, you must have an intolerably narrow viewpoint yourself.

Rockefeller: Why, Your Majesty?

HM: What good is your faith if you don't act on your convictions?

Rockefeller did not respond. The moderator announced a commercial break at this time. The panelists continued their discussion and tensions among them continued to rise during the break. When they came back on the air, Whitehead began the discussion again.

Whitehead: What about Algeria? Are they allowed to practice the Muslim faith?

HM: The Christian faith is encouraged but the local population is allowed to practice a benign form of the Moslem faith.

Johnson: Allowed?

HM: Yes, allowed. Fanaticism is not tolerated.

Rockefeller: Who manages the education system in Algeria?

HM: The Catholic Church.

Whitehead: Isn't imposing your religious beliefs on others immoral?

HM: It is if you assume religion is an entirely social product.

Whitehead: (Stung): So you believe Catholic Christianity is a dispensation from God?

HM: Yes, I do.

Johnson: That is a remarkable attitude this day and age.

HM: We must adjust our beliefs to be in accord with our Maker's will for the ages, not for the age.

Whitehead: Is it true you have a network of spies in every country in the world?

HM: Every other country has a network of spies in my kingdoms.

Whittemeyer: But yours is reputed to be the most effective intelligence gathering organization in the world.

HM: I sincerely hope so.

37

Johnson: Do you have spies in this city?

HM: Yes, we do.

Whittemeyer: In this studio?

HM: I cannot answer any more questions about our intelligence network. We must change the subject.

Johnson: You have a very large military force for a country the size of yours.

HM: We must always be prepared to defend ourselves.

Whitehead (*Scoffing*): No military force on earth is capable of overwhelming your kingdom, Your Majesty. I would suggest it is also a very effective foreign policy instrument?

HM: We have utilized our resources in that manner when other methods have failed.

Johnson: So you bluff your opponents by threatening the use of military force to achieve diplomatic objectives.

HM: We never bluff and we don't threaten the use of force to achieve any end.

Whittemeyer: Are you suggesting that when you say you are going to attack a country, an attack from your military is inevitable.

HM: Yes, it is.

Whitehead: And what circumstance could influence you not to go to war once you have made the decision?

HM: Our enemy's unconditional surrender.

Johnson: But you could achieve many of your aims without going to such extremes.

HM: We can more easily achieve our goals by diplomacy backed by a powerful military force and the certain knowledge that we will use it than by diplomacy alone.

Whittemeyer: That is true, but what about world opinion? You have few friends outside of Great Britain, Australia, New Zealand, Israel and your vassal states.

HM: That is why we must remain strong.

Johnson: Don't you think a little effort towards making your rule more popular might make a difference in alleviating the much of the world's hostility towards your government?

HM: If I may quote Napoleon, "If the king is popular, the reign is a failure."

Whitehead: Napoleon was a spectacular failure. He practically destroyed France.

HM: He committed military folly but many of his legislative and judicial reforms remain in place today.

Rockefeller: So you think it is a waste of time to cultivate world opinion.

HM: World opinion is a chimera. We might cultivate one and alienate many.

Whittemeyer: Nobody knows how you conduct military activities. Your government does not permit outside observers to be with your military during engagements or training exercises.

HM: Our military activities are secret.

Whittemeyer: But there are persistent rumors attesting to the brutality of your military in battle. Could you explain why?

HM: War is a brutal activity. It cannot be any other way.

Johnson: But your military has raised the bar.

HM: We do not make war for the benefit of our enemies.

Whitehead: But must they be so brutal, Your Majesty?

HM: In war, winning is everything and preventing the recurrence of war is most important. We do not wish to fight the same troops again.

Whittemeyer: There are also persistent rumors about how you brutally crushed the Algerian civil population.

HM: We pacified the civil population to prepare them to be a component of my kingdoms. We have a strong aversion to the kind of resistance the U.S. tolerated in its forays of this kind, like the Philippines, Vietnam and Iraq.

Whitehead: So you don't tolerate opposition to your government?

HM: No, we do not.

Whitehead: Even if it comes to murdering tens of thousands of innocent people who have the bad luck of honestly disagreeing with your plans for their lives?

HM: We are attentive to peacefully advanced complaints. We are intolerant of violence instigated by malcontents.

Whittemeyer: Have you regretted any decisions you made in regards to Algeria?

HM: Yes, I have.

Johnson: Which decisions have you regretted?

HM: I sent a force too small in my attempt to rescue our engineer.

Whittemeyer: In retrospect how big a force would you send?

HM: A regiment with another in immediate reserve.

Johnson (*Laughing*): They would have destroyed the whole Algerian military.

HM: Precisely.

Johnson: I've heard your military is changing from use of vernacular languages in favor of Latin. Latin is a dead language. Why?

HM: It provides a common language dedicated to military communications.

Johnson: So when an American on the street hears Latin, he or she knows it's a military command?

HM: Exactly.

Whitehead: Do women serve in your military services?

HM: Yes, they do.

Whitehead: And do you believe they are as capable as men in combat?

HM: The women in our services are as capable of performing the duties assigned to them as the men they serve beside.

Johnson: You mean you don't cut them any slack physically?

HM: None whatsoever.

Whittemeyer: What percent of your combat force is female?

HM looks to his aide: Aide: About five percent, Your Majesty.

Whitehead: That's not very many.

HM: We do not reduce our standards.

Whitehead: Maybe your standards are too high.

HM: War is not an appropriate enterprise for sociological experimentation and compromise. Our standards must be met. I should note that it is mandatory for men to serve in the military but all women who serve are volunteers.

Whitehead: Other countries disagree.

HM: You mean the militaries of the U.S. and western European countries?

Whitehead: The civilized countries.

HM: War is not a civilized activity. It is brutal and deadly, and as I pointed out earlier, there is no conceivable option but to win.

Rockefeller: Why is it not mandatory for women to serve?

HM: Women must first be mothers and care for their families.

Whitehead *(Indignant)*: Yours is an intolerably sexist society!

HM: Ours is a safe and productive society. American women have more opportunities for self-expression than U.S. women."

Whitehead: I don't believe you!

The moderator announced another commercial break but the off-air discussion did little to reduce the tension among the panelists. Alexander made it worse by appearing to be having a good time. Johnson started the next session in an attempt to keep things civil.

Johnson: Your Majesty, you and Queen Celeste are childless. Who is heir to the crown?

HM: My cousin George is in line to succeed me.

Whitehead: George? All he ever does is hunt, fish and play golf.

HM: George is an active participant in my government. He is present for all major decisions.

Johnson: Who is in line to succeed him?

HM: George's son, Prince Edward. He is a promising young man in whom we hold the greatest confidence.

Whitehead: That will be very interesting to see.

Whittemeyer: How many palaces do you have, Your Majesty?

HM looks to his aide: Aide: Seven, Your Majesty.

Whitehead: We've skirted an issue which we in the United States would like to have addressed.

HM: What is it?

41

Whitehead: Your Majesty, where is your legitimacy? You were never elected governor of that travesty called the 'Group States'. You were appointed to finish out your father's term and just stayed in the job until you declared yourself king. Then you arrogantly took over our name and proceeded to act as if it all belonged to you. Your Majesty, kings went out of style hundreds of years ago.

HM: I am legitimate because God has blessed me by his appointment. Even your government recognizes my government as legitimate.

Whitehead: I can't believe you're attesting to the divine right of kings.

HM: Where lies the legitimacy of your country's government?

Whitehead: Our government is by the will of the people who legitimize it at every election.

HM: So you confess confidence that wisdom and virtue lie in the hearts and minds of the common voters in your country.

Whitehead: Absolutely!

HM: My dear lady, that idea is convincingly refuted every time your country votes. Look at the shambles of this great city. Is this the fruit of good government?

Whitehead: What a scornful thing for you to say, Your Majesty.

HM: They are victims of their beliefs. Millions of innocent people throughout the world are unknowing victims of obnoxious little orthodoxies contending for their souls. As a result they are defrauded of their liberties and their treasure, even their livelihood by charlatans claiming to espouse good while offering only empty promises.

Whitehead (*Heatedly*): But these are individual failings, Your Majesty. The democratic process itself does no harm.

HM: By not doing good, it does evil.

Whitehead: What a despicable thing for you to say!

HM: Its true, Mrs. Whitehead, and you know it. You are part of this enterprise that assumes common people are dupes and fools. But they are not fools.

They are powerless in the face of malignant conspiracies arrayed against them.

The announcer signals there is time for one more question.

Rockefeller: Your Majesty, you have concentrated on bringing rural and industrial states into your kingdom but you have avoided the most populous municipal areas. Is this so? And if it is, why?

HM: You mean the Northeast Corridor, Florida and California?

Rockefeller: Yes.

HM: Populations in these areas are the least productive on the North American continent. They also contain the highest number of non-productive individuals and have the highest crime rates. We see no economic or geopolitical advantage in incorporating these areas into our Kingdom.

Whitehead: So, Your Majesty, you're saying we don't measure up to your kingdom's high standards!

HM: That is an unflattering way to put it, but you're right. Remember what happened to the German economy after they and the former East Germany were reunited. It would be an unwelcome sociological and financial burden on us if you were admitted into our country in your present state.

The camera briefly panned the angry expressions of the panelists before the screen switched to the moderator thanking His Majesty, Alexander, for this unprecedented and historical appearance on the show.

The King was burned in effigy that night in Times Square, Hollywood Boulevard, Miami, Florida and downtown Seattle. The world was unaccustomed to such confidence and public candor in a head of state. U.S. papers posted lurid headlines the next morning describing the remarks made by the American King.

There had been a lot of speculation in the news media and among the United Nations delegates as to what the King would discuss in his U.N. address. Consensus was he had decided to apply for membership in the United Nations. But seeing the backlash from his remarks in U.S. television, they were not sure what Monday would bring.

43

The next morning at ten forty-five, the King and Queen entered the U.N. chamber accompanied by his aide. The chairman escorted them to the podium where he seated the Queen and the aide to the King's right. He then made a short speech about this being an historical moment and introduced His Majesty to the seated delegates. He took his seat at the podium to the King's left. King Alexander began by recognizing important members and guests and thanking them for the opportunity to address this August assembly.

In spite of his advanced age, the king was a handsome man. He had a forceful speaking voice and his words were clearly enunciated in measured tones. After completing the formalities, he began his speech as the assembly waited in quiet anticipation to hear what he had to say.

"My Kingdom is a Christian country. I am a devout Christian. Queen Celeste and all of my family are devout Christians. We are devoted to the Church of Rome and support it wholeheartedly and faithfully. Unfortunately, I, my Queen and my government have become increasingly alarmed by actions taken by other governments which cause harm to His Holiness, his ministers and his faithful followers. I urge you today, members of this body, to desist in these acts at once. To encourage you in this matter, I am using this forum to publicly announce that from this day forward, my government will view any attack or hindrance imposed upon representatives of the Catholic Church in the same way we view such attacks on American citizens. We will take action against the perpetrators of these unseemly acts in the same vigorous, determined and forthright manner we would for our own people."

He paused to let that thought sink in before continuing. A low murmur passed over the seated delegates.

"Furthermore, my country's founding fathers emigrated from the British Isles. We have grown strong with many people from many nations and all have contributed their blood and sweat to make ours a great nation, but our ancestral home is in England. Today my government pledges that its grateful progeny, the American government, guarantees the integrity of England and Great Britain. Any attempt to do harm to her will place your governments in great peril."

He briefly paused again. The audience sat rooted in their places, stunned by the audacity of the American ruler.

"And last, my Queen, my government and I abhor the continued violence in our Holy Land. Within the hour, representatives of my government will be meeting with representatives of the governments of Israel and Palestine. My government will demand that

Israel discontinue all attacks against the Palestinians and deal with them peacefully on equal terms. The Palestinian government will be offered the option to treat Israel in the same manner. They will also be informed that continued attacks upon Israel will result in immediate annihilation by a Royal American force positioned two miles off their coast. My government's representatives will also meet with the governments of countries who have been supporting the Palestinian effort to destroy Israel and request they cease their support at once."

He looked out over the stunned delegates.

"Good day, Mr. Chairman, distinguished delegates, ladies and gentlemen. Myself, my Queen, my government and my people thank you for allowing me to address you on these important issues and I thank you in advance for your assistance in promoting peace throughout the world."

The chamber was so quiet you could have heard a pin drop as the King gathered his notes, took Queen Celeste by the hand and left the chamber with his aide following behind. The King had delivered a stunning ultimatum to the United Nations General Assembly. Its delegates were left speechless.

Tuesday's headlines blared; "King Alexander warns U.N. and world to keep hands off the Pope, England, Israel and Palestine." It was an audacious three-minute speech of exquisite clarity. And it shook the foundations of the world.

Panama was annexed in 2061. After a depressing series of failure prone governments and an alarming deterioration of the Canal, Alexander ordered seizure of the country. It was a bloodless occupation and the people of Panama almost welcomed the change. Newspaper headlines around the world deplored his action, but no foreign government made a formal protest. In a week the incident was forgotten.

In 2065, after years of advocating union then alternately pulling away, Mexico applied for and was admitted into Alexander's family of kingdoms.

45

Chapter Three

In 2066, King Alexander abdicated in favor of George Clark. The king was eighty-three years old so it was not unexpected. Under Alexander's guidance the kingdom had expanded to four-hundred-forty million subjects His military forces were feared worldwide, the economy of his empire was robust and his people enjoyed the highest standard of living on the planet. The new king kept Alexander's cabinet intact suggesting that with this first change of rulers he thought continuity of purpose was critical.

The king's cabinet shared some of the same concerns Mrs. Whitehead had voiced about George during the television interview with King Alexander. George was sixty-four years old but had been somewhat uninvolved and appeared uninterested in governing the kingdom. To say that they were unprepared was a gross understatement. The day after his coronation as King George the First, he became a ruling dynamo. His chief-of-staff and cabinet were pleasantly surprised when he chose to be an active ruler. But by the end of the first month, they were longing for the days of Alexander who, while very demanding at times, was nothing like George.

During his first one hundred days, George enacted the following:

- Ordered the placement of satellite weapons in space.
- Ordered his security services to develop the capability to alter other countries' spy satellite images without their knowledge.
- Ordered the building of a new government center in Kansas City, Missouri.
- Ordered the space agency to study establishment of a colony on Mars within ten years.
- Established new and elaborate court ceremonies.
- Formalized the aristocratic class with Earls, Dukes and Knights. Governors of states or provinces were appointed as Earls. Direct reports to Earls and Army, Marine Corps and Air Force generals were named Dukes. All other military officers were Knights. Upward movement of commoners into the aristocratic ranks was encouraged as a device to maintain the vitality of the ruling class. Upward migration of the labor class was possible but was not encouraged. This caused a frenzied drive on the part of many commoner parents to prepare their

children for elevation into aristocratic ranks. He also established a process where aristocratic children would be allowed to become commoners if they requested a change of status.

- Revamped the national legislatures to be elected by the two upper classes allowing equal numbers of lords and commoners. The king would provide the tie-breaking vote on controversial issues.
- Established a medal called the "Alexander Cross of Valor" for outstanding military feats.
- Established a civil medal called the "Queen Celeste Badge of Christian Service" for outstanding service to the Catholic Church.
- Authorized an improved identification chip which allowed communication via the auditory nerve and voice box with a centralized satellite tracking system.
- Posthumously nominated Alexander's mother as "Queen Mother Diane" and established the third Sunday in May as "Queen Mother Diane Sunday" in honor of the mother of the first king in the Clark dynasty.
- Ordered establishment of an "American Foreign Legion" to accommodate the flood of foreign nationals seeking to serve in the American military. They were commanded by an American general and they were trained to be the "toughest of the tough." They swore absolute fealty to the King. The training regimen was arduous to the extent that only twenty percent of the recruits completed the eleven month training cycle and twenty-two percent did not survive. They came to be known as the king's "junk yard dogs" and proudly wore a KJYD patch on their right shoulder.

After his first hundred days, King George went on an extensive tour of his domain and visited every country, state and province. His ten year old grandson, Prince Henry, accompanied the king everywhere he went.

New Hampshire was admitted into the Kingdom in 2068.

From his coronation until his death, King George actively worked, planned and pulled every string to make his kingdoms stronger, safer and more prosperous and his people happier.

In the spring of 2072, the king, queen and their grandchildren were vacationing at the Royal Retreat in Montana. Prince Henry and Prince William asked to visit a cattle ranch in the western part of the state to "see some cowboys." Both were horse lovers and very reckless riders when they could slip away from their attendants.

Arrangements were made for a week's stay at a ranch after Easter. Both boys were very excited and thought the day for their excursion would never arrive. When it finally did, they found themselves at the ranch, watching cowboys bringing in a herd of wild range horses to be broken. Henry asked to meet a "real cowboy" and the ranch foreman, who was their host, had one of his men get Slim. Henry and William were very excited when the thin, grizzled, bow-legged man in traditional cowboy attire was brought before them. The foreman introduced the boys to the old cowboy. Slim was not happy at being shown off like a circus freak and he let it show. He looked quietly at Henry, who at fourteen was almost as tall as he was. Henry's blond hair and blue eyes made him look like a young god.

"I ain't no subject to no king," Slim grumbled loud enough for everyone to hear. "We used to be free. Now we got a king! Ain't got no truck with no prince neither. You're jest another smart-aleck whippersnapper rich kid.

Then, to everybody's horror, he spat on Prince Henry. His spittle struck the center of Henry's shirt. Onlookers were struck dumb and momentarily rooted to the spot.

Henry looked quietly at the old man for a few seconds. Then he spat at Slim. The old cowboy looked at the front of his shirt, then back at the prince. The horrified crowd watched a grin slowly appear on the cowboy's face.

"Wal," he observed, "You might be a whippersnapper prince but you jest might make a cowboy."

Prince Henry broke the silence, "Sir, would you show us your horse?"

Slim reached out to shake hands with both boys. "Shore. You two jest follow me."

When Slim and the boys started towards the corral, their attendants moved to follow them but were stopped by the king.

"Let them go. It will be good for them to spend time alone with him."

For the rest of the week, the two boys spent every waking moment with Slim, insisting on eating with him and wanting to sleep in the bunkhouse with the cowhands at night. But the queen overrode the king and they slept with the royal party.

The king made an unannounced and unaccompanied visit to Slim and the princes mid-week to ask Slim how the boys were behaving.

"They shore are live wires and they're smart as can be. They don't let nothing slip by. That Henry always wants to ride the wildest hosses." The cowboy looked proudly at him, "Them he likes to ride is too rough for them other dudes."

"Make them behave," the king admonished the cowboy.

"I don't have no trouble with them. They do everything I tell'em to do and are right smart about it too."

"Good. I appreciate you taking time with them. They need to know the things you can teach them."

The king rose to go and shook Slim's hand.

"They's good boys. You don't have to worry about them none."

"Thanks," the king replied and took his leave.

Henry visited Slim every summer afterwards and in his eighteenth year spent all summer on the ranch without bodyguards or attendants. He continued to visit the old cowboy after he was crowned king when Slim was in his nineties.

In July, the English King William of the House of Windsor and Queen Anne made a state visit to America. It was the first royal visit of any kind since the Clarks came to power. With George's love of ceremony, it was a grand and lavish affair. Afterward, George decreed that he and his queen would be referred to as "His Royal Majesty" and "Her Royal Majesty" in correspondence to be abbreviated as HRM.

Then, in September 2072, disaster struck when King George was killed in a traffic accident. He had ruled the American Kingdom and Empire for only six years. But in those six eventful years he completed the transformation of his countries from a loosely aristocratic government to an absolute hereditary monarchy with established nobility, commoners and laboring classes. Like his predecessor, he did nothing to placate the world and for the most part ignored world opinion in all matters, insuring that America and her Empire was strong enough to defend itself from any outside threat.

He had been a stern but compassionate ruler and every corner of his realm mourned his passing. He left his son, Edward, a thriving kingdom and empire of five-hundred-ninety-four million subjects.

The Clarks had by force of will, made their possessions safe, orderly and prosperous. The rest of the world was increasingly disorganized, unsafe, lacking a collective unity of purpose and fewer and fewer ordinary people felt a kinship with their fellow citizens.

For the Clarks power came first. They could be generous, gracious and even benign. Their delightfully good-natured and easy-going attitude made them popular rulers. They were even admired by people in other countries. But at the slightest hint of internal turbulence, their taste for generosity gave way to ironclad conservatism. This characteristic was very strong in Alexander and one could even say it was the bedrock of his governing philosophy. George institutionalized it and Edward was to take it to its apex.

Their protectiveness of their subjects was legendary and no country hosting American tourists could ignore it. Let an American be maliciously injured or killed and the American government quickly escalated the incident to international proportions, ready at once to mobilize their formidable forces and deliver retribution with an iron fist. Even countries with a lackadaisical attitude toward such things were forced to adopt a different attitude in cases where Americans were involved. If they didn't punish the recalcitrant, the Americans would and in the process do considerable damage for which they would not admit responsibility for repairing. And in extreme cases, the Americans would take over the country.

Edward and Virginia were crowned king and queen at the end of September. He was forty-four years old and was just as stern and no-nonsense as his father and uncle had been before him. But Edward was ambitious and assumed the throne with plans to expand his kingdoms by political means if possible and by other means if necessary. Alaska, British Columbia, New Zealand, Australia and Saskatchewan were targeted for concentrated attention.

Immediately upon his ascension, he posthumously named his grandmother, "Queen Mother Rachel" and established her birthday, September twelfth, as "Queen Mother Rachel Holiday" in honor of the mother of the second king in the Clark dynasty.

Alaska was admitted in December, followed by British Columbia in mid-2073 with New Zealand being admitted in March 2075. Saskatchewan and North West Territories followed the same year. Alberta and Manitoba joined in 2076.

In 2077, Edward's oldest child, Princess Elizabeth visited South Africa as a private citizen, accompanied only by her personal servants. During a photographic safari, she and her party were captured by a group of native separatists and held captive for over a month. The South African government assured His Majesty's government of her prompt rescue but their attempt was ineffectual and resulted in a miserable, embarrassing failure.

When the king was informed of the situation his reaction was what you might expect from a Clark. He ordered the Foreign Legion to rescue them. Their commander reported to the king the lawless state of the country and the deplorable condition of its citizens. Two months later, South Africa had a new king and Elizabeth and her companions were back safe at home. Needless to say, her kidnappers were slaughtered along with their next-of-kin. The world had been afraid of Alexander and George, but this new king had turned out to be the most aggressive of all the Clarks. World governments began to communicate secretly among themselves about the need to resist HM government in future forays of this kind. King Edward's spies kept him informed of every move they made.

The United States was slowly pulling itself out of its helplessness in battling crime, managing its finances and began to invigorate its armed forces. They even persuaded His Majesty's government to allow them to import gasoline and diesel powered motor vehicles from American factories, including late model American tanks, without guns. American products were of the highest quality and durability. Of course, America did not export hydrogen powered vehicles or plasma weapons.

In 2078, Ontario, Newfoundland, New Brunswick and the Yukon Territories were brought into the Kingdom, leaving just Quebec and the Maritime Provinces to the Dominion of Canada. By now a lot of governments were profoundly disturbed by the American hunger for territory but were afraid to act.

In 2080, Saudi Arabia continued to meddle in the Palestinian-Israeli situation and the American government issued a stern rebuke. King Saud responded by freezing American assets, arresting American citizens in his country and placing a cordon of troops around the American embassy. Two weeks later the Royal Army invaded. In a surprise assault on his palace early on the first day, the Saudi king was captured along with most of his retainers. They were executed like the Algerian leaders had been. Eleven days later Saudi Arabia became another kingdom within His Majesty's empire.

Retribution was swift and brutal for those who mistreated or killed American citizens, including officers who gave the orders. The perpetrators, their immediate family members and all descendents were executed. Some high-ranking military officers escaped to neighboring countries but Edward demanded that the countries they fled to arrest them and turn them over to the American military. They were quickly caught and turned over to the Americans. There was no safe haven from a vengeful American government and no country wanted to be the next domino to fall.

By swift and determined action, the American King caught the world's governments by surprise and unprepared yet again.

It was election year in the United States. Fed up with continued humiliation at the hands of arrogant American kings, they elected a man to the presidency who promised to force a change in the continental balance of power. He was the candidate from the New Federalist Party and his name was Andrew Jackson. His platform was, "Reclaiming Our Manifest Destiny" and he won by a landslide. By now, the United States consisted of the District of Columbia, eastern Pennsylvania, Maryland, Delaware, New Jersey, Rhode Island, Connecticut, New York, Massachusetts, California, Washington, Florida, West Virginia, Hawaii, and Wisconsin; in all about 346 million people. Being on both coasts and having the two Midwestern states in the middle of American territory created logistical problems. But so far the Americans had been reasonable about allowing movement through their territory.

The problem for the U.S. was when in American jurisdiction, U.S. citizens were subject to American law and many careless United States citizens found themselves in serious trouble. The Americans didn't care what nationality you were. If you committed a crime on American soil, you received the same punishment an American would receive and there was nothing your government could do about it.

Foreigners were never allowed to accompany the Royal Army on campaigns or tactical training exercises. Everybody knew they trained often and vigorously but in a much dispersed manner because spy satellites never picked up any large-scale troop activity. In America, all able-bodied men and quite a few women were in the active reserve from eighteen years of age until they were sixty-two. The Americans were formidable adversaries in numbers alone. They could call up over a hundred million troops in a matter of days. In addition, they had clear superiority in equipment with their plasma weapons and hydrogen powered vehicles, but this was not apparent due to the lack of public information about military operations. Other countries coveted these weapons and vehicles, but nobody considered stealing one to reverse engineer, remembering the experience of the Chinese in '52.

Every country the Americans attacked had been overrun in a matter of weeks. When one considered their well-known brutality

52

towards their enemies, it was not a lightly taken decision to plan an attack on America.

The dearth of intelligence on American military doctrine and tactics had to be remedied before anything could be accomplished. The United States stepped up intelligence gathering in America with a priority on obtaining information about American military tactics.

President Jackson decided to start at the top. He ordered the CIA to find out what kind of men the king and crown prince were. They assigned a pair of double agents to learn details about King Edward and recruited a beautiful female agent to discover what kind of king Prince Henry was likely to be. They hoped he'd fall for her and take her with him on official trips, especially trips to view military training exercises. Somebody joked that she might sweep him off his feet and become the next American queen. Everybody had a good laugh over that. She was an intelligent, gorgeous, classy beauty, fully briefed and trained and she was ordered to sleep with the prince if that was what it took.

The big problem for the U.S. was the King's spies had infiltrated the highest echelons of the U.S. secret services and the King was warned in advance of every move they made. Further complicating matters, American double agents remained loyal to the Royal government and a fully briefed Prince Henry acted in a fashion which misled the female agent about his character. Although he was very handsome and athletic looking, she reported, he was also a shallow, alcoholic skirt chaser who was unable to perform in bed because of his drinking problem. Even though she tried everything in her considerable bag of tricks, she was never able to observe any military training exercises or even get on a military base because Henry pretended to loathe everything about the military. The only useful data she was able to report was the Royal military carried the ready reserve concept to its logical conclusion. Officers and men kept their military gear and weapons with them at all times, even when they traveled on vacation or business and government owned vehicles were always available for use in case of an emergency. All military personnel received half their military pay when not on active duty. She also reported morale of the population, the government and the military was very high and they were a supremely confident country. No good news for the United States came from their intelligence services about American military preparedness but the U.S. leadership beguiled themselves into believing that the Americans were a paper tiger.

King Edward died suddenly in January of 2084 of an aneurism. Twenty-six year old Henry ascended to the throne. He was the youngest king of the Clark Dynasty. The United States government did not believe he was like his father. They considered him to be a dilettante, an alcoholic, weak willed, indecisive and contemptuous of the military, an opinion based primarily on observations made by their female spy. They decided their best chance of success was to make a surprise attack on Good Friday, March 24, 2084 before Henry had a chance to acclimate to his new position.

Their objectives were to recapture Northern Virginia on a line from Leesburg through Fredericksburg to the mouth of the Rappahannock River. Essentially their goal was to regain possession of the Pentagon and Dulles Airport. If this attack succeeded, a second force was poised to strike out from western New York to capture the northern part of Ohio. The goal of this attack was recovery of the northern Ohio industrial cities bordering Lake Erie.

Preparations were made in secrecy as over a million troops traveled to assembly areas in civilian clothes while tanks and heavy equipment were transported in covered trains. Complete radio silence was maintained by units moving to the jump-off areas. Other radio traffic was kept at normal levels. Everything was ready on the evening of March 23, 2084. The world would know that democracy was alive and well by the end of the weekend. Easter celebrations were a big deal in the Kingdom. They wouldn't know what had hit them when they rose for their Easter prayers on Friday morning.

Chapter Four

The United States military force's moment of destiny had arrived. Four long years of preparation was about to pay off. It was a day for the United States to be proud of her soldiers again when they crossed their Rubicon in this long-awaited chance to erase thirty-six years of humiliation. The weather in northern Virginia was cold with a heavy frost. They waited nervously in the cold for orders to move out.

In private meetings President Jackson vented his animosity toward the Americans. He hated them. He hated everything they stood for. He loathed their rulers as pretentious, over-confident, arrogant sons-of-bitches and above all, he hated what they had done to the United States. His hatred was visceral, not from his heart or mind. It was from his gut. He had a special loathing for young King Henry, the silly, drunken, skirt chasing, selfish, indecisive rich kid who had ascended to the throne of a powerful country for no reason other than being King Edward's oldest son. The report from the CIA agent had confirmed his opinions about the man whose country he was about to attack without warning.

He had been careful not to vent his animosity in public, especially when he needed something from the Americans. Henry was proof of the reason monarchial rule had gone the way of the dodo bird. From Alexander to Edward, they had been effective rulers and anybody with a brain was afraid of them. But the line had petered out. It was time to change the continental balance of power.

When elected in 2080, President Jackson brought a new vitality to the United States. He had to fight every defense lawyer in the country to do it but he had cranked up the execution process and violent crime was way down. The economy had perked up and unemployment was down. The education reforms he introduced were bearing fruit. U.S. graduates, while not equal to the Americans academically, were at least better than those of third world countries. The military services had been reorganized and invigorated. They were better equipped than they had ever been.

It had been difficult but he and his military leadership had managed to keep this operation secret. Even congress was unaware of what was about to take place. This was mainly because it was an election year and the politicians were more worried about being re-elected than anything else. The government had to run itself during election years because those charged with that responsibility were busy maintaining their status. Opposition congressional leaders had been caught taking bribes again and the whole country was engrossed in the hearings. There were stories of drunken parties, expensive call girls assigned to members of Congress but paid for by lobbyists, lavish complimentary trips, luxury automobiles and even private planes complete with crews being provided in return for legislative favors.

A few trusted members of the resident's party had been told of the plan but they were sycophants who would never question their leader. If the president had informed the opposition leaders of Congress, the first thing they would have done would be blab everything to the press. Then every one of them would go public with their plan or try to postpone action and "negotiate" like fearful cowards.

Nothing had been leaked to the press. That had been nearly impossible; keeping the operation from those prying, lying, busybody, know-it-all bastards.

He had installed a gung-ho director of the CIA who identified the entire cadre of American spies in the country, fed them false information which, according to top secret reports, they dutifully forwarded to Kansas City. The CIA was confident that the element of surprise would be complete. This was confirmed by U.S. spy satellite images showing normal traffic patterns in targeted areas at the moment the attack started.

They deliberately chose the start of the Easter holiday for the attack. America was an extremely Catholic Christian country. Easter and Christmas were their two biggest holidays.

President Jackson's choice of commanding general for the attack was coincidentally ironic. His name was Grant, Major General Hugh B. Grant. He fell into the role with gusto, started smoking cigars, drinking from a whiskey bottle in public and a few days before the attack, he started wearing an old style Calvary hat like the one worn by the other General Grant.

Unknown to them, the other irony was the commander of the opposing American forces was Major General T. J. Jackson, ACOV, the Duke of Atlanta. Similarities in his case were few. For starters, he was black. But like the other General Jackson, he was an effective and aggressive commander.

General Jackson hated the United States with a vehemence that eclipsed the president's hatred of the American government. President Jackson would have been concerned if he had known about it. General Jackson grew up in a Boston slum and managed to immigrate to America by joining the Foreign Legion when he was eighteen. There

56

he distinguished himself by both his daring and his passion to succeed. He led the squad that rescued Princess Elizabeth from captivity in South Africa. He was awarded the Alexander Cross. Enlisted men who received the Alexander Cross were sent to the Virginia Military Institute. He graduated at the top of his class and now he was a Duke. He had been presented an opportunity to avenge his childhood.

General Jackson was also a serious man, much like the British Duke of Wellington. He was not the type of man who had a nickname. Nobody ever called him "Tommy" or "TJ". While units he commanded had never retreated an inch, nobody ever called him "Stonewall" either. Even his commoner wife addressed him as "Your Grace" in public.

One matter which ought to have concerned the U.S. commanders more than it did was they still knew little about American military tactics, organization and equipment. Although the American military trained a lot, no outsider had observed their military exercises. They conducted small live-fire exercises every year and two multi-state exercises involving over hundred thousand troops.

No reporters had ever been allowed at the front during actual engagements nor were there any public after-the-battle briefings. The only public notices that any fighting had occurred were terse American State Department announcements of the transfer of sovereignty of the latest country that had been overrun. No books or studies about any of their campaigns had been released.

The Algerian, Panamanian, Venezuelan, South African and Saudi Arabian wars were won and obviously studied in American military schools but no word of how they were won had been allowed to filter to the outside world. All that was known was these countries succumbed to American forces in record times. The few survivors of enemy military forces steadfastly refused to be interviewed, even when offered huge sums of money. By doing so they would risk discovery and thereby sign their own death warrant.

They knew the Americans were brutal and aggressive. Other than that, all they knew was they had a very annoying habit of winning every time. But President Jackson correctly pointed out that those victories were against third world military forces, none of which were a first rank force. Panama didn't even have an army and the Venezuelan military was "military" in name only. The Royal American military had never tangled with a front line country like the United States. It was time to show the world that there was a difference.

The secrecy of the president's operation prevented cooler heads from reminding him of the population disadvantage, the superiority of American mobilization capability and even more troublesome, the vindictive attitude the Americans had when even one

American citizen was attacked by a foreigner. The United States was attacking, without provocation, a whole country that was at peace with them.

The Americans' use of Latin for written and spoken military orders, operations documents, and correspondence was exceedingly strange. Alexander mandated the change when he was king and nobody could figure out why. Speculation was it had something to do with his conversion to Catholicism and his admiration of the Romans. How silly could they be! Something like that could never occur under a democratic government.

U.S. military objectives for the first day were to reach the Rappahannock River to the south and a line from the mouth of the Rappahannock through Fredericksburg then north to Leesburg. The United States government first goal was to capture the Pentagon and Dulles Airport.

Main attack routes were down Maryland Highway 13 into Virginia's Eastern Shore, an amphibious assault across the Potomac on Sandy Point, tank, mobile artillery and infantry assaults down Highways 301, I-95 across the Woodrow Wilson Bridge and all the bridges entering Virginia across the Potomac. The westernmost drive was south on Highway 15 out of Frederick, Maryland to capture Leesburg. Planners considered a second amphibious assault between Aquia and Dumfries but the proximity of Quantico Royal Marine Base and the likelihood of discovery in such a sparsely populated area caused them to reject it for the first wave. This assault was planned as a backup attack for the second day if things got bogged down. Confidence was high all the way from infantry privates to the Oval Office.

At precisely one o'clock a.m., 01:00 military time, all private traffic from Maryland's Eastern Shore to the West Virginia border was blocked as battalions of tanks accompanied by infantry began to move south. History was about to be made. The United States would demonstrate once again that she was proud and strong.

The first evidence that something was not right was when. the commander of the lead tanks noticed the absence of traffic from the south. When the first line of tanks exited the bridge into Virginia, it was ominously quiet and dark. Electric power was off, no streetlights, no traffic lights blinking at the early hour. It was eerie. The commander acted on his suspicions and broke radio silence to inform headquarters. Nobody knew what to make of it because there had been no mention of anything on television. American television and radio stations were broadcasting normal programs at this very minute. Nobody in headquarters noticed that U.S. spy satellite images were showing

58

lighted streets and civilian vehicles on the very routes that carried U.S. Army traffic.

After the first contingent of tanks crossed the bridge, infantry followed and began to fan out into Alexandria and adjacent communities. To their amazement, the city was deserted. Houses and businesses were closed and locked. Even convenience stores and all night interstate gas stations were closed and dark. Then to their surprise, Royal Army soldiers appeared out of the darkness and ordered them to surrender. A few random rifle shots were heard by the main contingent along I-95 but it was nothing to get alarmed about. Strict observation of orders for complete radio silence worked against them now.

Mobile artillery followed the tanks with about a mile of separation to allow the tanks room to maneuver if they met any opposition. As soon as the first U.S. tank battalion was a few hundred yards beyond the bridge, eight American armored vehicles advanced unnoticed up the ramps and moved quickly into position, four in the northbound lanes and four in the southbound lanes. Two in each lane turned their guns on the retreating tanks and the other two turned to meet troops and oncoming artillery units. The United States had not been able to develop laser weapons because of their inability to solve the power problems associated with laser weapon technology. They still fired bullets and shells from gun barrels like the world's armies had been doing for nine hundred years. American armor used electromagnetic beam weapons.

All eight Royal Army tanks fired at the same time. There was no loud bang as with cannons. There was just a violent "whoosh" and a stream of incandescent blue light flew at the closest tanks and gun transports. When the plasma struck its target, a super hot ball of energy enveloped it and exploded the fuel tank. That was followed a few seconds later by exploding ammunition inside the vehicle as it turned cherry red. U.S. troops caught close to the vehicles were severely burned while those farther away were in danger of being hit by exploding ammunition.

Traffic on the bridge was thrown into panicked confusion. By the time the U.S. tanks realized they were being attacked from the rear, American armor had destroyed the second row of tanks. The U.S. tank commander gave orders to turn and meet the attack from the rear but before they could complete the maneuver, other American armored units appeared to his front. The first blast from these American tanks destroyed the battalion commander's tank, killing him and throwing his force into confusion. Then the Americans began a systematic annihilation of U.S. forces. Royal Army hover platforms appeared and proceeded to attack troops and destroy military equipment on the bridge. Retreat was impossible because they simultaneously attacked north of the bridge entrance and the charred remains of vehicles prevented exit. The United States military and intelligence services were unaware of the hover platforms' existence. They had expected and were prepared for helicopter gunships. Their radar sighted guns were unable to lock on the platforms. Two were disabled by manually operated 50-caliber machine gun fire and they had to retreat but none were knocked out.

Meanwhile on the ground, the Royal Army was rounding up U.S. Army soldiers. U.S. units who quietly surrendered were disarmed and marched off to prepared holding areas. Units that resisted were slaughtered. That corrosive message spread like wildfire through the ranks along the entire front.

U.S. troops were terrified by the brutality of American troops. The Americans attacked with a savage ferocity and a seeming eagerness to kill. U.S. citizens still thought of themselves as being American "cousins" and deep down they could not believe an American soldier would really want to kill them. They learned the hard way that night that "cousin" or not, the Americans played for keeps in the fullest sense.

They had been told the Royal Army was equipped with plasma weapons but nobody knew how effective they were. The quiet swishing sound they made when fired was enervating and the wounds inflicted were horrible. And they never seemed to run out of ammunition. But still, the most unnerving aspect of the conflict was the savage brutality and lethality of the Americans in attack. Word got around quickly that those Americans actually wanted to kill.

The U.S. Marine amphibious attack at Sandy Point was another disaster. After allowing the first wave to come ashore, Hover platforms appeared and quickly destroyed landing craft, supply ships, troop ships, destroyers, two cruisers and a helicopter carrier. In spite to the carnage off shore, the U.S. Marines put up a stiff fight on the beach but they were outnumbered and outgunned. The pitiful remnants of this once proud force surrendered to the Americans at 03:15. They had suffered ninety-four percent killed. No one manning off shore units survived. Plasma weapon hits sufficient to destroy ships killed everybody inside and those outside within a fifty-yard radius.

With minor variations, these scenes were repeated along the entire front. All United States forces that had penetrated the American border were either dead or prisoners of war by 03:30. Unnoticed by the troops on the ground, the U.S. Air Force had been neutralized from the start but the battle was over so quickly nobody had time to complain.

Unfortunately for the United States, the Americans had known what was coming. They knew what was planned long before the U.S. attack came. They were supremely prepared to the point of having Empire troops in position for the counterattack and they were enraged because the U.S. government had engaged in treachery. The United States government was about to learn what a dangerous thing it was to make King Henry and his government mad. President Jackson and the whole United States would pay dearly for it. Even as U.S. forces were being systematically destroyed and survivors rounded up, Royal Army engineers were clearing all the bridges and routes into Maryland and Washington, DC in preparation for the American counterattack.

Chapter Five

With the invasion repulsed, the Royal Army prepared to strike back.

The American order of battle was as follows:

- First Royal Marine Division: Positioned on the left flank along the highway between Leesburg and Winchester. Two regiments were stationed in the spur of Virginia which juts into Maryland south of Brunswick.
- 6th Saudi Arabian Corps: Consisting of three infantry divisions and two armored divisions poised to capture Bethesda and occupy the area outside the I-495 corridor.
- 3rd Panamanian Regimental Combat Team: Attack parallel to the 6th Saudi Arabians and occupy the areas inside the I-495 corridor.
- 2nd Venezuelan Corps: Drive towards the Rock Creek Park area to occupy Langley Park.
- 3rd Royal Georgia Corps: Capture the Naval Observatory and occupy to Mount Rainier.
- 1st Algerian Corps: The position of honor; Attack out of Arlington, capture the White House and occupy the Federal District.
- 11th Royal Texas Corps: Attack across the I-395 bridge and occupy the Mall and the Capital.
- 2nd Royal Marine Division: Make an amphibious attack across the Potomac on the Washington Naval Yard and occupy up to Cheverly.
- 4th Royal Virginia Corps: Drive across the Woodrow Wilson Bridge into Maryland and occupy inside the I-495 corridor to Seat Pleasant.
- 1st Royal North Carolina Corps: Follow the 4th Virginia across the Wilson Bridge and fan out to the right to occupy the I-495 corridor to Largo.
- 7th Royal Ohio Corps: Attack up Highway 301 from Dahlgren and occupy St. Charles and Andrews Air Force Base.
- 9th Royal Illinois: Follow the 4th Ohio; attack and occupy Bowie.

- 3rd Royal Marine Division: Make an amphibious attack in the Scotland area and occupy up to the city limits of Annapolis.
- 82nd Royal Airborne Division: Air dropped north of the I-495/ 295 junction to occupy the area and contain movement to the north.
- 101st Royal Airborne Division: Dropped in an area southwest of Laurel along I-95 to occupy the area and block escape along that route.
- 5th South African Corps: Amphibious landing at Cape Charles to drive U.S. forces out of Virginia's eastern shore and occupy Salisbury.
- 218th Royal Commando Regiment of the Foreign Legion: Using hover vehicles, encircle and capture U.S. military Headquarters in the old Treasury Building.
- Royal Air Force: Maintain air superiority.
- Held in reserve: 5th Royal Tennessee Corps, 12th Royal Alabama Corps, 8th Royal Indiana Corps, 31st Royal British Columbia Regiment, 38th Royal New Zealand Corps, 39th Royal Saskatchewan Regiment, 46th Royal Minnesota Regiment, 42nd Royal Montana Regiment, 4th Royal Marine Division and the 122nd Royal Kansas Commandos.

The Royal American Navy supported the amphibious attacks and stood by to bombard if the need arose. The big guns never had to fire a shot. The Americans were fully aware of the impending U.S. attack. They were ready for the onslaught and had prepared a devastating counterattack on the seat of government of the United States.

As the U.S. High Command was beginning to realize the magnitude of the disaster they had suffered in Northern Virginia, word came that Royal Army troops were crossing the Potomac into Washington at all points. Reserves were quickly mobilized and units stationed in southeastern Pennsylvania, Maryland and Delaware were rushed south to defend the Capital. General Grant worried an attack might be made from western Pennsylvania if the area was denuded of troops. He didn't have to worry about it for very long.

American attacks targeted the front the U.S. forces had attacked, including a reverse amphibious attack originating from the Sandy Point area which obtained unopposed lodgment near Scotland and Coles Point in southern Maryland. It was as if the Americans had been privy to the U.S. plan and had developed a mirror image counter attack. To their utter dismay, the U.S. high command realized their spy satellite images were still showing normal civilian scenes in the area of the attack. Somehow the Americans had reprogrammed the U.S. spy network to show historical activity on the ground. They had no idea what was happening from a tactical or a strategic perspective. All they knew was the Royal Army was crossing into the District of Columbia and southern Maryland in force and so far nothing was able to stop them. They were still unaware that the pride of the U.S. force lay in smoking ruin in northern Virginia and its sons and daughters were either killed or captured. Or of the devastation which had been wrought upon their carefully developed and nurtured military machine.

Some U.S. units fought the invading Americans courageously and well but the lack of a unified command rendered their sacrifice useless in the overall picture while Royal Army units rapidly consolidated their gains. By daybreak the Americans were lodged in force in United States territory at all points along the front.

Pandemonium reigned in the Capital. At the first sign of trouble, President Jackson ordered the government evacuated to Camp David according to the emergency plan which had been developed. He also ordered the city evacuated. But by the time the order was transmitted, most of Washington and southern Maryland were in American hands. D. C. residents woke up to the sounds of U.S. gunfire and the unfamiliar, eerie "whoosh" and "swish" sounds made by American weapons.

The main offensive weapons of the American military were devices that projected a powerful burst of energy at the target. Their effect was similar to a lightning bolt striking the object. The technical name for the technology was "Electromagnetic Force Projection Enabler." Wounds were similar to injuries caused by being hit by lightning and were treated the same way. Combat wounds inflicted by these weapons on personnel were horrible. Hits on solid objects made by the plasma cannon were spectacularly destructive. The American military was the only military force in the world equipped with this technology.

American hand-carried weapons were particularly demoralizing. They were programmed to shoot short, one-inch wide streams of very high-energy plasma. The length of the plasma stream could be adjusted by the shooter. American soldiers had learned to set them for the longest plasma stream and move the weapon horizontally while firing. The plasma stream would fly like a thrown chain and would kill or wound as many as a dozen U.S. troops with one burst.

Smoking ruins of U.S. tanks and military vehicles littered Washington streets. By noon the entire capital, including parts of Maryland up to the I-495 loop, were occupied by the Royal Army. Forces driving up the peninsula captured Andrews Air Force Base stopping at a line along Highway 50. They did not enter Annapolis.

The capture of Washington, D.C. was the Royal Army's coronation gift to King Henry.

At a cost of less than five thousand American casualties, they had inflicted utter devastation on the U.S. military. U.S. casualties in the first two hours of the conflict exceeded 230,000 troops, over one-half of the attacking force. And eighty-six percent of the U.S. soldiers who set foot on American soil were killed.

At one p.m. a humiliated President Jackson ordered General Grant to offer a cease-fire to General Jackson and requested terms.

By the end of the first day, the Royal Army, Marines and Empire troops occupied the whole of Washington, D.C. and the Maryland eastern shore up to Ocean City. Having had no warning of the impending conflict, civilians were stunned to see foreign troops. They thought the Americans had attacked without warning because of belligerent remarks made by President Jackson. They didn't know that the United States had attacked first.

Diplomatic residents of Washington were just as stunned as ordinary U.S. citizens. First there was the sound of small arms and artillery fire and the unfamiliar "whoosh" of the plasma weapons. Then a very polite and very professional American officer arrived at their entrance informing them of the fighting and they, the Americans, had placed troops around their compounds to protect them. The officer also advised that movement outside of their compounds was not recommended. The French ambassador commented to his superior about it. He noted how fearful it would be to realize one was being attacked by an American Army and yet how comforting it was to be told they were protecting you. He commented favorably on the professionalism and discipline of the troops.

"The Royal Army captain who came to our gate spoke perfect French and she was both polite and reassuring. Throughout the day the soldiers guarding the compound displayed the same attitude. I observed a relaxed camaraderie between both officers and the ranks. They possess an élan unseen since Austerlitz. And, while the captain at our compound is a woman, stern and businesslike as any man, she could hold her own in the most stylish salons in Paris."

At twelve forty-five a.m., stunned members of Congress had received a communiqué stating, "The most glorious United States military achievement was about to occur." Then they were read a short press release announcing the attack and the victory to be disseminated to the media at six a.m.

The next communiqué they received was that the government would be evacuating to Camp David. By now they were vehemently vilifying the humiliated president.

At eleven a.m. there was another notice that the government and military headquarters would be moving to Philadelphia within the hour and the president had ordered General Grant to ask for terms. At days end a defeated U.S. military was retreating in disorder, closely pursued by American forces.

Terms were harsh. His Majesty demanded that all territory occupied by American forces at sundown be ceded to him and the president and his entire military and intelligence staff be arrested and surrendered to his government. A fair number of congressmen and senators were willing to surrender the president but they were loathe to give up Washington. They wrangled throughout the night in an indoor stadium in Philadelphia.

At first President Jackson was reluctant to reveal the magnitude of their military defeat and admit how outclassed the U.S. military had been. But an avalanche of bad news about losses in men and material forced him to reveal the truth.

The truth was appalling. U.S. troops never had a chance. In addition to being forewarned, prepared and having superiority in equipment and armament, the Americans were savage in attack, wiping out whole units if they resisted. The rumor was that every single U.S. soldier who fired at the Americans had been killed along with most of their comrades. Another grim reality was all those new guns and tanks now lay in smoldering ruins. Worse still, nobody was able to report a single American casualty.

On Saturday morning, a chastened U.S. government asked to meet with His Majesty's representatives in hopes of reaching some kind of compromise to end the fighting. President Jackson was not allowed to be present at the negotiations because congressional leaders feared the Americans would arrest him.

At nine a.m. on Easter morning negotiations began at Camp David between congressional leaders and General Jackson, Henry's Chief of Staff, Lord Walter Jones and their aides. It was over in forty-five minutes. The U.S. ceded Washington, D.C., Maryland and Delaware to the King. In return, the United States would be allowed to evacuate their remaining military forces and remove all operational

U.S. military equipment from the area. President Jackson would be removed from office by the end of the day. The demand for his arrest was dropped. After interrogations were completed, U.S. prisoners of war who wished to be repatriated to the U.S. would be returned.

The most humiliating two days in the existence of the United States finally came to an end. Royal Army troops moved to occupy the whole of Maryland and Delaware and established guards along the United States border. Panicked crowds of refugees clogged all roads out of the conquered areas and the Americans allowed them to pass by unmolested. They were posted along the borders to prevent outsiders from coming in. HM Government wanted those who wished to leave to go, but did not allow ingress for any reason, not even for those residents temporarily away from home on business or pleasure. They were told to complete a form and the legitimacy of their residence would be investigated before they would be allowed to return to their homes.

Foreign diplomats assigned to the United States were informed of the change in status of the U.S. Capitol. They were told they and their staff could continue to live and move freely where they were until the U.S. situation sorted itself out and they could make permanent arrangements. "All very civilized," commented an admiring French ambassador the next day.

Chapter Six

The swiftness of the U.S. defeat and the preparedness of the victor shocked the world. In the ceded territories American government spokesmen made regular announcements over the radio and television urging the population to go about their daily business and affairs as before. American troops were everywhere insuring that order would be strictly maintained. Over the next few days Royal Army officers met with local governments to prepare them for transition to aristocratic government.

Note: *[Latin]* indicates narrative spoken in the Latin language. By Royal decree, all American military commands were in Latin and it was used for informal conversation among upper class Americans. The reader can assume nobody else understood what was being said unless the narrative indicates otherwise.

Everybody knew it would be traumatic. For years the word was that Washington, D.C. was ungovernable. Now, HM government would give it a try. *The New York Times* taunted them in an editorial saying as far as the rest of the country was concerned it was good riddance and thanks for all the embarrassment and deficits.

On the nineteenth of April, General Sir Will N. Alston, Colonel Jerome Atkins and his staff met with Mayor Roosevelt Carpenter, council members and the heads of all city departments to work out details of the transition. The meeting began at nine o'clock with the mayor welcoming the conquerors.

General Alston was put off. "Mayor, are you suggesting you were a traitor to the U.S. government?"

He became flustered, "No, General. I was just trying to start off on a friendly note."

"This is a business meeting. We will address concrete issues in a businesslike manner. You and the other members of this government must come at once to the realization that from now on politics have no place in management of this city."

"But we were elected by the people."

"That is of no significance now. Today you will be appointees of His Royal Majesty, Henry the First for an indefinite period of time. You are charged with managing his city fairly, efficiently and according to his law."

Walter Hyde, one of the council members countered, "That will take some getting used to, General. When will we start the transition?"

"Your transition begins now and it will be complete at the end of this meeting."

"Suppose we can't make the changes you want us to make?" another council member asked.

"You will be replaced."

"But we were elected," he objected.

They were sobered by his remark. "Elections are a thing of the past for this city. You will be appointed and you will perform as expected or you will be dismissed."

"Tell us what we have to do, General," the mayor asked quietly.

"Your first priority is to make the city safe. You must control violence and illegal drug activity."

"How long will we have to make this change?" another council member asked.

The general looked at his watch, "You have until eighteen o'clock."

They were astonished. "General, we can't do it that quick. It will take time to get the word out," Hyde objected.

"The occupation troops are doing it now."

"Yes, but everybody knows they will kill you at the drop of a hat," the mayor replied.

"That is what your law enforcement officers must do too."

"That will take time, General."

"You have until eighteen o'clock," General Alston reminded them. "Occupation troops stationed inside the city will stand down at 18:00. We plan to turn the city over to your officers this evening. If it appears that you are losing control, all of you will be relieved and the troops will be redeployed until new city government officials can be appointed."

"General, our officers will not be able to do this."

"They must."

"Our officers have been trained to avoid confrontation and violence at all costs."

"Yes, I know. I have heard appalling accounts of the lackadaisical attitude your policemen have towards enforcing the law. Whole neighborhoods are unsafe."

The mayor shrugged, "Our hands are tied."

"Why?"

69

"We arrest them. Then they get right back out and go back to doing what they were doing."

"Why don't you keep them in jail?"

"We're not allowed to. Our jails are full."

"Why don't you execute the worst to make room?"

They were stunned, "That is cruel, General."

"It's not as cruel as law abiding citizens living in fear."

"Is that the way it is done on America?"

"We have no penitentiaries. His Majesty doesn't allow incarceration longer than fourteen days."

"No jails? Where do you keep criminals?"

"Criminals who commit capital crimes are executed. Non-violent criminals keep their regular jobs but live in barracks, are fined heavily, are not allowed any personal property and all their earnings go toward repaying their victims."

"We can't execute people."

"It is His Majesty's law."

"But, I can't. They're my constituents."

The general gave a sarcastic laugh, "Criminals are your constituents? I thought felons lost the right to vote?"

"They do."

"Then why do you care what they think?"

"They contribute to political campaigns."

"So they vote with their money."

"I'm still responsible for their welfare."

"I would consider the welfare of their victims a much higher priority."

"I try to look after them too."

"But your streets are unsafe."

"Listen General, I can't do everything and please everybody. It's a balancing act and I do the best I can."

"Your government has failed to protect your honest and law abiding people."

"But everybody has rights."

"Rights? To kill, and injure, to rob and steal and distribute illegal drugs which enslave thousands?"

"It's a complicated issue, General."

General Alston was becoming exasperated, "No, Mayor it is not complicated at all. This is what you will do starting at 18:00 military time." His aide passed a copy of a document to all the city officials at the table.

Order of the Day

By command of His Royal Majesty, King Henry, the following orders are given to civil authorities appointed this day, 19 April, 2084, for the governing of the City of Washington, D.C.:

- Individuals who flee from uniformed officers of the law are guilty of a capital crime and are to be executed on the spot by the arresting officer.
- Individuals found guilty of any crime of violence which could result in permanent injury or death are to be executed within fourteen calendar days from the date of arrest. This includes armed robbery, whether or not a violent act occurred.
- Individuals found with more than one dose of an illegal drug are declared dealers and are to be executed on the spot by the arresting officer.
- Individuals found in possession of one dose of an illegal drug are to be exiled from America for five years. They are to be told unapproved return is a capital offense.
- Looters are to be executed on the spot.
- Rapists, murderers and all other violent criminals unable to prove their innocence are to be executed within fourteen days of their arrest.
- Incarcerated criminals who committed violent crimes or sold illegal drugs are to be executed in fourteen calendar days from today.
- All other detainees in your jails are to be released today at eighteen o'clock.
- All jails in your city are to be closed within fifteen days. You are to maintain four (4) secure holding areas for those awaiting execution.
- Except as noted above, existing local laws will be observed and enforced until conversion to the Royal Code is completed.

(Sealed) Henry, REX, ROTR

The general continued, "You, your council and department heads will decide how best to accomplish what the King has ordered." Then General Alston added, "Implement these directives by close of business today."

They were stunned by the severity of the King's orders.

The mayor spoke for all of them, "General, we cannot do this! We must have due process."

"Due process is a device favoring criminal behavior. You have been given a direct order by the King. You must obey the King's directive."

"We cannot. It is against all humanity to do this."

"Mayor, it is against humanity to behave like savages. Control your people."

"But, we cannot," the mayor pleaded. "You are ordering us to kill our friends and neighbors."

The general sneered, "Friends? Criminals are your friends! Mayor this cannot be so?"

"We cannot." Then the mayor found his courage, "I was chosen for this office by the citizens of this great city and I will not do this!"

[Latin] "Sergeant, this man has refused to obey a direct order from the King. Remove him from this room. Take him to a private location and execute him."

The council members watched in stunned disbelief as a stern faced Royal Army sergeant took the mayor by the arm and ushered him out of the room.

"Where are you taking the mayor?" Hyde asked apprehensively.

"Mayor Carpenter has been relieved of his office."

"For what cause?"

"He refused to obey a direct order from the King."

There was silence in the room as they absorbed the importance of his statement. Finally, Hyde asked, "What will happen to him?"

The stern faced sergeant returned to the room alone.

"He has been executed."

They were terrified. Forebodings of doom filled the room. The general continued, "Gentlemen, ours is not a frivolous government. Your success is measured by the effectiveness of your efforts to do the King's bidding."

He fixed his gaze upon the police chief, "What is your name, Sir?"

"Arthur Carver, General."

72

"Police Chief Carver, you are now appointed Mayor Carver. Will you accept this responsibility?"

The police chief hesitated a few seconds before replying, "Yes, Sir."

"Do you have a second in command that is capable of replacing you as chief?"

"Yes, Sir, I do."

"Will you enforce the King's directive?"

Again he paused briefly, "Yes, Sir, I will."

"Arthur Carver, you are appointed chief executive of Washington, D.C. Everyone in this room reports to you. You are responsible for suppression of lawlessness and management of all civic and civil functions. You may choose your staff from those in this room or anyone in the city as you see fit. You must choose wisely from the best talent available to you. Government is a serious undertaking and you must chose capability over compatibility or friendship.

Govern the city by existing laws and regulations until the city's integration into His Majesty's Kingdom is complete. Colonel Atkins of the Civil Government unit," he paused and pointed to the colonel, "has been assigned as your advisor. The occupation troops will be available for ninety days if you need them, after which they will be withdrawn and the management of the city and the safety of its citizens will be wholly your responsibility.

Our experience has been it will take a minimum of five years for the population to acclimate to our form of government.

For you and your citizens, democracy is a thing of the past. Politics is the King's responsibility. For the rest of us, our duty is to do the King's bidding to the best of our ability."

He gazed around the room. The council members and the city department heads were in a state of shock.

"Are there any questions?"

None came.

"If not gentlemen, I bid you good day. And to you, Mayor, good luck."

The general and his staff left the room. The new mayor and the others stared at each other for a few minutes before silently filing out leaving Colonel Atkins and his subordinates alone in the room.

The first night 4,693 looters were killed in Washington, D.C. along with 2,219 others who were killed for failing to surrender to uniformed policemen.

The word got around quickly. Two things occurred. The hardened criminal element fled north. Those with roots in the city decided it was time to behave. Only one hundred and twenty-five were killed the second night. On the third night people were feeling so safe the city bustled with friendly activity. The lack of tension and fear was exhilarating and people were laughing. Similar scenes were played out in every locality in Maryland and Delaware with similar results.

Next was the societal adjustment to an autocratic government, a class society and an evolution of personal and family goals. For many, it would not be easy or pleasant.

Chapter Seven

Things got off to a bad start in Washington. When the mayor's council met the next day, the head of the sanitation department allowed himself to be bribed by a *New York Times* reporter so he could attend the meeting while posing as his aide. The reporter heard reports about the numbers of people killed the first night and managed to get one report out which resulted in lurid headlines about civilian massacres in the conquered territories. He was arrested and sternly escorted out of the country. The sanitation director was executed for treason.

Citizens of Washington, D.C. discovered early that His Majesty's government did not coddle them. Those who had been employees of the U.S. government would be allowed to emigrate if they wished. However, the American government desired to preserve U.S. museums and monuments within the city and those federal employees who wished to remain were employed in that area.

On the first of May, it was announced the District of Columbia would be dissolved and the city of Washington would be incorporated into the state of Maryland.

Citizens of Washington were amazed how quickly the city shaped up. Streets and sidewalks were repaired, public buildings and parks were spruced up and very soon an air of cleanliness and order pervaded the whole city. People were out a lot more and relaxed without the fear of being robbed or assaulted. Officials of the American Catholic Church came in on the heels of the occupation army and quickly established control over public and private education.

Everybody had to be tested to determine their societal status. Those eighteen years old and over who were assigned commoner or aristocratic status were required to personally swear allegiance to the King. They had heard about the way the Americans established a person's rank in society but were surprised at the seriousness in which it was held.

There were three classes: the aristocracy, commoners and laborers. The aristocrats were managers of society and were supposed to provide leadership. They were held to strict behavioral standards. Commoners were the workers, independent merchants and technicians. They were the middle class and provided a core of stability. Commoners were encouraged to prepare their children for advancement into the aristocracy.

The laborers were the lowest class and they provided street sweepers, domestic servants, construction labor and other intellectually undemanding forms of endeavor. They were limited in education and many were not allowed to have families. Upward advancement from this group into the higher classes was rare. Single members of the labor class lived in open government barracks and ate in mess halls. A few married members were allowed to live in government apartments. They were not allowed to own or drive vehicles or leave their assigned area without permission.

Imposition of a class society upon the citizens of conquered U.S. territory was to have significant and compelling impact upon everyone.

There were quite a few surprises once the testing began. Many of those held by their peers to be of low estate and esteem were elevated into the highest class while some who assumed automatic inclusion into the higher classes found themselves relegated to demeaning positions, even to the labor class, and were not allowed to have a family. Their shock at this turn of events was heartrending and profound. There was no recourse to alleviation of their misery except to request permission to emigrate. Many did.

One instance was particularly heartbreaking. Jonathan Forbes was a man on the move in Baltimore. His was a Horatio Alger life story. Born into ordinary circumstances, he had by force of will and intellect propelled himself into financial and personal prominence. He had a beautiful and cultured society wife. He was good to her and she genuinely adored him. They had two sons, eleven-year old Matthew and eight-year old Robert. Both were handsome and intelligent. They lived in a big house on Saint Paul Street in the Guilford neighborhood, had membership in prestigious clubs and all the amenities that go with outstanding personal and financial success.

Jonathan was infuriated by the ceding of Maryland and Delaware to the Americans. In his opinion it was weak-willed and cowardly. He complained to his wife about all those taxes down the drain when they just "gave us away like chattel."

He believed his success was made possible by the freedom and flexibility he enjoyed as a U.S. citizen and did not like what he heard about American society and their strict rules. He especially deplored the idea of military service and that members of the two upper classes were required to serve in one of the armed services. He was also opposed to swearing allegiance to anybody.

He and his family could have left Baltimore during the early part of the occupation but he could not force himself to leave the city he loved. Now emigration for them would be very difficult.

It was Sunday, May seventh and the youngest son was scheduled to take the test on Monday. It had forcefully dawned on them that their son's future in this new environment depended on the results

76

of a three-hour test. No member of his family could be present in the room with him. He would be on his own.

His wife, Katherine, was reassuring, "He's a good student, Jonathan. He'll do very well." She laughed, "He may do better than we do and we'll end up calling him 'sir'."

Jonathan did not think that was funny, "It's a damn bunch of crap. Why don't they just leave us alone?"

"We have to adjust to circumstances, Jonathan, or leave our home. A lot of things are better now."

"Like what?" he demanded to know.

"It's safer on the streets now. I don't worry now when I'm out alone and I like not having to worry so much about the boys' safety. They can play anywhere they want to. It's nice not to be concerned about that any more."

"Yeah," he replied with heavy irony, "Look at all the people they killed to make you safe."

"It sounds terrible, put that way, but I like it. You know the freedom from fear of muggers and vandals. And the city is cleaner than I've ever seen it."

"God damn! You sound like an American already!"

"Jonathan, we are Americans, whether we like it or not. We have to adjust. Besides," she added with a smile, "You're very intelligent. You'll do well and we'll survive and prosper. Why," she added putting on an aristocratic air, "we'll be Sir and Lady Forbes." She laughed, "Won't that be a hoot!"

"I am not going into the military. I've already decided."

"You'll be an officer. It ought not to be so bad."

"I'm not going."

"But they say you have to."

"I've made up my mind."

"You can't avoid it. All men of your rank have to go into the military."

"To hell with my rank. I'm going to flunk their damn test."

"Deliberately?" she was becoming alarmed.

"Hell yes. We've got plenty of money. We can stay here and live like we do now."

"But they say the laboring class lives in barracks and tiny apartments and eats in government mess halls."

"They don't have any money."

"It's not a good idea, Jonathan. We don't know what they'll do. I'm afraid for you to do it. Suppose they take your money away from you?"

"I am not going to be an aristocratic anything. We'll be okay. We've got plenty of money that they can't touch outside this stinking country."

"Jonathan, please don't do it," she begged. "It might not turn out the way you think it will. Please don't, for our sake."

"I am not going to be in anybody's goddamn army nor am I going to swear allegiance to any goddamn king! And that's final!"

Jonathan was the last to be tested. Both boys had scored high and were guaranteed academic opportunities and aristocratic rank on their eighteenth birthday. Katherine had scored well too and expected the letter confirming her nomination to the aristocratic class within the week. She was secretly pleased for herself and her sons but couldn't show it around her husband. He was still adamant about deliberately scoring low enough on the test to avoid military service. Still she hoped his natural competitiveness would take over and he'd take the test honestly.

He didn't. When he returned home after taking the test he bragged how he'd kept his score below eighty. He also mentioned the people administering the tests seemed to have a lot of curiosity about his score and had a private discussion among themselves before he was allowed to leave.

After dinner the following evening two American officials came to their home and introduced themselves as senior administrators of the Testing and Classification Service. They asked to speak to Jonathan privately and he took them to his study.

"Mr. Forbes, we have reason to believe you falsified the score on your qualification test."

"Why do you say that? I didn't use any notes or copy anybody else's answers."

"We believe you deliberately lowered your score."

"So what if I did?"

"Sir, you have no idea what a negative impact this would have on you and your family. Your score places you in the laboring class."

"Maybe I want to be a laborer."

"Mr. Forbes, let us not play games. You have not done manual labor in years. You are an intelligent, financially astute man and you know how to invest profitably. Aside from the work environment, your social contacts within the labor class will be enervating to say the least. It will be mental torture for you."

"I can take it. I grew up poor."

"But you have dedicated yourself to improving your lot in life. Why are you throwing it all away?"

"Because," he replied impatiently, "I will not be in anybody's army!"

"So, you're throwing away a lifetime of effort to avoid military service? Mr. Forbes, that is ill conceived and poorly thought out. You are a competent analyst. You must know the costs for this are far greater than the benefit you desire."

"I will not serve in the military," he repeated.

"But you would be an officer and a gentleman."

"That's a bunch of crap."

"Sir, do not demean a superior station in life, especially since you have one now."

"I am not going into the military."

They weren't making any progress, "Mr. Forbes, the purpose of our visit was to attempt to dissuade you from an unwise decision. If you persist in your determination to pursue this course, you and your family will suffer severe consequences. We are offering you an opportunity to retake the test and urge that you do and that you do your very best."

They rose and the speaker unsmilingly gave Jonathan his card.

"If you change your mind, Mr. Forbes, call me tomorrow by nine o'clock. And if you do not, may God be with you and your family."

Jonathan ushered them out and closed the door behind them.

Katherine was alone in the kitchen. She asked, "What was that all about, Jonathan?"

"They offered me a chance to retake the test."

"Will you?"

"No."

"Why not? They must have thought it was important to send two high ranking people out to see you."

"They thought it was important."

"But you didn't."

"I am not retaking the test, Katherine."

"Jonathan, listen to me. They are trying to help you, and us. I beg you to reconsider, if not for your sake, do it for my sake and your sons' sake."

"Katherine, no!"

"Please reconsider, Jonathan," she pleaded. "I'm afraid for you and for us. I beg you to retake the test."

"God damn it, NO!" he replied. Then he left the room and stomped upstairs leaving her sobbing at the kitchen counter.

Jonathan was scheduled to report to the Labor Coordinator's office Monday morning at eight hundred hours. He hated that way of telling time. It was just more military crap. Clocks everywhere were being changed over to those having twenty-four hour faces. One p.m. was no more. It was thirteen o'clock now.

He hadn't been able to avoid placement in the labor barracks, even with the efforts of the best lawyer in the city working on it. So far results were not good. These Americans were the most inflexible people he had ever dealt with. Katherine had cried all night and the boys were crying too when he boarded the bus.

He tried to remember the last time he'd ridden on a bus. He was in college. Maybe this had been a mistake after all and he ought to have listened to the two visitors. But it was too late now.

Things were not all bad. They had told him he was permanently assigned to the labor regiment adjacent to the one serving his home. He'd hoped for the one that was responsible for the Guilford area but he was not so lucky. He was within walking distance so maybe he could slip out to see his family when he had some free time.

He was both legally and financially helpless. He no longer had access to his money or property. Katherine was given total control of all of his assets. At least they hadn't confiscated everything and put her and the boys on the street or in some kind of barracks. The Americans wouldn't do anything like that. Private property was sacrosanct in America. She had already been told an aristocrat could not remain married to a member of the labor class. She cried for two days after hearing this news. Then he'd been told he could not spend any unsupervised time with his boys. They had even taken his driver's license away. He felt like a peasant.

When he walked into the barracks, a bluff, hearty commoner, whose embroidered nametag read "Spruill", greeted him.

"What's your name?" he asked. He was not unfriendly but there was a total lack of respect in the way he addressed Jonathan.

"Jonathan Forbes."

He called to one of the men wearing a drab gray uniform without any insignia except a nametag. "Reid, show Forbes to his bunk and locker, then take him to supply so he can draw uniforms and toiletries. After you finish getting him set up, take him to the infirmary."

A big, quiet man came up and motioned for Jonathan to follow him. They went up a flight of stairs into a big room about a hundred feet long with two rows of double-decker bunks arranged neatly along both walls. At the head of the stairs, an opening to the right had a sign over it that read "Latrine." He could see a row of sinks along one wall with a long shelf and a row of mirrors above them. At the far end of the room were two private rooms for the supervisors. Everything was immaculately clean and in a perfect state of repair.

There were twenty-eight double-decker bunks arranged between windows on both sides of the room. There was a small metal wall locker on each side of the bunks and two military style footlockers side by side at the foot of the bunks. Everything had a stenciled number on it. Each bunk had a placard attached with the position number. Bottom bunks had odd numbers and upper bunks had even numbers. The footlocker and wall locker on the left had an odd number corresponding to the bottom bunk and the ones on the right side had even numbers. It occurred to Jonathan that he could be quickly located anytime they wanted to find him.

He was shown to bunk number eight, the top bunk on the right side of the room in the exact middle. Then without saying a word, his escort motioned for Jonathan to follow him and they went back downstairs and outside toward a low brick building with a set of double doors on one end. A sign over the door read "Supply Room." The man behind the counter sized him up, went back to the shelves and returned with fourteen sets of shirts, trousers, boxers and T-shirts, a brown box labeled "Kit, Toiletries-L" and a duffel bag.

Then the man behind the counter asked, "Shoe size?"

"Ten and a half wide."

The supply clerk removed two boxes of work boots from a shelf behind him and placed them on the counter. Then he went back to the shelves, returning with fourteen pairs of wool work socks. The last item was a laundry bag.

"Wear clean clothes every day and wear your black boots on even numbered days and your brown boots on odd numbered days. Shine your boots every night. Shoeshine supplies are in the barracks. On Tuesday mornings, hang this laundry bag with your dirty clothes in it on the foot of your bunk. The clothes will be laundered and returned every Friday."

He looked at Jonathan, "Any questions?"

Jonathan shook his head. Then the quiet man picked up half of his clothes and motioned for him to pick up the rest and follow him. They went back to the barracks and the quiet man showed him how to arrange everything in the wall locker and footlocker. While they were doing this, three men came upstairs, discussing the menu for supper.

"Roast beef, mashed potatoes, butterbeans and egg custard pie!" one of the men exclaimed. "Man, it sounds good."

"You sure do like that pie, don't you?" one observed.

"Yeah, I do. I'll take yours if you don't want it."

"Naw. I want mine. The egg custard pie they make here is real good."

The third man chimed in, "I want mine too so don't bother to ask me."

Jonathan stared at the floor. So this was the level of conversation he'd have to endure. He hoped his lawyer could get this straightened out soon or else he'd go crazy.

The quiet man motioned for Jonathan to follow him again. "At least he doesn't make banal conversation," Jonathan thought.

Their next stop was another low, red brick building. This one had a sign above the door that read, "Infirmary." They went inside where a nurse got up from her desk and escorted Jonathan into an examination room. The quiet man took a seat in the waiting area.

"The doctor will be with you in a few minutes," she told him as she closed the door behind herself.

A sign on the inside of the door instructed him to remove his shirt and undershirt. Five minutes later, the doctor came in. He looked young, like maybe he had just graduated from medical school. Then Jonathan noticed his second lieutenant bars. He was a Royal Army doctor! He had an air of confident superiority and perfect grooming. God! How Jonathan hated these over-groomed and over-confident bastards who thought they were so much better than anybody else. Then he realized he'd be expected to address him as, "Sir."

"We have to do a ten minute procedure. We'll need to knock you out."

"What are you going to do?" Jonathan was not expecting anything but an examination. They hadn't even taken his temperature.

"We'll install a locator chip under a shoulder muscle to the right of your vertebrae."

"What for?"

"All of us have one except ours is in another location. Yours will be marked for the area in which you're assigned."

A nurse came in with a tray of surgical tools. After putting them down, she gave him a shot and he immediately lost consciousness. When he came to, the doctor was gone but the nurse was still with him.

"Are you feeling okay?" she asked.

He moved his shoulder and could feel the incision.

"Yeah."

"You'll be sore for a couple of days. They were very small incisions."

"They? How many did he do?"

"Two. One for the chip and one for the medication."

"Medication?"

"Yes, you have to be on medication."

"Why? What kind?"

"They know your IQ is much greater than your test result indicated. They've given you something to help you deal with frustration and boredom. This capsule will medicate you for about five years."

"So, they've given me a tranquilizer?"

"It suppresses your intellect a little too."

The magnitude of his mistake now dawned upon him. His refusal to bow to the conquerors had deprived him of everything; his wife, his children, his money and property, his station in life and now his mood and intellect would be chemically altered.

The nurse helped him up and made sure he was steady on his feet. Then she took him to the waiting area where Reid accompanied him back to the barracks.

"No time to do anything else today," he told Jonathan. "Just stay by your bunk. We'll go to the mess hall for supper at seventeen-thirty."

He sat on the footlocker, bowed his head and wept. It was the first time he had cried since he was eight years old.

Katherine sat on a stool at the kitchen counter. The men from the Testing and Classification Department had just left. They had come to inform her that her aristocratic status was confirmed and her sons were on track to achieve the same rank upon their eighteenth birthday. On the first of June, she would become Lady Katherine Anne Forbes in all official and formal communications and she would be expected to provide community leadership as befitting her class. They told her that she and her fellow aristocrats were not required to use formal titles in informal circumstances, even with members of the lower classes. They told her even His Majesty, Henry allowed the use of his first name in informal circumstances. She was to attend a class on the twenty-third where she would be taught the rules of aristocratic etiquette.

The news was good for Katherine and the boys but the news about Jonathan was disheartening. He'd been assigned to a local labor

83

battalion and his barracks was about six miles from their house. He was forbidden to leave his regimental area. She asked about visits by her and the boys and was told that visits of this kind were not normally allowed. When she pressed the issue, they told her they would see if they could arrange a visit for her but the boys visiting him was out of the question. They also reminded her that her marriage would be annulled the day of her admission into the aristocratic class and she would be free to seek another husband. Aristocratic women were expected to marry within their class but marriage to commoners was allowed in some circumstances where there was a perceived benefit to the Kingdom.

She put them off about another husband for the time being. She was too distressed about Jonathan to think about it. They had seemed understanding and did not press her on this matter. They also told her that due to the circumstances, a priest by the name of Father Jacob White had been assigned to her and her sons as their counselor and he would call on them in a few days.

The Americans seemed to know everything about her, Jonathan and their boys. The only questions they asked were questions like, "How do you feel about this?" They never asked for hard facts about anything. They seemed to be genuinely interested in their success as a family unit and in the boys' realization of their full potential as citizens. They were the most success oriented, positive attitude people she had ever met.

Jonathan's situation made her weep for many days and nights. She had finally been able to stop crying a couple of weeks ago and was trying to assess her situation logically in light of events. She still loved Jonathan but had to admit their separation was entirely due to his stubborn determination to avoid military service. She knew he had no idea how great his cost would be and suspected he now wished he had not been so stubborn. She had their sons to think of, and from now on, her focus would be on them.

The boys were doing great. They had new teachers and a new, challenging curriculum. Teachers were brought in from other parts of the Kingdom to fill in temporarily while local teachers went back to school to obtain credentials to teaching in American schools. It was a rigorous curriculum and she was glad the boys had been attending a good private school instead of a public school. The mandatory exercise program was good for them too. Matt, was excited about going to camp in Colorado the following year for the whole summer. She had to admit the boys were adjusting far better than she was. They were enthusiastic about the things they did and her youngest, Robert, couldn't wait to go into military service. He already understood what it meant to be an officer and he would be one someday.

Father White told Katherine she could see Jonathan on Sunday afternoon the twenty-fifth. When he saw her excitement at the prospect of seeing her husband, Father White warned her that he'd be different and his surroundings would not be what she was accustomed to.

When Katherine arrived at the compound at the appointed time, she was taken to a low red brick building with a sign above the door which read "Day Room." She was escorted inside where a number of workmen were lounging about on couches and recliners watching a baseball game on television. She was taken to a private room with a small table and two chairs and was told to wait while they fetched Jonathan. A few minutes later, he entered the room. Katherine was shocked at his appearance. She was prepared for the drab uniform but he looked subservient; not the fiery, vibrant man he used to be.

She embraced him, "Jonathan! What have they done to you?"

"Hello, Katherine. It's good to see you," he replied matter-of-factly.

She held him close for a few seconds before she stepped back and looked at him again.

"You are behaving differently," she observed.

"I'm on medication to keep me from getting upset."

"I've never seen you act like this."

"Has the lawyer made any progress towards getting me out of here?"

"I called him yesterday but he wasn't in and he didn't call me back."

"He probably doesn't have any news."

"I miss you terribly, Jonathan."

"I miss you too, Katherine. I wish I'd listened to you and the people from the Classification Bureau but I had no idea they really meant to do what they said they would."

"If we've learned anything, it is they mean what they say."

"Yeah, and now I'm in big trouble."

"How do they treat you?"

"Like I'm a very stupid laborer. I never would have believed how regimented we are. We are very organized."

"Have you discussed anything with the people here?"

85

"Katherine, we are just cattle. Nobody listens to cows. Cow's opinions get no respect."

"I'll try to see the lawyer tomorrow."

"It's my only chance. How are the boys?"

"They miss you but they're doing very well. They like school better now and they like the extracurricular activities a lot."

"I wish I could act normal for you, Katherine but my mind stays kind of numb all the time and I just can't seem to make myself care about anything."

Katherine broke down and began sobbing, "Jonathan, I love you. Why did you do this to me? I need you!"

"I'm sorry. I didn't know it would turn out this way," he replied with detachment.

"Our marriage will be annulled on Thursday!" she cried.

"Why?"

"Don't you remember, Jonathan? Members of the aristocracy are not allowed to be married to members of the labor class."

He was still detached, "I'm sorry."

"God! Is that all you can say? You're sorry!"

"Katherine, I'm on medication."

"They've already spoken to me about finding another husband!"

"They have?"

"Jonathan!" she screamed, "Is that all you can say? I want you back. I don't want another man!"

"I'm sorry, Katherine."

She was becoming distraught. An Army lieutenant came into the room.

"Lady Forbes, are you all right?"

"No, I'm not. I want my husband back," she demanded.

"Ma'am, there's nothing I can do about it and you can't either. He's permanently assigned to this regiment. He'll be here until the day he dies."

She stared at the young officer. "I must leave now," she said quietly. Then she embraced her husband.

"Goodbye, Jonathan," she whispered and left the room.

A few seconds after she'd left, Jonathan mumbled, "Goodbye, Katherine."

On the way home, she realized the American lieutenant had been the first person to call her by her aristocratic title.

She called the lawyer at eight thirty the next morning. "Katherine, there's nothing we can do. I spoke with the military governor of Maryland about this and he basically told me I was wasting my time. These people take this very seriously. He told me if Jonathan had been an American citizen he would have been charged with dereliction of duty and executed."

"But all he did was deliberately score low on a damn test."

"But from their viewpoint, he deliberately failed to do his duty and they are quite inflexible about it. In their, now our, society, failure to do ones duty is an extremely serious infraction."

"So you're saying Jonathan will never be allowed to return home."

"That's about it, Katherine. I'm very sorry. Jonathan always was headstrong and it worked in his favor for many years, but this time it has ruined him."

"Mail me your bill, John."

"There's no charge, Katherine. I wasn't any help. Sorry."

"I am too. Thanks for trying."

"Call me if I can do anything for you and the boys."

"Thanks, John. Goodbye."

She hung up the phone and went upstairs, lay across their bed and sobbed herself to sleep.

After they had hung up, John called his wife, "Ellen, go by to see Katherine today if you can."

"Why, what happened?"

"I just told her Jonathan will never come back home."

"How did she take it?"

"I couldn't tell. You know how controlled Katherine is."

"This is terrible. Jonathan was always so stubborn. I guess he's finally come up against something more stubborn than he is."

"Yes, he has."

"I'll go by this afternoon."

"I know she'll appreciate it."

"This is awful."

Her husband agreed.

Father White visited Katherine and the boys on Wednesday evening. The boys were in good spirits but Katherine seemed withdrawn and preoccupied. He knew she was distressed over her husband's plight and tried everything he could think of to brighten her spirits. Tomorrow was a fateful day. She would officially become Lady Katherine Forbes but her marriage would be annulled in the process.

He guessed that was on Katherine's mind. When he got back to the diocese, he spoke to his superior about it.

"She loved her husband very much," he told the bishop.

"This is such an unfortunate situation. Maybe if we'd been alerted sooner we might have persuaded him to turn from the path he chose."

"Is there anything that can be done?"

"No, unfortunately. He brought this down on himself by his pride and selfishness."

"I'll pray for them tonight."

"Yes, do, and so will I. You ought to go by tomorrow morning after breakfast and check on them."

"I'll go by first thing."

It was after midnight and Katherine couldn't sleep. She couldn't cry any more either. She was cried out and it did no good anyway. Normally Katherine was a down to earth practical woman but tonight was especially trying. At midnight her marriage to Jonathan had been annulled. Talk about her finding another husband revolted her. The very thought of another man touching her was repulsive and her sons calling another man father was too awful to contemplate. She absentmindedly looked out of her bedroom window and saw a man standing in the middle of the street under the streetlight. He was dressed in a drab uniform and seemed to be confused as if he was unable to decide what to do next. He turned and looked in her direction. It was Jonathan! She grabbed her robe and pulled it on as she raced down the stairs and threw open the front door. Just as she stepped out on the porch, a police car drove up and two policemen took Jonathan by the arm, ushered him to the cruiser and put him in the back. Katherine tried to scream at them to let her husband go, but the words would not come out of her mouth. Instead, she uttered a loud sigh, dropped to her knees and began to sob as the police car drove away.

Father White parked on the street at eight-thirty-seven, walked up to the front door and rang the doorbell. No one came and the house seemed quiet. He waited a few minutes and rang again. When no one came, he walked around to look inside the garage to see if Katherine's car was there. As he approached the garage, he heard the sound of an engine running inside the garage and immediately called the police. They arrived a couple of minutes later and broke into the side door where they found Katherine in her car with her head laid back on the seat and her arms around both of her sons. She and both boys were dressed as if they were going to a formal party. Her eyes were open, staring at the headliner and her makeup was streaked by tears.

That afternoon, Jonathan was summoned to the company commander's office and asked to sit.

"Forbes, early this morning your wife and two sons were found dead at their house," the lieutenant told him.

Jonathan tried to concentrate and think of something appropriate to say in a situation like this but the best he could do was, "That is very sad to hear."

Without asking any questions, he got up and left. On the way back to his barracks, he remembered that egg custard pie was on the menu tonight and Reid had promised to give him his slice.

Every day the newspaper and television commentators in the United States related lurid tales of cruel and inhumane actions taken by the American government against the citizens of Washington, D.C., Maryland and Delaware. Everything was heard second hand because U.S. reporters were not allowed into the newly acquired parts of America. Where facts were skimpy, imagination filled the blanks and every day brought fantastic tales of repression and bloodshed. Eventually this had to affect somebody and it finally did. On June third, Shonie Creamer and two friends hijacked an airliner out of LaGuardia and forced the pilot to fly them to Dulles Airport. It was the first airline hijacking in over sixty years and everybody was caught off guard.

Creamer's stated purpose was to draw attention to the plight of the "brothers" languishing in American jails. He and his partners were drunk and not very focused so it was hard to make any sense out of what they said. Their demands changed every five minutes. Still, they said they had guns and had threatened to kill everybody on the plane if the Americans didn't give them what they wanted.

The pilot tried his best to dissuade them from landing on American soil but they were adamant. They landed at Dulles at eleven-thirty-one. Military vehicles escorted the plane to an isolated tarmac. When it came to a stop, it was blocked from moving by Armored Personnel Carriers and surrounded by a company of the 104th Royal Commandos.

General Sir Will N. Alston happened to be in Dulles Airport after returning from leave. Being the ranking military officer in the

89

area, he was summoned to the control tower to take command. He was briefed and apprised of the resources at his disposal.

[Latin] "Make preparations to board the plane and prepare the robot for use," he ordered.

He then spoke to the pilot, "Can you brief me on the situation?"

The pilot started to say something but the hijack leader took the microphone from him, "We's come to get our brothers out of jail."

"To whom am I speaking?"

"Shonie Creamer. You got to let my brothers out."

"Out?"

"Out of jail, motherfucker."

"Sir, you have been terribly misinformed. No one is in jail in America."

"You're a lying honky."

"Sir, our laws forbid incarceration for more than fourteen days. If you give me a few minutes, I can show you the empty cells."

"I been told that you motherfuckers run a big fucking jail here and I come to give my brothers some relief."

"Sir, there are no prisons in all of America."

"It ain't what I heard."

"Pardon me, Sir, while I confer with someone."

[Latin] "What kind of imbeciles do we have here?"

[Latin] "They were intoxicated when they hijacked the plane, General."

[Latin] "Are there any Americans on the plane?"

[Latin] "No, Sir. But there are two women coming to meet their husbands who are U.S. POWs that requested asylum."

[Latin] "Does anybody know exactly what they want?"

[Latin] "They just want to get their 'brothers' out of jail according to Creamer."

[Latin] "Brothers?"

[Latin] "They're black hoodlums. Their buddies are referred to as 'brothers', Sir. Sixty-five percent of the prison population in the U.S. is black hoodlums such as these."

[Latin] "They needed to have three more."

[Latin] "Yes, Sir."

[Latin] "They obviously don't know our penalties for armed kidnapping?"

[Latin] "No, Sir. The pilot tried to tell them but they wouldn't listen."

"Mr. Creamer, this is General Alston. You have forced a plane to land on American soil, placing you under our jurisdiction. You and your friends have committed a capital crime in America."

"I knows dat, General. But iffen you wants to save any of dese folks lives you'll turn out all the brothers that is rotting in your jails and let us go back to the good old U.S."

[Latin] "Have we located their family members?"

[Latin] "Creamer's but not the other two."

[Latin] "How soon before we're inside the plane?"

[Latin] "Five more minutes, Sir."

"Mr. Creamer, that plane will not be going anywhere with you on it. You and your associates have committed a capital crime on American soil. The penalty is execution."

"You start anything and dese folks die."

"I didn't finish. Your blood kin will be executed too."

"What you mean by dat?"

"Your mother, father, brothers, sisters and your children."

"You mean you gone kill my fambly?"

"Yes."

"I got a little four-year-old girl."

"If she has your genes, she will be executed."

"They's in the U.S."

"U.S. authorities are arresting them as we speak and will turn them over to us this afternoon."

"That ain't fair. What about a trial?"

"There will be no trial. We know you're guilty."

Creamer didn't say anything for a few seconds.

"We done made a big mistake."

"Yes, you have," the General agreed.

[Latin] "The robot is on board, Sir."

"Who dat talking to you?"

"Colonel Wallace."

"I don't unner stand a word he's sayin."

[Latin] "Creamer is at the front of the passenger cabin using the stewardess microphone."

[Latin] "Where are the others?"

[Latin] "To his left, in the galley."

[Latin] "Who is armed?"

[Latin] "Looks like Creamer is the only one."

[Latin] "Get him first."

"What is you sayin, General?"

"I'm giving orders to Colonel Wallace."

Creamer was startled to see a small tracked vehicle moving up the aisle towards him. He started to say something into the microphone but just as he was getting ready, an oval bulb about the size of a softball rose up from the base on a telescoping pole. The last thing he saw was a blue light streaming directly towards his face. It hit him before he could duck. Then the oval rotated to the right and killed the other two hijackers.

A few days later, a busload of U.S. protesters crashed through the barrier on I-95 and got a mile inside of Maryland before they were stopped. They were all slaughtered before they could get off the bus.

The U.S. issued a formal complaint but HM government did not bother to reply. The U.S. could not attempt anything more concrete than a protest because they were thoroughly demoralized by the overwhelming power and savage brutality of the American armed forces. And there was not enough of their military remaining to back up any demands by threat of force.

The United States began to press for the return of their POW's. His Majesty's government appeared to be dragging their feet on the matter. Then in the middle of May the Americans agreed to return the POW's to United States territory on July fourth. This was an irony which could not fail to irritate the new U.S. president and congress. U.S. losses had been horrendous; a few over 31,000 POW's out of an original force of 230,000 who actually made it into American territory. Their loss percentages had been almost as staggering in Washington and southern Maryland, but most able bodied troops had managed to avoid capture and retreated into southern Pennsylvania while cease fire negotiations were going on. Some others managed to slip back when the U.S. was allowed to recover their military equipment from Maryland and Delaware. Pitifully few were returning and they would be arriving back on U.S. soil on Independence Day.

Some had requested American citizenship and 8,176 passed the classification test with scores high enough for commoner or aristocratic status. They became citizens of America and subjects of the King and by the first of June they had already been released from POW compounds and were in the process of moving their families to America. Because it was so many, the U.S. complained to the U.N., saying they had been coerced. Henry agreed for a U.N. body to be sent in to investigate. After interviewing a hundred, the U.N. investigators reported that they genuinely wanted to remain in America.

The Americans planned a victory parade in Washington for Sunday, July second. Victory parades and celebrations were usually held in Kansas City but the significance of the capture of Washington and the ceding of Maryland and Delaware to the King made this a special occasion.

The parade route was up Constitution Avenue from the Lincoln Memorial, past the former U.S. Capitol to Second Street. The reviewing stand would be across from the Ellipse on the side of Constitution Avenue which faced the Washington Monument. Representatives from all units that participated in the battle took part in the parade. The last elements of the parade would be the U.S. POW's, who after reaching Second Street, would be marched west on Massachusetts Avenue to the train station where they would board a special train to be transported to the border crossing where I-95 crossed into the United States. They would bivouac there and be in position to cross into Pennsylvania at nine o'clock on the fourth of July.

The victory parade, the victory banquet and ball were publicized in a manner guaranteed to irritate the United States. During the parade, the King would make a speech and present medals to those soldiers who performed heroically. Two would receive the Alexander Cross, the highest honor for any soldier in the American Military. Six unit citations for uncommon valor of a military unit would also be awarded, two of which would go to proud Algerian Infantry companies. It would be a big day in Washington, Maryland, formerly known as Washington, D.C.

The government was surprised and gratified that so many Washingtonians, Marylanders and citizens of Delaware were genuinely excited about the celebration. General Gates commented it was almost as if they'd forgotten that just a few weeks ago they were U.S. citizens. Of course he failed to note that many of those who might have objected had fled to the U.S., or they were dead.

Chapter Eight

In early June, King Henry made an unannounced visit to Washington and Baltimore. He traveled incognito around his countries occasionally. He did it with greater frequency than those responsible for his safety would have liked. His only close companion during these forays was his personal aide, Sir Carl Gillespie and a dozen plainclothes guards who were required to blend unseen into the background.

He had visited Washington with his father when he was a boy and they had toured all the museums and monuments. But it had been a public outing with everybody staring at them and there was all the news commentary on U.S. television and newspapers. He remembered the society page comment about the crown prince being "so cute" like he was an entertainer of some kind. He preferred to look around without celebrity fanfare.

This kind of media attention was not allowed in his countries. Sensational news was prohibited and American newspapers were strongly encouraged to stick to the facts. Of course, U.S. television and newspapers were available to everybody and they were widely read but American society thought them shallow and unreliable. The U.S. media's virulent animosity toward the American government and society caused them to go overboard and describe conditions that were evidently untrue to the most casual observer. They were useful as a negative educational tool for teaching American children how not to behave. Henry restricted his appearances in American media to official functions and tried to keep his personal life out of the news. Nobody outside his government knew he was coming.

Henry had never been to Baltimore and wanted to visit there after he made the rounds in Washington. He especially wanted to see the Inner Harbor area and tour the two-hundred and thirty-year-old USS Constitution which was moored at the dock.

He and Carl toured the ship and the harbor on the sixth of June, completing their rounds about eighteen o'clock. Carl asked the woman at the information desk to recommend a restaurant for dinner. She suggested Sabatino's Italian Restaurant on Fawn Street in Little Italy. It was an elegant five-star restaurant that was locally famous for the quality of its food and service. They followed her suggestion.

While they were waiting for their meal, a group of young people came in. Among them was a striking dark haired young woman wearing a sweater and long skirt. She caught Henry's attention and while he was giving her the once over she looked at him. Their eyes met and she gave him a sly grin. She was engaged in conversation with members of her party while they waited to be seated but she looked Henry's way several times. Every time she did, he was looking at her. An electric spark passed between them.

"Carl, do you see the tall, dark haired girl in line by the register?"

"There are several girls in the line. Which one?"

"The pretty one."

"All of them are pretty, Your Majesty."

"Don't call me that here. Call me Henry," he hissed. "The one in the gray sweater and long blue skirt."

"Oh, that one. She is quite attractive, Sir."

"Ask her to dine with us."

Gillespie went over to where the girl was standing and introduced himself. They had a few words after which she followed him to their table while her companions watched.

"Caitlin, this is Henry. Henry, meet Caitlin."

Henry stood and shook her hand. "I'm pleased to meet you, Caitlin. Would you join us for dinner?"

"I'm sorry but I can't. I'm with a group." She smiled, "But I would if I was free."

Henry's disappointment showed. "I wish you'd reconsider."

"I can't. Maybe another time?"

"I'm going back home on Monday."

"You're an American, aren't you?"

"Yes." Then he smiled, "Aren't you?"

She laughed, "I became one the first of this month. I am officially Lady Caitlin Rose York." Then she laughed again. "Isn't that something! What's your official name?"

"Sir Henry Clark and this is Sir Carl Gillespie."

"Well, Sir Henry, could we meet somewhere for lunch tomorrow?"

"You name the place."

"How about eleven-thirty tomorrow at the Crackpot Restaurant on Loch Raven Boulevard in Towson?"

"I'll be there."

She looked back toward her friends. They were motioning for her to come.

"I must rejoin my party. Should I curtsy now, Sir Henry?" she giggled.

He laughed, "Not in informal circumstances, Lady Caitlin."

As she turned to leave, she looked back over her shoulder. "See you tomorrow," she said as she smiled sweetly and rejoined her group. When they were going to their table, she looked his way twice more and smiled when their eyes met.

After she was out of sight, Henry observed, "What a gorgeous creature."

Carl had been watching his love struck monarch with humorous detachment. "She is quite attractive, Your Majesty."

"She's prettier than the CIA spy."

Gillespie laughed, "That is saying a lot, Your Majesty."

The Crackpot was a small restaurant. They decided Carl and one guard inside were enough protection and Henry asked them to sit at a separate table to give him some privacy. Unknown to them, two of Caitlin's friends were at another table.

She was five minutes late and apologized when she met him in line waiting to be seated. "I couldn't get off the phone with a customer," she explained. "I always try to be on time."

"It doesn't matter. I'm on vacation."

"Where are you from?"

"Kansas City."

"You must work for the American government?"

"Yes, I do."

"Are you in the military?"

"Sort of. My job interacts with all branches of government."

"What brings you to Baltimore?"

"I've always wanted to see the city."

"You picked a good time. June is one of our nicest months."

"The weather has been good."

The hostess led them to the pre-arranged table.

"There's a long line. You must have gotten here early."

"Carl made the arrangements."

"He's the man who was with you last night?"

"Yes."

"What does he do?"

"He's my aide."

"Your aide? I am impressed. A man with an aide! You must have a very important job."

He grinned, "It's fairly important. What do you do?"

"I work in a real estate office about fifteen minutes from here."

The waitress came to their table and they ordered.

"Where did you go to college?" she asked.

"NC State. Where'd you go?"

96

"The University of Maryland. Why did you go to NC State?"

"It's a tradition. My family originally came from North Carolina so all the sons go there and the girls go to Wake Forest University."

"I heard Wake Forest is a Catholic school now."

"Yes, it is."

"Are you a Catholic?"

"Yes, are you?"

"My family's Episcopal. Do you travel a lot?" she asked.

"Yes, quite a lot as a matter of fact."

"Out of the country?"

"That too. In my job I also have to deal with Empire issues."

She stared, "You must have a very important position."

He changed the subject.

"You are a most attractive woman."

"Thank you. You're pretty attractive yourself. I like the way American men take such pride in their appearance. From my point of view, neat and well groomed is always appreciated."

He laughed, "We're conditioned from birth to be neat."

"Americans certainly stand out in a crowd around here."

"It will change as Marylanders adjust to American ways."

"I know. Not everybody likes the American ways, but I do a little more every day. The absence of crime, clean streets and the order is nice. And I do not miss the panic subject of the day we used to have. People in general are a lot calmer now."

"How did your friends react to you meeting me for lunch?"

"They warned me to be careful. Debbie noticed how much I was attracted to you." She gave him a mysterious smile. "She and Eleanor are here just in case I need rescuing." She pointed to a table along the wall where two young women were watching them.

He laughed. "Carl and one of my associates are at that table." He pointed to a table in the back of the restaurant.

"So our friends are looking out for us."

They didn't say anything for a few seconds. Then the waitress came with their meals and they began to eat.

Henry stopped eating to ask, "Caitlin, will you go out with me?"

"Yes, I will. I was hoping you'd ask."

"Where would you like to go?"

She laughed, "What I'd really like is for you to take me to the Orioles game on Saturday." She paused, "But if you don't like baseball, we could go to a concert."

"What kind of music do you like?"

"Classical and pop. What do you like?"

"Classical and country."

"You know it sounds odd to hear that a man named Sir Henry likes country music."

"I like the theatre too, especially Shakespeare."

"Which will it be?"

"I'll take you to the ballgame."

"Are you sure?"

"I like sports too. I played baseball in college."

"I am an avid fan. I stand up and yell and everything."

"That's okay."

"There's one other thing."

"What?"

"You'll have to meet my family."

"Okay. It's old fashioned but its okay."

"I'm an old fashioned girl."

"I like old fashioned girls."

"My family is old fashioned too. We're so old fashioned that you've got to tell my daddy what you do for a living."

"I do?"

"Yes, you've been pretty vague with me about what you do but you'd better get your story straight for my daddy." She gave him a sultry smile, "You ought to be able to get it right in your mind between now and Saturday."

She looked at her watch, "I'd better get back to work. Why don't you come to our house for lunch on Saturday and we can leave from there to go to the game."

As they rose to leave, she gave him a card with her address and he accompanied her outside to her car.

"I'll see you Saturday about eleven," she said with a smile.

He replied with a sheepish smile, "I'll see you then."

"What kind of job does he have?" Caitlin's friend Debbie asked when they met back at the restaurant after work.

"He's got some kind of government job. He didn't say much about what he did but he has to travel all over."

"He must be a high official then."

"Maybe. He's got an aide who travels with him."

"That sounds pretty big but why would an aide accompany him on vacation?"

She looked at her friend, "It does seem odd doesn't it?

"He's not gay is he?"

Caitlin laughed, "He is definitely not gay. Maybe he's a duke or something."

"Maybe. I'm not very up on this aristocrat business anyway. He is definitely a hunk though. Tall, blonde, athletic build, blue eyes; if you decide it won't work out, send him to me."

Eleanor chimed in, "You two are letting your hormones take control of your brain. He's just a nice looking guy. There's nothing special about him."

"I bet you'd accept if he asked you out," Debbie retorted.

"In a New York minute!" she laughed.

They all laughed and finished their drinks.

Chapter Nine

Henry's Chief of Staff, Lord Walter Jones, called Henry early the next morning

"Your Majesty, you must explain to this girl who you are."

"Why? It's only a date to go to a ballgame."

"Carl has told me how infatuated you are with her."

"So? I'm excited about a pretty girl. Does that create a situation where my cabinet meets to discuss a date their king has with a girl in Baltimore?"

"Sire, everything you do is important to the realm."

"Not everything, Walter. It's only one date. What can be wrong if Henry Clark has one date with a pretty girl in Baltimore?"

"Suppose the relationship intensifies and she becomes candidate for queen?"

"Suppose it does? I'll tell her then."

"Don't you think she might be offended by your deception?"

"A little, maybe, but by then it ought not to matter if she likes me."

"Your Majesty, any deception weakens a relationship when it's discovered."

"She would get over it."

"Sire, you ought not to chance it. How would you feel?"

"I'd get over it."

"Nothing in my experience indicates that you have any tolerance for deceptive behavior."

Henry didn't respond.

"She comes from a good family. Her father was a state senator. He's been very helpful to us and has been appointed to the council. In September, he'll be named Duke of Cumberland."

"So, I chose well," he said sarcastically.

"Actually, you did. Remember, you're twenty-six and your realm needs an heir."

"Elizabeth is next in line."

"Elizabeth does not possess the mettle. She doesn't have children either."

"How about Rachel?"

"Sire, Rachel is much too spirited for the demands of Head of State."

"And William is too bookish."

"Exactly, Your Majesty. We need new blood."

"But it's just a date."

"I understand, Your Majesty."

"All the others couldn't forget my job and like me personally. They loved the King. The real Henry was something they wanted to leave in a closet out of sight."

"Maybe this girl is different, Henry."

"It would make me feel better if she liked me before she knew who I was."

"Your Majesty, do not deceive this girl. If she is the one, you, her and your subjects will suffer."

Carl contacted Caitlin that night saying Henry would like to meet her family Friday evening after dinner. She was mystified by this unusual request and had trouble concentrating at work while speculating about it. Both of her parents were mystified too. But these Americans were different and were sticklers for process.

Henry and Carl arrived at the York home at nineteen-thirty on-the-dot. Caitlin met them at the door and led them into the living room. After they were seated, she went to get her parents. She noticed Henry seemed quiet and subdued. It worried her a little which increased the mystery.

Caitlin introduced her parents to Henry and Carl. After introductions, Henry got right to the point.

"Sir Richard and Lady Francis, your daughter told me that before she could go out with me I had to tell you what I do for a living."

Her father nodded.

"Then, I'll tell all of you at the same time. But first I must apologize to Caitlin for concealing my true identity from her." He paused and looked at Caitlin. "My chief of staff and cabinet have been unanimous in advising me that I must correct any misconceptions I might have caused as quickly as possible," he paused again, looking at Caitlin to gauge her reaction. She was staring at him.

He addressed her parents first, "Sir, Lady," then he spoke directly to Caitlin, "and Caitlin, I am the King."

Caitlin's jaw dropped, "You're King Henry!" she stammered.

"Yes, I am, Caitlin. I apologize for not telling you before."

"Why didn't you tell me who you were?"

"I wanted to get to know you while you thought I was an ordinary man."

The Yorks became very flustered. Their King and the ruler of the third largest country in the world right here in their living room!

Carl tried to ease their stress, "Sir and Lady York, there are no protocol issues involved. In informal settings, Henry expects to be treated like anybody else. And His Majesty is sincerely attracted to your daughter."

Caitlin regained some semblance of composure, "When would you have told me?"

"After I knew that you liked plain old Henry Clark."

"I'd be mad."

Sir Richard found his voice, "She doesn't mean it like she said it, Your Majesty. She means she might be upset."

"Daddy, I'd be mad then. I'm upset now."

"My daughter is very outspoken, Your Majesty. Please don't take offense."

"Could the three of you please leave the room so Caitlin and I can discuss this privately?" Henry suggested, trying to keep it from sounding like an order.

Carl motioned for the York's to follow him into the foyer and they took him to their family room. Carl would try to put them at ease with the situation.

After they were alone, Henry continued, "Caitlin, when we're together I want you to be yourself and forget I am your King. I want us to be just Caitlin and Henry."

"How about when we go somewhere in public, like a baseball game?"

"We'll go like we planned."

"Will Carl be with us?"

"He'll be close but not so close we won't have privacy."

"What about guards? I thought you would have guards everywhere."

"They're inconspicuous. They blend in with the crowd."

"How many came with you?"

"Twelve."

"What should I call you?"

"Henry, when we're in private or in an informal group. If we're in a formal setting or a mixed group which includes commoners, you must address me as 'Your Majesty'."

"So, if my friends had been with us at our table, they could have called you, 'Henry'."

"Yes." He paused, "Caitlin, I'm sorry I misled you but I was afraid if you knew who I was you wouldn't want to go out with me, or worse, think you had to. I'm afraid of that now."

She looked at him. She knew he was sincere. And he was still handsome and very nice, in spite of being King.

She smiled, "I'll be okay, Henry. It will be quite an adjustment but I'll try if you want me too."

"I do. But right now I'm more concerned about what you want."

"Daddy was right. I say what I mean and don't care who I say it too."

"That's the way I want you to be with me."

She took his hand, "If you promise to be Henry to me, I promise to be Caitlin to you. And I assure you that I will never confuse the office with the man." Then she added, "If we don't hit it off, it's over, no matter who you are."

He laughed, "Agreed."

They looked into each other's eyes for a few seconds, "Should I still come to lunch tomorrow?" he asked. "If your parents are too upset, we could go out."

"Come here. I'll try to get them to calm down."

"They should treat me like any other young man who is interested in their daughter."

"It's easy for you to say but it won't be easy for them." She paused and smiled, "Daddy's been a politician all of his life. He won't ever forget who you are no matter what you or I say. Mama might get over it, but Daddy never will."

"Just try to get them to relax."

"I'll try."

"I suppose I'd better leave now and let them get over the shock."

"I wish you would stay but you're right, we ought to think of them."

She took his hand again, "Henry, thank you for telling me who you are and for being honest."

He grinned, "Thank you for not getting mad."

They went to the family room where Henry bade her parents good night before he and Carl left.

"How'd it go?" Carl asked.

"Pretty good. Walter was right."

"How did she take it?"

"She's okay. We're still going to the ball game tomorrow. She's got a mind of her own and a head on her shoulders too."

Carl didn't comment. He already knew the King was hooked.

"Her dad was a basket case by the time you two came in."

"Yeah, I hate that."

"Her Mom relaxed a little after I talked to them. Maybe they'll be able to get him calmed down a little."

"I hope they can before lunch tomorrow."

Henry rang the York's doorbell at twelve o'clock sharp. Caitlin opened the door and curtsied with a devilish smile.

"Welcome to our humble abode, Your Majesty," she said with mock seriousness.

Carl laughed. Henry was surprised how bold she was.

"I thought we were not going to play this game."

Caitlin laughed, "I'm joking, Henry. Unwind a little yourself." He grinned.

She escorted them to the dining room where her parents waited. Her mother greeted him as Henry but her father was still very nervous and greeted him without calling him anything.

Lunch was simple. Henry had been afraid they'd have a five course meal laid out and he was pleased by the modest lunch. After Lord York said grace they began to eat. Conversation was strained at first until Carl and Lady York began to discuss gardening. Carl was an amateur horticulturist and he commented on the beauty of the York's lawn. He and Lady York hit it off and got into an intense and detailed discussion about flowers and shrubs. That broke the ice and Lord York began to discuss legislative issues with the King. Henry learned that he was a deft politician. Caitlin was well informed herself and joined their discussion. Lunchtime passed quickly and soon it was time for Henry and Caitlin to leave for the stadium. Henry drove the car while Carl rode in the other car with the bodyguards.

After a few blocks Caitlin observed, "You don't drive a lot, do you?"

"No," he admitted.

"You're driven most of the time?"

"Yeah. I'm not scaring you, am I?"

"No, not at all, but you're driving too slow."

"Slow? I'm driving the speed limit."

"Nobody drives the speed limit, Henry."

"I have to."

"Why? You're the King."

"I'll be found out if we're stopped. I don't want to take a chance on losing my anonymity."

"If you keep driving this slowly they'll think you're drunk and pull you over."

Henry sped up a little as he eyed her slyly out of the corner of his eye.

They had bleacher seats mid-way up behind home plate. Caitlin noticed that, although the stadium was crowded, the seats to their right and left and those in the row behind them were vacant.

"Carl bought the vacant seats, didn't he?"

"Yes."

"Daddy wanted to get us a booth but I told him you wouldn't like that."

"It would have made us too conspicuous."

"I prefer these seats anyway. I can get the feel of the game here."

The opening ceremony began with the introductions of the players. Caitlin gave Henry an earful of information about each player. She knew their lifetime batting average, their average the last six games and the number of errors they had made this season. Then she gave him a Ph.D.'s worth of information on the two starting pitchers and pitching strategy. Then came a salute to the American flag and a local singer sang "God Save the King", followed by the national anthem accompanied by a high school marching band. When "God Save the King" was sung, Caitlin looked at him.

"How do you feel when you hear that?"

"I'm used to it."

"Do you think the people here mean it?"

"Some do, some don't."

"Does it bother you that some don't?"

"I would rather have my subjects respect than their love."

She didn't comment.

"Play ball" rang out over the speakers. From that moment Caitlin gave a running commentary on the game. She was a true baseball enthusiast, a diehard Orioles fan and an unofficial announcer for those within the sound of her voice. Most of the fans close by thought it was humorous the way she got into the game and the men enjoyed looking at her in her shorts and halter-top.

But one fan was annoyed. He was in the seat directly in front of Caitlin and before the second inning was over he had made several derogatory remarks about her carrying on, which she ignored. When the players were changing at the bottom of the third inning, he'd had enough.

He stood up, turned around, faced her and said, "Lady, shut the fuck up."

"It's a free country," she retorted. "I can say whatever I want to say."

"Yeah, it is. And I want to be free from listening to your lip so shut the fuck up so I can enjoy the game a little too!" Then he sat down.

She was fuming but didn't say anything for a few minutes. Henry was grinning inwardly as he appeared to concentrate on the game. He was amazed at the defiance of this spirited woman sitting next to him. Then the opposing team hit long into centerfield and the Orioles player dropped the ball. That set her off and she started yelling and shaking her fist. The man in front stood up, turned around and told her to shut up. When she ignored him he made a grab for her. Henry then stood up.

"Stay out of this, Henry. I can handle this jerk."

The man grabbed her arm and in a split second, Henry had him by the collar. Before anybody could think, three very strong men appeared, grabbed the man and ushered him out of the stadium. Two stadium policemen observed the commotion and rushed to them as they were taking him out. After seeing the bodyguards' ID they assisted in taking him outside.

"What'd I do?" he implored angrily. "All I did was tell that stupid bitch to shut the fuck up so I could enjoy the game too."

The stadium policeman told him he had to leave stadium property or face arrest.

"What the fuck did I do?" he kept mumbling to himself as he walked away.

Caitlin resumed her enjoyment of the game.

After the game was over, Henry took her home to change clothes and then they went to Sabatino's for dinner.

"I wanted to have dinner with you Tuesday but I needed to stay with my party," she told him.

"I was very disappointed."

"Why were you attracted to me?"

"I liked the confident way you looked at me."

"You must attract a lot of women."

"The King does. Henry's a face in the crowd."

"Henry's pretty attractive to me."

"I never think about it one way or another."

"You act down to earth. Didn't you grow up knowing you'd be King one day?"

"You wouldn't believe how strict I was brought up."

"I guess you were. They knew what burdens you'd face." Then she had a thought, "Is it a burden?"

"I like being King. I guess I was born to be one. But sometimes it would be nice to be an ordinary man and relax a little."

"You can relax around me."

"Thank you for letting me. I wanted you to think I was an ordinary man."

"Aren't you?"

"Yes, but I don't have an ordinary job."

"Henry, if we fell in love what would happen?"

"You'd be my Queen."

"You could marry somebody like me?"

"Sure. All of the other Clark queens have been Americans."

"I want us to be in love."

"I don't want a queen who doesn't love me."

"Then we agree on that."

"Yeah."

"I will expect my husband to respect me too."

"Caitlin, you won't have to worry about that no matter how this turns out."

She looked away like she was thinking about something. When she looked at him, she had a serious expression.

"Henry, I'm not a virgin."

"That's okay. But you must be faithful to me."

"If we fall in love, I will."

"I know you will."

"I won't sleep with you until we love each other."

"We're supposed to wait until we're married anyway."

"Is that a royal rule?"

"My cabinet doesn't want me sleeping around."

"You mean they advise you on that too?"

"They don't want to have any royal bastards to deal with."

"Oh," she murmured and then asked, "Have you slept with anybody?"

"Yes."

"Did they know?"

"They found out."

"What did they do?"

"Nothing. I don't always do what my cabinet advises me to do."

"You don't have any royal bastards, do you?"

"No."

"Don't start now."

"Why do you say that? Do you think I'm about to?"

"I see the way you look at me. You're not thinking kingly thoughts when you look at me the way you do."

He laughed, "Is it so obvious? I'm trying to be dignified."

"You are dignified, but I know what you're thinking."

"How?"

She pinched his cheek, "Because I'm thinking the same thing, Henry." Then she laughed too.

They went to a club where they danced the rest of the evening away.

"You are an excellent dancer," she observed.

"Part of my strict upbringing was I had to learn to dance well."

"That was money well spent."

"You wouldn't want to know how much it was."

He took her home a little after midnight.

"Could I see you tomorrow afternoon?" he asked.

"Yes." She paused, "I enjoyed this afternoon and evening, Henry."

"I enjoyed being with you very much, Caitlin."

"I enjoyed it a lot but this will take quite a bit of getting used to. I'll need time to think about it."

"I'm going back to Kansas City on Monday morning."

"Could you come tomorrow at fourteen o'clock?"

"I'd like to."

"We could go to a concert tomorrow night."

"Which one?"

"The Baltimore Philharmonic." She laughed, "The program will be United States patriotic music."

He grinned, "That's okay."

"How about dinner at our house?"

"As long as it's a regular meal, nothing lavish."

"My sister and her husband will be here."

"That's okay."

"Me having a man as my guest is unusual."

"It shouldn't be." He was thinking it was because he was king.

"I've never had a man as my guest for dinner with my parents before."

"That's surprising."

"Can I tell my sister who you are?"

"Will they keep it to themselves?"

"I believe so."

"Okay."

She kissed his cheek, "Goodnight, Henry."

"Goodnight, Caitlin."

Chapter Ten

Caitlin's sister was stunned by the news about who Caitlin was bringing to dinner. Who wouldn't have been? Ashley, like her father, was uncomfortable dealing with high ranking people. Her mother tried to calm her down after she mentioned being afraid of being beheaded if she offended the King with something she said.

Her husband, Brent, took it all in with a bemused smile as he watched his wife agonize about what to wear and coached him about proper table etiquette all the way to her parent's home.

"Why in the world would Caitlin subject her family to something like this?" she asked.

"I doubt if she did it deliberately, Ashley. It just happened."

"You can believe that if you want to but I know everything Caitlin does is deliberate. She never 'just happens' to do anything."

"Now, Ashley, how could Caitlin have managed to meet the King on purpose?"

"I don't know but I know her and she is 'Miss Organized' to the nth degree."

"Well, it's a pretty big stretch to think she set this up."

"Caitlin always was odd, you know. She's not like a normal person."

"She's always acted pretty normal around me."

"You don't know her like I do. When she makes up her mind about something she sticks to it no matter what."

"I like that about her."

"You haven't been around her like I have. She is the most insufferable person on earth when she sets her mind on something."

"You mean like baseball?"

"Yes, think about it! A high society woman that is wild about baseball. You ought to see the way she carries on at games."

"How do you know how she acts?"

"I went with her once."

"You did?"

"Yes, but I'll never do it again."

"Why? What did she do?"

"She's a regular baseball facts encyclopedia. I bet she knows the jock strap sizes of every player in the American League. And it's so embarrassing to see how she acts during the game, like standing up and yelling and carrying on all the time. More people watch her than watch the game. Especially the men when she wears short shorts and a halter-top. It is embarrassing I can tell you."

"Well, she's always acted okay around me."

"You don't know her like I do. She probably thinks she's about to hook the King but she'd better not let him see how she acts at baseball games. It would be over by the second inning of the first game he took her to."

"Caitlin is very personable and very attractive, Ashley."

"You say that, but you don't know her like I do."

When Henry and Carl arrived Sunday afternoon, Caitlin ushered them into the York's living room. After the greetings were over, Carl and Lord and Lady York adjourned to the family room leaving Caitlin and Henry alone. They talked for a few minutes about general subjects.

"Would you like to go somewhere?" he asked.

"Clifton Park is nice this time of year."

"You drive."

As he rose to leave Caitlin asked, "Aren't you going to tell Carl you're leaving?"

"I ought to."

She left to bring her car around while he told Carl and her parents where they were going. Carl ordered two of the bodyguards to follow the King and the other one would remain at the York home.

After arriving at the park, they walked around the perimeter and then sat on a bench overlooking the floral gardens.

"This is a pretty place," he remarked.

"I think so. I come here when I need to be alone."

"Everybody needs a place where they can be away from their normal life."

"Do you have one?"

"I go to Montana when I need to be by myself."

"To be alone?"

"That and to see my best friend."

They sat quietly for a few minutes, each absorbed in their thoughts.

"Henry, I told you I was not a virgin, but I don't want you to think I sleep around."

"It hadn't occurred to me that you did."

"It happened when I was seventeen."

"It's none of my business, Caitlin."

"We were at the beach and I had this huge crush on a boy staying in the cottage next door. He came over one afternoon when I was alone in the house and one thing led to another and we had sex."

"Don't worry about it."

"He wouldn't have anything to do with me afterwards. I was crushed. After that I vowed never to sleep with a man unless both of us were in love."

"That's a good way to look at it."

"I haven't been with anybody else, Henry."

He looked at her. She returned his gaze, "I wanted you to know."

He couldn't get over how beautiful she looked when she was being serious.

"We need to leave in a few minutes. Would you like to walk some more," she asked.

"I'm okay sitting here with you."

"Mom said my sister was more upset than Dad was."

"I hate that. There's no reason for her to be concerned."

"I know. But she's always worries about everything anyway."

"And you don't worry?" Henry asked.

"No. I take life as it comes. I believe fate is neutral. It doesn't care one way or another. You ought to make the best of what comes your way."

"That is an excellent way to look at it."

"Fate brought us together, didn't it?" she said.

"Yes, it did."

"What we make of it is up to us, isn't it?"

"Yes, Caitlin. It is up to us."

"My heart is already telling me I love you."

"Mine is too, Caitlin."

"My mind is yelling at me to cool it!"

Henry laughed, "So is mine."

"Our hearts and minds are miles apart."

"For the time being, we ought to heed our minds."

"I know. But I've never felt this close to anybody before."

"Yeah, I could just stay here with you forever," he said quietly.

"It would be nice, wouldn't it?"

"Yes."

"What time will you leave tomorrow?"

"Nine."

"Could I see you off?" she asked.

"I don't know why not."

"Where will you eat breakfast?"

"At the Officers Mess in the airport."

"Which airport?"

"Andrews Air Force Base."

111

"Could I join you?"

"I'll have Carl get you a pass."

She looked at her watch, "We need to get back. Ashley and Brent should be arriving about the time we get home."

They held hands on the way back to her car.

Ashley actually liked Henry and was soon at ease with him. She told her mother while she was helping in the kitchen that she thought the King was easy to get to know.

"Your father is still very nervous around him."

"You know how Daddy is. He's always worried about making somebody mad. He'd be the same if it was a gardener or a mechanic."

"Now he's worried what will happen if Caitlin makes him mad. You know how she can tic people off."

Ashley laughed, "I think it'll be over by the first inning of the first baseball game he takes her to."

"They've already been to one."

"You're kidding! And he's still interested?"

"Apparently."

"That's amazing. She must have behaved differently around him than she did the time I went."

"She almost got into a fight with a man. His guards intervened and hauled the guy off," her mother said with a smile.

"He must really like her!"

"They seem to get along. She likes him a lot."

"Do you think it's because he's the King?"

"I don't think so. You know she never cared anything about what people were. I believe she views his being King as a handicap."

"I think so too," Ashley said. "Never any privacy to vent."

Francis laughed, "That won't bother Caitlin one bit."

Ashley giggled, "You're right. This will be interesting."

"Caitlin always kept the other men she dated at arms length. I know that two of them liked her a lot, but she kept her distance. She's different with Henry. She likes to be close to him."

"Like I just said, this will be very interesting. By the way, why isn't she helping us?" Ashley wanted to know.

"She's with him. She's always been good about helping me but when he's here, she's with him and I don't believe she even thinks about helping me."

Ashley put her hand to her mouth to suppress a giggle, "Mama, I believe Caitlin is in love."

"I liked your sister and her husband," Henry commented on the way to the concert.

"She wasn't as bad as I was afraid she'd be."

"You mean about me?"

"Yes, she warmed up to you pretty quickly."

"I tried to put her at ease."

"It worked in this case. I'm glad too."

"You seem quieter than usual," he observed.

"You're leaving tomorrow."

"I'll be back on the thirtieth."

"You will?"

"We're having a victory parade on the second of July and I'll be here to make a speech and review the troops."

"Will you have time to see me?" Caitlin asked.

"I'll make time."

"Will you be busy?"

"Very. Would you sit with me on the reviewing stand?" he asked.

"I don't think so. I'm not ready for that yet."

She saw he was disappointed, "But I'll be out in the crowd watching you."

"Then you can monitor my speech and tell me how good or bad it was."

"Don't you have people doing that already?"

"I'm never sure they're truthful. I know you'll tell me the truth."

"Henry, it's not that I don't want to be up there with you. It's that I wouldn't feel right about it. We just met."

"I understand."

"I'm not ready to be a queen."

"There'll be a formal banquet Sunday evening. Would you accompany me to it?"

"I don't know," she replied.

"There'll be a fancy dress ball afterwards."

"That sounds more interesting."

"Will you go?" he asked.

"If I don't, you'll be dancing with everybody else won't you?"

"I have to dance with the wives of the notables at least once."

"How many will that be?"

"Fifteen at the most. Your mom will be one of them."

"Is it open to the public?"

"The galleries will be open."

"Will they be able to dance?" she asked.

"Only if invited by an official guest."

"I bet every social climbing single woman in a thousand miles will be lined up to dance with you."

"Probably."

"Then I'd better go. I don't want any royal bastards either."

"Lady York has arrived, Your Majesty."

"Please escort her in, Major."

When Caitlin was brought to him, Henry noticed she was well dressed.

"Do you dress like this for work?"

"Heavens no, Your Majesty."

"You look exceptionally beautiful this morning."

"One must look one's best when one is dining with one's king." she answered with a smirky smile.

He grinned, "Yes, I suppose one must."

Carl came up to them and greeted Caitlin, "Good morning Lady York. It's good to see you again."

"Nice to see you again, too, Lord Gillespie."

"You look very nice today."

"Thank you. His Majesty thinks so too."

Carl laughed, "I'm sure he does."

They were called to their tables. Caitlin was seated to the king's right and Carl was to her right. General Sir Horatio Gates, commanding general for the Occupation Army in Maryland, was seated to the King's left. General Gates made a short speech about the honor of having their King share breakfast with them and made brief complimentary remarks about the officers invited to attend this occasion. He then asked the Bishop of the Catholic Diocese of Maryland to say grace. The prayer focused on the special occasion, thanks to God for the goodness and dignity of their King, expressed the hopes of the people of Maryland and asked for divine guidance for His Majesty. He ended with thanks for the meal and for the presence of the King's beautiful guest. Caitlin discretely slipped her hand into Henry's during the prayer. He squeezed it when the bishop said "Amen."

After they began eating, Caitlin commented to Henry, "This is delicious. Is it always this good, or is it because you're here?"

"It's supposed to be this good all the time whether I'm here or not. They are required to use fresh ingredients if possible."

"I've been told there are public mess halls all over America."

114

"There are. In urban areas we try to have public mess halls no more than four miles apart."

"Is it free?"

"Yes, all you do is walk in and show your ID."

"Will we have them in Maryland too?"

"They should be up and running in the new territory within two years."

"I bet a lot of people never cook at home."

"I've heard that."

"What is your favorite breakfast?"

"I won't tell anybody."

"Why not?"

"If I do, it'll be menu everywhere I go."

"I suppose you're right."

"My father said he let it slip out once that he liked deviled eggs."

"What happened?"

"From that day forward, deviled eggs were prominent items on the menu every where he went, including Saudi Arabia and Algeria."

She laughed, "I bet he got tired of them."

Then General Gates got the King's attention and spent the rest of the meal briefing him on occupation and territorial administration details.

Caitlin looked over the officers in the room and noted several high-ranking women officers, including one general.

"Does the military have a lot of women in it?" she asked Carl.

"Quite a few."

"What do they do?"

"The same things a male officer would do."

"How about enlisted?"

"It's the same there. The only difference is all men of military age are required to serve but all the women are volunteers. Women are not required to perform military service."

"Are they discouraged in any way?"

"No."

"Will I have a few minutes of privacy with the King before he leaves?"

He smiled, "Yes, Caitlin. I've reserved a conference room adjacent to this dining room until the King boards the plane."

"Thank you, Carl." She smiled, "You think of everything don't you?"

"Not in this case. His Majesty ordered me to reserve it."

115

"Thank you for telling me."

"Are you enjoying your meal?"

"Very much."

"How do you like the military atmosphere?"

"It's different. But I think I could get used to it."

"The King likes it better than a civilian atmosphere."

"Does he have a military rank?"

"He is Commander-in-Chief."

After the meal was finished, the King mingled with his officers for a few minutes until they began leaving. Carl had told Caitlin she should stand with the King. She was a little uncomfortable about it but everybody was friendly and several made small talk with her. One was the female Royal Air Force General.

"Are you a pilot?" Caitlin asked her.

"I was a fighter pilot."

"I bet that was exciting."

"Oh, it was. Flying along at four thousand miles per hour gets your adrenalin up."

"When did you decide to be a pilot?" Caitlin asked.

"I was a tomboy when I was growing up and always wanted to be a fighter pilot.

"Were you in combat?"

"Yes. And I'm an Ace."

"Wow. I'm impressed."

"It was nice to meet you, Lady York. Are you with the Royal Party?"

"No. I'm the King's friend."

She gave Caitlin a knowing look, "Then it has been my pleasure to meet you. And maybe I'll see you again soon."

Henry's official duties were finally over and he led Caitlin into a conference room down a hall from the main dining room. Refreshments, including chilled wine were on a table in the corner.

"Did they think we were going to eat in here?" she commented laughing.

"They go overboard when I'm around."

"Thank you for letting me come."

"Thank you for coming."

They faced each other awkwardly for a few seconds.

"I know it's been a short time, but I'll miss you, Henry."

"I'll miss you too."

"You know, we haven't kissed."

"No. We haven't."

"Would you kiss me goodbye?"

He took her into his arms and kissed her. Then he kissed her with more passion. She pushed back.

"I won't be able to sleep for a week now," she whispered.

"Will you see me on the thirtieth?"

"You know I will."

"Caitlin, I...," he paused as if he was trying to formulate his thoughts. He continued, "I can't wait." He still looked like he wanted to say something else but didn't.

"I'll count the minutes, Henry."

Carl knocked on the door.

"Your Majesty, it's time to go."

He took her into his arms and kissed her again.

"Goodbye," he said.

"Goodbye, Henry," she whispered.

She accompanied him to the plane and stood outside the hangar watching it taxi and take off. She watched until it disappeared into the distance.

Carl observed her watching them. "Your Majesty, I believe Lady York likes you very much."

"Yes, she does. And I like her very much too."

Chapter Eleven

They hadn't discussed how much and how often they would communicate but Caitlin expected Henry to call her after he returned to Kansas City. By Wednesday, she was worried. Did he like her like he said he did? Or did his cabinet suggest he not pursue a woman who had recently gained aristocratic status? Was the past week a dream and she was waking up?

Carl had left his card with her and seemed sincere when he told her she could call him anytime. She called him Thursday night.

"I thought Henry might have called me," she said when he answered.

"We have a situation with Namibia," he told her. "Some missionaries are missing and the locals are not being cooperative in helping us locate them."

"Oh."

"He's been very busy."

"That's okay. I was wondering if everything was alright."

Carl read between the lines, "Caitlin, the king is sincere about his interest in you and your relationship with him. He will contact you at the first moment he has the time to do so."

"I'm sorry. I didn't mean to be childish about this."

"You continue to be prominent in his thoughts, Lady York."

"Thank you, Carl. I'm sorry I bothered you."

"Call me anytime, Caitlin."

Henry called five minutes later.

"Carl said you were worried."

"Not worried, Henry. I needed a reality check."

"A reality check?"

"I hadn't heard anything and I was beginning to wonder if it was real."

Henry didn't reply at once. She thought they might have been cut off. "It's real," he said quietly. "Caitlin. I think about you every free minute."

"But you haven't had many free minutes?"

"No, I haven't."

"I don't want to appear childish."

"You're not. I ought to have called."

"Is it okay if I call occasionally?"

"I'll have Carl send you a phone you can use to call me direct."

118

"Thank you."

"You can use it anytime. I won't answer it if I'm busy and can't talk."

"Henry, talking to you is nice but I want to see you."

"I want to see you too, Caitlin."

"I want you to kiss me again."

He was quiet, "Don't think because I'm not available that I'm not interested. I'm as interested as I was when we were together on the park bench."

"Thank you for telling me."

"It's true. Will you be okay now?"

"I feel much better." She paused, "I'll try to be more patient."

"I'll see you as soon as I can arrange it."

But he wouldn't see her until the twenty-ninth of June. By then the missionaries had been rescued and he was Emperor of Namibia.

He was as good as his word about calling and called her at odd times a couple of times a week. She tried to be disciplined about calling him. She'd called him once with the phone Carl sent but she could tell by the way he sounded that he was preoccupied and she wished she hadn't bothered him. But he did thank her for calling.

On the twenty-ninth she was getting ready for bed when she remembered her book was downstairs. When she went down to get it, the doorbell rang. She opened the door and there was Henry. Without saying a word, he gathered her up into his arms and kissed her. Then he let her go and stood back to look.

"You are more beautiful than I remember."

She was embarrassed, "Henry, you surprised me. I'm not made up and I'm dressed for bed."

"You are beautiful."

She got her wits about her a little, "Won't you come in?"

He came inside and closed the door. Her mother called down from upstairs.

"Who's there, Caitlin?"

"Henry."

"Henry who?"

"Mama, it's Henry Clark."

"Do I know him?"

"Mama, it's the King!"

"Oh!" There was a short pause before she said anything else, "Tell him we're glad he's back." Then they heard her parent's bedroom door close.

She laughed, "Mama's embarrassed."

They went into the living room and sat on the couch.

"I know it's late but I had to see you."

"You're early. I expected you tomorrow."

"I couldn't wait."

She smiled at him, "I feel happy all over when you're around."

"I can't stay long because I've got to get ready for tomorrow."

She took his hand, "Do what you need to do, Henry. I can be flexible. But I do want you to spend some time with me."

"My official business will be finished on Thursday afternoon. Would you like to go with me somewhere? I don't have to return to Kansas City until Monday morning."

"You mean we could spend three whole days together?"

"Yes, if you would."

"Three uninterrupted days?"

"Yes, three uninterrupted days."

"I want to."

"Where would you like to go?"

"The beach?"

"That's fine."

She kissed his cheek, "What will our sleeping arrangements be?"

"We'll be in separate suites."

She was both disappointed and relieved, "I'm okay with that."

"We must be disciplined because I don't want to get you pregnant. It would be a terrible scandal if we had a child out of wedlock."

"Oh. No royal bastards again, right?"

"Right. No royal bastards. My council would be very upset."

"I would be too. I don't want to have an illegitimate baby."

"Caitlin, you are so very beautiful."

"Thank you, Your Majesty. I'm very glad you find me attractive."

"I've got to go."

"Where are you staying?"

"The Hilton at Dulles Airport."

She kissed him, "And you came all the way up here to see me for ten minutes?"

"Yes, I did. I've got to be back in twenty minutes."

"You'll never make it. It takes over an hour from here."

"I'm on a Hover Platform."

"Oh." She didn't know what it was but didn't want to waste their precious time together with him describing something she'd never seen.

He stood up, "I'd better go. Will you join me for breakfast tomorrow?"

"Sure. Where?"

"At the Hilton."

"What time?"

"Seven."

"I'll have to leave at five o'clock to get there."

"No, you won't. I'll have you picked up."

"What time?"

"Six-thirty."

"I guess I'll fly."

"Yes. What time are you supposed to be at work?"

"Nine o'clock."

"I can get you back by then."

They walked to the door together. He took her into his arms and held her.

"My heart still tells me I love you, Henry."

"Mine tells me the same about you, Caitlin."

He kissed her, opened the door and left. She looked out into the street and saw a squat oval machine with Army markings in the driveway entrance. When Henry approached, a gull-wing door lifted up from the center and Henry got in. She saw another man inside and assumed he was the pilot. The door closed, it made a whirring sound, and then it lifted off and was out of sight in seconds.

When she went upstairs, her mother met her outside her bedroom.

"I'm sorry I didn't catch who he was. Was he upset?"

"No, Mama, he wasn't."

"I'm glad. He seems to be very nice."

"Mama, he's the nicest man I've ever met."

"You like him a lot, don't you?"

"I love him, Mama."

"Already?"

"Yes."

"Does he know?"

"I've told him my heart loves him but my head tells me to cool it."

"What did he say?"

"He feels the same way about me."

121

"Both of you need to listen to your heads for a while."

"We know."

"Could he marry you?"

"Yes, he can."

"I'm surprised. We're nobodies really."

"All of the Clark Dynasty kings have had American wives."

"But you only became an American on the first of June."

"He said it didn't matter."

"So he can do what he wants to do?"

"He can, but he pays attention to his council."

"Do they know about you?"

"Yes. They're the ones who persuaded him to tell me who he really was the night they came over."

"He sounds like a very careful man."

"He wanted to know that I loved him for himself and not as the king."

"I can see how he'd be concerned about that."

"They persuaded him to be truthful with me about who he was."

"Why would they care?"

"Their thinking was if I ended up to be the one he wanted to marry he ought not to start off by lying about who he was."

"They certainly look ahead about things."

Caitlin laughed, "They don't want to take any chances which could result in royal bastards."

"I thank them for that. But you've always kept your wits about you in those matters."

"I have, Mama. But I've never been in love before."

"I know you'll always try to do the right thing, Caitlin."

"I will and he tries too."

"Caitlin, your father and I love you very much, no matter how this turns out. We'll always be here for you if you need us."

"Thank you, Mama. It seems so unreal. I love a man who rules a third of the world. I have to pinch myself and then I still have trouble believing it's happening to me."

"If anybody can deal with it, you can. I don't know of another young woman as level-headed as you are."

"Thanks for your confidence, Mama. I'll try to keep things in perspective."

"I know you will. When will he see you again?"

"I'm having breakfast with him tomorrow morning at seven."

"Where?"

"The Dulles Hilton."

"Good lord, you'd better get to bed. You'll have to get up at three a.m."

"He's sending for me at six-thirty."

"You'll never make it, even without traffic."

"He's sending some kind of Army thing to pick me up. It looks like a flattened football and it just swooshes through the air."

"I guess he could since he is the king."

"I can't wait to ride in it. It looked so neat when he left. It just swooshed away into the night."

"Caitlin, always remember your father and I love you and always want what's best for you."

"I know, Mama. I love you and Daddy too."

Lieutenant Gibson rang the York's doorbell at exactly six twenty-five. Caitlin opened the door.

"Lady York, I'm here to take you to breakfast with His Majesty."

The Hover Platform was not designed to carry passengers she had trouble getting into it. Finally, she asked Lieutenant Gibson to look the other away so she could hike up her dress and climb in.

It was a thrilling ride and quiet enough inside the vehicle to allow normal conversation. Gibson called ahead to ask for a stool when they landed so she could exit the craft with a little more dignity. Twelve minutes later they were landing in the parking lot of the hotel. Lieutenant Gibson escorted her to the hotel entrance where Carl met her.

"Good morning, Lady York. It's nice to see you again."

"Good morning Carl, nice to see you too." She noticed the crowded hotel lobby. "Why are all these people here?"

"They are having breakfast with the king."

She hadn't thought about a crowd. She had assumed the group would be about the same size as in the Officer's Mess when she ate with him the last time.

"How many are here?"

"Two hundred and fifty seven, Lady York."

"I hadn't thought there would be so many guests."

Carl sensed her unease, "Don't worry, Caitlin. You'll be all right. You are quite beautiful this morning."

"Thank you. I hope so. I'm glad I dressed up this time too." She laughed, "He didn't tell me how to dress. Suppose I'd worn jeans?"

"His Majesty would have thought you were beautiful, Lady York." Then he added, "You will sit on His Majesty's right again. Lady Pamela Hastings will be to your right."

"Who's she?"

"She's the Royal Air Force general who was with the King on his last visit."

"Oh, I spoke with her when she was leaving."

"I'll take you to His Majesty now. You must bow to the King when I present you to him."

They threaded their way through the crowd and approached a group of dignitaries. When they saw Carl they parted to allow him and Caitlin to approach the King.

"Your Majesty, Lady York has arrived."

Caitlin bowed as instructed, "Good morning, Your Majesty."

Henry smiled, "Good morning, Caitlin," and took her hand.

"I didn't expect such a crowd, Your Majesty."

"I'm afraid it will be a crowded week until Thursday. But I wanted you beside me this morning."

"And I wanted to be beside you, Your Majesty." She gave him a sweet smile.

The onlookers observed their verbal ballet with quiet curiosity. One of the ladies whispered, "Who is she?"

The other whispered back, "I don't know. I've never seen her before."

The King's steward called the group to breakfast and the guests in the lobby moved into a dining room. Henry and the royal party sat at a long head table on a platform. It allowed them to look out over the crowd and the crowd to look up at them. The newly installed Royal Governor of Maryland, Lord Thomas Whitford, rose to greet the dignitaries and their King. Henry was invited to speak and he made a few complimentary remarks about how much progress had been made toward integrating the new territories into his kingdom and thanked everybody present for their part in the enterprise. Then the Bishop of the Maryland Diocese said grace, adding effusive thanks for their wise and loving King. Henry held Caitlin's hand during the prayer.

During the meal, Henry divided his time between the governor on his left and Caitlin. The governor apparently understood Caitlin was a special person to the King and did not invoke his right of first place by rank to the King's attention. When Henry and the governor were engaged in conversation, Pamela Hastings and Caitlin chatted.

"It's nice to see you again, Lady York. How have you been?"

124

"I'm fine. And it's nice to see you too, Lady Hastings. I haven't been doing anything special or interesting, just working and visiting with my friends. How about you?"

"It's been pretty exciting on my end. I got back from Namibia on Tuesday."

"Carl told me there was some kind of emergency with Namibia."

"Not any more. Namibia has been annexed. It's part of His Majesty's Empire now. Since Sunday, he's been Emperor of Namibia."

"That was quick."

"The Namibian dictator was a mean, grubby little man who terrorized his people. His favorite thing was to cut limbs off of anybody who so much as looked at him the wrong way. There are thousands of Namibians missing parts of their bodies because of his cruelty. A village chief cursed him once and he had the feet of every man in the village cut off."

"What a terrible thing!"

"We went in to rescue two nuns and a priest who'd been arrested but when His Majesty was informed about conditions in the country, he ordered us to remove the governing body by force, execute the top three tiers of government officials and establish a Royal administration until the population could recover from all those years of irrational cruelty. The whole population acts like a whipped dog. It will be at least a generation before they recover any pride and self confidence."

"Are the nuns and the priest okay?"

"Yes, they're fine but they had a few harrowing days."

"Then Henry was very busy."

"Yes, he was. Henry's decisiveness and ability to choose the proper solution makes his kingdoms successful."

Caitlin laughed, "He is decisive."

Pamela smiled, "Yes, he is and he is quite taken with you. Insiders are already betting that you will become our Queen."

Caitlin blushed, "It's a little early to think about that. We just met."

"I know, but the way he acts when you're around it is evident that he is quite attached to you already."

"We do get along."

"You are the only woman he's behaved this way over."

"He must have a lot of women after him."

"He's mobbed everywhere he goes. But their goal is to be with the King. He hates it."

Caitlin laughed, "The night he told me who he was, I told him if we didn't hit it off, he was history no matter who he was."

Pamela laughed out loud, "That is great! I like you, Caitlin."

Henry heard Pamela laugh, "What's so funny?"

"I told her what I said to you in our living room the night you came over and confessed that you were King."

He looked at Pamela and grinned, "She has her own opinions, Lady Hastings."

"I think it's wonderful, Your Majesty," Pamela replied with a smile.

Henry returned to his conversation with the governor while Caitlin and Pamela began what was to become a lifelong friendship over breakfast that morning.

She didn't get to work on time. Carl called on her behalf to inform her office she'd be late. She also had precious little time with Henry before he had to leave. When they were alone in an adjacent conference room for a few minutes he apologized for his hectic schedule.

"I'll be okay as long as we can have the three days you promised me," she told him after they kissed.

"You will. I promise. And I want some quiet time for us much as you do."

"Where will we go?"

"I have a place in North Myrtle Beach."

"That's fine."

"My security would much prefer we go there rather than a public resort."

"Will people be around us all the time there too?"

"Just the servants and Carl."

"But we can be alone where we can talk?"

"Yes."

"I feel like I'm in a whirlwind now. I'm not ready for all this queen talk. All I want to do is get to know you."

"We'll have three days starting Thursday."

"When will I see you again?"

"How about a private breakfast tomorrow?"

"Just you and me?"

"Just us."

"Where?"

"Here."

"Will I be picked up again?"

"Sure."

"That was so neat," she smiled.

"It doesn't have to be as early."

"Seven o'clock is fine with me."

"Then seven it is."

"Kiss me, Henry."

He called a little before bedtime and told her he'd missed having her by his side all day.

At six-twenty-five Lieutenant Gibson rang her doorbell again. This time he had brought a stool. The lobby was almost empty when Carl escorted her up to Henry's suite for breakfast. A table had been set for them beside a window overlooking Dulles Airport. The room furnishings were lavish and the table was set with very expensive china and silverware. Henry was dressed in slacks and a loose sweater.

"You look very handsome," she told him after they kissed.

"I don't have any meetings until ten."

A very well dressed woman wheeled in a cart with their food. After she set out their meal and left, Caitlin asked if she was a hotel employee.

"She's my personal servant, Rebecca. Regular hotel employees get so excited about the prospect of serving me they sometimes spill the food. Then they're mortified and cry about it no matter what I say. It's kinder to do it this way."

"Henry, how on earth could you have kept up the façade about being an ordinary guy?"

"I realize now it wouldn't have worked."

"Sometimes I think it would have been easier myself. You're so busy and you're never alone."

"We have to manage with things like they are."

"If we fell madly in love but I couldn't handle the public life part to the point that it was either me or the Kingdom, which would it be?"

"The Kingdom," he replied without hesitation.

She was quiet for a few seconds, "Thank you for being honest with me."

"Thank you for being honest with me. Neither of us can have the luxury of illusions in this matter. I am King and being the King must always come first, no matter how I feel personally."

She turned her attention to her food and ate while staring out towards the airport.

127

"I guess it can't be any other way," she said quietly almost as if she was talking to herself.

"You are a very intelligent woman. You can do anything you make up your mind to do."

"But will it be worth it to me?"

"Caitlin, that is a question only you can answer."

"I still want us to love each other like we would if you weren't King."

"That's what I want too, Caitlin. What I want more than anything is have a wife who loves me, to be the mother of my children and my Queen."

"Actually, loving you is not difficult. And if we do work things out I would be happy to have your children. I just have to make up my mind about being queen."

"You're as qualified to be my Queen as any woman in my Kingdoms."

"I may be, but it will still be a very big adjustment."

He took her hand, "If you want to, I know you can do it. And you must know that I want you to."

She started to become emotional. Tears came into her eyes, "I know you do, Henry. I want to be yours with all my heart but it hurts because it's so one-sided. I'm the one who has to adjust. I am an important person too."

He took her hand, "Yes, you are. You are most important to me. Don't worry about it now. We have plenty of time to work things out."

She wiped her tears with her napkin, "Thank you, Henry."

They spent the remainder of the meal discussing his schedule. They tried to eke out a few private moments together over the next four days without much success. He kissed her tenderly before she had to leave.

Chapter Twelve

The sun rose Sunday to a perfect, cloudless, summer day in Washington. Everything was in readiness for the parade.

Local citizens in the new territories had never seen an American victory parade so they looked forward to the event with mixed feelings. On one hand, life in the former United States capital was decidedly better. The city was cleaner, everything was in repair and nobody complained about feeling safe when they ventured out into the city. But a lot of them missed the freedom of living in a democratic society. Those of a more observant nature knew they had a better chance to realize their individual family and career goals under the monarchy. But the monarchy was all business, with a no nonsense attitude about everything. The adjustment to a class society had taken a toll on many lifelong relationships and in some isolated cases even separated husbands and wives. For most of the new Americans, the formality of this new society was a very difficult adjustment.

Making it harder were the opportunists. They appeared in greater numbers than one would ever have guessed and they embraced the new ways with an unsettling, unbearable fervor. Unfortunately monarchy has historically produced more sycophants than any other form of government other than totalitarian dictatorships. And from the new territories, sycophants appeared in every nook and cranny. To listen to them, they had been against democratic government since the sighting of Plymouth Rock. But for normal people, the event would be a new gauge on which to contemplate life in a new and very different political environment.

Across the Potomac, citizens of Virginia had already been a part of the Kingdom for a generation and simply saw it as a chance to see their young King for the first time. Knowing he was unmarried and that he needed a queen, many Virginia belles pulled every string possible to obtain invitations to the Celebration Ball. Society pages of the Richmond Times Dispatch had been filled for weeks with pictures of His Majesty in various poses and settings, and detailed conventional wisdom as to what qualities of feminine pulchritude and intellectual attributes he might desire in his queen. Every ambitious single woman within the aristocracy and quite a few commoners considered themselves the perfect candidate. The problem was how to catch His Majesty's eye. As a result, obtaining invitations to the ball became a frenzied quest and many young military officers succeeded in seducing the most alluring of Southern goddesses by holding out the possibility of an invitation to THE BALL.

It would be an affair to remember for many reasons.

Caitlin attended the pre-celebration breakfast with the King. It was more crowded than the one on Wednesday morning but she got to sit beside him again and he held her hand while the Bishop prayed. This was the only informal contact she would have with him until the ball. Pamela sat to her right again and they could talk when Henry was otherwise occupied. But, it was "His Majesty" again today and not "Henry" as Caitlin preferred.

People were beginning to notice her and those of a more perceptive nature realized Caitlin was more than pretty furniture sitting beside their King. He was obviously solicitous of her and went out of his way to have her beside him whenever possible. Society was beginning to wonder who she was and how she fit into the royal scheme of things.

They were even more puzzled by the seating arrangements on the parade reviewing stand. The seat to the King's right remained vacant as if it had been reserved for someone important who could not attend.

By seven o'clock the parade route was cleared of all traffic. When the middle of the procession was adjacent to the reviewing stand, the parade would stop, do a right face and stand for the King's address. Big screens had been placed along the route to allow those unable to be near the center to see and hear the King. Even the prisoners of war would hear his address. By sunrise the city was already crowded and by seven-thirty all places along the parade route were taken. People were hanging out of windows and along rooftops. Security was tight but unobtrusive. The King did not wish to be observed always surrounded by guards and often mingled with the crowds, shaking hands and speaking personally to his subjects.

The celebrated Algerian Infantry in their colorful native costumes stepped off smartly at nine o'clock. Their officers were mounted on white Arabian chargers festooned with silver breastplates and colorful banners. Troops of each nationality proudly wore native garb and tried to outdo the others in spit and polish. Every unit had different dress uniforms so parade watchers could easily distinguish between the First Royal Marines, the Third Royal Georgia and the 3rd Royal Panamanian Regiment. The 11th Royal Texans were all mounted on identical black quarter horses, each having a white stocking on the left front leg. Naturally, the 5th Tennessee rode high-stepping Tennessee walkers. It was a spectacular military parade and it provided visiting dignitaries and the foreign press a look at the proudest, most confident and deadliest military force on earth.

Caitlin squeezed in among the first row of onlookers directly across from the reviewing stand where she could watch Henry. The Washington Monument dominated the skyline behind the podium. The parade stopped when the exact mid-point was in front of the stand where the King stood. When it stopped, the troops did a smart right face and all of the bands played "God Save the King", followed by the national anthem.

When the songs ended, General Gates presented the King. "Fellow soldiers, officers, ladies and gentlemen, I present to you His Royal Majesty, Henry the First, King of America, Canada, Mexico and New Zealand. His Excellency, the Emperor of Algeria, Panama, Saudi Arabia, South Africa, Venezuela and Namibia."

Henry stood to the thunderous applause of Army, Marines, Air Force and Navy troops and from the crowd of bystanders. Caitlin saw he was wearing his Commander-in-Chief uniform.

After the applause died down, he made formal greetings to General Gates, the Royal governors in attendance, (taking special notice of the new governors from Maryland and Delaware), to the Corps Generals, his troops and the members of the public. Then he began his speech with a civics lesson:

"The first priority of any national government is to protect its citizens from outside threat. All of you, even those in the new territories must know that your government is always prepared to provide this protection from any foreign aggressor.

For those whose safety is threatened from an outside source, my government will rush to any place or any country, friend or foe to defend and rescue any of my subjects. And for those who would attempt to harm one of you, be assured that retribution will be both fierce and swift.

The second priority is to provide an educational environment that prepares our children for life. This includes an appreciation for cultural, occupational and military issues with a focus on development of the whole person to enable them to venture out into life with the skills needed for success in their family, career and intellectual lives.

The third priority is to provide a stable environment for everyone to live free from medical concerns, personal safety concerns and also foster a business climate where each of you can prosper to the limits of your ability. It is my government's goal to insure prosperity for everyone according to their ability and effort, not for a favored few.

Our fourth priority is to care for our people who are unable to care for themselves, whether it is due to age, infirmity or injury.

Our fifth priority is to provide an environment and facilities for you to enjoy life. Public mess halls dot our cities and the countryside; never more than twenty minutes away from any settled area. We have stadiums for athletic events, auditoriums for concerts, theatres for plays and many parks designed and maintained for your enjoyment of nature. Inexpensive public transportation is available for travel to any of my kingdoms and all of you are encouraged to visit its farthest reaches to experience the rich and varied cultural and natural delights that are yours to enjoy.

I am proud to be the Commander-in-Chief of the finest military organization the world has ever seen. Our enemies tremble at our might and determination to prevail. Our friends bask in a sure confidence that we will stand beside them in their time of peril and the weight of our power, skill and determination makes them safe from any external hazard.

I am the proud ruler of a Christian nation, devoted to the True God and to seeing His will done as far as my poor human condition allows. I am a proud champion of my Church and resources in all of my kingdoms are dedicated to insure that the Christian faith is carried to the very ends of the universe.

To you my people, I am proud that God has seen fit to appoint me as your ruler and may my rule be remembered as just and fair for as long as records are kept on earth and in heaven.

And last, I salute our newest heroes, those whose extraordinary measure of individual and unit heroism made this moment possible.

Thank all of you for this opportunity to share time with you.

Thank you. General Gates, I turn the podium back to you."

It was twenty minutes before the cheering subsided, after which General Gates called forward those who were to receive awards. As soon as they were in place, General Gates escorted the King to each recipient and the King placed the ribbon holding the Alexander Cross around the necks of two soldiers. He then presented plaques to commanders of the units honored for their extraordinary courage in battle. Then the general and the King returned to the podium where the general gave the command, "Left face" and the parade resumed its progress along Constitution Avenue.

Prisoners of war on their way to the Pennsylvania border for repatriation to the United States were the last contingent of the parade. They presented a melancholy contrast to the joyous and exciting spectacles which had preceded them. Most of the onlookers were gone by the time they began to pass. While they appeared to be in good health and physical condition, all of them looked depressed, defeated and sad. They marched staring straight ahead, looking neither left or right. They even looked as if they were mildly frightened because any sudden noise startled those closest to the source. The contrast between the United States prisoners of war and the American troops could not have been greater. Caitlin observed this with interest and wondered what made the POW's seem so uniformly sad and uneasy. She decided to ask Henry the next time they were alone.

She watched Henry as he mingled with those who had been with him on the reviewing stand. She had noticed the vacant seat beside him and thought it had been his way of saying he wished she were beside him. She thought about going over to see him but decided against it.

Henry looked in vain to find her but had been unable to pick her out in the crowd. Caitlin made her way back to her car and drove home to get ready for the ball.

Henry arrived at exactly eighteen o'clock. Her mom and dad had already left being afraid traffic might hold them up. Caitlin was alone in the house when Henry rang the doorbell.

When she opened the door, Henry stood outside looking at her before he said anything.

"My, you look gorgeous tonight."

"Why thank you, Your Majesty. Won't you please come in?"

He came inside and she closed the door, "I can't kiss you. I'm already made up. We'll be late if you mess up my makeup."

"I missed having you beside me today."

"I know. I saw the vacant seat beside you."

"I was hoping you'd change your mind and sit with me."

"I'm not ready for that, Henry. I'm sorry."

"I looked for you in the crowd but didn't see you."

"I was directly across the street from where you stood but I didn't wave or do anything to get your attention. I thought it might look odd if I waved at you like a clown." She paused and added, "You looked very handsome in your uniform."

He laughed, "I was? Was my speech okay?"

"I thought it was very good. You have an excellent speaking voice and you certainly got your message across to anybody who was listening."

"So you liked it?"

"Yes, especially because it was short. Political speeches in the U.S. are long, boring and pretty meaningless. What you said in a few words covered more topics than a month's worth of their speeches."

133

"So," he smiled. "After listening to such a fine speech you'd follow me to the ends of the earth?"

She returned a coy smile, "I'd go anywhere with you if you stuttered."

"We ought to leave. I can't be late to my own function."

"I'm ready. Let me get my purse."

Henry had a driver this time so they sat together in the back seat.

"Henry, I liked the parade except for the POW part. They looked so depressed and sad when they marched past us."

"Their demeanor didn't matter. They have little reason to be happy. Many of their comrades are dead and I'm sure they were shocked by the violence of the fighting."

"But they're going back home, aren't they?"

"Yes, but a defeated army going home is a sad thing."

"Weren't they treated well in the POW camp?"

"They got the same food and medical attention our troops get except they were medicated with a behavior modification implant."

"What does it do?"

"It reduces aggression and makes them easier to manage."

"So that's why all of them had the same expression when they passed by."

"Yes."

"When will it wear off?"

"The implanted medication lasts five years."

"Five years! Isn't that a little harsh?"

"They attacked civilian areas without warning. They won't do that again, at least for five years."

"Can U.S. doctors remove the implant?"

"It is invisible to medical imaging devices and the medication would make the POW's resist its removal."

"Henry, that's cruel."

"Those men will never attack America again. We have seen to that."

She looked at him. He had no sympathy for the defeated and demoralized men. It was disturbing for her to know that he was not remorseful.

"I wish you hadn't told me that, Henry."

"When we are attacked, we defend ourselves vigorously and we make certain that our enemies will think twice before they attack us again. Actually, Caitlin, they're lucky to be alive."

"I heard that your government demanded the president and his whole cabinet be arrested and turned over to you."

"They traded Maryland and Delaware for them."

"What would have been done to them?"

"They would have been executed as war criminals."

She was appalled.

"Henry, that's terrible! I can't believe you'd do a thing like that to the president!"

"He ordered an attack on us when we were at peace with his country. He would have killed thousands of American civilians if we hadn't known ahead of time and evacuated them. They broke every existing law of civilization by doing so."

"Henry, must America so be hard?"

"We must be to survive in a hostile world."

"I'm getting upset. We need to change the subject."

"I'm sorry. If you are to be my Queen, you must accept what we do."

"Right now, I don't even want to think about it."

He took her hand while she looked out the window for the remainder of the trip to the stadium where the Victory Ball was to be held.

All was bright and glittery at the stadium. Searchlight beams swept the sky. Music was heard everywhere. Every kind of music imaginable was being played by impromptu bands that simply picked a spot and started playing. It was a cacophony of sound, jarring, silly or profound. All of it was in honor of the occasion and every participant hoped to catch a glimpse of the King. He had, uncharacteristically, given permission for three outside news agencies to be present at the banquet and ball and to take photographs, including pictures of himself.

When Henry and Caitlin exited the car a photographer snapped a photo of them. Within minutes the digital image was on television screens all over the world. At that moment, Caitlin's anonymity was lost.

Carl escorted them to the place where Henry was to receive the guests of honor. Included were Caitlin's parents, the Royal governors of Delaware and Maryland, the mayors of the major cities in the new territories, Lord Walter Jones, Chairman of the Kings Council, commanders of military units who fought and the commander of the occupation army.

During the reception, the king mingled with the crowd with Caitlin by his side. Everybody wanted to meet her and find out who she was, including those jealous social climbing women who had come in hopes of catching the King's eye.

The reception, banquet and ball for the invited guests were held in the playing field of the arena. The stands were full of noisy onlookers, curiosity seekers and ambitious but uninvited young women hoping to catch somebody's eye in hopes they'd be invited to the ball. Some of them were scandalously dressed in costumes leaving very little to the imagination as to what charms they possessed. It promised a harvest of delights for the young officers and gentlemen who were invited guests.

At the beginning of the formal dinner, the King made a brief speech and the Bishop of the Delaware Diocese lead the prayer. The Marine band played during the meal. Carl and his wife were to Caitlin's right and Pamela Hastings and her husband were to their right. The stadium concession provided free drinks, hotdogs and hamburgers to the occupants of the stands. The stadium was full, with twelve hundred invited guests plus the many thousands filling the stands.

After dinner was over, the guests mingled while the playing field was converted to a dance floor. The special guests were assigned tables on a raised platform at the 50- yard line and it was made ready first. The King and Caitlin shared a round table with her parents, General Gates and his wife, Lord and Lady Whitford, governor of Maryland, Lord and Lady Hamilton, governor of Delaware, Lord and Lady Pickett, governor of Virginia. Lady Hamilton was a loquacious woman who was blatantly pretty and she was the type of woman who flaunted her good looks. Caitlin noticed her openly flirting with the King and developed an immediate dislike for her. It didn't help to know that Henry was supposed to dance with her at least once.

The dancing began at twenty-one thirty with military bands providing the music. The dance floor was divided into four sections with the Air Force band playing waltzes, the Army band playing swing, the Marine band playing rock and roll and the South African band playing pop tunes. From their vantage point on the platform they could watch the crowd and were close enough to the four dance floors to allow their special guests different varieties of music to choose from.

The Air Force band led off with a waltz. Henry and Caitlin danced the ceremonial first dance. When it was over, they bowed in the four directions of the compass to the cheers of the crowd. Caitlin squeezed his hand as they bowed and continued to hold it as they moved to the rock and roll section. As they were walking, every band began playing , the dance floors filled and the dancing began in earnest. Henry and Caitlin stayed out on the floor for a few more dances before he began his obligatory dances with his honored guests' wives. He told her his great uncle, Alexander, started the tradition and it had continued through his grandfather's reign and his father's. He danced with Lady

Gates first and set a pattern of dancing with each of the wives once and Caitlin twice. Caitlin's mother was the second in line to be followed by Lady Whitford, Lady Hamilton, Lady Pickett, Lady Jones and Lady Gillespie, Carl's wife.

When he danced with Lady York, she commented on what an excellent dancer he was.

"My father thought it very important for me to be a good dancer. I had the finest dance instructors the Empire could provide."

"Do you enjoy dancing?"

"Yes, but not as much as Caitlin does."

"Well, Caitlin is a little extreme over things she likes."

He laughed, "You mean like baseball?"

"That too. She's very fond of you, Your Majesty."

"I'm very fond of her too."

"I don't mean to sound disrespectful, but I hope it works out for the best for her."

"I share your hope in that respect."

"She's never been like this about anybody else."

"I haven't felt like this about anybody else either, Lady Francis."

"You seem to be such a gentleman. It's hard sometimes to think of you as a King."

"I want Caitlin to have affection for the gentleman."

"She's never cared much about what somebody was."

"Her attitude in that respect is very appealing to me."

The dance ended and he escorted her back to their table. Caitlin was not there and her father told the King she'd gone to the powder room.

A young woman from the floor approached Henry, bowed and asked, "May I have this dance, Your Majesty?"

Caitlin was in a stall when she heard two women come in.

"Have you danced with His Majesty yet?" one inquired of the other.

"Not yet. Lady Whitford is next in line and then he'll dance with that woman he's with." Caitlin recognized Lady Hamilton's voice.

"Who is she, Emma?"

"Caitlin York."

"I've never heard of her. Is she from Kansas City?"

"She's from Baltimore."

"How'd he meet her?"

"Nobody knows. She showed up beside him at breakfast on Friday morning. Her father was a Maryland state senator. He's been appointed to the Maryland governing council."

"She sure sticks close to him."

Lady Hamilton laughed, "Wouldn't you?"

"Lord, yes! He is the sexiest man I've ever seen. I get wet just thinking about dancing with him."

"He is very attractive," Lady Hamilton observed.

The second woman giggled, "I think I could have an orgasm if he touched me anywhere."

"Surely not!"

"I'll probably have one when we dance."

"You're oversexed."

"No, I'm not. He is so very attractive. I read that kings used to have mistresses. Does he?"

"I haven't heard anything but he is very private."

The other woman giggled, "I'd volunteer to be his mistress any day of the week."

Lady Hamilton laughed, "What would Roger say?"

"I wouldn't care. He could watch as far as I'm concerned."

"I'd better get back. Stewart will be wondering what took me so long."

"Me too. I needed to touch up my makeup before I dance with him."

Caitlin heard them leave and the door closed. She was fuming. Henry was at their table waiting for her.

"Do you have to dance with all of the dignitary's wives?" she whispered as she sat down beside him.

"Yes. It's my job. Why do you ask?"

"I think it's a silly tradition."

He looked at her. She was staring grimly into the distance, "Is something bothering you?"

"I'll be okay in a minute," she replied and squeezed his hand.

They danced the next two numbers and as soon they returned to their seats, Caitlin heard a familiar voice behind them.

"Your Majesty, I believe it's my turn now."

Caitlin didn't turn to see who it was. She kept looking out over the crowd. When Henry left to dance with the dignitary's wife, Carl came to the table and asked her to dance with him. While they were out on the floor, he told her not to worry about women flirting with the king. He reminded her that Henry was accustomed to it and everywhere he went women like her clustered around him like flies to honey.

Caitlin was amazed at how perceptive Carl was. How could he know what she had been thinking?

After Carl put her mind at ease, Caitlin relaxed and began to enjoy the evening, even to the point of allowing Henry to dance with some of the many aspirants who came to their table requesting a dance with their sovereign. They didn't get home until four in the morning.

She snuggled up to him on the ride back. "That fancy ball was not nearly as romantic as the ride back," she remarked as they turned into her parent's driveway.

"It was work for me."

"For the crowd it's glamour, but for you, it's your job?"

"Yes it is. What happened to upset you?"

"I overheard a woman telling Lady Hamilton how much she'd like to get you into bed."

He laughed, "Being King must be the make-out occupation of all time."

"You could have had her last night."

"She's married."

"She said her husband could watch as far as she's concerned."

"I'm glad you're not like them."

"Don't think I'm immune to your charms, Your Majesty, I am more enthralled than any of the others," she said with a sweet smile.

"But you don't throw yourself at me."

"I'm waiting for you to throw yourself at me," she teased.

"Don't tempt me tonight."

They went inside. He took her into his arms and kissed her. She pressed her body to his for a moment and then pulled away.

"I like this but we better stop," she whispered.

He stepped back. "I have to go. I have a meeting at nine."

"Thank you for not inviting me to that one. When will we see each other again?"

"I'll call this afternoon and let you know."

They kissed again before he left. She stood outside and watched as the car drove away.

Henry called Sunday night at bedtime and invited her to lunch the next day. He had to be in Delaware on Tuesday and wouldn't return until late Wednesday. He also invited her to accompany him to Delaware but she declined, saying she wasn't ready to be queen. He would have her picked up on Thursday afternoon for their trip to Myrtle Beach. She was looking forward to some time alone with him. She hoped it would allow them to get to know each other.

The forlorn expression of the U.S. POW's still stuck in Caitlin's mind. On Tuesday, July fourth, a little before nine o'clock she was at the Pennsylvania border.

Americans were obsessed with schedules and timetables. The POW's were lined up in formation to begin crossing over at precisely nine. There were a handful of American onlookers like her and an American military escort. You couldn't exactly call them guards because the prisoners had no inclination to escape. Two companies were escorting 23,024 men. The American soldiers were disciplined and alert and the contrast between them and their captives was stark. The U.S. military across the line suffered in comparison too.

A long line of buses were parked on the shoulder of Highway 29 and a lot of doctors and nurses waited for the exchange to begin. There was no conversation between the Americans and the United States contingent. Caitlin noticed that while there were a lot of U.S. military officers waiting for the exchange, there were no United States government officials welcoming the men home. This omission was callous and cowardly.

At precisely nine o'clock the first row of prisoners crossed into Pennsylvania. They shuffled into home territory without any noticeable change in expression; keeping the same bland melancholy look they had worn the day of the parade. Caitlin looked in vain for any recognition that they were free and at home. Swarms of medics, doctors and nurses met them and were greeted with the same hangdog look they had while they were in American hands. Caitlin wondered where their relatives, wives, children and girlfriends were. Didn't anybody tell them their loved ones were returning home? Did nobody in the United States care anything for these poor men who had risked their lives on a foredoomed attack which was bound to fail? And what about the 198,000 U.S. soldiers in common graves in America? They had given up their lives in vain and nobody in the United States cared about their sacrifice.

At that moment Caitlin appreciated the American government more than she ever would have imagined. They had proven many times how each and every American citizen was precious and would risk lives and treasure to protect them, even to the point of going to war on their behalf. And when they returned to American soil there was rejoicing. The contrast was sobering and for the first time she was ashamed of the United States.

On the way home, the plight of those poor U.S. troops haunted her in a most profound manner.

140

Henry called her every evening while he was in Delaware. His schedule allowed them to leave for Myrtle Beach on Thursday afternoon, so he sent a car for her to join him for lunch at the Langley Officer's Mess before they departed. It was a small gathering this time and she was thankful. Pamela and a few other military officers were there. Lord and Lady Hamilton were there too and Lady Hamilton flirted openly with the King as usual. Caitlin wondered if she had had an orgasm when she danced with Henry at the ball.

Having people around him all the time was getting on her nerves. That, plus deciding what to take to wear about wore her to a frazzle. Nobody would tell her what the King's friend should wear at the beach. Carl was no help. He told her whatever she chose the King would think she was beautiful. She toyed with the idea of testing that theory by taking flip-flops, tank tops and cutoffs but decided against it.

At thirteen-thirty they and a four plane fighter escort took off from Andrews Air Force Base in one of the King's planes. He had one for formal state occasions with the American flag on it and it was designated "Royal Air Force One". The one they were in was much smaller and it didn't have distinctive markings. But it had the fanciest furnishings she had ever seen in an airplane even though she had ridden in Air Force One with her dad and the U,S. President once. She sat beside Henry on a couch and Carl was in the easy chair facing them. Two servants, three bodyguards and the aircrew were the only other people on the plane.

Everything about the plane and the service was first class. She stirred her coffee with a golden spoon, in an exquisite cup with matching saucer trimmed in gold. Debbie and Eleanor's eyes would have popped out at all this finery. She had to be circumspect in what she told them because she didn't want her friends to get the idea she was bragging.

She listened as Henry and Carl discussed empire matters. Henry was easy to talk to. Even though he was king, he didn't discourage divergent opinions. Listening to them talk in calm, measured tones made her think about the contrast in these discussions and similar ones in the United States where nobody was candid and everybody tried to manipulate the discussions to prove their particular point of view. Whatever else this monarchy was, it allowed constructive discussion of important issues. Decisions were based upon reality and they were made at the top.

They landed at Myrtle Beach Airport instead of the airbase. A car was waiting to take them to the royal compound.

She didn't know what to expect. She half expected to see a palace but it turned out to be an ordinary beach house. Three adjacent houses completed the compound. They too were ordinary beach homes and housed the royal staff.

A servant escorted Caitlin to her room and told her she had been assigned to care for her needs while she visited the king. She introduced herself as Kathy O'Donnell. While she was dressed casually, she was as well dressed and groomed as the servant who served them at the Dulles Hilton. The king's livery was first class.

Caitlin's room was on the second floor and looked out over the Atlantic. It had French doors that opened onto a balcony. While Kathy unpacked her things, she stepped outside to look at the ocean. The balcony extended across the whole ocean side of the house. As she stood leaning on the rail basking in the ocean breeze, Henry came out of the doorway adjacent to hers. Without saying a word, he came to her, took her into his arms and kissed her.

"How do you like it?" he asked.

"I like it. I didn't know what to expect and thought it might have been a lot bigger."

"A palace would be out of place here."

"It is tasteful. How many palaces do you have?"

"Nine plus two Royal retreats. Another palace is under construction in Namibia."

"Where are the retreats?"

"One is in Montana, north of Lewistown on the Missouri River. The other is at Lake Louise in Alberta."

"Do you ski?"

"Love it."

"Could we go skiing sometime?"

"We have some excellent slopes on the retreat."

"Could I invite my girlfriends?"

"Sure."

"I guess your palace in Kansas City is the biggest?"

"No. It's second largest. The one in Mexico is the biggest and most lavish."

"How many rooms are in the one in Kansas City?"

"One hundred and nine."

"It must be an expensive place."

"Over two million a day for all of them."

"So your houses cost over $730 million a year."

"Actually, almost $800 million."

Kathy interrupted, "Your Majesty, when will you want dinner?"

"Twenty o'clock."

"Will you and Lady York wish to go to the beach before dinner?"

"Caitlin, would you like to?"

"I'd love to."

"Yes, Kathy. We'll go to the beach in a few minutes."

"Then I'll lay out Lady York's swimsuit. Would the Lady wish to have assistance dressing?"

Caitlin answered, "I'll dress myself, thank you."

"I'll tell Rebecca to lay out your swim trunks, Your Majesty."

"Thank you, Kathy," Henry said.

"This will take some getting used to." Caitlin observed. She was glad she hadn't brought the tank top, flip-flops and cutoffs.

Chapter Thirteen

They were seated in beach chairs with their feet in the surf. Henry was wearing navy swim trunks with an "H" inside a circle embroidered on the right leg. It looked like a cattle brand, the "Circle H." Caitlin was wearing a navy two-piece swimsuit.

"Without even trying, we match," she observed.

"You are much more beautiful in yours."

She smiled, "You're pretty sexy yourself. Debbie told me after we had lunch at the Crackpot that if it didn't work out for us she'd be glad to step into my place."

"But she didn't know who I was at the time."

"It wouldn't matter to her."

They were quiet for a few minutes, enjoying the solitude and not thinking of anything to say.

"Where are we going from here, Henry?"

"What do you mean?"

"Can I actually be your wife?"

"If we love each other, you can."

"Suppose somebody objects, like Walter? I'm not a native born American."

"He's already heard enough from Carl to think you are definitely queen material."

"Will I have to embrace the Catholic faith?"

"Yes, you will."

"Suppose I don't?"

"You won't be queen."

"Even if you love me?" she asked.

"Even if we're madly in love."

"Could I be your mistress if I don't become your wife?"

"I don't want a mistress," he said.

"What other conditions will I have to meet?"

"You must learn Latin."

"Why?"

"If I'm incapacitated for some reason, my Queen becomes Commander-in-Chief of the armed forces."

"Who on earth thinks I'd know what to do?"

"I have a capable staff to advise you."

"Suppose they disagree and are evenly divided?"

"You are the tie breaker."

"So I'd be on the spot."

"Make a common sense judgment. You have a lot of common sense."

"I can see why you don't want to muddy up your life."

"How's that?"

"All those decisions you have to make. Simple issues are resolved long before they get to you. You get the hardest ones."

"That's why I'm king."

They were quiet a few more minutes.

"You know if you were an ordinary man, we wouldn't be sitting out here like this," she said with a devilish smile.

"Yeah, it would be a lot simpler."

"We'd be sharing a room too."

He grinned, "I'd like that."

"We wouldn't be sitting out here with everybody watching us either."

"Oh?"

"We'd be in the room doing what every other young couple in Myrtle Beach is doing."

"I wish we could," he said wistfully.

"Can't you?"

"My behavior must be beyond reproach."

"And if I'm to be your Queen, mine has to be above reproach too?"

"I'm sorry, but it has to be that way."

"Sometimes it's hard to come up with a good reason to be a Queen." Then she added, "Except I love you."

"Do you? Are you sure?"

"I'm positive. If I didn't, I wouldn't be here now."

Rebecca interrupted them, "Your Majesty, dinner will be served in forty-five minutes. How will you dress?"

"Slacks and a golf shirt."

"What will the Lady wear?"

Caitlin answered, "The white sundress and my white sandals."

"Will you need Kathy's assistance?"

"She can lay them out. I'll dress myself."

"Thank you Lady York and Your Majesty," she said as she bowed and turned to go.

Caitlin thought to say something disparaging about all this formality but held her tongue. Henry had never known anything else. She realized that he thought this was informal. He wouldn't know what she was talking about.

A Catholic priest was present to say grace before the meal began. Caitlin made a mental note to ask if priests always said grace before royal meals. The table seated ten. Henry sat at the head of the table with Caitlin to his right and Carl to his left. The priest was to Caitlin's right and the captain of the guard to his right. The mayor of Myrtle Beach, his wife and two teenage daughters completed the table. The place at the end of the table facing Henry was vacant, the seat where the queen would normally sit. The two teenage girls were beside themselves and their excitement was palpable. Henry held Caitlin's hand under the table while the priest prayed.

Conversation centered on the gorgeous weather and entertainments available at Myrtle Beach. Nobody ever asked Henry what he did. Caitlin decided it was because everybody knew what he had done. The mayor suggested they attend a "Grand Ole Opry" style show the next evening and Henry agreed. They decided to tour Brookgreen Gardens the next afternoon. They had also been invited to lunch at the Pawley's Island home of the Governor of South Carolina. Henry asked for the lunch to be informal and when they toured the gardens they wanted to be treated like ordinary tourists.

After dinner was over, Caitlin and Henry took a moonlight walk on the beach. She knew everybody watched them all the time. When he took her hand, when they stopped to look at a seashell, if he put his arm around her waist, somebody noticed and thought it was important. Love in a fishbowl was an unrewarding experience. Pamela's comment about insiders betting she'd be queen still stuck in her mind and she knew it made people try to figure out what kind of queen she'd be. All she wanted to do was love Henry and be his wife. She hated it when people watched them measuring her while they speculated in their minds how they ought to behave around her. The fishbowl was getting on her nerves.

A local musician came at twenty-three o'clock and serenaded them on the balcony. After he left, they were alone except for the ubiquitous servants who popped out of the woodwork every few minutes to inquire if His Majesty or the Lady needed anything. Henry had grown up having all this attention and didn't think it was a nuisance like she did. To her immense relief, Henry dismissed Kathy and Rebecca at midnight and they were finally alone.

She was still in her sundress but had slipped out of her sandals when they walked on the beach. He was barefoot too.

"Let's go back to the beach," he suggested.

"Let's. I'll change."

"No! Go like you are now!" He jumped up.

They raced downstairs and ran all the way into the surf with her holding up her dress so she could keep up with Henry. They ran straight into the water until she was up to her waist with the light waves up to her chest. He pulled her to him and kissed her. Then they began to frolic, chasing and splashing water on each other. They played like this until almost two o'clock and both were soaked from head to toe. They finally grew tired and started back to their rooms. The moon was full and bright. Her wet sundress and sheer bra didn't hide much of her anatomy. They stopped outside her door and kissed passionately in their wet clothes. Then he stood back to look at her.

"Caitlin, you are a most beautiful woman."

She stuck out her chest, "Why thank you, Your Majesty. And you are the handsomest of men." Then she giggled and motioned him to come to her finger. He took her into his arms again and they kissed.

"Henry, we ought to get out of these wet clothes."

He looked at her with a grin but then his expression changed to serious, "Yes, we should, Caitlin," he paused, looking solemnly at her, "I want to be with you tonight but we must not."

She looked at him, saw his need for her and loved him all the more in his agony. She knew how he felt because she wanted him too. "I know," she said sadly, "And the future queen must also be above reproach."

He kissed her on the lips again and turned to go to his room.

"I love you, Henry."

"I love you too, Caitlin."

It was a long time before either of them got to sleep.

Kathy came into Caitlin's room the next morning while she was still asleep. She picked Caitlin's wet clothes off the floor and took them to the laundry. She smiled secretly to herself, trying to visualize what had gone on between her King and Lady York after they had been dismissed last night.

Rebecca woke Henry up at eight-fifteen. "When do you and Lady York want breakfast, Your Majesty?"

He yawned, "About nine." Then he added, "We were up pretty late. She may not want breakfast."

"I'll have Kathy ask her, Your Majesty."

She came back into his room a few minutes later, "She wants to dine with you at nine, Your Majesty."

Caitlin was smiling and giggly at breakfast. The uninhibited play time they had in the ocean relaxed her and made her feel closer to Henry. In the right circumstances, he was fun to be with.

Henry responded in kind and held her hand openly when the priest said grace. Carl, Rebecca and Kathy watched them with growing amusement. None of them had seen their king behave this way and they were pleased.

After breakfast, Caitlin and Henry were relaxing on the deck enjoying the view and the ocean breeze. Carl interrupted them at ten o'clock with the day's dispatches. Caitlin looked out over the Atlantic while they discussed the day's issues and the king made his suggestions and gave the orders. She noted how businesslike and confident Henry was in dealing with matters of government.

Kathy approached her to ask how she would dress for the luncheon with the governor.

"How should I dress?" Caitlin asked.

"Your blue flowered dress would be appropriate."

"Must I wear heels?"

"Your matching low heels are fine for this occasion. A string of pearls would be appropriate also."

"I didn't bring any jewelry."

"Then I'll get a pearl necklace from the purser for you to wear."

"Purser?"

"He's the custodian of the royal jewels. He has a very nice pearl necklace that belonged to His Majesty's great grandmother."

"Is there anything else?"

"No, Milady. I'll lay your outfit out for you. Will you need my assistance dressing?"

"You could help me with my hair. I was in the ocean last night."

"You look lovely," Henry commented on the way to Pawley's Island.

"Why thank you, Your Majesty. Kathy fixed my hair."

"She did an excellent job."

Henry had sent word that he was on vacation and did not want a formal luncheon with many guests. When Governor and Lady Tucker met them at the entrance they realized their hosts had trouble toning things down. Henry frowned when he saw fifty people waiting inside to catch a glimpse, or maybe even shake hands with their King. Everybody was overdressed. The royal party was the most casually dressed of the group, including the servants. Caitlin knew Henry was displeased but noted that he didn't do or say anything to indicate his displeasure.

The women zeroed in on Caitlin. Rumors about her and the king had been flying since late June and they wanted a measure of the woman who had caught the king's fancy. They listened to her when she spoke, memorized what she wore, observed her tiniest gestures and noticed the confident way she looked at and spoke to her monarch. When the ubiquitous priest said grace, some kept their eyes open and saw the king take her hand during the prayer.

At least there were no speeches. After lunch Henry and Caitlin mingled with the governor's guests until it was time to leave. After changing clothes at the beach house they toured the gardens and returned to the royal compound for a quick dinner before going to the country music show on the strand. The mayor, his wife and Carl accompanied them. They got back at the beach house a little after twenty-three o'clock.

Henry and Caitlin took another moonlight walk on the beach. Tonight Caitlin couldn't get the U.S. POW's out of her mind.

"Did you have to medicate the U.S. prisoners?" she asked Henry as they walked holding hands.

"Yes, we did."

"They had been defeated in battle. Wasn't that traumatic enough?"

"They attacked our country without warning. We were at peace with their country. They would have killed or injured thousands of innocent American civilians if we hadn't known about the attack and evacuated them."

"But Henry, they were doing what they were ordered to do."

"That doesn't matter. They attacked American citizens."

"Must America be so harsh?"

"It is my constitutional responsibility to protect my countries and my people from foreign hazard. What I authorize on behalf of foreigners and enemies in keeping that charge is not subject to restriction. But I am required to do whatever is necessary to guard from future recurrence.

"They got off light. They are physically healthy and in five years they will revert to their normal psychological state."

"But you could have moderated their punishment."

"Yes, I have the authority to do it."

"Do we always treat defeated enemy soldiers this way?"

"No. In other engagements, the enemy armies were annihilated. We even offered American citizenship to the U.S. soldiers. Over eight thousand are Americans now."

149

"And the others didn't want to be Americans?"

"That or they didn't pass the placement tests."

I don't suppose you came up with the medication idea but you could have cancelled it?"

"General Jackson's staff came up with the idea because of our common heritage with the United States."

"But you could have cancelled the order?" She was becoming more upset.

"Yes. I could have."

"Without any repercussions?"

"None, other than the chance we could be fighting those same men again in the future."

Caitlin had become quite upset. "Henry, why didn't you cancel that order?"

"I thought the suggestion was generous and humane. It allowed them to live and provided adequate protection to Americans."

"But you took five whole years from their lives!"

"It was a proper and humane approach in this circumstance, Caitlin."

"Henry, how could you allow it? It was a terrible thing to do to those poor men. "

"Caitlin, it's my job!"

She started to say something else but didn't. She was too upset by now to formulate rational arguments. While they continued to hold hands, they didn't say anything else for the rest of their walk. When they stopped at her door, she quietly bade him good night without a kiss or a word of affection. The next morning over breakfast, she asked if she could go home. She was on a plane within the hour and that afternoon, Henry returned to Kansas City.

Chapter Fourteen

Caitlin's mother and father knew she was upset when she got home and wondered what had happened. Lord York knew how outspoken Caitlin could be and guessed she had angered the king. She kept to herself the rest of the week without saying anything to either of them about what had happened.

Her mother came into the kitchen on Friday morning while Caitlin was having a piece of toast. "What happened between you and Henry, Caitlin? Your father and I are worried about you."

"We had a disagreement, Mama. That's all."

"Is Henry angry?"

"No, Mama. It's me who's upset."

"What about?"

"I'm upset over what they did to the U.S. prisoners, Mama. They medicated them to make them timid and fearful for five years!"

"But they didn't permanently injure them, did they?"

"No. But Henry could have cancelled the order and didn't."

"He did what he thought was best, Caitlin."

"But, Mama, those poor men looked so depressed and forlorn."

"They're lucky to be alive."

"Mama, you didn't see them when they were turned over to the United States. Nobody from the U.S. Government met them. No family or friends met them. Nobody cares about them any more and they are medicated to make them sad and afraid."

"Caitlin, what the United States did or did not do is not His Majesty's responsibility."

"Mama, it was awful and Henry is not even regretful."

"How do you know that?"

"He let them do it, Mama."

They sat quietly for a time while Caitlin looked out the window.

"Caitlin, didn't you tell me that you promised him you wouldn't confuse the man with the office?

She stared at her mother, "Yes, I did."

"Aren't you doing just that?"

Caitlin sat her cup of coffee down and without responding to her mother's question, got up from the table.

"I'd better go. I can't be late for work." Then she picked up her briefcase and purse and left.

She tried to call Henry the next evening just before she went to bed but he didn't answer.

Carl called her at work on Monday.

"His Majesty said you called him?"

"Yes, I did, Carl."

"What did you wish to say to him, Lady York?"

"I wanted to tell him I realize I broke my promise to him and I'm sorry."

"What promise did you break, Lady York?"

"I promised him I'd never confuse the man with the office and I did just that when we were at the beach."

"I'll pass it on to him, Lady York."

"Tell him I am truly sorry and I'll try my best to never let it happen again."

"I'll tell him what you said.

"Thank you, Carl."

"You're welcome, Caitlin. Goodbye."

"Goodbye, Carl."

Carl called her Wednesday at bedtime.

"His Majesty would like for you to accompany him on a trip to Montana on July 27th."

"What's the occasion?"

"He visits an old friend from his childhood on his friend's birthday.

"When will I leave?"

"You'll be picked up on the twenty-sixth and you'll go with him to his Montana retreat on the twenty-seventh."

"How should I pack?"

"Kathy will call you with the wardrobe requirements."

"Tell him I accept his invitation."

"I will." Carl was quiet.

"Is there something else, Carl?"

"I apologize for speaking out of turn, Lady York, but we in the Royal party are pleased that you called His Majesty."

"Thank you, Carl. My mother pointed out to me that I was wrong and I am sorry for what I did."

"Goodbye, Caitlin."

"Goodbye, Carl and thanks."

152

Carl called her the next day at work to ask if Caitlin's mother would be able to accompany her. She was a little puzzled about this request but after consulting with her mother, she called him back to say her mother would be honored to accept the king's invitation.

Kathy called Caitlin the next evening and gave her a list of what to wear while visiting with the King. She told Caitlin when they arrived in Kansas City her mother would be taken to the palace to be met by the Queen Mother. Caitlin would be taken to the government building where Henry's office was.

They flew to Kansas City on the same plane she'd ridden to Myrtle Beach on. Her mother was very impressed with the furnishings. Kathy had come from Kansas City to accompany them on the trip. Neither of them had ever been in a royal palace of any kind so both were curious and a little nervous about this trip. Lady Francis was more than a little nervous about meeting the Queen Mother.

Upon their arrival, two hover platforms were waiting to take them to their separate destinations. A car would transport Kathy to the palace with their luggage. Steps were provided this time and Caitlin's mother got the thrill of her life on the ride from the airport to the palace. When the hover platform landed on the palace grounds, a uniformed servant was waiting to assist Lady Francis exit the craft and then escorted her to meet the Queen Mother. Queen Virginia was waiting just inside the entry.

She took Francis' hand, "Lady York, it is such a great pleasure to meet you."

"I'm very pleased to meet you, Your Highness."

"I have been dying to meet the mother of the young woman who has caused such a stir within the Royal family."

"Oh, she has?"

"Yes, she has. We have all been dying to meet her and when I found out she was coming to visit Henry, I asked him to invite you. This way, I can get to know both of you."

"What on earth has His Majesty told you about Caitlin?"

"Nothing, nothing at all. Henry is most uncommunicative about his personal affairs. If I learn anything it's from other sources."

"Henry does try to keep his personal affairs private."

Her Highness laughed, "I depend on Carl, Rebecca and Kathy to tell me what Henry is up to."

"And they have told you about Caitlin?"

"Oh yes. And it has been so intriguing to hear about her and her delightful independence. But pardon me. How thoughtless of me.

You must be tired from your trip. May we adjourn to my sitting room where we can continue?"

Lady York followed Queen Virginia to an elevator. They went up to the third floor and down a wide hall to a set of double doors. A servant opened the door for them. They entered a big sitting room with windows giving a view of the plains west of Kansas City. Queen Virginia led Lady Francis to a comfortable chair in the center of the room and chose another facing it for herself. Another servant offered Lady York a cup of coffee.

Queen Virginia continued, "I am so pleased Henry has met someone who is not a shallow social climber and has opinions of her own. It has been very difficult for him to meet a girl not fixated on his rank."

"Well, he hit the jackpot in that respect with Caitlin. She is truly her own person." Then she added, "She is a little trying to be around sometimes but her father and I love her dearly."

"Well, I have heard nothing but good things about her from Carl and Kathy. It was just wonderful how she stood up to Henry when they disagreed. You know, very few people disagree with a king."

"But I told Caitlin she was wrong."

"And that was even better because she was open minded enough to listen to advice and she had the courage to admit to Henry she was wrong."

"Caitlin always tries to do what's right, even if it hurts her."

"The more I find out about her, the more I like her and I haven't even had the pleasure of meeting her yet."

Kathy came in, "Your Highness, Lady York's luggage has been placed in her suite."

"Lady York, may I call you Francis?"

"Certainly, Your Highness."

"You may address me as Virginia in informal settings. We can continue this discussion later." The Queen Mother paused, "There is a formal state dinner this evening and Henry wishes for you to attend as his guest."

"I didn't bring any formal clothes."

"Lady O'Donnell has taken care of that. We would like for you to attend. I apologize for putting you on the spot like this but we felt it to be poor taste not to invite you since you are the king's honored guest."

"I will be pleased to accept the king's invitation."

"Thank you, Francis. You are very gracious. We must get ready and you may need a little relaxation after your trip. Kathy will show you to your suite."

Queen Virginia rose and took Francis' hand, "I will see you at dinner. It has been wonderful to meet you and get to know you a little."

Francis followed Kathy out and down the hall to another set of double doors. A servant opened the door and she entered a spacious and elaborate suite.

"Dinner will be at twenty o'clock. Lady Jane will assist you in anything you need. It will be a state dinner. We have taken the liberty of providing a formal gown and jewelry appropriate for the occasion."

Kathy turned to leave, "If you need to speak to me about anything ask Jane to contact me, Lady York."

Francis was overwhelmed, "Thank you. I can't think of anything at the moment, Kathy."

Kathy left the room. Francis wondered if Caitlin knew about the formal state dinner.

The hover vehicle with Caitlin landed on the roof of a big stone building in downtown Kansas City. Carl was waiting to meet her and take her to the King's office.

"Welcome to our capital city, Lady York." Then he added, "It's great to see you again."

"It's good to see you too, Carl. How is Henry?"

"Henry's fine." He paused and then added, "He was quite upset when you left so you can expect him to be a little formal at first. He has brightened considerably since you called. I think everything will be alright in a few days."

"I hope so. But if it doesn't work out, it doesn't work out. A lot of people have broken up over less of a disagreement than this."

"Caitlin, I admire your clear grasp of reality. And I know Henry always appreciates your candor."

She laughed, "Always, Carl?"

He grinned, "Well, almost always, Caitlin."

They went down the stairs from the roof and into a long, wide hallway with double doors leading off from both sides at rather long intervals. Most were numbered with a system identifying the floor and suite number. They came to one with a golden crown painted on the door and entered an anteroom furnished with very expensive furniture. A handsomely dressed man sat at a desk in the rear of the room. When they approached him, he greeted Carl.

"I see that Lady York has arrived, Lord Gillespie."

He rose and shook her hand, "Welcome to His Majesty's office, Lady York. I am Lord Edward Short and I am pleased to meet you."

"Pleased to meet you, Lord Short," Caitlin replied.

"Please have a seat. I'll tell His Majesty you have arrived."

Short went into the office while Caitlin took a seat.

Portraits of the Clark family adorned the walls of the anteroom. She got up to look at them, pausing before each to study it. Alexander was the first one on the left from the entry, followed by George, Edward and Henry was the last. On the right side were portraits of Alexander and George's parents, the ones who initiated the dramatic changes that resulted in the Kingdom. First on the right was a portrait of Graham Clark, Henry's great grandfather. Henry's resemblance to him was uncanny. The next portrait was one of Henry's great grandmother Rachel. It depicted her in her early forties and she was a very beautiful woman. Her eyes were captivating and she was wearing an expensive looking diamond necklace with matching earrings and bracelet.

"They must have been very rich," Caitlin thought.

The next portrait was of William Clark who was clearly a bigger version of his younger brother followed by a portrait of his wife, Diane.

While Caitlin was looking at the portrait of Diane, Emma Hamilton emerged from the king's office. Caitlin was so startled to see her she almost dropped her purse. When Emma saw Caitlin she came over to greet her.

"Lady York, it is such a pleasure to see you again," she gushed.

Caitlin was surprised by her overly friendly approach, "It's good to see you too, Lady Hamilton" she stammered. "I'm surprised to see you."

"Well, I'm not surprised to see you. The palace has been abuzz since it was announced you were coming to visit His Majesty."

Caitlin immediately didn't like for Lady Hamilton to know so much about her business. "Oh, they are?" Then it occurred to her that Emma Hamilton might have been alone with Henry. She didn't like that at all.

"Yes, they are. Everybody here thinks you will be their queen someday. Just think, Baltimore, Maryland producing the queen of America."

"It is thought provoking, isn't it?"

"Oh, it is! And I was with the Royal party the first time you were publicly beside him at an official function."

Lord Short rescued her. "His Majesty will see you now, Lady York."

She said goodbye to Lady Hamilton and followed Lord Short into Henry's office. She was relieved to see Lord Hamilton sitting with Henry at a conference table. Henry rose and embraced her briefly.

"It's good to see you again, Caitlin. I have a few more items to discuss with Lord Hamilton and then we can talk. Please have a seat over there." He pointed to a couch near a window with a panoramic view of the western part of the city.

Lord Hamilton rose and shook her hand, "It's nice to see you again, Lady York."

She took a seat and tried to relax. Had he been cool to her because of Lord Hamilton's presence or was he cool to her because he was still upset? She was surprised when Henry embraced her at all in front of somebody else. He could have shaken her hand.

Five minutes later, Henry and Lord Hamilton got up from the table, Hamilton stuffed some papers into his briefcase and they shook hands. On the way out, he told Caitlin he'd see her at the dinner tonight.

As soon as the door closed, Henry announced on the intercom he was not to be disturbed. He marched to where Caitlin sat, lifted her up, took her into his arms and kissed her passionately. Then he released her and stood back to look at her.

"You are more beautiful every time I see you."

She laughed, "I guess you aren't mad at me?"

"A little. But my affection for you has not diminished."

"It's good that we can disagree without disliking each other."

"As I said that evening in your parents' living room, I always want you to be honest with me. In all matters, whether they are personal or business."

She took his hand, "My affection for you has not diminished either, Your Majesty."

They sat on the couch.

"I do want to say one more thing about the matter of our disagreement and then put it to rest."

"Okay."

"As a matter of long standing policy, our military tries to kill all enemy combatants. This policy was relaxed in the conflict with the U.S. because of the common heritage we have with them and because there are many cross border family connections. If it had been anybody else, there would have been no POWs to return."

She looked at him a few seconds before replying, "That's king stuff, Henry. I love Henry. What the king does is his business."

He took her into his arms, "I love you too, Caitlin." Then he sat back and regained his business expression.

157

"There is a formal dinner this evening for some South American heads of state. I didn't tell you about it because I wasn't sure how you felt about us. I want you beside me."

She looked away while she thought about it, "Okay. But I didn't bring any formal clothes."

"Kathy has taken care of that. A formal gown is already in your suite along with appropriate jewels."

"If I'm with you, I'll be alright."

"Then you'd better go to the palace and get ready." He grinned, "I want my guests to see my beautiful friend."

He rose, took her hand, pulled her to him and kissed her again before he called Lord Short to arrange transportation to the palace for Lady York.

Kathy met Caitlin when the Hover Platform landed and escorted her to her suite.

"Your mother is in the suite next to yours and there are connecting doors so you can go to her suite without entering the hallway."

"Will Mama be at the dinner too?"

"She'll sit beside the Queen Mother."

"Isn't it unusual for us to attend formal state functions as special guests? Henry and I are not even engaged and everybody is treating this like it's a done deal."

"There are no precedents to guide us. Henry is the first American King to ascend to the throne as a single man. He is the one who insists that you sit with him. His mother tried to talk to him about it but he told her you would be by his side unless you objected." Kathy smiled, "Caitlin, His Majesty is quite taken with you."

"It still looks like we're rushing things."

"Not as much as you think. The place to his right is for a favorite guest. The place of honor would be at the opposite end of the table facing him. If you notice, it is always vacant unless his mother attends the function. It's where the Queen would sit if he had one."

"Then I prefer the place of his favorite guest to the place of honor so far away from him."

"His Majesty feels the same way, Caitlin." Kathy smiled at her. "It is wonderful to see how His Majesty lights up the moment you enter the room."

"Love in a fish bowl is not much fun," Caitlin observed.

"You are handling it very well," Kathy replied.

"I didn't bring a formal gown."

"I have one for you."

"Will it fit?"

"It was custom made for you for this occasion."

"So you know my sizes?"

"Yes."

"What about jewelry?"

"We have the perfect set. It belonged to His Majesty's great grandmother." Caitlin wondered if his great grandmother was the only one who had any jewelry.

"I saw the portrait of her in the anteroom of Henry's office. She was very beautiful."

"The story was that before she met His Majesty's great grandfather, she dated an Arab Prince and he presented her a beautiful diamond necklace set." Kathy opened a jewelry case and Caitlin saw the necklace Henry's great grandmother was wearing in the portrait. She picked it up, moved to a mirror and held it to her neck.

She smiled, "It looks good on me too."

"Yes, it does. You will look like a queen tonight, Lady York. His Majesty and his guests will be most impressed."

"How much is it worth?"

"The purser lists its value at over three and a half million."

"Wow!"

"We must get you ready for dinner. You start your bath while I get ready to do your hair."

"Could I speak to my mother?"

"Sure. But don't take more than ten minutes. She has to get ready too."

Kathy opened the door between the two suites. Caitlin's mother was sitting in the chair having her hair done. She introduced Caitlin to Lady Jane.

"Did you know about the dinner?" Lady Francis asked.

"No. Henry told me when I got to his office. Are you okay, Mama?"

"Yes, Caitlin. I'm overwhelmed but I'm okay."

"I'll have to behave tonight, won't I?" Caitlin remarked with a grin.

"Yes, you will."

When she went back into her suite Caitlin commented about an aristocrat doing her mother's hair.

"All of us are aristocrats. The king's personal servant is Lady Rebecca Forsyth, the Duchess of Houston."

"Then you must be one too."

"I'm Lady Kathryn O'Donnell, Duchess of Vicksburg."

159

"But you live here?"

"Being the Duchess of Vicksburg means I am the Royal Patron of the city and I represent it on the council. I also receive a percentage of the tax revenues for my financial support."

"I suppose you let me call you Kathy because I wish to be informal."

"Henry encourages the use first names in informal circumstances. We like it too. Sometimes all these titles can get pretty cumbersome."

"Yes, they do. I'll take my bath now."

"I'll do your hair and makeup and help you dress as soon as you are ready."

Chapter Fifteen

Kathy didn't let Caitlin enter the room until all the other guests had arrived. When Caitlin entered, a hush fell over the crowd as she made her way towards Henry. She was regal in a strapless midnight blue satin gown and diamond necklace, earrings and bracelet. Walter observed her entry and whispered to Carl that she looked every inch a queen.

Everyone watched and listened as Caitlin approached Henry, bowed and said in a clear voice, "Good evening, Your Majesty."

"Good evening, Lady York," he said with a smile. "You are beautiful this evening."

"You're pretty handsome yourself," she replied. Then she added, "Your Majesty."

Those close enough to hear the conversation and observe her behavior noted the confident manner in which she spoke and looked at him.

"You do look absolutely gorgeous," he remarked.

"If beautiful dresses and expensive jewelry help, I must be gorgeous," she replied laughing as she took his hand.

"You'd turn my head in overalls, Caitlin."

"I'll test your theory one day, Henry."

"Do," he replied with a smile. "I must introduce you to my mother."

"She's here for the dinner too?"

"Yes. She decided to come when she found out you would be here. She's been hounding me to let her meet you for some time now."

"She has?"

"She wanted to come to Myrtle Beach."

"I'm glad she didn't. It would have made things worse when I left."

"Not for her. She appreciates your independence. She was pleased that you didn't cave in to me."

"So, I have one highly placed ally in the palace."

"Three."

"Three?"

"My mother, Carl and Kathy."

"Oh."

"Come, my mother is dying to meet you. I'll introduce you two before dinner begins." She presented her arm for him and they moved through the crowd to where the two mothers were speaking to other guests. Queen Mother Virginia saw them coming and met them. "So this is Caitlin?"

"Yes, it is, Mother. Caitlin, meet my mother, Queen Virginia."

Caitlin curtseyed, "Pleased to meet you, Your Highness."

"I have been hearing so much about you. It is wonderful to finally meet you."

"It's nice to meet you too, Milady."

"We must spend some time together before you return home so we can get to know each other better."

"Yes, we should, Your Highness."

"Henry, she is so cultured and well mannered."

Henry laughed, "She can be at times."

His mother laughed too, addressing Caitlin, "Yes my dear, I have heard about your wonderful independence of mind."

Caitlin wanted to ask if they didn't have something better to discuss but held her tongue, "They do say I am outspoken."

They were interrupted by the master of the table, calling all guests to dinner.

Queen Virginia took her hand, "Caitlin, we will continue our discussion later in more private surroundings."

Henry led her to the head table where she sat to his right. Queen Virginia had changed the seating arrangements so she could sit beside Caitlin and Caitlin's mother sat to her right. The High Governor of Mexico was to Henry's left and the governors of Venezuela and Panama to his left. Carl and the Cardinal of Mexico completed the head table.

Henry made a short speech thanking the heads of state of the South American countries for attending the conference and contributing to the discussions on how to improve relations between his government and their respective governments. He told them the intent of the conference was to find ways to improve the economic lot of every nation in the western hemisphere. Then each head of state said a few words thanking His Majesty for hosting the event and complimenting him on his kingdom's hospitality. After they finished, the Cardinal said grace and they began to eat. The High Governor of Mexico occupied Henry's time throughout the meal so Caitlin and Virginia continued their conversation.

"Are your quarters comfortable?" the Queen Mother asked.

"Very."

"How do you like the palace environment?"

"It would take a lot of getting used to."

"Henry doesn't especially like living in the palace. He takes every opportunity to get away from the palace atmosphere."

"I prefer an informal atmosphere myself."

The queen looked away as if she was thinking about something, then she turned to face Caitlin, "Caitlin, do you like Henry? I mean do you like him as a man, not as king?"

Caitlin thought this was unusual timing for such a question but decided to answer truthfully because the subject obviously bore heavily on the Queen Mother's mind. "I love Henry, Your Highness. I don't care very much for his position."

Queen Virginia was quiet afterwards and didn't say anything until dessert was served. She reached over and took Caitlin's hand, "Thank you for appreciating my son, Caitlin. I thank God he has found someone like you."

Caitlin looked at her. There were tears in the Queen Mother's eyes.

After the meal was over, Caitlin stood beside Henry as he thanked everyone for coming and wishing them a safe journey. Caitlin was the star attraction.

The High Governor of Mexico spoke to her. "Lady York, it is a pleasure to meet you. It is wonderful to see our king as happy as he is when you are by his side."

"I like to be beside him too, Your Grace."

"Well said, Lady York. You must persuade him to bring you to Mexico where we can show you some fine Mexican hospitality."

"I would enjoy visiting Mexico, Your Grace."

He smiled and shook her hand before moving to bid the king goodbye.

"I'm glad that's over," Henry said as they rode to the palace.

"Me too, but it was nice to dress up. I've never worn anything this beautiful in my life."

"Did you like it?"

"It's gorgeous."

"You're gorgeous. The clothes are only an accessory accenting your beauty."

"You saying that makes me want to take them off," she giggled.

"Don't start that please. Mom will be watching us tonight."

"Oh, she will?"

"She wants us to have a perfect courtship."

"Oh, she does?"

"Without any scandal, like you getting pregnant."

163

"Don't we want it too?"

"I do, most of the time." He grinned at her, "Then I think about you in the wet dress on the porch at the beach sticking your chest out at me."

"I wanted you more that night than I ever imagined I could want a man."

"We must not give in. We must control our passions."

"I'll try. I want it to be right for us too." She paused, "It helps when people are around us all the time when we're together. You're used to it, but I am very conscious of everybody watching us."

"I'm aware of it too. I try to ignore them."

"I love you, Henry."

"I love you, Caitlin."

They left for Montana early the next morning accompanied by Carl, Rebecca and Kathy. The ubiquitous guards had already left and were waiting for them at the royal retreat.

The Montana retreat was a big log house on the south side of a mountain outside Lewistown. Viewing rooms with picture windows faced in every direction, allowing scenic views any time of the day.

After unpacking, they drove for four hours to the cabin where Slim lived. Henry planned to visit with Slim until his bedtime after which they would return to the lodge. It would be a long day. Carl and one guard were their only companions on the trip.

"Who is Slim?" Caitlin asked when they started out on the drive west.

"He's a cowboy I met when I was fourteen."

"You must like him a lot to go to this much trouble on his birthday."

"He taught me about ordinary people and how life is with few of the trappings of civilization." Then he added, "He taught me what is important in life."

"How old is he?"

"We think he's ninety-three."

"You think?"

"He won't tell anybody how old he is."

"Can't you find his birth certificate or something?"

"He won't tell us where he was born."

"How do you know when his birthday is?"

"We don't. The date changes sometimes."

"He sounds like a crank."

"He is the ultimate crank. And he hates the monarchy."

164

"But he likes you?"

"Sure. But he never admits I'm King. I'm his friend. That outranks my being King in his opinion."

"That's my attitude too. You being king is a handicap as far as I'm concerned."

"You and Slim will get along just fine."

She laid her head on his shoulder and took his hand. "Thank you for inviting me."

"I wanted you to meet him. He might not be around another year."

They arrived at Slim's tiny cabin a little after fourteen o'clock. It was perched on top of a low mountain and boasted a porch on the south side. There was another house nearby. Henry told Caitlin it was where the people who cared for Slim stayed.

"This looks nice. You fixed it up for him, didn't you?"

"Yes. And I pay the people who care for him too."

"Does he have any money?"

"Not a dime. He never saved a cent in his whole life."

When they got out of the car, Slim came out to meet them. He stood straight and strong, bowlegged as he was. And he was still wiry. He met Henry with a grin.

"Howdy, Henry."

Then he spied Caitlin, "Who's the purty thing you got with you?"

"Slim, this is Caitlin. She's my friend."

"You goin to marry her, ain't you? She's too purty not to marry."

"We're thinking about it, Slim."

"Wal, don't take too much time thinking. She's so purty I just might make her an offer myself."

Caitlin extended her hand to Slim. He took it and held it gently in his coarse, hard hand.

"Pleased to meet you, ma'am. Henry's a real good boy. It'd be real hard for you to find yourself a better boy than he is."

Caitlin laughed, "Pleased to meet you too, Slim. I think he's a good boy too."

Slim addressed Henry, "Where's my presents? You did remember it's my birthday and brought my presents didn't you?"

Henry laughed, "Yes, Slim. Carl is getting them out of the car now." Then to Caitlin, "See what I mean?"

165

They followed him inside where Ted and Alma Walsh, the couple who cared for Slim met them. The kitchen was decorated and a birthday cake was on the table. Caitlin noticed neither of them smiled about anything and were all business in their dealings with Slim. Henry introduced her to them and they shook her hand. Other than that they ignored her and Carl. She decided whatever deference they gave Henry was solely because he paid them. What a dreary pair they were.

She watched as Slim opened his gifts from the king. He was like a child in anticipation as he opened each one. She watched Henry too as he humored and catered to Slim, appearing to listen reverently as the old man gave the king advice about "hosses," "wimmin" and "likker'. She was touched by Henry's affection for the old man.

After opening presents and eating some birthday cake, Slim invited them to take a walk with him. They walked along a trail leading down the mountain and towards another low building where Slim kept his horse. He couldn't ride any more but he still kept a cowpony to remind him of the days when he was "wild and free and could whip anybody in a hundred miles" as he told Caitlin.

The day was spectacularly beautiful with a cool temperature at this elevation. They walked briskly to keep warm. Slim told Caitlin and Henry, (Who had already heard these tales many times), stories of the west and the mountains and all the heroes of days gone by. He told of the day he met Henry when he was a "young city squirt" but Henry had loved "hosses" too and his love of those wild range bred horses endeared him to Slim.

"There won't no Cayuse too wild for Henry here," he told Caitlin with evident pride. "He rode hosses some real cowboys was skeered of."

Caitlin was amazed at the old man's vigor. They didn't get back to the cabin until right before dark.

The birthday supper was Slim's favorite; beans, bacon and biscuits with cornbread and molasses for dessert. After supper, they took their leave. She knew it was sad for Henry because he knew the old man might not live another year. Still, he was tough and might live to be a hundred. Henry hugged the old man. When Caitlin hugged Slim, he kissed her cheek.

"You take care of Henry," he admonished her. "He's a good boy but he needs advice sometimes. I can tell you're real smart and can give him some when he needs it."

Then to Henry, "You better marry her real quick, Henry. She's so damn purty some gent's going to steal her if you don't move fast."

"I'll work on it, Slim," Henry laughed. "See you next year."

"Hope I'll be around. You can come anytime, Henry. I'm always glad to see you."

"I'm glad to see you too, Slim."

"Next time you come, be sure to bring her with you."

"I'll try."

"You better! She's too damn purty to leave by herself somewhere. I told you some dude'll make off with her if you ain't kerful," he warned.

"I'm not worried, Slim."

"I reckon not. She likes you."

"Take care of yourself," Henry said as they got into the car.

"Goodbye, Slim," Caitlin said.

"See ya'll next year," Slim shouted as they drove away.

"What a character!" Caitlin observed.

"Yeah, he is."

"Where'd you find that stern old man and battleaxe woman to care for him?"

Henry laughed, "When I decided Slim needed caring for, we sent a nice looking middle aged woman to look after him. She lasted two days."

"What happened?"

"He was after her all day and all night for sex. He even threatened to tell me she was stealing crown property if she didn't give in. She had to lock herself inside the house to get away from him."

"He is a scoundrel, isn't he?"

"Next, we tried a married couple. The husband was a big man. They lasted a week with the husband telling Carl if Slim touched his wife one more time, he'd kill him. Then we tried the Walsh's."

"How long have they lasted?"

"Almost six years."

"I guess they're tougher than he is."

"I think the woman knocked Slim down a few times until he finally got the idea."

"When will we go back to Kansas City?"

"Sunday."

"So we have two whole days to play in the mountains."

"Yes, we do."

"I noticed my room is some distance from yours," she said with an ironic smile.

"Everybody is trying to keep us pure."

"So they'll be watching us every minute."

167

"Every minute."

"Suppose we did it anyway, with them looking."

"They wouldn't say anything," he said quietly.

She thought a few seconds before she said, "If we did, I know we'd wish we hadn't later. I still think we ought to wait."

"I do too, Caitlin."

Alone at last! Rebecca and Kathy remained out of sight except at mealtimes and just before they retired. Carl gave Henry his daily briefing at mid-morning. The rest of the time they were left to themselves. She realized the servants knew what they were doing because the proper clothes were always laid out for her, no matter what she needed to wear. This was easy duty for the guards because of the remote location and satellite surveillance let them know if anyone entered the property, so they stayed pretty much out of sight. The compound contained over a half-million acres.

On Friday afternoon they rode horses and when she went to her quarters after lunch to dress, her jeans, her plaid shirt and a new pair of perfectly fitted, sixteen-inch leather lace-up riding boots were set out for her. When Henry escorted her to the stables, a groom met them and led her to a pretty roan mare standing inside the corral. Another groom was holding a big, fiery black horse she assumed was for Henry. As soon as she saw the horse, she realized what Slim had been talking about. The horse was prancing, tossing his head and pawing the ground impatiently.

"What's his name?" she asked, half expecting Henry to say something like "Satan" or "Devil" because he looked wild and mean. The horse cut his eyes at her when she spoke. The way he looked at her, she knew that he was jealous.

"Blackie."

"Well, he is black," she observed.

Henry laughed, "The trainer and groom have different names for him I'm sure. He's tough to handle."

"Why won't he stand still like my horse?"

"He'll leave without me if the groom lets him go."

"Sounds like he's still wild."

"He is. He would revert to a range horse in five minutes."

"So that's what Slim was talking about?"

"Yeah, I impressed Slim when he saw how I liked to ride horses like Blackie."

Henry helped her mount, then mounted Blackie and they started up a trail towards the mountain to the west of the house. Her horse was docile and disciplined as they cantered along the road but Blackie kept trying to break away. After about a mile, Henry had to let him go.

"I've got to let him unwind," he explained. "I'll be back in a few minutes."

He released the reins and Blackie took off like a shot, disappearing quickly over the hill in front of them. She saw them top another low hill in the distance with the black horse stretched out in a headlong gallop. A few minutes later, she saw them coming back over the hill at the same breakneck speed. Minutes later they were beside her again and Blackie was much calmer.

"I've never seen a horse behave like him before."

"He's part thoroughbred and part wild mustang. He's got the Thoroughbred size and gait and the mustang temperament."

"Was he raised in the wild?"

"He didn't see a man until he was two."

"Which parent was the Thoroughbred?"

"The stallion. He was a descendent of Secretariat."

"So he was bred especially for you?"

"Yes, I picked the stud and the mare myself."

"He's pretty but he's not much of a pet."

"I didn't want a pet."

She laughed, "Is that the way you like your women too, wild and independent?"

He grinned, "I hadn't thought about it, but I guess I do."

When they arrived at the peak of the mountain, they stopped and dismounted to rest the horses. He took her into his arms and kissed her. She clung to him a moment before releasing him. Then they sat on a rock holding hands while looking at the magnificent panorama spread out before them.

After a half hour they remounted and started back to the lodge. Henry wasn't much of a talker when they were alone. Even at official social functions, he didn't engage in small talk. He was unfailingly polite and his remarks were carefully chosen but light conversation was not his bailiwick. She knew he liked to be alone with her but theirs was not a verbal communion.

It was wild rides on ATV's the next afternoon. Caitlin was more at home on the ATV than the horse. They raced up and down trails and across the flat range to the east of the compound. By the end of the day, they were very tired and went to bed early.

The next day, they would be picked up after lunch for the trip back to Kansas City and then she and her mother would return to Baltimore. She wondered how her mother and the Queen Mother had fared while she and Henry were playing. Just before they were to be driven to the Royal Airport, Henry came into her suite and kissed her.

"So you won't forget about me," he said with a smile.

"Don't worry, Henry," she whispered.

Afterwards, he accompanied them to the Royal Airport.

"When will I see you again?" she asked.

"Can I see you Saturday?"

"Sure. What would you like to do?"

"Anything private."

"Could we go out to dinner and invite Debbie and Eleanor?"

"Yeah."

"Then you and I go dancing until the wee hours?"

"Yep."

"How about lunch at my parent's house on Sunday?"

"Okay."

"When will you return here?"

"Sunday afternoon."

"Who'll accompany you?"

"Carl, Rebecca and three guards."

"Then they are invited to lunch on Sunday too. But it's only the two of us on Saturday night."

He grinned, "You, I." Then he added, "And one guard."

He followed her onto the plane and thanked her mother for coming and told them both goodbye.

They began a pattern of her coming to Kansas City on alternate weekends and him going to Baltimore when she didn't come to Kansas City. This continued through the remainder of summer and into the fall and winter. They went to Montana again in the fall when the leaves were at their peak of color.

She accompanied him to New Zealand for a state occasion where she was mobbed by a crowd chanting, "Kate Lin, Kate Lin". Henry was upset about it and put out an order restricting demonstrations when she was with him.

They spent Thanksgiving in Kansas City and he was in Baltimore for Christmas from the twenty-third until the twenty-seventh. She attended the Royal New Years Eve and Ascension Ball in Kansas City celebrating the thirty-sixth year of the monarchy. Caitlin was resplendent in a sleeveless, v-neck emerald gown of silk made especially for her. She wore matching long gloves, an emerald necklace with diamonds surrounding the emerald and matching earrings. Her hair was up and held in place by hairpins with sparkling emerald heads.

170

Kathy again had her wait until everyone else had arrived and Caitlin made another grand entrance to greet the king. Gossip was rampant that she would soon become their queen.

During this time, both were falling more and more in love. On a few occasions when he was occupied and couldn't see her on the weekend, he made a trip during the week to be with her an hour before he had to return. Once when he couldn't manage to come at all, he had her picked up after work, brought to see him and ferried back in time for her to get to work the next day. He was so disciplined and duty oriented that it never occurred to him to have her quit her job, move to Kansas City and ensconce her in the suite she used on each visit. She wondered why he hadn't thought to suggest it but was glad he hadn't.

She admired his discipline and loved him all the more for trying to set an example for his subjects and his kingdom. She thought it exemplary and at the same time wanted him to relax sometimes and let go, especially when they were close and alone in sweet embrace. She knew she would be his anytime he wished. And she knew it was only a matter of time. She hoped it would be after they were married. She did not wish to bear the first royal bastard of the Clark dynasty.

In mid-January they went to Lake Louise for a long weekend ski trip. He invited her friends, Debbie and Eleanor to accompany them. The lodge was a stone building on a mountaintop with a magnificent sweeping view in all directions. It had a glass domed room facing north with spectacular views of the night sky and the Aurora Borealis. There was a fireplace on each end of the room and all the furniture was covered in fur. Caitlin and her friends loved the lodge. They stayed up every night into the wee hours sipping wine, looking at the northern lights and the starlit sky. Her friends were surprised and pleased when each of them was assigned a servant who helped them dress, do their hair and make up and even suggest the proper attire for each function. On their way home on the king's plane both were outspoken about how much they enjoyed being waited on. Caitlin did not agree with their enthusiasm but did agree that it was helpful at times.

Caitlin liked the ski lodge so much that Henry, at Kathy and Rebecca's suggestion, invited her to spend the week of February eleventh at the lodge for skiing and relaxation. Since Wednesday was Valentine's Day she thought it was a nice touch. He personally delivered flowers to her bed before she got up. Then they had a wonderful morning on the slopes. At lunch he gave her a ruby necklace. Then they were on the slopes again in the afternoon. That evening, they had a special Valentine dinner with fine wine.

After dinner, they adjourned to the dome room to watch the night sky. It was a spectacularly beautiful night. After midnight, Rebecca asked if she and Kathy could be excused and Henry released them for the evening.

Henry had been restless all day. Carl had told him of potential problems which could erupt at anytime in Saudi Arabia and Argentina. There was also troubling intelligence that the Russians had made a breakthrough in their beam weapons program. Henry was thinking about all this while he tried to entertain Caitlin.

Caitlin was cuddling under an ermine robe on a sofa in the middle of the room. She had been giggly all evening, something Henry attributed to the amount of wine she had consumed. Every time he looked at her she was smiling and doing a lot of squirming around under the robe. He was absentmindedly looking toward the east when a big meteor shower lit up the sky. It was followed by two more in quick succession. He called her to him to watch. She giggled and told him she couldn't come. He insisted that she come and got a little testy when she giggled again and refused his request.

"Caitlin, come here."

"What for, Henry?"

"I want you to see this with me."

"I can see it from here, Henry."

"But I want you beside me."

"I can't, Henry," she insisted while giving him a sweet smile.

"Why not?" he asked evidently irritated.

"I can't," she giggled again.

Henry started to get mad. He turned, walked to the couch and looked down on her.

"I want you to stand beside me at the window."

She giggled again and gave him a sweet smile, "Henry, I just can't."

"And why not?" he insisted.

"I don't have any clothes on, Henry." She giggled again.

He was flabbergasted, "No clothes!"

"Not a stitch."

"What are you doing?"

"The fur feels so good on my skin that I undressed so I could feel it all over. Fur makes me feel very sexy."

She kept smiling at him. He remembered all the squirming she had been doing. She expected him to grin at her like he always did when she surprised him about something but he didn't smile this time. He stood there looking sternly down at her. His expression was almost unfriendly. He looked at her for a few seconds without saying anything.

172

Then he reached down, lifted the robe and looked at her. She felt his stare but was not embarrassed with him looking at her.

"I love you, Henry," she said quietly.

He dropped to his knees and began kissing her while his hands roughly caressed her. Then he stood up and began tearing off his clothes. She sat up and helped him undress and soon they were locked in sweet embrace.

He was not gentle.

As they lay in each other's arms afterwards, Caitlin whispered, I love you, Henry."

"I was rough. I'm sorry if I hurt you."

She put her finger to his lips, "I've been ravished by my King and I loved every minute."

"We shouldn't have, you know."

"I know. If I'd kept my clothes on this wouldn't have happened."

"I lost control. I'm sorry, Caitlin," he said despondently.

"Don't be sorry, Henry. I love you and I know you love me."

"But, we should have waited."

"We can't change what has happened. God loves us anyway."

"But, you might get pregnant."

"I can take a pill if I need to."

He got upset, "No! You must not!"

"Why not, Henry?" She didn't understand why he was so upset.

"You can't. If you're pregnant, you must have the baby."

"Why? Lots of women keep from getting pregnant that way."

"You're not 'any woman' and the child is legally protected."

"Henry, we just made love."

"It's against the law for you to do anything." He was becoming more upset.

"Against the law?" She was trying not to get upset herself because he was visibly agitated by their conversation.

"My dear Caitlin," he whispered. "It is treason to deny the kingdom a potential heir to the throne."

That was a stunning piece of news and she stiffened her body as she lay close to him. She thought to ask if she'd be executed if she took the pill but decided she already knew the answer. It took a while for her to regain control of her thoughts.

She looked at him with a solemn expression, "Then, if God wills it, I shall bear the first royal bastard of the Clark dynasty."

"Caitlin, I am so sorry. I wanted us to wait but I lost control." He was quite upset now.

"Don't blame yourself, my darling. It was as much my fault as it was yours." She took his face in her hands and kissed him, "Henry, I love you with all my heart."

"I love you too, Caitlin," he whispered.

He kissed her gently and pulled her closer to him and soon they drifted off to sleep in each other's arms.

He woke up at four and looked at her. When he moved, it woke her up and she smiled sleepily at him.

"You are so very beautiful," he whispered.

They kissed and began to explore each other and soon they were locked in sweet loving embrace once more. After a short nap, they rose, slipped on a few clothes and carried the rest to their rooms. He kissed her outside her door.

"We love each other, Henry. We'll be okay, no matter what happens."

"I hope so," he answered with a worried look.

She went inside and leaned on the door, deep in thought about their sweet love and the worry it had caused. Then she lay across the bed and went to sleep.

He stood outside her door thinking about joining her but remembered that he was King and went to his room for a fitful few hours of sleep.

When Rebecca came in to check on him at seven o'clock, she found him already awake.

"Are you alright, Your Majesty?"

"I'm okay. I was thinking about a few things."

"I know the situation in Argentina and Saudi Arabia is tense. Is there something else?" Rebecca knew him well.

"I was thinking about Caitlin."

"Your Majesty, Kathy and I see how happy you are when you are with Lady York. I hope things are going well between you two."

"We love each other, Rebecca."

"That is good news, Your Majesty, but Kathy and I already knew that you two were in love. I was concerned you'd had another disagreement."

"No, our relationship is fine."

"Thank you, Your Majesty. I didn't mean to pry."

"It's alright, Rebecca. You know me too well."

"Will you want breakfast at the regular time?"

174

"Yes."

"Will the Lady?"

"I'm sure she will."

"Thank you, Your Majesty."

Rebecca and Kathy watched them closely during breakfast to assure themselves that things were in fact all right between King Henry and Lady York.

"They seem closer," Kathy remarked after Henry and Caitlin left for their morning walk.

"Yes, they do." Rebecca replied. "He was awake early this morning and I was afraid they'd had another disagreement."

"Ever since they met, it has been evident they enjoyed being together. The king seems like a different person when she's with him."

"Yes, he does. He's always so stern and businesslike. It's good to see him relax like he does when she's with him."

"I like Lady York myself," Kathy admitted. "She's forthright and down to earth about everything. And she is unusually genuine for an aristocratic woman."

"She is brutally honest, even with herself."

"The king appreciates that aspect about her."

Rebecca laughed, "Our king likes many things about Lady York. From a man's point of view, she has great appeal."

"She is very beautiful."

"Yes, she is. Carl told me when His Majesty first saw Lady York he told Carl she was prettier than the CIA spy."

"I couldn't stand her, even giving her the benefit of being an enemy spy."

"She acted like she wanted him to make her his queen," Rebecca observed.

"It was so funny when they assigned Wilma to be her servant. Wilma couldn't pick out the proper gown in a warehouse full of pretty gowns. Remember the night her hose clashed with her gown and the gown was so thin you could see her hose?"

"And the time she wore rubies with a red dress!"

Kathy laughed, "I bet Walter deliberately chose Wilma because he knew she couldn't choose the correct handkerchief to wipe her nose with."

"The whole episode was hilarious from the start with everybody knowing she was a spy and Henry playing along with the gag."

175

"It's a wonder to me how she never noticed all those people laughing at her behind her back."

"She was too stuck on herself to notice anything like that. She was like all U.S. citizens, shallow and uncomprehending. She thought all she had to do was be pretty and seduce the crown prince."

"She certainly didn't know our Henry."

"No, she didn't, thank God," Rebecca sighed with relief. "I'm surprised at the restraint His Majesty has displayed regarding Lady York."

"What do you mean?" Kathy asked.

"They are passionately attracted to each other."

"Oh, that. I am too. But she doesn't like us being around them all the time. They have had very little personal privacy. It probably reduces the opportunity for intimacy."

"She made sharp remarks to him at the beach about how difficult it is to love somebody in a fishbowl."

Rebecca laughed, "She's certainly able to express herself with exquisite clarity, isn't she."

"Oh, yes and she is fearless. I still can't get over how boldly she behaves around the king, even in public. When she bows to him on ceremonial occasions, everybody knows she's putting on a show."

"Carl told me about what she said to him in front of everybody right after they met."

"What did she say?"

"He invited her to have breakfast with him and a group of military officers and other dignitaries at the Andrews Air Force Base the day he was returning to Kansas City. She marched straight up to His Majesty and bowed, keeping eye contact with him when she did, and smiling like a naughty child. When he complimented her on her attire, she replied 'One must look one's best when one dines with one's king.' Carl said she had a most devilish expression when she said it."

"What did His Majesty say?" Kathy asked.

"He laughed and said, 'I suppose one must'."

"So he likes her irreverence?"

"I don't think she's trying to be irreverent. She enjoys playing with the king."

"Well, he certainly likes to play with her. They are like children when they are together."

"They certainly play hard when they can get away. I'll need a week's vacation to recover when she goes home Sunday."

"Me too, but the king will expect me to be around," Rebecca said without relish.

"I bet he asks her to be his Queen before the end of the year."

"I bet he does before spring," Rebecca countered.

"You do?"

"You should have seen the way he looked this morning when he spoke of her."

"Oh."

"Uh oh, here they come. Look at the happiness on their faces and holding hands like two teenagers."

"They're going skiing. I'd better lay out her outfit."

"Yes, I'd better get him ready too, as soon as Carl finishes his briefing."

Caitlin and Henry skied the morning and afternoon. But after last night, they were not as enthused about skiing. They did it more as a matter of duty to occupy themselves during the day.

And Henry was also preoccupied with the news from Saudi Arabia. He told her over dinner how radical Islamists were creating unrest in Saudi Arabia. His spy reports indicated they were using the Hajj pilgrimage to Mecca to collect all the radicals in the vicinity and try to inflame the pilgrims. They planned to start an uprising during the Eid-ul-Adha Festival of Sacrifice next week.

"We know they have infected some Arabian Army units with their poison and are not absolutely certain of their loyalty. They will be tested if we have to put down an uprising."

"How will you test them?"

"They will be sent in first. If they don't fight on our behalf, loyal units will cut them down."

"Isn't that a little extreme?"

"Every citizen in my countries has sworn loyalty to me. Disloyalty is a capital crime."

"Will you go to Saudi Arabia?"

"Maybe. I'll know early next week. We are arresting the most vocal radicals and sending them out of the country. I've also forced the Moslem television stations to tone down the rhetoric."

"How?"

"I ordered them to comply or be shut down."

"You can do that?"

"I can shut down any broadcast medium that I choose."

Henry and Caitlin exercised unbelievable restraint Friday night and succeeded in keeping their clothes on. Bad weather on Saturday kept them inside but they were never alone during the day.

177

After dinner, they couldn't stand it any longer and decided he would sneak into her room after one o'clock.

He knocked on her door at one o'clock. She let him inside and was kissing him passionately before he could get the door closed. In moments, they were in her bed. Afterwards they lay entwined in a lovers knot.

"What will we do now, Henry?" she asked. "I'll simply die from wanting you when I get back home."

"I don't know. But we can't keep making love like this. You'll get pregnant."

"Are you sure I can't do something?"

"Positive. We can't break laws I must enforce on others."

"But I love you so much. And I need you now," she implored.

He was as desperate as she was, "I know. I need you too. I barely slept a wink last night thinking about you."

"God, how I wanted you last night!"

"We must get control of ourselves before something happens." They became quiet.

"I'll try," she said finally without any enthusiasm or determination.

"We must try, Caitlin. We've got to," he dejectedly hoped.

He stayed with her until five o'clock and they made love again before he went back to his room.

They left for Kansas City the next morning and she was to be ferried to Baltimore on his plane after he was dropped off. Everyone got off to give them some privacy to say goodbye.

"Will you come next weekend?" she asked.

"Yeah, if I can."

"I hope you can. I'll be a basket case if you don't."

Then they embraced like lovers do when they separate.

"I love you," she whispered.

"I love you too. I'll see you as soon as I can." Then she took his hand as he left the plane and Kathy re-boarded to accompany her on the trip home.

"You and His Majesty seemed closer these last few days," Kathy observed.

"We are closer than we've ever been."

"The king loves you."

"I know," Caitlin said dreamily. "I love him too."

"I'm glad the two of you are sensible about everything."

"We're trying."

"It would cause irreparable harm to the monarchy if there was a scandal."

"Well, I certainly wouldn't want to have that on my conscience now, would I?" Caitlin replied with heavy sarcasm.

"No, you would not," Kathy replied seriously. "Over eight-hundred million people depend on the king every day of their lives. You would not want to do anything to diminish their trust in their sovereign."

"I guess it makes me the eight-hundred million plus one in line for His Majesty's time and attention."

"No, Caitlin. You are first in his affection. But if you become his queen, you will find yourself with over eight-hundred million souls looking to you for protection and guidance just as they look to Henry."

"Sometimes it's hard to come up with a good reason to be queen."

"Milady, you will make a wonderful queen. Even Walter thinks so."

"He's only agreeing with Carl."

"No. He never parrots Carl's opinions. He is very astute about people."

"I just want to be Henry's wife."

"My dear Caitlin, what you desire is impossible to achieve. You can in truth become his wife and love him, but the price you will pay is you must also become his queen."

"Somehow it always comes back to that. I love a man. He happens to rule one of the largest kingdoms on earth. If I become his wife, I take on a job I have never aspired to and find unappealing in the extreme."

"Lady York, you will be a wonderful queen. And I think it will not be the onerous assignment you fear it will be."

"I certainly hope not because I am deeply in love with His Majesty and I fear that if he asks me to marry him I will accept his offer."

"I sincerely hope you do. I both believe and hope that you will find the happiness you desire."

"I pray that you're right."

The plane began its descent to Andrew's Air Force Base where a military driver would take her home.

"When will you see Henry again, Caitlin?"

"Next weekend I hope."

"Things are looking pretty bad in Saudi Arabia. He may be busy."

"Then I know he'll come as soon as he can."

"I'm sure he will, Your..." Kathy corrected herself. "Caitlin."

Caitlin knew she was about to call her "Your Highness." How could they be so damn certain about everything?

Kathy bade her goodbye and boarded the plane for the flight back to Kansas City. A sergeant drove her home and helped her take her luggage inside. Home. How nice it was to be in these friendly unofficial surroundings. No servants, no protocols, nobody watching over her day and night, not finding just the right outfit laid out for her to wear, nobody to answer any question or meet any personal need expressed or unexpressed. She needed a break. But she needed Henry too. And she loved him with all her heart.

Chapter Sixteen

Henry called her that night. "Are you okay?" he asked.

"As good as I can be separated from you."

"I miss you too," he confided. "We've got to deal with Saudi Arabia though. I'll try to call everyday, but if I don't you shouldn't worry."

"I'll try not to. It's hard being away from you, Henry. I keep thinking about us on the couch."

"Me too. But we need to cool it. If you're not pregnant, I don't want to get you pregnant before we get married. It would be such a scandal."

"Kathy reminded me of that on the plane."

He was alarmed, "Do they know?"

"No, they don't. We were speaking in general terms. But if I am pregnant it will certainly make me appear two faced."

"When will you know?"

"You mean my period?"

"Yeah."

"The middle of next week."

"So we've got ten days to sweat it out?"

"More or less."

"You seem calm about it."

"It wouldn't do any good for me to get excited would it? I'm either pregnant or I'm not."

"Yeah, I guess so. That's something I especially like about you."

"What?"

"You are so logical and think in concrete terms."

"Is there any other way?"

"As far as I'm concerned there's not, but very few people think as clearly as you do."

She laughed, "Clarity failed me at a critical moment last week."

"When?"

"When you started kissing me on the couch and I helped you undress."

He laughed, "I thought it was an exquisitely clarifying moment."

"But we thought nothing of the consequences."

"I wouldn't trade anything for that moment, Caitlin."

She sighed, "I wouldn't either. I only hope I'm not pregnant."

"Me too."

181

"I miss you, Henry."

"I miss you too, Caitlin. I'd better go."

"I love you."

"I love you too."

He hung up the phone.

On her way upstairs to bed, she thought about the irony. The King of America and Emperor of the American Empire had told her he loved her. How many millions of women in the world would be supremely envious of her?

Kathy called on Monday night to tell her that His Majesty had gone to Saudi Arabia.

"Does he have to go to every trouble spot?" Caitlin asked.

"He likes to be on top of things. But he's good about not meddling. He lets those he has placed in charge dispense with their duties without interference."

Henry called her after she'd gone to bed. "You okay?" he asked.

"I miss you. Other than that, I am."

"I'm in Saudi Arabia."

"I know. Kathy called to tell me."

"It's about to get pretty bad here."

"I guessed it was or else you wouldn't have gone."

"I might not see you this weekend."

"I'll miss you terribly."

"I'll miss you too."

"I love you, Henry."

"I love you too, Caitlin. I've got to go."

He hung up.

[*Latin*] "The troops are in position, Your Majesty."

[*Latin*] "Then we are ready?"

[*Latin*] "Yes, Your Majesty, we are ready."

The Royal Saudi Arabian Army had surrounded Mecca. Moslems around the world howled at the sacrilege. As a precaution, a Royal South African Army stood in reserve. American strategy was always to have overwhelming strength at all points of contact. Algerian forces had also been mobilized for rapid deployment if needed. Signs had been placed directing all pilgrims to exit the Mecca area through military checkpoints. Leaflets had been dropped telling peaceful worshipers they would be allowed to leave unmolested. Militants were identified and rewards were offered for information that could lead to their arrest. The MP's had recent photographs of all the agitators, along with their names and aliases and were ordered to arrest and execute any who tried to leave.

As groups began to converge on the checkpoints, a few militants tried to slip out along with peaceful pilgrims but were spotted and arrested. Then they were executed in plain sight of everybody. A roar swept through the crowd but a careful observer could see some people were not angry. They were simply terrified. As a consequence there was a general hesitance about approaching the checkpoints. Loud speakers exhorted those with peaceful intent to leave and guaranteed their safety.

When peaceful pilgrims tried to approach the checkpoints, militants tried to intimidate them and persuade the peaceful ones to join with them. Royal Army sharpshooters began to fire stunning shots with their plasma weapons at anyone seen hindering those who were trying to leave. Mass confusion reigned with the check points being alternately mobbed by those desperate to get out, then virtually abandoned while another wave of mass hysteria swept the mob.

Gradually the stunning shots began to immobilize enough fanatics and intimidate the others to allow peaceful pilgrims to leave in an orderly fashion. Still a few militants tried to slip out, only to be pulled out of the line and executed.

Soon the militant leaders realized their game was lost and offered to negotiate. Their offer was ignored and it gradually dawned upon them that none would be allowed to leave alive.

They reacted in unpredictable ways when they realized they would soon meet their fate. First, those with guns formed into groups and charged the Royal Army. They were cut down before they got into effective range of their rifles. Then they laid down in groups on the hot sand sending loud wails up to heaven begging rescue from their almighty. The Royal Army let them lie in the hot sand until they died from the heat and lack of water. Some slipped back into the city to hide, only to be rooted out and executed by Royal Army commandos.

For his part, Henry was pleased with his Saudi Arabian Army because it had stood the test of loyalty to the crown. Because of this, he ordered only Moslem commandos to enter the holy city to finish off the fanatics. Not a single Royal Army casualty resulted from the battle. It was all over by Sunday.

On Monday, Henry met with his Saudi Arabian Army commanders and the Saudi ruling council to compliment them on the way they managed the operation. He ordered them to extract

183

commitments from the Egyptian, Jordanian, Syrian and Iraq governments to extradite to Saudi custody all members of the militant groups within their borders who were responsible for the disturbance so they could be executed. The South African troops were to remain until this was accomplished in case there was resistance. Henry returned to Kansas City on Wednesday.

He called Caitlin on Wednesday night after she'd gone to bed.

"Henry, I have missed you so much."

"I missed you too. I'm sorry I couldn't call every night."

"I miss your calls but I knew you were busy and would call if you could."

"I'm glad you don't get upset when I don't call."

"I'm not pregnant, Henry."

He was quiet for a few seconds before he answered, "Are you sure?"

"I started this morning."

"God is smiling on us in spite of our carelessness."

"God loves us, Henry. I believe He means for us to be happy."

"Caitlin," he paused before he continued, "When we were at the beach and we were standing outside your door in our wet clothes, I loved you for a thousand reasons."

"And I loved you in return, Henry," she whispered.

"I know." He paused again, "Tonight I love you without reason and without limit."

"Oh, Henry," she whispered, "That is so sweet. I wish you were here."

He was quiet again. It was so long before he said anything else that she thought the connection might have been broken. She was about to ask if he was still on the line when he popped the question.

"Caitlin, will you marry me?" he asked quietly.

"Yes, I will."

There was another long period of silence before he asked, "And will you be my Queen?"

"Yes, I will be proud to be your Queen."

Another period of silence followed, "I'm sorry I can't offer you the normal life you desire."

"I love you, Henry and I want to be your wife no matter what."

"I want you beside me always."

"I love you with all my heart, Henry.

"And I love you, Caitlin."

"What happens now?"

"I'll discuss it with the council tomorrow morning."

"When will we tell our parents?"

"Can I come tomorrow night?"

"Come for dinner. I'll tell mama and daddy you'll be here."

"They ought not to go overboard. Just a normal meal like they'd have without me."

"How about your mom?"

"You can come to Kansas City this weekend and we'll tell her formally. She'll know by then from other sources but she'll be okay. You haven't met my sisters and brother either."

"I can't wait to see you."

"I apologize, but it's going to be a circus from the time it's announced until we're married."

"I know. I'll be okay, Henry."

"I can't wait until you're beside me every night."

"Don't start me thinking about that."

"Yeah, me either."

She laughed, "I know what's been on your mind."

"You certainly don't have to be a mind reader to figure it out do you?"

"No, I don't. But it's on my mind too."

"I've got to go. I have a busy day tomorrow."

"I won't sleep a wink tonight."

"You'd better get all the rest you can because it will be hectic after the announcement."

"I'll try. Goodnight, Henry. I love you and I can't wait to be your wife."

"I can't wait either." He hung up.

It was a long time before she got to sleep. She thought of many things, including how much she loved Henry but she neglected to ponder the fact that this was the very last day of her life as a private person.

On the far side of the world another person was having trouble sleeping. His name was Fawzi Kibur and he lived in the shadow of the pyramids. Two of his cousins were turning to dust in a common grave beneath the sands of Saudi Arabia where they gave their lives in protest of defilement of the most holy place in Islam. If his father had not prevented it, Fawzi would have shared their glorious fate.

Fawzi dedicated time every night to hate the American king and pray to Allah to punish him for his evil deeds. On this night Allah

185

came to him in a dream. In his dream, Allah beckoned him and he followed, riding on a magic carpet to America where he saw someone who looked exactly like himself standing beside the infidel Christian king. Suddenly, there was an explosion and the infidel king was no more and in the place where he stood was a bloody mass of human debris.

Fawzi was gone too and he understood his remains were mixed in with the remains of the hated one. Then he saw two angels appear and he was lifted up and carried towards Heaven, the angel's voices singing sweet songs of praise.

Fawzi sat up with a start. His cousin, Sabri Salama, lived in Baltimore, Maryland, and he had an uncle in the Egyptian diplomatic service. Fawzi had read in the English language newspaper that the king had fallen in love with a woman who lived in Baltimore.

Kathy called Caitlin at work after nine o'clock. "Rebecca told me he asked you last night."

"Yes, he did."

"And you accepted?"

"Yes."

"I'm so excited. I know you'll be good for His Majesty."

"I love him and this is the only way for us."

"Everybody will be pleased about this."

"I hope so."

"The bets have been on you since last summer."

"I didn't like hearing all the speculation."

"It was all in your favor. He's meeting with the council now."

"Do you think anybody will object?"

"Not at all. Walter has been preparing them for months now."

"But Walter's not been around me much."

"Walter observed the way you conducted yourself during the Victory celebration and was very impressed. He's also very good friends with General Hastings. She has been another staunch advocate for you at court."

"I like her too and we get along well."

"Queen Virginia likes you too."

"She likes me because I have affection for Henry, not the crown."

"She told me that. She is another ally."

"What if nobody liked me and objected to Henry's choice?"

Kathy laughed, "Caitlin, it wouldn't matter to Henry. He would make you his Queen if it made everybody in the empire mad."

"I'm that way about him too."

"I've not been told yet, but I expect I'll be coming with His Majesty tonight."

"What for?"

"I'll be assigned to take care of you."

"Already?"

"When the announcement comes out, the world will be camped on your doorstep."

"I hadn't thought about that."

"A company of guards will be assigned to you too."

"I hadn't thought about that either."

"Caitlin, a Royal Air Force unit at Andrews has already been ordered to provide aerial surveillance everywhere you go."

"I guess I'm really in a fishbowl now, aren't I?"

"You'll have to learn to ignore it and live your life as if it wasn't there."

"I guess Henry's used to it."

"He's had it since he was born." Then Kathy added, "I probably ought not to say this, but you've had protection since last July."

"I have?"

"Henry ordered it."

"Why?"

"He wanted to protect you, but he also wanted to shield your privacy. A lot of people knew about you by then and he meant to keep it out of the papers."

"I wondered why nobody ever bothered me."

"They stopped a CIA recruiter from coming to see you."

"You're kidding!"

"No, I'm not. He was arrested and quietly deported. Henry sent a message by him for them to leave you alone."

"They would have been wasting their time anyway."

"The U.S. Government has the opinion that many in the new territories wish to be reunited with the United States."

"I don't know anybody who feels that way. They appreciate all the benefits the monarchy has brought and can't wait to be completely assimilated."

"We know it, the U.S. Government doesn't."

Someone in the background said something to Kathy. "The council has approved your marriage to Henry. They're discussing protocol and ceremonial issues now."

"I don't suppose anything will be simple, will it?"

187

"No, Caitlin. This is the first time an American monarch has wed. Yours will be the wedding of the century."

Someone else spoke to Kathy. "I've got to go. I'll see you tonight."

Caitlin realized the whirlwind was about to engulf her and her life would be forever changed. It was all because she loved the most powerful ruler on earth.

Henry arrived alone at her home a half-hour before dinner. They retired to the living room where they could talk.

"Are you okay?" he asked after they kissed.

"If you mean, do I still want to marry you, the answer is yes. I'm adjusting to the other. I'll be okay, Henry."

"We've got to do a lot of things you aren't used to."

"I know. Kathy told me this morning."

"Good. I'm glad she did. She's waiting to come here when I let her know its okay."

"Its okay, Henry. I like Kathy and I trust her."

"Can she stay in the bedroom next to yours?"

"It's Ashley's room. I'll have to ask Mom but I believe it will be alright."

"She'll help you deal with the public and advise you about ceremonial and protocol issues."

"This is going to be pretty complicated, isn't it?"

"Yes. There are many details about being in the royal family you've got to learn."

"I'm sure there are."

"She'll be with you everywhere you go in public."

"Like Carl is with you?"

"Yes. For example, you're not to be seen paying for anything. Kathy will pay for everything you buy, even if it's lunch or a candy bar."

Lady Francis came into the room to tell them dinner was ready. After they were all seated, Lord York said grace and they began to eat. Caitlin's parents sensed there was some purpose for this sudden visit. Henry made small talk during the meal and didn't broach the subject of his proposal until dessert had been served.

Then Henry laid down his fork, took Caitlin's hand and said, "Lord and Lady York, the purpose of my visit tonight is to tell you I have asked your daughter to marry me and become my Queen. She has accepted my offer. We wish to have your blessing."

They could tell by her parent's reaction they had already guessed the reason for the visit, "Yes, Your Majesty," her father replied. "You and Caitlin have our blessing. We know she loves you and we believe you love her. Because of that, we believe God will bless your marriage."

"Thank you, Your Grace and Lady York. I love your daughter. And I must apologize in advance for the disruption our marriage will cause you and your family."

"We know there will be many of things we must deal with because of your position and the position Caitlin will assume."

Then they got down to business. Henry assured them any extra expense incurred by the marriage would be borne by the Crown. Kathy was to be given the use of Ashley's room until after the marriage. They would need a place for the royal staff to stay. Her father suggested the possibility of renting the Forbes' house directly behind the York house. A guards company would be posted at Fort Meade and provide twenty-four hour protection to the compound.

The date for the marriage was set for the twenty-first of April in the Royal Cathedral in Kansas City. Pope Paul VII would perform the marriage ceremony on Saturday at fifteen o'clock and Caitlin's coronation as Queen on Sunday at fifteen o'clock.

Henry called Kathy to let her know she could move into the York home. Caitlin, Henry, her parents and Kathy spent the evening discussing the many things to be planned and accomplished prior to the wedding. Before Henry left, he and Caitlin went to the living room to say goodbye.

"Where will we go on our honeymoon?" she asked.

"Wherever you want to go," he replied. "After our honeymoon, we will do a progress through all of my kingdoms and empire so my subjects may see their beautiful new Queen."

"Didn't you say your palace in Mexico is the nicest?"

"It's the biggest and most lavish."

"I want to go there for our honeymoon."

"The High Governor of Mexico will be most pleased with your selection."

"I don't care about him," replied with a seductive smile. "I want us to have plenty of room."

He grinned, "I'm sure you will find the Mexican palace big enough to meet our needs."

He took her into his arms and kissed her, "I've got to go. We'll tell my mom Saturday night. She already knows but she'll act surprised."

"Apparently my parents had figured it out too. By the way," she asked, "don't I get a ring?"

He frowned. "I hadn't thought about the ring." He smiled, "Certainly. I'll present it to you on Saturday afternoon."

"When will it be announced?"

"It will be in the papers Sunday."

"Then I'd better enjoy what privacy I can for the next two days."

"Yes, you ought to. The next seven weeks will be like a whirlwind but when it's over, we'll be together. I can't wait to get to Mexico."

"I'll dream about it every night until we're there."

He kissed her again, bade her parents goodbye and left.

Caitlin had never met Henry's sisters and brother. Elizabeth, who was two years older than Henry, was married to Lord James Blake, a diplomat who was the ambassador to Argentina. Rachel was three years younger than Henry. She was pursuing a doctorate at Harvard and William was a freshman at NC State. All of them would be at the palace this weekend to meet her. Henry's mother planned a private dinner in her suite Saturday evening for the three of them. The rest of the family would meet for lunch in the big dining room on Sunday after mass. Kathy gave her a rundown on Henry's siblings.

"Elizabeth is nice but she doesn't act like royalty. She doesn't even have a personal servant. Her husband is a brilliant man and a talented diplomat. He's on assignment in Argentina to look after our considerable interests. She's pregnant with their first child and I've heard it will be girl. She is not suited to rule. She's very softhearted and would give an enemy the shirt off her back.

"Rachel is a twenty-three-year-old wild child. They are embarrassed by her shenanigans but haven't done anything to restrain her. She's very pretty and she has been wooed by some pretty high-ranking men but she's very stubborn, willful and predatory. She leads men on, bleeds them dry financially and emotionally, then she haughtily discards the husk.

She can be very personable when she wants to be. She and Henry get along in spite of their different attitudes about life. Walter's nightmare is she's the most viable heir to the throne if something happened to Henry and he didn't have an heir.

"William is a nerdy bookworm. He has a very high IQ but he can't make up his mind which door to leave the room by.

"They're actually a very nice family in the commonest sense of the word. There's not a mean bone in the whole crowd of cousins, uncles and aunts. Henry was groomed by his grandfather, King George, to be a king and he did a very thorough job. Henry is every inch a king."

"How do you think they'll react to me?"

"I predict Elizabeth will be cordial but a little distant at first. I think you'll end up liking each other.

"I think you and Rachel will hit it off. Both of you have vibrant personalities and both of you are fearless. She won't be jealous. She has no aspirations to be head of state. She enjoys flaunting herself before all the men of the world too much to want to rule."

"William will be so detached he won't even know you're in the room."

"Thank you for telling me what to expect."

"It's my job."

"Who chose you to be my servant?"

"Walter."

"So he really is on my side. He could have assigned somebody who made me look bad."

"He could have."

"Has he ever done it?"

"Yes. The U.S. sent a woman spy to woo Henry when he was crown prince."

"Oh, they did? Was she pretty?"

"She was very beautiful. Walter assigned her a klutz named Wilma and it was hilarious."

"Well, I'm glad he likes me. I'll have to thank him sometime."

"Walter is all business and he works day and night to make the government run smoothly and keep our enemies at bay. He would certainly appreciate a word of thanks from you. His interpretation of your expression of gratitude will be that you have a good mind and are able to appreciate his decisions."

Caitlin laughed, "He is all business isn't he."

"He is and he is devoted to Henry."

Caitlin, Kathy and two guards rode to Kansas City Saturday morning in a different plane. It was as well furnished as the other plane and but the color scheme was softer.

"Why did he send a different plane?" Caitlin asked.

"This is your plane. It will be stationed with its crew at Andrews until the wedding."

"My plane?"

"Yes."

"And I can go anywhere on it?"

"Yes."

"Suppose I want to invite Debbie and Eleanor to go to the beach with me one weekend?"

"All you have to do is say the word."

Caitlin was quiet. "Maybe being Queen won't be so bad after all," she observed to herself.

Henry greeted her at the curb when the car drove up to the palace. He embraced her, took her by the hand and led her into a small room off the entry foyer. As soon as they were inside, he took her into his arms and kissed her. Then he invited her to sit at a small table in the corner. After they were seated, he took a small ring box from his pocket and sat it on the table.

"Open it," he said.

She smiled, "I'm so excited, Henry," she said as she fumbled to get the box open. The box contained a single solitaire diamond engagement ring. It was a very high quality three carat diamond. She'd been afraid it would be something huge and was pleased he'd chosen a reasonable size stone. He took it out and slipped it onto her finger.

"It fits!" she exclaimed. "Now I feel engaged." She got up, came to him, kissed him and sat on his lap with her arm around his neck.

"Do you like it?" he asked.

"I love it. I'm glad it's not some huge thing. I'd feel funny wearing something big and gaudy."

"I don't like gaudy jewelry."

"Is it an heirloom?"

"Yes. It was my great-grandmother Rachel's engagement ring."

"Was she the only Clark woman who had any jewelry?" Caitlin asked.

"No, but hers seems more appropriate for you."

"She looks happy in the portrait in your office. I want to be as happy as she looks."

Henry laughed, "She had a shorter engagement than we'll have."

"She did?"

"Six days."

192

"She must have been in a big hurry to marry your great grandfather."

"He proposed on Monday and they were married the following Sunday."

"I wish we could."

"It would be nice, but it's impossible in our case. The cabinet wanted us to wait until September."

"And you insisted on an earlier date?"

"I proposed the thirty-first of March."

"I guess the diplomatic issues make it hard?"

"We have to give our important guests enough time to choose and procure an appropriate gift."

"Who asked the Pope to perform the wedding?"

"He volunteered. When Walter told him about it, he insisted he would do the wedding and the coronation."

"I guess everybody in the world will want to see it, in person or on television."

"Walter wants to relax our media rules and allow the foreign press in."

"Why? I like the media restraint that we enjoy."

"The cabinet thinks it will increase the popularity of the monarchy."

"So our marriage will be a big media-political event."

"Caitlin, from the day of our wedding announcement, everything we do in public will be a political event."

"You know I won't like that."

"I'm sorry. But it's the way it will be."

She smiled, "When I said I'd hate it, I didn't mean to imply that being your wife wasn't worth it."

"I understand."

"I love you with all my heart, Henry."

"And I love you too, Caitlin. We'd better go. Mom's waiting to see you in her suite."

"Will you stay with me?"

"She wants to have some private time with you before dinner."

Caitlin was apprehensive, "Alone? Why?"

"She wants to prepare you for what's ahead. She knows how much we dislike formality and she wants to encourage you to endure the publicity and political trappings because it will be good for the kingdom."

"I'm enduring it for us. The kingdom is a distant second."

193

"You can tell mom what you just said. She'll understand and appreciate how you feel. My mom likes you a lot, Caitlin and she will do everything she can to help you."

"My goal is to be the wife of a wonderful husband."

"We'll have that too, Caitlin. Play the game. We'll be okay."

"I'll try because it's the only way I can become your wife."

"I know you will. We'd better go. Mom's waiting."

Queen Virginia tried to make a social occasion of their meal. Henry was glad the two women got along. Caitlin tried to relax during dinner but was having trouble until Virginia mentioned Slim and how much Henry doted on the cranky old man.

"It was touching to see Henry cater to the old rascal," Caitlin told her.

"Henry's been like that about Slim since he was fourteen years old. He spent his eighteenth summer with him. I was very much against it but his grandfather insisted the old coot could teach Henry a thing or two."

Caitlin laughed, "What did he teach you, Henry?"

"How to control a spirited horse, how to rope a steer and how to cook beans and bacon on a campfire."

"I thought he taught you about 'wimmin' and 'likker'?" she replied with a smile.

Henry grinned, "That too."

They went on about Slim for a few minutes before the subject changed to the wedding. The Queen Mother was very excited about it and was looking forward to all the balls and formal dinners associated with their wedding.

"You will be crowned with my old crown," she told Caitlin, "And you'll look very regal and queenly, my dear."

"Thank you, Your Highness. I'll try."

"Dear Caitlin, you already look like a queen. I've thought so since I first met you."

Caitlin blushed, "Thank you, Your Highness."

"When we're in private circumstances you can call me 'Mom,' my dear. And do feel as if you can relax around me."

Caitlin tried to relax and became more comfortable by the time dessert was served. After the meal was over, Henry escorted her to her suite and kissed her goodnight.

"I want you, Henry," she whispered as she clung to him.

"We must not," he answered without any conviction.

"Then we must be strong, my darling," she said, with even less conviction.

"Yes," he agreed. "We must be strong."

"When we're together like this, I die for you."

"And I for you. We'll make up for it in Mexico."

"I lie awake every night dreaming of Mexico."

Rebecca appeared and asked the king when he would retire for the evening.

"As soon as I wish Lady York a good night," he said a little impatiently.

Rebecca smiled, "Then I'll lay out your pajamas, Your Majesty," and went into the king's suite.

"She's trying to help us," Caitlin whispered.

"Yeah," he replied grumpily, "Sometimes I get too much help."

Caitlin laughed and pushed him away, "Good night, Your Majesty. I'll see you in the morning." Then she added with a sweet smile, "And I won't sleep a wink for thinking about Mexico."

"Me either," he agreed morosely.

She opened the door to her suite and saw Kathy turning down her bed.

She kissed him on the cheek, "We didn't have a chance anyway," she whispered.

They parted until morning and a new round of festivities.

The family attended early mass at the Royal Cathedral. It was the first time Caitlin had been inside the church. It was of traditional design and very beautiful. Afterwards they socialized in the Queen Mother's suite until lunchtime. Kathy's observations had been right on the mark. Elizabeth was cordial but distant. Her husband, Lord James Blake, was a remarkable man, handsome, brilliant and with a habit of command. Caitlin realized at once that his marriage into the Royal family had been a career move for him. His manners were impeccable and he spent time with Caitlin in order to get to know her. She decided she wouldn't be surprised to discover he kept a mistress but he was attentive to his wife in a dutiful way.

Rachel was a study in the vagaries of royalty. She was pretty, regal and haughty but she managed all three in a way that made her pleasant to be around. She and Henry had an easy relationship and Caitlin decided she was the only one of his siblings who was capable of understanding the problems of governing. It meant that among the Royal family, there was only the Queen Mother and Rachel for Henry

195

to call upon in time of trouble. Rachel's servant was a man, a handsome commoner. Caitlin noticed them exchange meaningful glances several times during the afternoon. She had a certain type of beauty and attitude that could drive men wild. It would be just plain bad luck for a man to actually be in love with her. She was an engaging conversationalist, something Henry was not. From the outset Caitlin enjoyed her company.

William was a nerdy, sweet guy who kept a book under his arm the whole time he was in the room with his family. Caitlin got the impression he'd rather be reading his book than socializing. Still, he was friendly to her and seemed to accept her entry into the Royal family without misgivings or animosity.

The luncheon went well and Henry's family welcomed her into their midst without visible rancor. The only ones she really liked, besides Henry, were his mother and Rachel.

On the way back to Baltimore, Kathy produced a copy of the Baltimore Sun. The headline occupied the whole front page. It read, "Baltimore Woman to Wed the King!" The first five pages of the paper contained nothing but information about her. Accompanying the text were a surprising number of photographs of her alone and with Henry. There was one of her and Henry at the Orioles' game with her standing up shaking her fist. Then one of her and Henry on the park bench and pictures of her at most of the functions she'd attended when he was in town. But the one that surprised her the most was one of her right before she lifted her dress to get into the Hover Platform in her parents' driveway the time she went to meet Henry at the Dulles Hilton.

"You will need an aide, Caitlin."

"Can't you do it?"

"I won't have the time with all the other things I have to do and I'm not particularly good with the public, especially if I don't like the person I'm dealing with."

"Will Walter assign someone?"

"He suggested somebody. You have to agree."

"Who?"

"Emma Hamilton."

"That...." she started to say "slut" but bit her tongue. Instead she corrected herself and said, "I don't like her."

"I know, but she is the most talented person we've come up with. You need somebody from around Baltimore."

"But she gives the impression of being a loose woman."

"That's an act. She likes to tease men. She adores her husband and has never been unfaithful to him."

"What will people think if I choose her?"

"People who know her will applaud your decision. She is the brains behind her husband's success."

"You'd never know it the way she acts."

"She admires you too."

"Oh, she does?"

"Yes, she's been in your camp since last July."

"I'm surprised to hear that."

"She's an ardent booster for the Maryland-Delaware area and takes great pride in the fact that the king has chosen someone from the area to be queen."

"She's more politically astute than I thought she was."

"Lady Hamilton is a very politically astute person. In my opinion, you couldn't find a better spokesperson and advisor in the whole Empire."

"I'll have to think about it," she said and turned to look out the window of the plane.

"Okay. But don't take too much time making up your mind. People are already camped out along the whole route from Andrews to your house waiting to see their new queen."

"They are?"

"Lined up six deep, I've been told."

Her ordeal had begun.

Chapter Seventeen

At breakfast the next morning, Caitlin asked Kathy to arrange an interview with Lady Hamilton. Then she left for work like she used to do before she became a celebrity. But today, the whole route between her parent's home and her office was lined with people. Some were holding signs with messages like "Go Girl" and "We're proud of you Caitlin." In twenty-four hours her name had become a household word. Cameras from all the major American and U.S. networks recorded her driving into the parking lot and parking her car. Kathy escorted her into the building while her guards kept the crowd at bay. She refused to speak to any of the half dozen reporters thrusting microphones into her face. After they were inside, the guard's commander asked if she wanted them to clear the crowd off the parking lot where she worked.

"Let me speak to my boss first," she replied.

Madeline Watson was the owner of the agency and Caitlin's boss. She was not amused by the crowd or the notoriety.

When Caitlin entered her office, she looked out the window and said, "I knew it would be like this when I saw the paper yesterday."

"I'm sorry. What do you want me to do? My guards will clear the lot if I ask them to."

"They'll congregate next door."

"I'm sorry I caused this."

"Do you actually need to work, Caitlin?"

"I don't need the money, but I wanted to enjoy my normal life for a few more days."

"I wish you could, but as you can see it's going to be impossible."

"I know," Caitlin said sadly. "I'll leave."

Her boss hugged her, "Caitlin, you've been an excellent employee. I'm happy for you in your upcoming marriage. And I am proud to have been associated with our new queen." Then she added, "I hate to lose such a good employee."

"Thanks for giving me a job and letting me off after I met Henry."

"You're welcome. We're all very proud of you."

"Thank you," she said sadly. "I'll go back home."

Caitlin and Kathy were back at home before nine.

She called Henry. "I couldn't work today because of all the publicity."

"There's nothing we can do about it. We discussed ways to keep a lid on it but decided it would be impossible. Instead, we opted to try to get as much favorable publicity from it as we could."

"There were U.S. reporters there too."

"If you think the Sun's treatment was overdone yesterday, get a copy of the New York Times."

"You mean it was worse?"

"Eleven pages worth. I was amazed at the number of pictures they had."

"The one with me about to get into the Hover Platform in our driveway surprised me."

"I guess a freelance photographer took them on the chance they'd be worth something someday."

"Well, the privacy was good while it lasted. I'm grateful for you keeping a lid on it as long as you did, Henry. It was very thoughtful of you."

"I don't like it any more than you do."

"I'm interviewing Lady Hamilton tomorrow."

"She'll do a good job, Caitlin."

"It was a big surprise when Kathy told me Walter recommended her for the job. I thought she acted like an empty headed flirt."

"She's very effective and very astute."

"So her acting that way is a sort of disguise."

"You could say that."

"In spite of the hustle and bustle, I love you Henry. And I keep the vision of us all alone in our big palace."

"I can't wait," he replied. Somebody said something to him in the background. "I've got to go. I'll call you tonight."

"Bye, Henry."

Caitlin and Kathy spent the remainder of the day working on plans for the wedding. That evening Caitlin went out to dinner with Debbie and Eleanor. The crowds were present but they stayed at a respectful distance. The twenty-three o'clock news focused on her two trips away from home that day. Everything she did now, no matter how trivial, was news. For the next seven weeks Caitlin's life would fluctuate between infuriatingly mundane periods and social events of intoxicating intensity. Whatever else could occur, she and Henry had absolutely zero chances for intimacy. If she didn't know he loved her already, she couldn't have made it. When she was down, she conjured up images of them in that lavish Mexican Palace all alone and away from the maddening crowd. Marrying a king was hard work and the ordeal would strike fear in the stoutest of hearts. But through it all, she kept foremost in her mind how much she loved Henry.

Lady Hamilton arrived for her interview at nine o'clock. Kathy met her at the door and led her to the dining room where Caitlin waited.

"Good morning, Lady Hamilton," Caitlin said when she greeted her. "Thank you for coming on such short notice."

"This is certainly a surprise to me," Emma replied. "You could have knocked me over with a feather when Lady O'Donnell called me yesterday." Emma was dressed more conservatively than she had been the other times Caitlin had seen her. But still, she was dressed to the nines and would have stood out in any gathering.

"I prefer to use our first names in private conversations like this. May I call you Emma?"

"Yes, you may."

"I'll come right to the point, Emma. I need a spokesperson; someone who can deal with all the publicity associated with my marriage to Henry and advise me on how to act when I'm in the spotlight."

"Why me? I'm as new to the kingdom as you are. There must be somebody in Kansas City more qualified than I am."

"Walter thinks you are the best candidate."

"Why?"

"Because you are from the same area and you've demonstrated outstanding ability doing this on behalf of your husband."

"But I know my husband and it's easy for me to judge what works best for him."

"I'm sure you can do as well for me."

"I'm still surprised. I didn't think you liked me."

"I didn't at first."

"What didn't you like?"

"Your flirting with all the men, including Henry."

"Oh, that's just an act."

"I know it now. Kathy told me."

"You'd be amazed what a woman can find out if a man thinks she's interested in him."

"I hadn't thought about it, but I guess you're right."

"Another advantage is people don't think a flirty woman is especially intelligent."

"You sound absolutely Machiavellian."

"Exactly."

"Have you been in an awkward situation where the man thinks you're serious and expects something from you?"

She laughed, "You mean sex? I smile and remind them that I'm married and Stewart would not approve."

Caitlin smiled, "You play to win, don't you?"

"Is there any other way?"

"I suppose not. My problem is I don't have any political street smarts. I need somebody to coach me and intercede when I need it."

"Caitlin, do you actually believe I'm the best candidate?"

"Yes, I do."

"You know, I was unaware you didn't like me until somebody told me. I've liked you from the start. You're genuine, intelligent and you have a presence that is rare in a woman. I think you'll make a great queen."

"The queen part is secondary as far as I'm concerned. I love Henry and I want to be his wife."

"You'll be good for him. It is wonderful to see how much he brightens up when you're with him."

"Will you take the job?"

Lady Hamilton looked away for a few seconds before answering. "Yes, I will, on two conditions."

"What are they?"

"That I'm allowed to help Stewart as long as it doesn't interfere with my job and you accept what I say as honest advice given in my best judgment, not taking anything as personal criticism of you and your convictions."

"I agree. I will always want your honest opinion."

"Then, I accept. And I will do whatever you ask me to do on your behalf to the best of my ability, even if you don't follow my advice."

"Thank you."

"I will pledge my devotion to you, now as my employer and as my Queen after the wedding."

"I want you to understand I will always want your truthful opinions. I will never penalize you in any way for telling me the truth."

"You sound like Henry."

"Henry and I share many characteristics. When can you start?"

"Now."

"What is the first thing I need to do about all this publicity?"

"Get an office downtown. Then you can deal with the media and the public away from here and it will give you and your family a little peace and quiet."

"That is your first assignment."

"Milady, I will move on the matter at once."

On Thursday, Lady Hamilton found an office suite on Pratt Street overlooking the harbor. Caitlin approved it after a quick walk-through.

"Three plane loads of furniture and fixtures are being loaded as we speak," Emma told her. "The floor above is part of the package. It'll be quarters for a contingent of guards."

"When will it be ready?" Caitlin asked.

"You can occupy it on March eighth."

"How? The place is bare and it needs cleaning and painting."

"The best architectural firm in the city is on the project. The interior decorators I use in Wilmington will be here this afternoon and a coordinator has been assigned from the palace maintenance organization. Crews will work twenty-four hours a day to get it ready."

Caitlin smiled. "Walter was right about you."

"Thanks for the compliment. When is His Majesty coming to see you?"

"Tomorrow evening."

"Ask him to bring Walter. We have a lot of things to discuss. You need to be in the discussions too."

"I'll ask him."

"Kathy also ought to be in the meeting with us."

This woman was a dynamo, Caitlin thought. And the contrast between her in private and in public was amazing. "I'll see to it," she replied.

"Could we have dinner somewhere private this evening where we could talk?"

"Eat with us. A Royal chef helps Mom now so another guest won't be any problem. We can meet in the living room after dinner."

"That will be fine. I'm installing a small kitchen and dining facility in your suite for occasions such as this."

"Very good."

"I need to go to Wilmington after we talk. Can the Air Force furnish me some transportation?"

"Use my plane."

"Your plane? You've been assigned a plane already?"

"Yes."

"Caitlin, Walter must like you."

"Why do you say that?"

"He's so tight-fisted with the royal treasury you'd think it was his money. I have no restrictions on this project either. His only orders were to make it fit for a Queen."

After dinner, they adjourned to her parent's living room where they talked until late evening. Emma gave Caitlin so much advice her head was buzzing by the time Emma left.

"You have two lives now, Caitlin," she told her. "For your own sanity, you must be yourself in private circumstances and with close associates. But you must always be Queen in public. They aren't interested in Caitlin. They want to see their Queen. So remember, in public you are Queen and you must always behave like one. And you need to start behaving like the Queen now. I'm going to tell the guard commander to have the men guarding your house wear dress uniforms and come to attention when you approach. You're not a military officer and you don't have to salute but you must acknowledge them with a nod. It must be a regal nod indicating that you are of superior status.

In public you must always stand straight and proud no matter how you feel. It's okay to smile at someone in the crowd but do it in a queenly way. Never laugh at anybody in public, no matter how silly the occurrence. When all else fails, be dignified. You can always indicate disapproval by simply looking away.

"You'll soon be appearing before groups and the media, making speeches and appearing on television. The palace is already being bombarded with requests for you to appear on national television here and in the U.S."

"I haven't made a speech since I took a public speaking course in college."

"We'll start slow, something like the Baltimore Woman's Club. Your audience there will be favorable and proud that their future Queen came from their midst. And they'll be mature women so you won't have to deal with screaming teenagers. Then maybe we can do the Baltimore television station's Sunday morning talk show."

"Suppose I can't make it come off right?"

"Don't worry. You'll do very well Caitlin. You have a presence about you that makes people respect you without knowing you. You come across as genuine. You'll actually be an asset to the monarchy. Alexander was the last king to have much of a public personality. Your quick wit and strong convictions about right and wrong will carry you through like a champ. Be yourself and act like a queen."

"I'll try."

"It won't be as difficult as you think, Milady."

"I certainly hope not."

"You'll do fine."

"Thank you," Caitlin said.

"It's my job, my future Queen. And I know you will be the greatest Queen America has ever had."

Henry arrived at her house in time for dinner. They had a few minutes of privacy in the living room before the meal started. He took her into his arms and kissed her. She clung to him and kissed his neck.

"I love you," she whispered.

"And I you," he replied. "How are you holding up?"

"I'm okay. And you?"

"I've got this and my regular job. I'm pretty busy myself."

"We will have privacy in Mexico, won't we?"

"A whole week to ourselves. Then our subjects will get to see their queen."

"A week is not much payback for all we're going through."

"It won't be so bad. The progress will be sort of like an extended honeymoon mixed with government business."

"So we'll be able to mix relaxation with me being queen?"

"Absolutely. And I dare to predict you'll enjoy being queen too."

"That's a stretch!"

"I bet you will. You already seem like a Queen to me."

She laughed, "But you're in love. You're not rational."

"Maybe that's it," he laughed. "I do feel very happy at the prospect of having you beside me all the time."

She gave him a sultry smile, "Beside me? How about on top of me."

"Don't start that!"

"Why not?" she giggled.

Her mother came into the room to inform them that dinner was ready. They grinned at each other as they rose to go to the dining room.

They met Sunday afternoon in a conference room on Andrews Air Force Base. Caitlin had never seen Walter except on social occasions so she was surprised how crusty he was. He was all business, even when he spoke to the king.

Emma proved all over again that she was a master of organization and focus. In discussions about the wedding, the coronation and all events leading up to it, she was clearly Caitlin's advocate in every aspect of the issues involved. Most of the talk was about political and publicity issues to be dealt with but she always tempered the discussion towards the needs to the bride and groom. "It is their wedding," she reminded them on several occasions.

When the discussion was winding down and they were reviewing their notes to be sure everything had been covered, Emma made a statement. "In our effort to publicize this momentous event on a worldwide stage, we must not forget the entire basis of this opportunity to enhance the prestige of the monarchy is the wedding of two young people who are very much in love. The single most important item on which to focus our attention is them and their future happiness. Let us not forget this in our work on the political aspects of this wedding."

Caitlin observed Walter while Emma was speaking and watched as he laid down his pen and looked at Emma. Caitlin thought he might have been in disagreement with Emma's reminder, or thought it superfluous and overly sentimental.

"Lady Hamilton," he said, without any change of expression. "Your point is very well taken. The happiness of our King and Queen must be always uppermost in all our minds as we grapple with affairs of state." Caitlin couldn't tell if he genuinely agreed or he was only saying it because he ought to say something like that.

Then he turned to Caitlin, "Lady York, I look forward to the day when you will be my Queen and the happy wife of our monarch. I know that he will be happy with you beside him as his wife and his queen."

Then he abruptly adjourned the meeting, after which he and Henry closeted themselves in another room to discuss an issue involving Argentina. After dinner, in a restaurant with everybody staring at them, Henry had to leave for Kansas City. She was to join him there the next Friday accompanied by her mother, Kathy and Emma.

Fawzi was upset. All of his planning and the diplomatic service had failed him. After his dream, he had asked his father for permission to visit his cousin in Baltimore. His father had enthusiastically approved his request and uncharacteristically promised him ample funds for an extended stay. His father thought his nephew was doing very well in America and he was weeks from becoming an American citizen.

On visits back home, Fawzi's cousin had been enthusiastic about becoming an American, an aristocrat and an officer in the Royal Air Force. In three short years, he had become rich by Egyptian standards. After the American conquest of Maryland, things were even better with the crime rate almost non-existent. His skill as a computer programmer guaranteed him a promising future in the American Kingdom.

Fawzi was offended by his cousin's constant praise of the infidel Kingdom of Satan but Fawzi kept his true feelings concealed in order to achieve his mission. If his cousin had sold out to the infidel, that was his problem. Allah would deal with him when the time came. Fawzi had made a promise to Allah and if it meant playing up to his infidel cousin, he would do that too. He even acted as if he was interested in following his cousin's footsteps and applying for American citizenship.

Fawzi had a lot of trouble obtaining a bomb. The Egyptian government would certainly want no part of his plan. Even though they hated the Americans, nobody was foolish enough to risk making them angry. They had only to be reminded of the fate of Algeria and Saudi Arabia to quell any thoughts of taking an action that might be construed as hostile by the Americans. The Americans played hardball and they played for keeps.

The best he could buy an old World War II hand grenade on the black market. He persuaded his uncle in the diplomatic service to have it delivered to him at his cousin's home after he had arrived in America. He told his uncle he had some extra money his father didn't know about and wanted to spend some of it in America.

"I hear that the American women are most beautiful and spirited," his uncle said with a sly wink.

It had sounded so simple but the fools at the Egyptian Embassy didn't attach any significance to a small heavy package to be delivered to a nobody living with his cousin in Towson, Maryland.

Getting into America had been easy because of Fawzi's cousin's connections. He filled out the form and indicated he was considering citizenship. He was issued a plastic card with his picture and a barcode. He was told it must be on his person at all times, even when he was taking a bath. It came with a cord and they suggested he wear it like a military dog tag.

The king was in town this weekend to see the woman. Fawzi had been able to get as close as thirty feet from the king. Fawzi believed he could have gotten as close as he needed because there were no guards around the king and it was said that Henry liked to move freely among his subjects. The package came the day after the king went home and Fawzi did not know when he would return.

Staying with his cousin was wearing on Fawzi's nerves too. It was getting harder and harder to listen to his cousin sing the praises of this infidel country and its contemptible Christian king. To make it all the more unbearable, his cousin was talking about marrying the

206

`daughter of a rich American Lord. But the worst thing of all was his cousin was studying to become a Catholic!

Allah appeared to Fawzi again that night. He stood with him in the crowd close to where the king had stood. Allah pointed to the woman by the king's side. "Her death would hurt him more than his own death," Allah whispered to him. Fawzi woke up in a cold sweat. He now knew what he had to do.

On Friday, Kansas City turned out for their king and his queen–to-be. Crowds lined the streets as the motorcade made its way from the Royal Airport to the palace. Signs everywhere welcomed Caitlin. There would be little chance for privacy this weekend with most of the time spent selecting her wedding dress, coronation gown and the jewels to be worn with each.

Henry met Caitlin when she and her entourage got off the plane and rode with them to the palace. They had dinner in the formal dining room with the cabinet and the Queen Mother. Caitlin sat to Henry's right and he held her hand when the priest said grace. They shared breakfast in her suite the next morning. Kathy and a servant were present the whole time but they were allowed to relax and enjoy each other's company for almost two hours before she met with the fashion experts and dressmakers. She let Kathy, Emma and her mother guide her on matters surrounding the wedding dress and coronation gown but she would to choose the jewelry herself.

Caitlin didn't see Henry at lunch. Dinner was in the main dining room that evening with all the governors and their wives. Emma sat beside her husband and was dressed less provocatively than she usually dressed at functions such as this.

Caitlin and Henry breakfasted again in her suite on Sunday morning and after early mass they went to the royal vault to see what jewelry was available for her to wear. Walter had told her that if she didn't see anything she liked; she could buy jewels selected especially for this occasion. Henry gave Walter a questioning look when he said this. Later he told Caitlin how surprised he was when Walter offered the suggestion, commenting that Walter was usually very tight with the purse strings.

The royal vault was bigger than Caitlin imagined it would be and there was a lot of jewelry on display, representing every precious stone and precious metal.

For her coronation jewelry, Caitlin chose the necklace set Henry's great grandmother had worn in the painting. She chose a less extravagant set for the wedding. Emma complimented her on her choices.

"You have excellent taste, Milady," she whispered as they left the vault.

Next Caitlin selected the dressmakers for her wedding dress and coronation gown. She chose the exclusive Parisian fashion designer, Le' Chic for her wedding dress and Dallas dressmaker, Claire's for her coronation gown. By the time they left for the airport, she was longing for the peace and quiet of home. She and Henry rode to the airport in a separate vehicle so they could have some time alone.

"Can we relax next weekend?" she asked.

"Yeah. Meet me at the beach."

"That is a deal," she whispered and kissed his cheek.

"I can't wait."

"My office is supposed to be ready Thursday," she told him.

"I bet it will be fit for a Queen."

"I've been so busy this weekend I couldn't think about us in that fancy palace in Mexico."

"Don't stop thinking about that," he grinned. "I haven't."

"Henry," she sighed, "I am about to die to be yours again."

"Caitlin," he said quietly, "I need you too. We must be strong next weekend."

"I'm not worried. We won't be able to because we'll have so many people around us. It's like we've got chaperones with us all the time."

"In a few weeks it won't matter."

"I cannot wait!" she replied emphatically.

He followed her onto the plane and kissed her goodbye.

Caitlin's office was ready for occupancy Thursday morning. It was lavishly, or more correctly, royally decorated with plush furniture and fixtures and the magnificence of her temporary office was astonishing. Two guards in dress uniform bracketed the entry. They came smartly to attention as she approached. The entry doors were double eleven foot walnut of classic woodwork. Inside was an entry foyer about thirty feet long and sixteen feet wide. Arranged along the left wall was the York family coat of arms. Facing it across the room was the Clark family coat of arms. There were also portraits of them facing each other across the room. Her portrait had been borrowed from her mother and somebody had painted one of Henry the same size. At the desk at the far end of the foyer was a well-dressed man she had never seen before. Emma introduced him.

"This is Lord Roger Dickens," she said. "He's your receptionist and appointments secretary."

"Pleased to meet you, Lord Roger," Caitlin said.

"I'm pleased to finally meet you, Milady," he replied.

Lord Dickens rose to open the door to Caitlin's office. When she entered, she was surprised by its size and the luxurious furnishings.

Emma sensed her surprise. "You need an office such as this. You'll be meeting a lot of people here that you want to impress."

"I am very surprised. This is temporary, isn't it?"

"We'll probably keep it for your use when you visit after the wedding."

"This is a far cry from what I had at the real estate office. My desk here is bigger than my office was there."

"Lady York, on April the twenty-second you will be the second highest ranking person in the kingdom and empire."

"It's still hard for me to realize what I'm getting into."

"Milady, you are every inch a Queen."

Caitlin stared at Emma for a moment, "You say so, but I'm still just Caitlin York, soon to be Caitlin Clark."

"It's good for you to think about it like that. It keeps your position from going to your head. Your greatest strength is your firm grasp of yourself. You're genuine, Caitlin. Don't ever lose that."

"Henry's like I am in that respect."

"Yes he is. That's why he's a great King. You two are the perfect match and everybody who knows you, realizes it's true."

"Both of us believe that God brought us together."

"I believe it too, Milady. God blesses our countries and empire in so many ways. He gave us our good King and now He's giving us a wonderful Queen to be his companion and helpmate."

Caitlin laughed, "Don't forget the heir. That's all Walter thinks about."

Emma laughed too. "He is concerned about it. His worst nightmare is something happening to Henry and Rachel would become our monarch."

"He might be surprised about Rachel. I like her."

"Caitlin, that's one of your most precious gifts."

"What?"

"Your ability to size people up. You are the only one, besides Henry, who accords Princess Rachel the respect she deserves."

Her office had a big desk and leather executive chair. She had but to turn around to look out over the Baltimore Harbor. To the right of her desk was a ten-person conference table with matching chairs. Paintings adorned the walls and luxurious drapes framed the windows.

An area by the window facing the harbor was set up like a living room with a leather couch, five upholstered chairs and a coffee table. There were two phones on her desk.

"Why do I have two telephones?" Caitlin asked.

"The white one is a direct line to His Majesty."

She picked it up. It rang once. Henry answered.

"Hello, Caitlin."

"Henry, it's so nice and so very big."

"I hope it's fit for my Queen."

"Oh, it is!

"Lady Hamilton did an excellent job getting it ready so quickly."

"She helps me a lot."

"I knew she would."

"Thanks, Henry."

"I'd do anything for you, Caitlin."

"Anything?" she giggled.

"That too," he laughed. "But we must wait."

"I know, but I think about it every time I'm alone and have time to myself."

"Forty-five more days."

"Seems like forever."

"Yeah."

"I think I'll give Ashley my car. I can't drive it anywhere now. People try to take stuff off of it for souvenirs."

"You can have a personal car, you know."

"I know. But right now it's a bother."

"Things will calm down after we're married."

"I hope so. I want to see you, Henry."

"I could come for a couple of hours tonight."

"No, that's too hard on you. I'll wait for the weekend."

"I love you, Caitlin."

"I love you too, Henry."

"I've got to go."

"Bye."

She hung up. When she did, she remembered Emma was still in her office and had heard everything she said.

"I forgot you were here, Emma."

"That's okay, Milady. You must learn to ignore us and say whatever you want to say."

"It's hard to do."

"You don't have to worry about any of us divulging anything you say. It is treason for me or Kathy to divulge your private conversations."

"Even to Henry?"

"Even to Henry."

"This is still hard to get used to."

"You're doing fine." She laughed, "It's so wonderful to hear the way you speak to His Majesty. He can't help but love you."

"I can't help loving him either," she mused. "If I could, my life might be normal again."

"Milady, you are about to marry the man you love and you are going to be the greatest Queen America has ever had."

Caitlin looked at her with a solemn expression, "I love Henry with all my heart, Emma."

"I know you do, Milady."

Caitlin looked out the window at a ship leaving the harbor, "Loving Henry is easy. It's all this other stuff that's hard."

"You will find the other stuff is not so bad either."

"I hope you're right. Emma."

"You're doing fine. Now let's get to work."

Caitlin met Henry at the Myrtle Beach compound Friday afternoon. If she thought people had watched them the first time she was here, it was claustrophobic now. She had Kathy and Emma plus another servant assigned to her when she was at the beach. Even though she was not yet part of the royal family, everybody treated her like she was. Emma made it worse by telling everyone to treat her with the utmost respect and consideration.

Every time she and Henry slipped into some private place to kiss and cuddle for a few minutes, somebody interrupted them. Finally Caitlin exploded at Kathy after she and Henry had been playing in the water. He had followed her into her room laughing, pinching and hugging her when Kathy interrupted them to ask her something.

"God damn it," Caitlin blurted out, "Will you please leave us alone for a few minutes!" Kathy blushed, apologized and left them alone.

Henry was astonished at her outburst, "Kathy was only trying to do her job."

"Henry, I came to the beach to be with you! I didn't come to be watched and waited on every minute. I know you're used to all this but I'm not and there are some times when I want to be private with you and nobody else."

211

"I'll speak to Rebecca and my staff. You'll need to speak to your staff."

She calmed down and gave him a little smile, "I'll apologize to Kathy. But first, go back to what you were doing before we were interrupted."

After Caitlin had changed out of her swimsuit, she went to Kathy's room. When Kathy opened the door Caitlin said, "I'm sorry, Kathy. "I'm not angry with you. But all this attention is getting on my nerves."

"I understand, Milady. And I know you and His Majesty need time alone."

"I'm sorry I flew off the handle."

"I was inconsiderate. There's so much to do now and I sometimes forget the romantic part of your engagement." Kathy smiled, "The way you and His Majesty carry on when you're together is so sweet."

"We can't seem to have much time alone lately. I thought it was bad before but it's worse now. I hope things calm down after we're married."

"It will, Milady."

Henry and Caitlin held hands during prayer, played in the ocean, sunned on the beach and enjoyed what little privacy they could. Emma forbade any interviews or visits by local officials and they didn't go to any outside entertainment during the whole weekend. The only business interruption was when Carl gave Henry his briefing at ten every morning. When they parted, Henry followed Caitlin onto her plane to tell her goodbye.

"In forty-one days, you will accompany me wherever I go."

"I cannot wait!" she whispered as he kissed her. "I need you Henry and nobody will leave us alone long enough."

"I know. I need you too."

"I know we need to wait, but I'm about to die the way you touch me all the time."

"I try to cool it, but I can't keep my hands off you when we're together."

"Well, everybody ought to be damn pleased that we didn't do it again."

He wanted to laugh but didn't because she was so serious, "I love you, Caitlin."

"I love you, Henry. I guess it's Kansas City next weekend. Emma said I needed to handle some things. And we won't have any chance because more people will be watching us."

"But by then, it will be only thirty-five days away."

"You say it like it's nothing. In my present state, thirty-five minutes is too long." Then she laughed and kissed his cheek, "I'll be okay, Henry. I only get this way when I'm around you."

He brushed her cheek with the tips of his fingers, "I like you this way." Then he kissed her and left the plane. Pressing business awaited him in Kansas City.

Chapter Eighteen

Caitlin's first public activity was a visit on the fourteenth of March by a third grade class from Cedartown, an Eastern Shore community. In addition to the Baltimore television station and a reporter from the Sun, a CBS news crew would film the visit. Caitlin's scheduling had been transferred to her office and Lord Roger had to bring in three people to handle the traffic. Emma kept a tight rein on Caitlin's schedule and eased her into her public life slowly. She encouraged Caitlin to make time to visit her friends, Debbie and Eleanor, and to let them know that their friendship was very valuable to her. Caitlin was amazed by how busy she'd become, even with Emma, Roger and Kathy at her beck and call.

Henry called her Monday morning to say how much he missed her and told her he might have to go to Argentina sometime soon.

"Will this be another annexation?" she asked.

"Maybe. We're trying to work it out so we won't have to do it. Russia, Europe and several middle-eastern countries are pretty upset with us over the action at Mecca last month. They're talking about a mutual defense treaty."

"Why are they so upset?"

"The Europeans are worried about their oil supply."

"What are our interests in Argentina?"

"We have a lot invested and they may be about to elect a president pledged to confiscate our property and holdings."

"Isn't anybody running against him?"

"Yes. But he's not very popular and we can't provide him any overt support because of the strong feelings against us in the international community."

"It looks pretty bad, doesn't it?"

"We're mobilizing."

"Do we have any allies?"

"England and Israel. Of course we have the Empire countries but they're not allies. They're us.

She heard Walter greet him.

"I've got to go."

"Love you."

"Me too. Bye."

She went out to dinner with Debbie and Eleanor Tuesday night. At least one guard and Kathy or Emma accompanied her everywhere she went. She began to worry about her friends being in the spotlight with her but they seemed to like it. Debbie especially liked it and told her so. After dinner, she took them to her office to give them a private tour. Eleanor laughed when the guard on duty came to attention as Caitlin approached.

"You're really somebody now, aren't you?"

"I'm the same person you've always known."

"How does it feel?"

"Sometimes I just want to be left alone," then she added smiling, "with Henry, of course."

"He was so handsome when he met you at the Crackpot. I didn't have the foggiest idea he was king," Debbie observed.

"I didn't either."

"It was good of him to come clean about who he was, especially the way things have turned out," Eleanor said. "Who'd have guessed in a million years this would have happened?"

"Not me," Caitlin replied.

"Debbie said you had a plane now?"

"Yes, I do."

"Is it as nice as Henry's?"

"Yes, it is."

"And you can just pick up and go anywhere you want to?"

"Kathy said I could."

"Could we go with you?"

"Yes, you can."

They became quiet, standing inside her office suite with the guard still holding the door open. The night secretary came up to Caitlin and bowed, "Can I help you, Milady?" he asked.

"I wanted to show my friends my office."

"Then I'll show them around Milady, if you please?'

"Please do."

Debbie and Eleanor gave each other the look and then both smiled at Caitlin.

"Thank you, Milady," Debbie said with a devilish smile.

The last room they were shown was Caitlin's office.

"This is awesome!" Eleanor gasped in astonishment when she saw the size, the furnishings and the view from the window.

Debbie and Eleanor tested all the furniture by sitting on it, giggling all the while and saying, "Milady this" and "Milady that" in every sentence. Caitlin laughed at their antics and Kathy suppressed a smile at their exuberance.

"How will Caitlin be addressed after she marries the king?" Eleanor asked Kathy as they were leaving.

"She will be called 'Your Highness'."

On their way home, Debbie asked Caitlin if they would still be able to be friends after she married the king.

"Yes, of course. I want you two to continue to be my friends just like you are now."

"Can we come to see you in Kansas City?"

"I'll send for you."

"Most importantly, can we go with you to Lake Louise again?"

"Certainly."

They rode quietly for a few minutes before Eleanor said, "Debbie and I are very proud of you, Caitlin. I know you'll find this an astonishing statement coming from us, but we believe that you will be a great queen."

Caitlin didn't reply immediately.

"She will be a great queen," Kathy agreed.

"I'm glad you think so. And thank you for being my friends."

"We love you, Caitlin," Debbie said solemnly, "And we are very proud and grateful that you consider us to be your friends."

On the day of the school children's visit, Emma was tied up all morning with the two television stations setting up. The media people accepted an invitation to join them for lunch in the dining room. The U.S. people were quite impressed with everything, including the meal. Over lunch, Emma, Kathy and Caitlin reviewed her brief welcoming speech and remarks to be given when the class was settled in her office.

The school children arrived at thirteen-thirty. Caitlin and Emma met them as they got off the elevator. Caitlin greeted the children, their teacher and chaperones. After each child was introduced to Caitlin by the teacher, each girl curtseyed and the boys bowed when their names were called. When introductions were complete, Caitlin led them on a short tour of the suite before gathering in the living room area of her office. As they were sitting down on the carpet before the picture window overlooking the harbor, one of the boys asked what the white telephone was for.

"It's my direct line to the king," Caitlin replied.

"You can talk to the king just like that?"

"Yes, I can."

"Wow." He elbowed the boy next to him and whispered loud enough for everybody to hear, "Did you hear that? She talks to the king any time she wants to."

"She's going to marry him, dummy. It's like your mom talking to your dad."

Everybody laughed. The teacher shushed the boys.

"Thank you for visiting me," Caitlin began. "This is my first public appearance since I became engaged to the king. And it's my first time ever on television.

"I grew up here in Baltimore and went to college at the University of Maryland. I met Henry last June and we have been seeing each other since then. In February he asked me to marry him and I accepted. We are to be married April the twenty-first.

"Becoming a member of the royal family is a very complicated thing to do and I am learning as I go. At times it is interesting, at times it is frustrating and sometimes I wish we could run off and elope. But I love the king and I must do all these things to become his wife." She paused and looked at each of the children, "That's it in a nutshell. Now you may ask me questions. Afterwards, we'll go to the dining room where the royal chef has prepared refreshments for us and each of you will receive a small present from me and His Majesty."

Emma instructed them to address Caitlin as "Milady".

A girl in the front row raised her hand first, "Milady, we are so proud that our king picked you to be his queen. We think it's so neat that our Queen grew up in Maryland."

"Thank you," Caitlin replied.

A boy asked, "Will you live in a palace?"

"Yes, I will."

"Is it big?" another boy asked.

"Yes. It has 109 rooms."

A girl asked, "Have you been in it?"

"Yes, I have."

"Is it nice?'

"It is very nice."

Another asked, "How many palaces does the king have, Milady?'

"Ten."

"Have you been in them all?"

"Only the ones in Kansas City and in New Zealand."

A girl in the back asked, "Milady, does he have any other houses?"

"He has homes at Myrtle Beach, Lewiston, Montana and Lake Louise, British Columbia."

"Which do you like the best?"

"The one at Lake Louise."

"What's it like, Milady?"

"It's built of stone and it sits on top of a big mountain. But the neatest part is the big glass dome where you can watch the Northern Lights and stars at night."

"Wow!"

A boy in back raised his hand, "Milady, do you really like the king?"

"I love him."

"My mama says the king is a mean man."

The teacher was aghast and was about to reprimand the boy but was prevented from doing so by Emma.

"The king has a very hard job," Caitlin answered calmly, "Sometimes he has to do things that other people don't like."

The boy wanted to say something else but the child next to him elbowed him when he saw the teacher shaking her head.

Another boy asked, "Milady, can I be one of your guards when I grow up?"

"You can certainly apply to be one."

A girl asked, "Milady, can I be a queen like you some day?"

Caitlin laughed, "You have as good a chance as I did."

"What will people call you when you're queen?"

"Your Highness."

"Is that what the king will call you too?"

"The king calls me Caitlin."

"What do you call the king?"

"Henry."

"I can't wait until you are our Queen, Milady," the first girl said.

"Thank you. I can't wait to be your Queen either."

Emma signaled that time was up.

"Emma tells me that refreshments are ready. If you'll join me in the dining room we can have a snack and each of you will receive a present. Thank you for coming to see me."

The girl in front stood up and smiled, "Thank you, Milady. We are thrilled to be the very first class to meet our new queen in person."

"How'd I do?" Caitlin asked Emma after the children and their chaperones had departed.

"You did fine. It will be boring television but everybody has been clamoring for something and this ought to satisfy them for a few days. I'm sure every second of it will be aired worldwide tonight."

"At least I didn't flub up."

"Your reply to the boy was great. And you are very photogenic. I watched the monitors and you have quite a screen presence." Then she added thoughtfully, "The wedding will be a spectacular show and the eyes of the world will be upon you."

"And to think, all I wanted to do was marry Henry Clark."

"Milady, you are going to be a star!"

"What will I do next?"

"The Sunday morning talk show on Channel 6 here in Baltimore."

"Henry's coming this weekend."

"He'll be in the audience."

"The audience? Why can't he sit beside me?"

"It's your show, Milady."

"What are the rules?"

"They are not supposed to ask any intimate or highly personal questions. If they do, simply refuse to answer."

"Will I have to make a statement?"

"No. The moderator will make the opening statement and then open it up to the panel."

"Who will be on the panel?"

"The reporter from the Sun who was here today, the society editor of the Richmond Times Dispatch, the evening news anchors from Channel 6 and the president of the Baltimore Woman's Club."

"What a crew," Caitlin observed laconically.

"You will be the star of the show, Milady."

"What's next?"

"We'll go to Kansas City on the twenty-third and you'll appear on national television on the twenty-fifth."

"That big already?"

"Milady, by then you will be a pro and you'll knock'em dead."

"I bet."

"No, really. You will. You are a natural."

"I'll decide about that later."

"I think you ought to appear on NBC's 'Meet the Press' on the first. They've already reserved the slot and are waiting for your decision."

"That's April Fool's Day."

Emma laughed, "What better time to show the U.S. a little class."

"Maybe we should," Caitlin replied thoughtfully. "It would be gratifying to make them a little jealous of us poor conquered peasants in Maryland and Delaware."

"Milady!" Emma replied gleefully. "Those are my thoughts exactly."

"We could rub it in a little, don't you think?"

They both laughed, "Milady, you are a woman after my own heart. Let's make the U.S. turn absolutely green with envy."

"I could take twelve of my tallest, handsomest guards in their finest uniforms and have both you and Kathy dressed like queens yourselves."

"And we could have a special dress made for you that would knock out every man's eyes. It would make all women in the United States yearn to look like you."

"Let's not overdo it."

"Milady, it ought to be an exquisite ensemble which highlights your great beauty. We'll show them some class!"

"I'll wear some nice jewelry."

"Oh yes! And very expensive looking too."

They continued this discussion and decided they had better run it by Walter before making their final decision.

Walter would approve anything which might irritate the United States as long as it could not be construed as diminishing the monarchy. In the conversation, Caitlin asked Emma if she thought it would be a good idea for her to learn Spanish so she could converse with the Mexicans on their honeymoon.

"It would be a nice surprise for them," Emma agreed.

Henry arrived in time for dinner on Friday. He stayed on Andrews Air Force Base and they dined the Officer's Club. This gave them more privacy and allowed them to relax. Afterwards they went to a dance on the base before he took her home. They also attended the Orioles game on Saturday. Since everybody was watching them, Caitlin stayed calm for most of the game even though she kept up a running dialog with Henry the whole time and only jumped up twice when the Orioles made home runs. The Orioles won. The president of the Orioles organization presented them permanent passes as they were leaving after the game was over.

Emma reminded her that she had to prepare for the Sunday morning talk show. After dinner at her parent's house they visited a few minutes in their living room before Henry had to leave.

She clung to him, "Will the day ever come, Henry?"

220

"In thirty days."

"Then we can relax?"

"And make love."

"I've been so busy I haven't had much time to even think about it."

"I've been pretty busy myself, but I think about it a lot. You'll do fine tomorrow. All you have to do is relax and be Caitlin."

She smiled, "I'll try. I love you, Henry."

"I love you too, Caitlin." Then he gave her a sweet good night kiss and left.

She would rather have thought about them together in their Mexican palace but instead she went to bed thinking about her busy day tomorrow.

The program was taped before a live audience an hour before it was to be aired. The auditorium was packed and people were standing everywhere. The station manager told them this was the biggest studio audience they ever had. Emma and Kathy were with Caitlin and two of her guards. As part of their plan for the NBC event, Emma had picked the two guards for Caitlin's appearance on the program.

Roslyn Townsend, the evening news anchor for the television station was the moderator. Stephen Clayton, reporter for the Sun, Elizabeth Ann Lee, society editor for the Richmond Times Dispatch and Abigail Fitzgerald, president of the Baltimore Woman's Club made up the panel members. There was a small informal rehearsal to put everybody at ease prior to the taping session. Henry sat in the top row of seats in the back with the studio audience. Those next to him had trouble concentrating on the show when they realized their monarch was sitting next to them. Caitlin wore a conservative, navy blue business suit with a knee length skirt, a light blue long sleeve silk blouse and a pearl necklace and earrings. She was stunning.

The lights came on and the camera panned the individual members of the panel and the audience before it focused on Mrs. Townsend.

"Members of the panel, studio audience and all of our viewers, the moment we have been waiting for these long days has finally arrived." She paused for effect. "The future Queen of America, Canada, Mexico and New Zealand; the future Empress of Panama, Venezuela, South Africa, Namibia, Saudi Arabia and Algeria is here. Please welcome Lady Caitlin Rose York!"

The audience roared in appreciation and the panel stood and applauded when Caitlin made her entrance, bowed to the audience and the camera before taking a seat opposite Mrs. Townsend.

Mrs. Townsend spoke, trying not to gush, "Welcome, Lady York. We are so excited. We're excited for you and about you and the wonderful news that you will become our Queen."

"Thank you," Caitlin replied.

"This city and the whole state are united in our pride that one of our own will be at our king's side."

"Thank you for inviting me."

"For the benefit of the audience, let me say that Lady York grew up in Baltimore where she attended Baltimore schools and the University of Maryland. She is the daughter of Lord Richard and Lady Francis York, the Duke and Duchess of Cumberland. She has one sister, Ashley, who is married to Sir William Brent Churchill." She paused to catch her breath. "And now, Lady York, we are dying to find out how you met His Majesty."

"I was having dinner with some friends at Sabatino's in Little Italy and we spotted each other."

"You spotted each other?"

"I saw him giving me the once over." The audience laughed.

"And what did you do, Lady York?"

"I gave him the once over." The audience laughed louder.

Mrs. Townsend laughed, "And what happened then, Lady York?"

"He sent his aide to ask me to dine with him."

"And did you?"

"No. I went to his table to meet him but I told him I couldn't because I was with friends."

"So you refused to dine with the king because you were with friends."

"I didn't know he was the king at the time. But it wouldn't have mattered if I had."

Clayton asked, "Who did you think he was?"

"He introduced himself as Henry Clark. That's his real name," she added.

Mrs. Lee: "So he was trying to be incognito?"

"Yes."

Mrs. Lee: "Did you dine with him later?"

"We met at the Crackpot in Towson for lunch the next day."

Mrs. Fitzgerald: "When did you find out he was king?"

"He came to our house on Friday night and told us who he really was."

Clayton: "Why did he do it then?"

"His advisors thought it was a bad idea for him to deceive me about who he was."

Fitzgerald: "What did you think?"

"I don't like to be deceived. I was pretty upset."

Clayton: "About him being king?'

"No. About him not telling me who he was."

Lee: "Why did he do it?'

"He was tired of women wanting to become his queen without caring anything about Henry."

Fitzgerald: "Then my guess is you care about Henry."

"I do. Being queen will be my job."

Clayton: "How did your parents react when they discovered the king wanted to date their daughter?"

"They were quite agitated about it. Finding out the man standing in their living room was the king was very upsetting to them."

Lee: "I suppose they've gotten over it by now?"

"Yes. They like Henry a lot."

Townsend: "We know about some of the times you have been with him in public but tell us about being with him in private."

"Since last July we've been together every weekend except when he was out of the country on business. I went with him to New Zealand. It was the first time people turned out to see me. It upset him when they did. Henry is very private and doesn't like publicity. I also went with him to Montana for his best friend's birthday. We had a good time on that trip. I loved Montana and the horseback riding."

Clayton: "The king likes horses?"

"Yes. He loves ride his black thoroughbred and mustang mix."

Lee: "Is he a good rider?"

"Yes, he's very good. If he wasn't, he'd fall off Blackie; he's so wild and frisky."

Townsend: "Who was the friend?"

"Slim."

Fitzgerald: "Slim?"

"I don't know his last name. He's an old cowboy Henry met when he was a boy."

Lee: "Cowboy?"

Caitlin laughed, "Slim told me Henry was a good boy. But he needed advice once in a while."

The audience laughed.

Clayton: "So cowboy Slim advises the king. What kind of advice does he give him?"

"He gives the king advice about 'likker', 'wimmin' and 'hosses'." The audience howled. "He also told Henry to marry me quick before some dude ran off with me." The audience laughed again.

Fitzgerald: "It is touching to hear that the king is devoted to friends like Slim."

"He loves Slim. It was so sweet to see how he catered to the cranky old man."

Clayton: "You like Slim too, don't you?"

"Yes, I do. He is the genuine article. There is no pretense in Slim."

Lee: "Which of the places he's taken you is your favorite?"

"The lodge at Lake Louise."

"Tell us about it."

"It's a gorgeous stone house in a beautiful setting. But the main reason it's my favorite is because it's the place where I decided I wanted to marry Henry."

Fitzgerald: "So it's where you realized you loved the king?"

"No. It's where I decided I wanted to marry him. I've loved him since the weekend after we met."

Lee: "So, it was love at first sight?"

"Yes."

Fitzgerald: "For both of you?"

"Yes."

Lee: "We are so proud of you, Milady. And it's so nice to know that you have such a wonderful sense of yourself."

"I can't be any other way."

Fitzgerald: "My dear that is what makes you so very special. And it is obvious that our king appreciates you too."

The red light went on.

Townsend: "Our time is up. Lady York, we, along with the management of this station, our sponsors, the studio audience and all of the people who are watching this broadcast thank you for sharing this time with us."

"Thank you for inviting me."

The audience applauded, the credits began and the camera played on the panel who were shaking Caitlin's hand. The king then joined them on the stage.

That evening excerpts from the program were shown in newscasts throughout the world. Most of the stations in America and the United States played it in its entirety during prime time.

Emma was beside herself, "You were wonderful, Milady!"

224

Henry stood beside her with his arm around her waist, "You were very good, Caitlin."

"Thank you, Your Majesty," she said with a smile.

People from the studio audience crowded around them shaking hands and enjoying the opportunity for close association with their king and future queen. It was a magnificent public relations success.

Henry had to leave early for Kansas City so he and Caitlin said their private goodbyes in the studio manager's office.

The Royal Security Service Satellite Observation Unit was located in the Cheyenne Mountain complex in Colorado. Their function was to monitor satellite-derived locations of people close to the Royal Family. Every American had an identification and locator chip implanted behind their right ear. Foreigners in the country were required to wear an identification card which contained a locator chip with the visitor's name, country of origin and other information such as date of entry. A technician alerted the duty officer.

[*Latin*]"The Egyptian is back."

[*Latin*] "Where?"

[*Latin*] "He's outside the television studio where Lady York is appearing on television."

[*Latin*] "The king is inside the studio too."

[*Latin*] "Yeah, I know."

[*Latin*] "Have you passed it on?"

[*Latin*] "Yeah. I've alerted the guards."

[*Latin*] "Do they have his description?"

[*Latin*] "Yeah."

[*Latin*] "It looked like he was testing to see how close he could get to the king on the fourth. Is he behaving like it now?"

[*Latin*] "Yeah."

[*Latin*] "Is he carrying anything?"

[*Latin*] "He's got something in his pocket. It's not a gun or a bomb. It could be something flammable or chemical. I can't tell what."

[*Latin*] "The king is about to leave the building. If he moves into the pink zone, arrest him."

Fawzi was standing across the street when Henry and Carl exited the building. He hadn't heard the king was in town and was surprised to see him. He cursed the missed opportunity because the king was out of the building, in the car and gone before Fawzi could

225

react. He moved across the street to get a little closer to the entrance. He felt the grenade in his coat pocket and put his finger in the ring. There was a crowd outside the studio. He didn't notice the two men in business suits who followed him across the street, one on his left and the other on his right, each staying about twenty feet away.

[*Latin*] "Lady York and her party are about to leave the building."

[*Latin*] "Where is he?"

[*Latin*]"He's moved across the street closer to the entrance."

[*Latin*] "How far from the door?"

[*Latin*] "A hundred and seven feet."

[*Latin*] "Who's closest to Lady York?"

[*Latin*] "Parker."

[*Latin*] "He's new. Why is he assigned to close protection?"

[*Latin*] "Lady Hamilton ordered it."

[*Latin*] "Who in hell does she think she is? That's the guard commander's decision."

[*Latin*] "Lady Hamilton insisted and he agreed."

[*Latin*] "That woman has far too much influence."

[*Latin*] "They're coming out of the building."

[*Latin*] "Are our people in position?"

[*Latin*] "Yeah."

Fawzi noticed the crowd becoming excited and moved a little closer to the entrance. He guessed the king's bride-to-be would emerge from the center door and moved in front of it. That way, if she came out of one of the other doors, he could easily adjust. His heart started pounding when he saw a man open the door and hold it open. Then he saw her approaching.

Fawzi was getting light headed from the tension as he focused on her to the exclusion of everything else. As she exited the door, he decided to move quickly. At his first step, out of the corner of his eye, he saw a man start running towards him. He had to act now! He took the grenade from his pocket, pulled the pin and lobbed it in the direction of the woman as she stood smiling at the crowd. He heard the grenade hit the pavement just as the man tackled him. Then another man was on him and he was pinned to the ground.

Caitlin had exited the building and turned to speak to Emma when she saw something falling toward her. Then she heard a metallic "clunk" when it hit the pavement about three feet away. Before she could react, the guard holding the door threw himself on the object and two other guards shoved her roughly back inside the building, positioning themselves in front and behind her with weapons drawn. Then she heard a "pop" like a firecracker had exploded and saw smoke emerge from under the guard on the ground. In seconds, nine guards had surrounded her with weapons drawn. The guard commander ran up and ordered them to move Lady York into the conference room off the lobby while he sorted things out.

National television cameras had recorded the whole scene. One of the guards urged Caitlin to sit down. She looked around for Emma. Emma and Kathy were standing behind her with ashen looks on their faces. The guard commander came in.

"Lady York, an Egyptian has made an attempt on your life."

"Why?"

"We don't know yet but we will know within the hour. He has been arrested and is being taken to detention."

"What did he throw at me?'

"A grenade. It turned out to be an old training grenade but he thought it was the real thing."

"Was the guard who threw himself on it injured?"

"No, Milady. He was wearing body armor and it was like a big firecracker explosion."

"Suppose it had been a real grenade?"

"He might have been killed, Milady."

"Bring him to me."

"Right away, Milady."

The guard commander left and a moment later returned with the guard. The front of the guard's suit and shirt were smudged and burned in spots but otherwise he appeared to be all right. He came to attention in front of Caitlin.

"You sent for me, Milady."

"Yes, I did. What is your name?

"Agent Parker, Milady."

"What you did was very courageous."

"I have sworn to defend your life with mine," he replied.

"Then today, you have proven both your courage and your devotion to me."

"Thank you, Milady."

"I wish you to be my personal bodyguard from now on."

"Thank you, Milady," he stammered and dropped to his knees before Caitlin and bowed his head. She extended her hand. He took her hand and kissed it.

He was overcome with emotion, "You do me great honor, Milady," he said with a trembling voice. Cameras recorded the whole scene while the crowd applauded and cheered.

Then Henry burst into the room. He was frantic. His guards were in despair because they knew that he might have been targeted too but they had been unable to contain him in his rush to be back at his beloved's side.

"Are you okay, Caitlin?" he asked all out of breath.

"I'm okay, Henry."

"You're calm. You're calmer than I am."

"There's no reason for me to get excited. My guards protected me."

He relaxed a little, "They will pay for this. Whoever set this up will pay."

Then he asked the guards to clear the room.

After they were alone, he took her in his arms. "I was so afraid for you when they told me."

"I didn't have a chance to be scared. It was over before I could get upset."

"I hate to leave you at a time like this, but I do have got to leave."

"I know. Thank you for coming back to me."

"I love you, Caitlin."

"I love you too, Henry."

They kissed and left the conference room. The crowd cheered and applauded when they emerged.

At the cabinet meeting the next morning, Walter played the recording of the television program and the assassination attempt. When it was over, he sat back, folded his arms and grinned.

"What did I tell you?" he gloated. "She is every inch a queen!"

Chapter Nineteen

Fawzi lay on the floor of the vehicle. It was moving but that was all he knew. His arms were pinned to his sides with a band of plastic wrap like that used to hold cardboard boxes on pallets. His nose itched and he couldn't scratch it. Two men were in the compartment with him. He knew they were hard men. That was what was difficult to understand about these Americans. No passion. If he'd been in Egypt they would be beating him now. But they sat there ignoring him while they stared out of the vehicle windows.

Sabri had commented on it too. Americans were unfailingly friendly and generous. They were honest and open, he'd told him, but if you messed up, you were an instant pariah. He told of a man who worked with him who was very personable and well liked by everybody. Then this man was accused of molesting a child. He disappeared, his office was cleaned out and no vestige of his presence remained. Nobody mentioned his name anymore and it was like he had never existed among them. He left a void that nobody noticed.

Fawzi wondered what would happen to him. He'd heard there were no prisons in America. Then he thought about his failed mission. He had failed Allah and now Allah had turned his back on him. Maybe that is what had happened to his cousins. Maybe Allah had turned his back on them too. In spite of his fervent love of Allah, maybe he had not loved Allah enough and Allah had turned his back on him.

The vehicle came to a stop, the doors were opened and the two men lifted Fawzi to his feet and ushered him into a solid looking, brightly lit room without windows. It had a cot, a lavatory, a commode, a table and one chair. He was led to the chair and motioned to sit down. They did not remove the plastic wrap. Nobody said anything. A nurse came in, pulled the plastic wrap off his left shoulder and gave him a shot in the muscle of his upper arm.

He noticed she didn't disinfect his skin before inserting the needle. A chilling thought occurred to him. He wouldn't live long enough for an infection to develop.

Fawzi felt an irresistible urge to talk. It was like he couldn't keep from talking. The larger of the two men uttered the first words directed to him since he had been knocked to the ground.

"Tell us why you did this and who helped you."

Fawzi started talking. He couldn't shut up. He even remembered the name and address of the black market dealer who sold him the grenade.

It was eight o'clock in Cairo and President Abdullah Ibrahim was sitting down to dinner with his family when an aide rushed in and whispered something in his ear. He frowned and excused himself and left with the aide. The American ambassador was waiting in his office with some very alarming news.

When the ambassador was escorted into the president's office, he got right to the point. "An Egyptian citizen has attempted to assassinate Lady Caitlin York, the king's fiancée."

The president was speechless for a moment, "This is terrible!" he said, "How could this be?" he asked, while thinking of an intelligent question to ask.

"He was a religious fanatic, a member of the sect that caused the trouble at Mecca in February."

"I hope that Lady York was not injured."

"She was not injured."

"Then I thank Allah that he has spared Lady York. I can assure you that my government did not participate or condone this in any way."

"We know that."

How could these Americans know everything he thought? "Then I will arrest and punish any Egyptian citizens who participated in this in the slightest fashion."

"His Majesty has requested that you arrest them and turn them over to us."

"But they are not Americans, they are Egyptian citizens. It is our responsibility to dispense justice to our citizens on our soil."

"His Majesty insists you turn them over to us."

"There are international laws which forbid this."

"American law is above international law in this case."

He tried to buy some time, "We'll have to investigate the matter and identify the culprits."

The ambassador handed him a list with seventy-nine names on it. "These are the individuals you are to deliver to us."

He glanced down the list. There was a senior member of his diplomatic staff on it and the heads of two prominent families in El-Uqsor. "There are women and children's names here."

"American law requires that the parents and siblings of violent criminals be executed."

The president was appalled, "I cannot do this!"

"The king demands that you deliver all the people on this list to the American Airlines gate at the Cairo Airport at nine o'clock on the twentieth."

"That's the day after tomorrow."

230

"That is correct," the ambassador confirmed coldly.

"I must confer with my advisors on this matter."

"Time is short. The first and third Algerian armies will be at your western frontier by tomorrow afternoon. Three Saudi Arabian armies and one South African army will be posted on your eastern border by midday tomorrow. The Foreign Legion; the 82nd and 101st Royal Airborne Divisions are boarding planes now for immediate deployment. Advise me of your decision by nine tomorrow."

The American ambassador stood up, bowed to the president, turned on his heel and took his leave.

The president sat quietly at his desk. It would take his army a month to mobilize. Then he realized no matter what position he took, the people whose names were on the list were doomed. Even if the Americans didn't invade his country and take it over, they would hunt them down and assassinate all of them where they lived. Those damned fanatics! Why did this idiot have to be born an Egyptian? And those damned Americans! Why had Allah allowed them to become so all-powerful? Were they Allah's punishment for those of insufficient piety? He had forgotten to ask what they planned to do with the man they had arrested.

Sabri had gone in to work early Sunday morning. He was behind on his project because he'd vacationed with Denise at her parents lodge in Colorado and returned two days later than he'd planned. He had to make up the time before Friday.

Things were going very well for him career-wise and socially. He had asked Denise to marry him and she accepted. They hadn't asked her parents yet but he was confident they would welcome him into the family.

He got home at seventeen o'clock. He was supposed to take Denise to dinner this evening.

Denise had left terse a message. "I can't go out with you tonight." That was all. No explanation. No suggestion for him to call her. He was puzzled.

He called her home and a servant answered. "I'd like to speak to Denise."

"Lady Templeton cannot speak to you."

"Why not?"

"Haven't you seen the news?"

"No. I've been at work all day."

"Watch the news tonight. Then you'll know why. Do not call Lady Templeton again."

He was stunned. What could possibly have happened? He turned on the television. A newscaster was in the middle of a report of some kind.

"...And an Egyptian, a man named Fawzi Kibur," the American mispronounced Fawzi's first name, "Has been arrested and is being questioned by the Royal Secret Service this afternoon." Then he went on about how Fawzi had thrown a bomb towards Lady York, the king's betrothed. Luckily it was not a real bomb and the Lady had not been injured. One of her guards had behaved with great valor and covered the bomb with his body to prevent injury to his charge. He was a national hero and was certain to get a medal. Then the scene where he knelt before her and kissed her hand was played with much commentary about how much like a Queen the lady behaved already and she was certain to be the greatest Queen America had ever had.

Sabri turned the television off. His promising new life had turned to dust. He knew enough about American law to know he'd be arrested and if not executed, he'd be deported. At the moment deportation seemed as bad as being executed.

At nineteen o'clock the police knocked on his door. When no one answered, they broke the door down and found him in the bathroom sitting in the tub. He had slit both wrists and bled to death. Fastidious to the end, he had held his hands under the running faucet and there was not a drop of blood in the tub. One of the policemen turned the faucet off and called his supervisor.

Fawzi had finally talked all he wanted to and they told him they had recorded everything he said.

"What will you do with me?" he asked, afraid of what the answer would be.

"You will be executed at one minute past midnight."

He absorbed that for a minute, "Will you untie me so I can pray to Allah?"

"No."

"What will you do with my body?"

"It will be cremated and your ashes dumped into the sewer."

So, all his dedication to Allah came to this. Allah had truly abandoned him. There would be no heavenly reward and he had found little happiness in this life. He would have been twenty years old next month.

Walter brought in the head of the Secret Service.

"His Majesty has ordered you to eliminate the leaders of the sect Kibur was a member of."

"Everywhere, or just in the Middle East?"

"Everywhere."

The Egyptian Foreign Minister called on the American ambassador at eight o'clock.

"The president will comply with your king's demand. All of those on the list will be delivered to American custody at nine o'clock tomorrow morning at the designated place."

"Thank you. Inform your president he made a very wise decision."

If Caitlin thought the publicity was bad before she was famous, she was in for a revelation now. The switchboard lit up like a Christmas tree on Monday with requests for her to appear on some program, make a speech somewhere or grant an interview. Even the BBC called. She appreciated Emma more than ever with her ability to say no without making the callers mad.

"We'll stick to the plan we made before all this happened. We must leave some time for you to have a life for yourself. You don't owe anything to the world and you must not neglect Henry."

Caitlin heartily agreed.

The planet went wild over Caitlin. The scene with her sitting in the chair and Parker on his knees before her making his speech was played worldwide over and over again until she thought everybody ought to be sick of it. But it kept on playing. Somebody in the United States wrote a song about her and it topped the charts immediately.

When Caitlin arrived in Kansas City on Friday afternoon, the whole city was decked out with banners and flags welcoming their future queen to her future home. She was treated like a goddess during the televised panel discussion on Sunday morning. She looked like one too. Emma and Kathy worked themselves ragged to present her in the best possible light. She was asked where she and Henry would honeymoon and she revealed they would spend their honeymoon in Mexico. The Queen Mother toasted her Sunday night when Henry and Caitlin dined with her in her suite.

"Caitlin, you are making us famous. And you're doing it in the best way imaginable."

"Thank you, Your Highness," Caitlin replied. She was glad Henry's mother was not jealous.

233

Henry was proud of her.

When she returned to Baltimore Sunday evening, they began preparing to enter the jaws of the lion in New York City the next Sunday. Walter and Emma had discussed the plan for hours and he was tickled to have an opportunity to put the Royal Family in good light on U.S. television.

The High Governor of Mexico was on the phone to her first thing Monday morning. He was very pleased to hear that the royal couple would honeymoon in his country. He told her the people of Mexico had been celebrating in the streets since they heard about it.

At the last minute NBC switched moderators for her "Meet the Press" appearance. They replaced the regular host with Gerry Anderson, a talk show host who specialized in making people nervous. Emma smelled a plot.

"They're trying to trim your sails, my dear," she told Caitlin the minute she got off the phone. "Your new popularity has upset somebody in the United States."

"I don't care what they think about me."

"That's okay. But we must not let them get the upper hand."

"Are you worried?"

"Not in the least, Milady. Your quick wit and screen presence will stand you in good stead. No matter what happens, the audience will be on your side. Our polls show U.S. citizens admire you in overwhelming numbers. Maybe that's what bothers the U.S. media people so much."

Henry traveled to New York with her on Saturday afternoon. Crowds lined their route from the airport to the Waldorf Astoria where they were staying. The royal party occupied the entire upper floor plus a sizeable chunk of the floor below. Security was very tight. They had dinner at the hotel and attended a play on Broadway. The U.S. president and his wife met them at the airport and accompanied them to dinner and the play. Crowds cheered them everywhere.

"You are the most popular politician in both of our countries," the president observed to Caitlin.

Henry and President Richardson got along well enough to agree to set up a series of low-level meetings aimed at reducing the animosity caused by the war.

Emma obtained a copy of a report their undercover operative at the network had prepared.

"They're going to hit you with the aftermath of the assassination attempt," she told Caitlin.

234

"Like what?"

"The execution of the assassin. There was no public trial."

"We don't have public trials."

"They know it. They want to make us look brutal."

"Not much for them to work on is it?"

"Not much. They're struggling to make you and Henry look bad in the U.S. My guess is you'll be asked some probing questions of a personal nature."

"I won't answer any intensely personal questions."

"Don't. Be yourself and you'll do fine. Your honesty will work against their shoddy tactics. This woman is a real bitch."

"Who else?"

"Samuel Crowell, editorialist for the New York Times. They hate us and he hates us. Melanie Griffin, reporter for the Boston Globe. She'll be fair-minded. I can't say the same for the one from the Inquirer. Arnold Speck is a virulent critic of the monarchy."

"Don't they have anything better to do than pick on us?"

"We're an easy target because we don't respond to their provocations." She laughed. "They're still mad about Alexander breaking away thirty-six years ago."

"To make it even more galling, you are from a recently integrated territory and you're blowing away their theories about those poor downtrodden Marylanders under the conqueror's brutal heel. The publicity about you has shown way too many cheerful looking Marylanders in the background. Expect cheap shots from Mrs. Anderson."

Caitlin sighed, "I was getting tired of all the public adoration anyway."

Emma laughed, "You are one in a million, Milady."

The audience cheered when Caitlin walked onstage. The panel members stood and applauded as she took her seat.

Anderson: "Welcome to 'Meet the Press', Lady York. We are so pleased that you found the time to share these few moments with us in the United States."

Caitlin: "Thank you for inviting me."

Anderson: "I find it remarkable that one year ago you were a citizen of our country and today you are a subject in a monarchial state and about to wed its ruler."

Caitlin: "I find it pretty remarkable myself."

Griffin: "Lady York, do you realize that after you're married you probably won't cook another meal, clean a house or iron a shirt?"

Caitlin: "I hadn't thought about it. I like to cook but I won't miss ironing. I hate to iron."

Anderson: "We saw how calmly you reacted when you were attacked two weeks ago. I'd like to know how it affected you after you had time to reflect on the danger you were in."

Caitlin: "I don't think I'm any different. I'm not a worrier."

Speck: "So you haven't changed your routine or felt any apprehension when going about your daily affairs?"

Caitlin: "No. I haven't."

Griffin: "You must be a very psychologically secure person."

Caitlin: "If I worried about everything, I couldn't be a good wife to Henry."

Griffin laughed, "Well put, Lady York."

Crowell: "What changes have been made in your protection?"

Caitlin: "None that I'm aware of. I was protected then and I feel safe today."

Anderson: "Is the young man who so gallantly risked his life with you today?"

Caitlin: "Yes, he is."

The camera panned to show Agent Parker standing at attention, handsome, perfectly groomed, in his tailored suit.

Anderson: "Your guards are exceedingly handsome, Lady York."

Caitlin: "They're just typical American men."

Anderson: "I don't believe you, Lady York. You are just showing off."

Speck: "It was a very moving scene when you called for him and he knelt before you."

Caitlin: "Yes, it was. I have been surprised at the play it has received worldwide."

Griffin: "It was a very touching scene. I think people have reacted to it so favorably because it was genuine."

Anderson: "Do you know what happened to Kibir?"

Caitlin: "He's been executed."

Speck: "We haven't heard anything about a trial."

Caitlin: "He didn't have a trial. Everybody knew what he did."

Anderson: "You Americans are so brutal. I bet he wasn't even interrogated."

Caitlin: "Yes, he was. They had to find out who helped him."

Crowell: "Was he tortured to make him talk?"

Caitlin: "They gave him medication."

Griffin: "Truth serum?"

Caitlin: "Something like that."

236

Griffin: "You said you and His Majesty will honeymoon in Mexico?'

Caitlin: "Yes, we will."

Anderson: "Why did you choose the Mexican palace?"

Caitlin: "I've been told it's the nicest."

Anderson: "It is very lavish. We were allowed to film it last week. We were even allowed to photograph the king's suite. It is a most lavish dwelling."

Caitlin: "I've never seen it."

Anderson: "We could give you a private showing of the recording after the show."

Caitlin: "No. I'd rather see it myself when we go there."

Anderson: "We're not allowed to broadcast them until after the wedding and you are in Mexico.

Speck: "Lady York, there have been persistent rumors somebody is assassinating the leaders of Kibur's sect. Can you address that?"

Caitlin: "They have a lot of enemies in the Arab world."

Speck: "Arab assassins don't possess the skill of the people who are doing this."

Caitlin: "You don't know that."

Speck: "Lady York, the most professional secret service on the planet answers to your fiancé."

Caitlin: "Are you suggesting it's a bad thing to have an effective secret service?"

Speck: "No, I'm not, Lady York. I'm only pointing out a coincidence."

Caitlin: "If we are, it's for a good reason."

Anderson: "That's what your government always says on matters such as this. Lady York, do you condone the execution of people without a public trial?"

Caitlin: "I condone the execution of violent criminals."

Crowell: "But your hasty process could cost the lives of innocent citizens."

Caitlin: "American judicial processes have safeguards to deal with doubtful situations."

Speck: "But you are so brutal."

Caitlin: "Until Kibur was executed last week, there have been no executions in Maryland since last September." Then Caitlin added a kicker, "Nobody is imprisoned in America either." She looked at Anderson. "Your prisons are full."

Crowell: "But everybody in America must be living in fear."

Caitlin laughed: "Marylanders don't have to lock their homes or cars anymore. They can leave the keys in their cars on busy streets. They don't worry about being robbed at a money machine or having their purse snatched. If a woman accidentally leaves her rings in a public lavatory, she can most likely find them where she left them or have them saved for her to claim."

The audience applauded when she finished.

Caitlin: "Besides, every American man and a lot of American women are armed everywhere they go. They are required to be armed because they are in the military service."

Anderson: "What about those poor people in the labor class?"

Caitlin: "They would equate to your chronically unemployed and permanent welfare population. Ours are clean and well fed, given entertainments they can appreciate and they are productive members of society." Then Caitlin added, "They are law abiding citizens."

The audience displayed their approval again.

Crowell: "I understand that very few people emigrate from America?"

Caitlin: "My interpretation of that is few want to leave." She struck again, "But lots of U.S. citizens are trying to immigrate to America."

Speck, ignoring her cut: "We heard that it's difficult to emigrate and your government questions people extensively about their reasons for wanting to leave."

Caitlin: "Maybe the government wants to know why a person wants to leave in case there's something they can do to make things better."

Anderson: "Lady York, you're stretching here," she said with heavy sarcasm.

Caitlin looked to see if Carl was offstage and saw him sitting beside Emma. "Carl, you know everything. How many people have emigrated from America this year?"

"About three hundred."

"Do you know why they emigrated?"

"Most of them were American women who had married foreigners."

Then Caitlin bit back, "Why are you asking me all these political questions? You agreed to confine discussions to my courtship and wedding."

Anderson became angry and discomfited, "Very well, Lady York, do you actually love the king or are you simply another extremely attractive social climber?"

The audience booed.

238

"That is a stupid question!" Caitlin answered angrily. Then she regretted her sharp reply. "Of course I love the king. I wouldn't be on this show if I didn't love Henry."

The audience applauded.

Anderson: "Lady York, have you been intimate with His Majesty?"

The audience booed.

Griffin: "Gerry, that is inappropriate!"

Caitlin heard Emma say "Bitch!" loud enough for the microphones to pick it up.

Caitlin smiled sweetly at the audience, the camera and then at the moderator, "That is none of your business!" She stood up. "Good day Miss Anderson." Then she walked proudly offstage, looking like a queen with every step.

The studio audience cheered and began to chant, "Kate-Lin, Kate-Lin."

"I'm not sure we won that skirmish," Emma observed after they left the building

"I'm sorry. I lost it there for a minute," Caitlin replied.

"You were far more dignified than they were."

"I thought Mrs. Griffin handled herself well and tried to stick to the subject."

"Yes, she did."

"I think I'll write her a thank you note."

"That would be appropriate, Milady."

Henry hugged her and said he was very proud of her.

Even the New York Times was ashamed. The front page headline on Monday read "SHAME" and chastised NBC and Gerry Anderson for an infuriating lack of taste. NBC ran a hasty and heavily edited version of the taped session. It made the audience appear to be applauding for Anderson when they had actually applauded for Caitlin. Nobody from the American contingent hung around to assist or approve the edited version. The lead editorial in the Times remarked that whatever progress made in the effort to reduce tensions between the two countries had been nullified by a tasteless performance by the NBC crew. Melanie called Caitlin on Monday to apologize and told her Gerry Anderson had been fired along with her boss and producer. Crowell and Speck called later in the day to apologize.

"Maybe we won after all," Emma observed.

Walter called Caitlin and complimented her on her discipline and added, "You defended our policies like a seasoned professional."

Caitlin and her entourage flew to Kansas City on Thursday. She was to be the honored guest at the Kansas City Woman's Club the following evening. She was to do the same on Tuesday in Houston. She and Henry had very little private time together.

"It's like my job is keeping me away from you," she complained. "And I'm not even Queen yet."

On Wednesday she was in Great Falls, Montana and in Atlanta, Georgia on Thursday. When they got back to Baltimore on Thursday evening, she, Emma and Kathy were worn out.

Caitlin's friends had planned a private bridal shower for her on Saturday afternoon. At least she'd be able to relax at this event. No reporters, no cameras and no strangers wanting to meet their Queen-to-be. She asked her friends to have a gag gift exchange rather than traditional gifts for her. It seemed like bad manners for her to accept presents considering her status. Kathy and Emma were invited guests too.

No public appearances were scheduled for her the following week as they had to prepare for the wedding. They left for Kansas City on Wednesday, taking an extra plane for luggage. The palace sent Henry's plane for her parents, Ashley and Brent.

Caitlin was getting excited. In three days she would be Mrs. Henry Clark and on the next day, she would become Queen Caitlin. The day after that, they would be all alone in their big fancy palace in Mexico.

The Queen Mother hosted a bridal party for Caitlin on Thursday night. All the wives of high government officials and the royal governors attended.

Rehearsals began on Friday. Debbie was to be maid of honor. Ashley and Eleanor and three college friends were to be her bridesmaids. Emma sent Caitlin's plane to Baltimore to pick them up in time to attend the bridal party. Caitlin asked them to stay in her suite so they would have more time to visit. Her things would be moved into the king's suite on Saturday.

From here on out everything would be a very big deal. The royal governors and their families were invited guests to all events, including the rehearsal dinner on Friday, as was the King and Queen of England and the President of Israel and his wife.

240

The U.S. President and First Lady would attend the wedding, as would the Chiefs of State of every country in the world. Both husbands and wives attended the rehearsal dinner on Friday.

A full range of entertainments were available for all invited guests, ranging from golf outings, cultural tours, musical concerts and skeet shooting. There was even a carnival with midway rides for the youngsters. All restaurants in the city were on the royal tab to provide food and drink for the guests. All one had to do was flash their invitation. The Pope and his entourage arrived Friday morning and were greeted by a crowd as he exited the plane at the airport. His Holiness said grace at every formal meal during the whole affair. The King and Queen of England, the President and First Lady of Israel and the U.S. President and First Lady were provided suites in the palace.

Over his mother's strenuous objections, Henry invited Slim and assigned him his own personal suite in the palace. Slim had never flown in an airplane and they had to give him a sedative to keep him in his seat. When he was brought to the palace he told Henry that he had a "real nice place."

As the Queen Mother's revenge for Henry inviting Slim, Wilma was assigned to look after him while he was visiting the king.

Chapter Twenty

The Royal Wedding-Schedule of Events

Thursday April 19, 2085

09:00-17:00: Arrival of guests

18:30-19:30: Open reception on the palace grounds

19:30-21:30: Bridal Party Dinner- Invited guests

Friday, April 20, 2085

08:30-09:30: Bride and Groom's Breakfast - Royal Governors and their wives

09:30 -11:00: Free time

11:00-13:00: Governor's Wives Reception and Luncheon for the Bride

13:00 -17:30: Rehearsal - Bridal Party

18:30-19:30: Reception for the Bride and Groom- Palace Grounds

19:30-21:30: Rehearsal Dinner- Main Dining Room in the Palace- Bridal Party

22:00-02:00: Spring Ball – Palace Grounds

Saturday, April 21, 2085

08:30-09:30: Stag Breakfast for the Groom at the Ritz Carleton - Male guests

10:30-11:30: Bridal Brunch at the Willow Green Botanical Gardens – Female guests

11:30 -13:30: Stag Picnic at the Kansas City Golf and Country Club – Male guests

15:00 -17:00: Wedding of Lady Caitlin Rose York to Sir Henry George Clark at the National Cathedral; His Holiness, Pope Paul VII officiating

17:00 -19:00: Reception in the Cathedral Assembly Hall

19:30 -21:30: Dinner for guests at the Ritz Carleton

22:00 – 02:00: Royal Wedding Ball at the Ritz Carleton

Sunday, April 22, 2085

08:30 -10:30: Empire Breakfast at the Main Government Dining Room
Hosted by Lord Walter Jones- Invited guests

11:00 -13:00: Ladies Brunch in the Main Dining Room of the Palace
Hosted by Lady Emma Hamilton

15:00 -17:00: Coronation of Lady Caitlin Rose York Clark as Queen of America, Mexico, Canada, New Zealand and Empress of Panama, Venezuela, South Africa, Namibia, Saudi Arabia and Algeria
The National Cathedral
His Holiness, Pope Paul VII officiating
Invited guests

17:00 -18:00: Swearing of Allegiance Ceremony
Lord James Whitmore, Chief Justice of the Realm
and Empire presiding

19:00 – 23:00: Coronation Banquet in the Main Palace Dining Room
Hosted by the Queen Mother, Princess Elizabeth and Princess Rachel

08:30 -10:00: King and Queen's Breakfast
Hosted by Her Royal Highness, Queen Caitlin and His Royal Majesty,
King Henry
Main Palace Dining Room.

13:00: The King and Queen depart for Mexico

There was little time for Caitlin and Henry to be alone and it began to wear on her. After traveling all over the country to appearances the week before and now with people around them all the time, she was a little testy when he came into her suite after the bridal party on Thursday. She'd let her hair down, flung off her gown, hose and shoes and was sitting on the side of the bed in her slip when Kathy announced the king wished to visit her. She looked at the time. It was twenty-three o'clock.

"Send him in," she replied. She didn't bother to put anything else on.

He came in smiling, lifted her up off the bed and kissed her. "You were gorgeous tonight." He stepped back and looked at her, "You're more gorgeous now."

"I don't feel very gorgeous," she grumbled.

"What's wrong?"

She regretted her despondent reply and put a smile on her face, "Nothing you can't fix."

He grinned. "I'll fix you Saturday night."

"That's good. I'm too tired to be fixed tonight anyway."

"Then I'd better go and let you get some rest."

"I'm sorry, Henry. I love you but the pace of these last few weeks has gotten me down."

"Me too. It'll be over in three more days and we can be normal again," he grinned, "Except you'll be with me every night."

"I've been dreaming about it since last July. Sometimes I wonder if it will ever happen."

"It will. And you will share my bed Saturday night. Just think, two more nights alone and then we'll become one."

She put her arms around him, "I can't wait," she whispered.

He kissed her and took his leave. "Two more long days," she reminded herself and she would be his!

At formal dinners, Debbie and Eleanor were always seated to Caitlin's right. After breakfast on Friday as the guests were starting to leave, the High Governor of New Zealand, Lord Charles Morris and his wife Lady Gwendolyn, made their way to Henry and Caitlin followed by a young Army captain.

After greeting Henry, Lord Charles addressed Caitlin, "Lady York, my son, Garrett would very much like to be introduced to your friend, Lady Eleanor."

"I would be most pleased to do so, Your Grace." She took Eleanor's hand, "Captain Morris, I'd like for you to meet one of my best friends, Lady Eleanor Lewis."

The captain bowed, took Eleanor's hand, kissed it and said, "Pleased to meet you, Milady." Then he stood and asked, "Would you do me the honor of accompanying me on a walk through the palace gardens?"

As they were leaving, Eleanor looked over her shoulder at Caitlin and Debbie and grinned.

When Eleanor got back to Caitlin's suite, she commented, "He is very nice." Then she asked if it would be possible for him to be seated to her right at the rehearsal dinner. She added, "He's going to be my date to the Ball tonight."

Debbie was jealous. "He's so cute! You and Caitlin just reel them in, leaving poor me all alone out in the cold."

"Don't worry, Debbie," Caitlin assured her. "I've noticed a couple of great looking hunks checking you out."

"I'll be an old maid," she pouted.

Then all three of them started giggling.

Slim came to the rehearsal dinner in jeans, black spit-shined cowboy boots and a plaid shirt with pearl buttons. Everybody else wore tuxedos and fancy ball gowns. To suggest that Slim stood out in the crowd would be a stupendous understatement. He had a voice that carried and then there were his mannerisms. He was not bashful or retiring among the dignitaries, speaking as an equal to governors, generals, dukes, earls and even to Henry.

Slim made it a point to greet Caitlin first. When he came up to her, he dropped on one knee, took her hand in his and kissed it. Then he stood and winked at her, saying loud enough for those around them to hear, "I knew you'd git'im," and laughed his cowboy laugh. Then he greeted Henry with a slap on the back saying, "You sure done good when you picked her, Henry." The Queen Mother was close enough to hear it and rolled her eyes "listening to the old coot," as she told it later.

After the rehearsal dinner, a dapper young man who introduced himself as Matthew Jones struck up a conversation with Debbie. He was the grandson of Lord Walter Jones. Now she too had a date for the ball.

As the evening progressed, there was more visiting and renewing acquaintances than dancing. It was the first time Caitlin had met all the royal governors and their wives, so she and Henry spent time with them instead of on the dance floor. As the evening wore on, the dance floor gradually filled as the crowd developed a party mood.

Slim stayed remarkably sober. Henry had warned him about his behavior and he tried his best to mingle. Princess Elizabeth avoided him but Lord Blake spent some time with Slim and appeared to enjoy their conversation.

Slim was vocal to everybody about his part in helping Henry decide to marry Caitlin. "I told him he'd better marry the purty thang before some dude run off with her," he was overheard telling a number of people.

Slim and Princess Rachel hit it off at once. The band struck up a number while they were talking and before she knew it he had her on the dance floor. It was a sight; her in an elaborate ball gown and he in jeans and cowboy boots with his bowlegs. He could dance and was a natural at learning new steps.

After dancing with Princess Rachel, Slim sauntered over to the bandstand where he asked them to play a two-step. Then he marched straight to Caitlin and asked her to dance as soon as the music started. A dozen or so couples came out on the floor to dance with them but seeing the old man dancing with their Queen-to-be was so intriguing they stopped dancing to watch them. Slim was smooth and graceful as he led Caitlin over the floor with a style that belied his age. By the time the dance was over, everybody in the room was watching them and the crowd applauded when the tune was over.

When Slim delivered her back to Henry, he remarked, "She shore can dance."

Henry escorted Caitlin to her suite after the dance was over. "This is our last night apart," he whispered when he kissed her outside her door.

She held onto him. "I love you, Henry."

"Even with all the formality and politics?"

"I'll endure anything to be your wife."

"I can't tell you how good it makes me feel to know you love me so much."

"I want you, Henry."

"I want you too, Caitlin."

"I can't wait until tomorrow night. Sometimes it seems like it will never get here."

She opened the door to her suite and saw Kathy turning the covers back on her bed. Kathy had already laid out her clothes for the Bridal Breakfast. Debbie and Eleanor had not returned.

"I won't see you again until I march down the aisle," she said wistfully.

"I'll have the most beautiful bride in the world," he whispered in her ear.

"And I'll have the handsomest groom." Then she added, "But best of all, afterwards I'll have a wonderful husband and we'll be together at last."

"See you tomorrow."

He kissed her and held her close, then turned to go. Before she closed her door, she reminded him that she loved him.

Saturday morning was a blur for both of them. When Carl gave Henry his morning briefing it was the first time his monarch had seemed un-attentive. Luckily the country and empire were calmer than usual. Secret Service depredations against the Islamic sect were beginning to bear fruit and the organization was gradually disappearing.

In spite of Caitlin's apprehension, the hour of their marriage arrived and by fourteen o'clock the cathedral was already full. Camera crews from all over the world were setting up for the marriage of the century. Kathy, Emma and three extras were busy getting Caitlin ready to walk down the aisle. She was flushed with excitement realizing the moment she'd been longing for these last months had finally arrived. Rebecca was struggling to get Henry ready. She could tell he too was excited and was not as easy to please as he usually was.

Carl was Henry's best man. Lord James Blake, Elizabeth's husband, Henry's brother William, Brent Churchill, Lord Zachary Hastings, Pamela's husband and two of Henry's college friends were groomsmen.

Debbie was Caitlin's maid of honor. Her bridesmaids were Ashley, Eleanor, Princess Elizabeth, Princess Rachel, Kathy and one of her cousins from Baltimore. Her father would walk her down the aisle.

People lined the route to catch a glimpse of them as their respective entourages made their way to the cathedral. The Pope was in the first cavalcade, Henry and his group in the second and Caitlin was last. By the time she passed by in an open vehicle, the crowd was in a frenzy.

Stadium sized screens had been erected at the civic center and several other places where groups could gather to watch the wedding. Local television stations had been providing constant coverage since early morning. Foreign television stations focused on the dignitaries from their respective countries until the Pope, the bride and groom entered the cathedral. A hush fell as the groomsmen began to seat the invited guests. It was a who's who of worldwide proportions. Then Lady Francis York was seated and after she was seated, the Queen Mother was escorted down the aisle. The sanctuary glittered with jewels of untold value. Finally the groomsmen assumed their positions in front. All was ready when Henry and Carl took their positions.

The bridesmaids began their procession down the aisle and when the bridal march began, the guests stood and Caitlin started her long walk down the aisle on the arm of her father. Her face was flush with excitement as she made her way slowly while smiling at everyone. She was followed by the ring bearer who was the seven-year-old son of one of Henry's cousins. Henry waited expectantly for her.

They remembered it in a blur, the routine repetition of, "I will's" and "I do's" and hearing His Holiness telling Henry he could kiss his bride. There was the brief peck on her lips, their march together up the aisle and into the entry foyer with all the cameras. They posed for pictures prior to their mandatory appearance at the reception and the Royal Wedding Ball, which they left promptly at twenty-two thirty.

Finally they were alone in their bedroom. His pajamas were neatly folded at the foot of their bed alongside her chemise. He took her into his arms and kissed her.

"Welcome to our home, Mrs. Clark," he whispered.

She clung to him, "I love you, Henry."

He reached down and flung his pajamas and her gown on the floor, "We won't need these tonight."

She giggled and they began pulling their clothes off, each helping the other until they fell on the bed in each other's arms, laughing and kissing.

Rebecca looked in on them at eight thirty. Seeing them asleep in each other's arms, she quietly closed the door. When she checked an hour later, both were awake.

"Your Majesty, would you and Her Highness like breakfast?"

"Yes, Rebecca."

"Should I serve it in here?"

"Yes."

She saw they were very happy. Henry was the happiest she had ever seen him.

When Rebecca exited the suite, Kathy and Emma were waiting outside the door, "How are they?" Kathy asked.

"They look very happy."

"We'll help you with their breakfast. We're dying to see them."

The king's suite had two dressing areas adjacent to their bedroom, one for him and one for his Queen. Kathy had engaged additional staff to help her with Caitlin; Lady Tia Chin as her wardrobe manager and dressmaker, Sir Lance Rogers as her hairdresser and Lady Chrysie Le Penn as her cosmetologist.

The Queen's dressing area was three times the size of the King's and Rebecca was Henry's only personal staff member. Now that Henry and Caitlin were married, Kathy moved her office into Caitlin's dressing area.

Henry and Caitlin had put on their robes by the time Rebecca, Emma and Kathy served them breakfast. During the priest's blessing of their food, they held hands. They didn't seem to notice his prayer was long, thanking God for the king's happiness and for the happiness of their Queen-to-be. After serving them, Kathy, Emma and Rebecca left them alone. They couldn't help but peek in on them and saw them kissing between bites of food. When Rebecca came back to remove the dishes, she reminded them that at eleven-thirty they needed to start dressing for the coronation.

Caitlin wore Henry's great grandmother's diamond necklace set for her coronation. It was a much more solemn affair than their wedding. She was crowned with the same crown Queen Celeste and Henry's mother had worn. This was a media event at least equal to the wedding and the crowds were just as big. It was very moving when the Chief Justice led the swearing of allegiance to the new Queen.

On the drive back to the palace, the crowd took up the chant, "Kate Lin, Kate Lin," as they drove by in the open car, wearing their crowns. The king and queen made a ceremonial appearance at the coronation banquet then excused themselves at twenty-one o'clock. They would leave tomorrow for Mexico City.

His Majesty and Her Highness presided over the coronation breakfast the next morning where they thanked their guests for sharing their joyous event. Henry made it a special point to speak to Slim who assured Henry that he had, "done good by marrying that purty thing."

After wishing their guests Godspeed on their return journeys, Henry and Caitlin retired to their suite to get ready to begin their honeymoon. Emma asked Caitlin for leave to spend a month in Delaware with her husband.

"You're not the only one who needs to spend some private time with her man," Emma remarked when she made the request.

Chapter Twenty One

If they thought Kansas City was raucous, Mexican crowds made them seem placid in comparison. The Mexican people went beyond anything Henry and Caitlin had imagined in demonstrating their adoration for their king and his beautiful queen.

Henry and Caitlin rode in the High Governor's open car, dressed in travel attire. It didn't matter to the Mexicans as they stood twenty deep along the route from the airport to the palace. When they arrived at the palace, Henry led Caitlin up to a second floor balcony facing the street where they waved at the crowd and made a few remarks. Caitlin made hers in Spanish. This was the first time the Mexicans knew Caitlin could speak their language and they were overjoyed.

Then Henry gave her a tour of the palace while Rebecca and Kathy moved their things into the king and queen's suite.

"I never dreamed it would be so beautiful," she remarked when they got back to their suite.

"I'll show you the grounds tomorrow."

Caitlin was standing like she had that night at Myrtle Beach when she was in her wet sundress, "We could tour them today," she suggested with a demure smile.

He pulled her to him, "I had something else in mind, my dear."

"And what was that, my darling?"

He kissed her in a way that answered her question.

When Henry visited Mexico in the past, he had moved about the city publicly and went somewhere every day. This time he and Caitlin remained secluded in the palace for four whole days.

Making matters worse, the priest who said grace at mealtimes was a garrulous man. Every day the priest told of seeing the joy and sweet affection that the royal pair displayed openly before him. He also told of that first evening when the Queen refused to sit at the Queen's place at the far end of the table and ordered that her place be moved to the King's right so that they could hold hands while the priest said grace. He spoke of their smiles: saying that he had never seen their king so happy and that the Royal couple's happiness was infectious to everybody around them.

Then there were the house servants, who giggled while whispering of seeing their scantily clad king and queen chasing each other up and down the corridors of the palace, laughing when one caught the other, and of the kisses and caresses. And those tantalizing tidbits, like each morning finding pillows and cushions in odd places about the palace. Each whispered tale spread like wildfire, embellished with every retelling.

On Friday, the High Governor called upon the Royal couple. He timed his visit so that he would arrive as Carl finished His Majesty's daily briefing. He told the king that he had come with the greatest love and admiration for his Queen and King. But this time he had a most urgent request and asked to speak to them together. Lance and Chrysie had to be summoned in haste to prepare the queen to meet the governor. When Caitlin walked into the room attired in a flowing spring dress, the governor was moved.

"Your Highness," he said as he bowed, "You are even more beautiful as my Queen."

"Thank you, Your Grace," she replied as she took her seat beside the king and took his hand in hers.

The Governor got right to the point, "My beloved King and Queen, I have come on a mission of utmost gravity. If it had not been of such importance I would not have interrupted your honeymoon."

"What is this matter of such great importance?" Henry wanted to know.

"Your Majesty and Your Highness, my people are to the point of open rebellion if they do not see their beautiful Queen very soon. I respect your wish for privacy in your joy but my people cry out for you."

"What would you have us do?" Henry asked, slightly annoyed.

"Could you please make a public appearance this weekend for your loyal subjects who so love both of you?"

They looked at each other. Caitlin said, "Its okay with me, Henry."

"What do you suggest, Jorge?" Henry asked.

"Would you attend the bullfight at the arena tomorrow evening?"

"I've never seen a bullfight," Caitlin said.

"Is it okay?" Henry asked.

Caitlin replied, "Yes."

"We will go," Henry said to Jorge.

"Thank you, Your Highness and Your Majesty. If you don't object, we will have a parade and approach the arena by a circuitous route. That will afford more people a chance to see their Queen."

"Whatever you chose to do is fine," Henry replied.

"You and the Queen are very gracious, Your Majesty."

"Brief Carl on the arrangements."

"I will. And thank you so much. The Mexican people are overjoyed because you chose to honeymoon with us," he smiled at Caitlin, "They know that you suggested it and love you all the more for choosing to be with them in this joyous time."

"Thank you, Your Grace," Caitlin said with a smile.

The governor rose, bowed and took his leave.

The bullfight was scheduled to start at twenty-one o'clock. They left the palace at eighteen o'clock. The route took in almost all of the main thoroughfares in Mexico City. They rode in the open car with Lord and Lady Cardenas. The crowds were joyous.

Even Henry was struck by Caitlin's beauty as he observed her during the ride through the streets filled with adoring subjects. She was radiant. He couldn't decide if she was more beautiful because of their love or if the ministrations of Kathy's assistants were taking effect. He asked her why she seemed more beautiful than ever.

"Because I married the man I love, silly," she replied with a sweet smile. Still he had to admit that her dress was perfect for the occasion and her hair and makeup accented her natural attractiveness. He decided to thank Walter when they returned for assigning Kathy the responsibility for Caitlin's care. It had been an inspired choice.

Lord Cardenas's personal Guards Battalion held the crowd back to provide a passage for the Royal couple to enter the arena while a Mexican soldier stood at attention every ten feet all the way to the governor's box. Banners were everywhere welcoming the King and Queen and television camera's recorded their exit from the car and followed them all the way to their seats. Big screens on all four sides of the arena gave everybody a close up view as Henry and Caitlin took their seats.

"Nobody ever turned out like this for me," Henry commented, making sure that no microphone was close enough to pick it up.

"But you discouraged celebrations like this, didn't you?" Caitlin suggested.

"Yeah. I guess you're right."

"Emma told me that you are very popular."

"I try. Could this be a result of my suppression of celebrations and now everybody's going overboard?"

"I think that our marriage is what got everybody excited. It was the first royal wedding on American soil. It was a significant event," Caitlin suggested.

He looked at her. Was this untutored beauty that he fell in love with becoming politically astute? "I guess you're right. Walter wanted

253

to use it to increase the monarchy's popularity. He's getting what he wanted."

"Yes, he is, in spades."

The Mexican National Choir had assembled on the field and at twenty o'clock began singing the National Anthem. It was followed by, "God Save the King" and then "God Save the Queen". When the singing stopped, the Archbishop of Mexico took the microphone to pray. After he finished, a hush fell over the crowd and the announcer requested that the King and Queen advance to the center of the field to receive a special gift. Eight sharply dressed Royal Mexican Commandos escorted them to where the Mayor of Mexico City stood beside a high school girl in a white dress holding an elaborate case. The mayor bowed and the girl curtseyed.

"Your Highness," the mayor intoned in his most official speaking voice, "The people of Mexico present this to you as a token of our love and respect."

The girl advanced to Caitlin and opened the lid of the box. It contained a beautiful and very elaborate Aztec style gold necklace. Caitlin's hand went to her mouth as she beheld the beautiful work of art. She picked it up and held it so the crowd could see it. The cameras caught its glitter on the screens in the arena and on every television screen viewing the spectacle. Then she handed it to Henry.

"Henry, please put this on me." The crowd loved the way she addressed their king by his given name.

She turned and Henry removed the necklace she was wearing, put it into his pocket and then put her new necklace around her neck. When he did, he realized that Kathy must have known about the ceremony and gift because the new necklace complimented her attire. After he fastened it about her neck, Caitlin stood for the camera, turned and bowed to the four points of the compass.

"Thank you so much," she said to the adoring crowd. "I will treasure this lovely token of your affection and this moment for the rest of my life."

The crowd gave a thunderous cheer and as Caitlin and Henry turned to be escorted back to the governor's box, the now familiar chant began, "Kate-Lin, Kate-Lin".

"You are a star," Henry observed as they moved up the steps to their places.

She looked back and smiled. "I'm your star."

They returned to the palace after two-thirty, retracing the earlier route, smiling and waving at thousands on the way back.

"Mexicans know how to party, don't they?" Caitlin observed.

"Yes, they do," he agreed.

When they got to their suite, their sleeping attire was laid out for them. Henry swept it onto the floor, pulled her onto the bed and ordered, "Be my star."

On Sunday they attended Mass at Our Lady of Guadalupe church and afterwards toured the shrine. The Mexican crowds were present as before but refrained from chanting on the Sabbath. It was obvious that the Mexican population adored Caitlin. She spoke to several elementary school children while they were at the shrine and signed the little notes that they handed her with trembling hands. Caitlin had a way with children and she always made eye contact with their parents.

Of course, everything she said and everything she did in public was broadcast all over the world. By now she was the most viewed personality on international television. It seemed as if the world could not get enough of her. Her popularity eclipsed that of the world's models and movie stars and she set an example of behavior that was both moral and responsible. Fashion magazines ached to find a way to put her on their covers. She looked genuinely happy every time she appeared in public. And she was very beautiful.

The Cardenas had the newly weds to lunch at the governor's palace and then on a sightseeing flight over the Mayan ruins in Yucatan. They had dinner Mayor of Mexico City that evening.

On their way back to the palace Caitlin remarked, "Being Queen isn't so bad after all."

"I told you that you were a natural," Henry reminded her.

She snuggled closer to him, "Being your wife is the most fun."

He grinned but didn't say anything.

"You sexy hunk, will I get to wear a gown tonight?"

"Probably not."

She squeezed his hand, "I hope Walter never finds out how much money he wasted on honeymoon gowns for me."

"Me too," he laughed.

The next week consisted of visits to principle cities in Mexico starting with Chihuahua, Monterey and Guadalajara and ending up in Merida.

They were feted at every turn. By the time they returned to the palace Friday morning, they were ready for some down time. They slept in Saturday morning and had a late breakfast. On Sunday after mass in a church close to the palace, they packed to leave for Panama City. They stood by the window while Kathy and Rebecca supervised removal of their luggage.

"It was even more wonderful than I imagined it would be," she observed. Then she added, "And I knew it would be wonderful with you."

He put his arm around her waist, "I'm glad."

"I love you, Henry."

He took her into his arms, "I love you too, Caitlin."

"I enjoy the queenly attention more than I thought I would. But I could chuck the queen stuff. I could not bear separation from you."

"That's what I liked about you from the start. You understand what is important."

Crowds lined their route to the airport bidding them farewell.

The same tumultuous welcome greeted them in Panama City. Crowds lined the streets along the route from the airport to the palace. Governor and Lady Kincaid met them at the airport where they were greeted by a chorus of high school students singing a song of adoration that they had composed in honor of their new Queen. Caitlin was touched and applauded when it was over. She took time to speak to each member of the chorus and their parents. The boys solemnly bowed as she approached and the girls curtsied with shy smiles.

The governor's guard held the throng back at the palace door. Henry and Caitlin went up to the balcony where they spent a few minutes conversing with people in the crowd. On occasions like this, Henry stood aloof and dignified. He was not unfriendly and he smiled but there was no electricity. It was different with Caitlin. She interacted with her admirers in a most appealing way and the crowds loved it. They saw how relaxed and easy she was with their sovereign, how she took his hand, put her arm around him and called him "Henry" in front of everybody. They also noticed how she laughed and how genuine her smile was when she made eye contact. First she won the hearts of all Mexico. Now, in these few minutes, Panama was eating out of her hand.

The Panamanians generously allowed the Royal couple three days of seclusion in the palace to honeymoon before the governor called with an urgent request. The Panamanian servants were not shy about discussing their observations of the two lovers and the whole country was inflamed in their desire to see more of their king and queen.

The governor organized a parade that began and ended at the palace. The route would take them to a park beside the canal where a picnic and entertainment was to be held which would allow the Royal couple to mingle with their people. Henry enjoyed meeting his subjects like this but it taxed his and now, Caitlin's security. They knew all too well that there were governments and groups that would like nothing better than to read headlines announcing the king's demise. But the Governor and Henry were determined to ignore the risk.

At nine on Saturday morning the parade began with the Royal Panamanian Commando's stepping out smartly, followed by another specially selected high school band, the Mayor of the city and his wife, the Governor and his wife and finally Caitlin and Henry in open cars followed by a battalion of Royal Panamanian Infantry. Panamanians lined the streets along the route waving flags and holding signs expressing their joy at seeing their King and Queen pass by.

At the picnic, Henry and Caitlin conversed with commoners and aristocrats alike. Caitlin made it a point to speak to their children and hold babies in her arms for proud parents. It was late when they returned to the palace where they had a light supper after which they went to bed. After mass on Sunday they left on a road tour of the cities in Panama and returned on Friday. The Governor and his wife hosted a formal dinner and a ball on Saturday night. On Sunday afternoon they left for Venezuela, waving to the throngs of well-wishers as they drove to the airport. They landed in Caracas in mid-afternoon.

It was the same in Venezuela. The Governor and Lady Barrus met them at the airport, followed by the cavalcade where they waved to the crowds from an open car and the informal give and take from the balcony. Caitlin was becoming a pro at mesmerizing the crowds of admirers. At a gathering open to the public on Saturday, a pair of teenagers appeared with a gift from the people of Venezuela. It was an amber necklace and earring set. Kathy had again been prepared and when Henry put the necklace around Caitlin's neck, it matched her outfit perfectly. Lance appeared to help her with the earrings.

On Monday of the second week, Walter came from Kansas City to brief the king on some pressing issues. Henry asked Caitlin to sit in. After greeting them Walter got right to the point.

"Your Majesty, our work of eradicating Islamic fanatics is causing unfavorable moves by several countries."

257

"Like what?"

"France, Germany, Russia, Greece and Turkey are discussing some kind of alliance to consider a concerted action against us. They have also engaged the U.N."

"Why? They suffer at the hands of the militants more than we do."

"France, Germany and Turkey have large numbers of Islamic sympathizers within their borders."

"What about Russia? They don't coddle the militant extremists."

"The Russians will do anything to hinder us. They are our main competitor on the world stage."

"Like the U.S.?"

"They are more determined."

"Aren't we using Russian nationals on this project?"

Walter laughed, "There are three teams of Russian assassins working for us."

"What about Italy?"

"Italy is our friend."

"What do you think will happen?"

"U.N. censure for eliminating the fanatics' leadership."

"So what. And after that?"

"France, Germany and Russia are discussing formation of a military alliance against us."

"We're not planning to attack any of them."

"The alliance would come to the defense of any country that we might target."

"Like Argentina?"

"Yes."

"That won't hinder us. We will be finished before they know what's happening."

"They will retaliate by attacking a more vulnerable point of the Empire."

"Algeria is closest to them."

"That's what I think too."

"We'll defend the Empire."

"They want us to do that."

"Why?"

"They wish to draw us into a big war."

"They can't win. Their weapons are obsolete."

"The Russians are deploying their portable advanced beam weapon."

"So soon? They only recently tested the prototype."

"It's a political decision."

"Have we developed defensive measures?"

"We have built a similar weapon in our laboratories that uses the same technology. We have made some progress in development of defensive measures but it does alter the combat landscape negatively for us."

"Have we obtained one to study?"

"No. But we have drawings and specifications."

"That's better. How does it compare to our weapons?"

"It uses a tremendous amount of power. They have two versions but they haven't miniaturized it to where it can be carried by a man."

"How much power?"

"One firing consumes more electricity than two one hundred car high speed electric trains."

"Over four thousand amps?"

"Yes."

"How is it deployed?"

"One would fill the role of heavy artillery and anti-aircraft defense. It is mounted on a tractor-trailer rig with a separate tractor-trailer power unit. It is capable of projecting a line-of-sight beam one hundred and ten miles for a period of sixty seven seconds. It takes two minutes for it to recharge. Attempts to fire them faster results in severe overheating, reduced range and destructive power."

"How does it work?"

Walter laughed, "The Russians have built the world's biggest, and heaviest capacitor."

"Capacitor?"

"It weighs five and a half tons."

"So its discharge powers the beam accelerator?"

"Yes, Your Majesty: high school basic electricity."

Walter laughed again, "A plasma beam hit on a charged capacitor results in an explosion with the power of a two-thousand pound bomb."

"Do you think they know that?"

"They don't know."

"What about the smaller unit?"

"It is mounted on a three-quarter ton truck for use against troops and thin skinned vehicles."

"Is it effective against hover platforms?"

"It destroys them."

"What defensive measures have we come up with?"

"We're working on an electronic defense shield."

259

"Does it work?"

"Only if the platform is more than a mile away."

"What is its range?"

"Three miles."

"We'll have to modify our tactics."

"We already have."

"How much risk has this added to our forces?"

"Not as much as they think it does. Their new weapons generate more of a psychological than operational threat. They are bulky, cumbersome, and expensive. They also require a lot of manpower to operate and maintain."

"So, with the Alliance's inefficient operational strategies plus the length of time it takes them to mobilize, they cannot prevail."

"That's the way I see it and the council and joint chiefs see it the same way. But the Alliance countries think they can. They believe that with the addition of the Russian beam weapons, added to their combined population advantage and military might that they are more than equal to us."

"If we can keep China and India neutral, we will be okay."

"China and India would like to see Europe and Russia humbled."

"Israel will support us militarily. What about England and Italy?"

"England will be with us. Italy is leaning towards a closer alliance with us."

"Then the European alliance with Russia cannot prevail."

"I don't see how, Your Majesty."

"What should our next step be?"

"The U.N. Secretary General has asked to confer with us on the matter of our activities against the Islamic fanatics."

"How many remain to be eliminated?"

"One hundred and sixty-eight."

"How much longer?"

"Five weeks."

"Tell the Secretary General that we will meet with them after the queen and I visit England at the end of our honeymoon."

"That will allow plenty of time, Your Majesty."

"Anything else?"

"Argentina continues to seethe."

"I thought we bought him off."

"We did. In spite of his heroic rhetoric, he's another greedy politician on the take."

"So the good Christians in Argentina continue to suffer?"

"They suffer grievously, Sire."

"And the country is at the point of anarchy?"

"Yes. He has asked us to deposit ten million in a Swiss Bank for him."

"It will be deposited in our Swiss Bank?"

"Exactly."

"Order the Joint Chiefs to plan for operations in Argentina and for simultaneous defense of Algeria."

"As you wish, Your Majesty."

"Might Russia attack across the Bering Strait?"

"They may."

"Prepare orders to defend our northwestern borders too."

"Should they attack will we wish to retaliate by conquering part of Siberia?"

Henry walked over to a map of the world on the wall, studied it a moment and pointed to a spot inside Russia. "Make plans to occupy to the sixteenth parallel."

Walter grinned, "Well done, Your Majesty." Then he rose, bowed to the Queen and bade them good day."

"So that's what they like about you," Caitlin observed after Walter had left the room.

"What?"

"Your quick decisions and clearly expressed orders."

"I can't afford to be indecisive. The world is not our friend. We will be overrun if I lose the upper hand."

"It was an education for me. Thank you for the invitation."

"You are my second in command."

"I still love you."

"Was there any doubt?"

"No, not really: but I love the King now," she said with a demure smile.

He grinned. "Isn't it about time we resumed our honeymoon?"

They rose and walked outside into the palace gardens. The morning air was clear and it was warm. The gardens were beautiful as they wandered down the flower-bordered walkways holding hands and talking. They stopped at a bench overlooking a mountain valley. It was a beautiful vista of spectacular mountains and tropical green. They sat for a while drinking in the splendid scene.

"Remember the last time we sat together on a park bench?" he asked.

"Yes, it was in Clifton Park."

"You said you loved me then."

"Yes, I did. I couldn't believe I told you so early."

"I loved you too."

"I knew you did," she replied. "I felt like I had known you all my life."

"God brought us together that day."

"Yes, He did."

"God has blessed us with much happiness and joy, Caitlin."

"I love you with all my heart, Henry."

"And I you, Caitlin."

He took her into his arms and kissed her. Then he began caressing her. His caresses became more urgent. She responded to his need.

"Should we here? What about the servants?"

"What about them?"

He was touching her now and she wished she didn't have on so many clothes.

"Nothing," she sighed and began unfastening her dress.

He removed his jacket and laid it on the grass. Then they lay on his jacket fumbling with their clothes.

"Hurry up, Henry," she urged.

He was trying to be gentle.

"Hurry Henry, please," she whispered again urgently. "Love me please!"

He moved on top and she pulled him to her in ardent passion, whispering of her need for him.

The birds in the trees interrupted their song as they watched and listened, oblivious to the human attributes of the occasion.

The day before they were scheduled to leave Venezuela, Caitlin was sitting on the west side porch enjoying the morning view while Carl was giving Henry his daily briefing downstairs. One of the servants approached her and bowed.

"Your Highness, the King requests your presence in his office."

Caitlin rose and followed the servant downstairs to the room facing the east where Henry did business in the palace. When she walked in, Henry was looking out the window. He didn't turn to greet her when she entered. She thought that was odd. Carl looked a little strange too when he greeted her, like he was holding something back.

"I'm here, Henry," she said quietly, wondering what this was all about.

262

Henry turned and when he did she thought he was trying not to laugh. He didn't reply.

"His Majesty asked me to tell you something, Your Highness."

She thought to ask why Henry didn't tell her himself but when she looked at him, he still looked as though he was trying to keep from laughing. "What does Henry wish to say, Carl?" she asked.

Carl started to say something but was obviously having trouble saying it himself. He got up and walked to the window and looked outside.

"Your Highness, Lady Wilma Blankenship has requested permission to marry Slim."

Caitlin's jaw dropped. She didn't reply at once. "Are you serious?" she asked, astounded.

Henry started laughing so hard that he had to sit down. Carl broke up too. It was quite a while before either of them could stop laughing long enough to say anything.

Between guffaws, Henry managed to say that it was true.

Caitlin had to take a seat herself but she didn't think it was all that funny.

"Both of you ought to be ashamed. It's not funny. What on earth did that old coot do to make her request such a thing?"

"We don't know," Carl answered. "Rebecca spoke to Wilma and she is serious. I also asked her to speak to Slim. He wants a quick wedding."

"I bet he does."

Henry found his voice, "Tell her the best part, Carl."

"And what is the 'best part', Carl?" Caitlin wanted to know.

"He wants you and Henry to attend."

"Surely you aren't surprised? How old is Wilma?" Caitlin asked.

"Thirty-six," Carl replied.

"Slim is almost sixty years older than she is!"

"Something like that."

"What are you going to do?" she asked Henry.

"I don't see any reason to disapprove it." He was about to start laughing again.

"Henry, I can't believe you'd let her go and live with that old rogue. There's no telling what he'll do, other than die before she's forty."

"Caitlin, Wilma wants to go. Rebecca said that she told her that she was in love with Slim."

"I bet Slim didn't say he was in love with her."

"He told Rebecca that she was a 'right purty filly'." Then Henry and Carl had another spate of hard laughter.

"Knowing him, I guess that's the best he'll ever do. What does your mom think?"

"She assumes that I'll disapprove it and hasn't commented."

"I bet she'd be mad if she knew how you two are taking it."

"She might."

"Henry, are you serious? Wilma's an aristocrat and Slim is a commoner, an old one at that."

"I don't see why not. Wilma is not very well liked by rest of the palace staff. It would give her some time away from the palace and being with Slim would add a little spice to her life."

"Its more like add a little spice to Slim's life."

"I'll keep her on the palace payroll."

"I don't know, Henry. You have no idea how Slim will treat her."

"I bet he'll treat her like his queen."

"He's such a rapscallion."

"Caitlin, what would you have me do?"

She thought a minute, "I'll have Emma speak to both of them. If she says its okay, I'll agree."

"Get in touch with her today. She ought to discuss it with them face to face."

"I think so too. I'll call Emma now."

When she left the room, Henry and Carl started laughing again. She had married a king who acted like a boy sometimes.

Emma thought it was funnier than Henry and Carl did. She laughed so hard that she had to lay the phone down. After she came back on the line, Caitlin made the request and apologized for interrupting her well-deserved vacation.

"If it's okay, I'll take Stewart. We'll just add it to our vacation," she said while barely suppressing laughter.

"That's okay. You can stay at the lodge if you like."

"Thank you, I believe we will for a couple of nights."

"You can use my plane too and stay in my old suite at the palace when you're meeting with Wilma."

"Thank you, Your Highness. How's the honeymoon?"

"It's been very nice."

"How about the queen stuff?"

"Some of that's been fun too. I got some beautiful jewelry."

"I read about that. The public loves you everywhere you go. All we read about around here are the latest 'local gal makes good' anecdotes. They can't get enough of you."

"I'm feeling a little more relaxed in front of a crowd."

"You're a natural, Caitlin. And Lance and Chrysie are doing an excellent job of making you as appealing as possible."

"People seem to think that I'm attractive."

"Your Highness, you are the most beautiful Queen since Helen of Troy."

"I hope I won't be kidnapped by some foreigner."

"God help anybody that laid a hand on you. The Trojans got off light compared to what Henry's reaction would be."

"Yes. Henry can be very hard."

"Henry is a king in the fullest sense of the word."

Henry came into the room and kissed her cheek, "Speaking of Henry, he's come for me. I've got to go."

"Enjoy your honeymoon, Milady."

"Oh, I am!" she said as she hung up the phone.

"Who was that?" Henry asked.

"Emma."

"She'll check on Wilma and Slim?"

"She's going next week. Stewart's going with her. I told them to stay at the lodge. Is that alright?"

"Yes, it is," he said as he started kissing her neck. "You're so beautiful."

"I'm glad that you think so," she whispered and let him continue his explorations. A few minutes later they were seen smiling and holding hands on the way to their suite.

On Sunday afternoon they left Venezuela to cheers and accolades. With the speed of the plane and the time difference they arrived in New Zealand one hour local time after leaving Venezuela. The High Governor and his wife and all the state governors met them at the airport. After a short welcoming ceremony, there was another cavalcade to the palace in an open car. They followed their new routine of coming out on the second floor balcony so they could converse with the crowd. Henry made a short speech thanking them for their affection and formally introduced them to Queen Caitlin. He told them he hoped they adored her as much as he did. Then Caitlin made a short speech about how honored she was to be their queen. Everybody had seen the televised balcony appearances from Mexico, Panama and Venezuela so this crowd was primed for "The Caitlin Show".

Caitlin's exchanges were with ordinary people if they could be distinguished from reporters. Even though reporters were allowed to film everything, the media honored her desire to keep it a "people" conversation.

A woman asked, "Your Highness, on your first trip here did you have any idea that you might one day be our Queen?"

"Yes, by then we already knew that we loved each other."

A man asked, "Your Highness, my wife wants to know if you iron the king's shirts?"

Caitlin laughed and gave him a devilish smile, "Sir, look at me. Do you think that the king married me to iron his shirts?"

Laughter rippled through the crowd.

"Your hair always looks great. Who does it for you?" a woman asked.

"Sir Lance Rogers."

"Can I get him to do mine?"

"You could if you can afford it."

She bantered with them for almost half an hour. They loved it and they loved their queen. She ended it in her own way.

"His Majesty and I are on our honeymoon and as much as I enjoy this, I must go. One must not keep one's king waiting."

The crowd erupted into cheers and hurrahs, finally ending in the familiar chant, "Kate Lin, Kate Lin".

Kathy and Rebecca were standing inside the doorway listening to them.

"She has been so good for His Majesty," Rebecca observed.

"They are a wonderful match. I've never seen him so happy."

"God blessed us with a wonderful king and now He has given us a wonderful queen."

"It does seem like a miracle," Kathy agreed.

They had two days of privacy before the formalities began. For the remainder of the time spent in New Zealand, they honeymooned privately on alternating days and visited with their subjects the other days. On Saturday night there was a formal ball at the palace where the winner of the national spelling contest presented them with a king-sized fur blanket made of twelve kinds of animal pelts. They were arranged in a way that the York coat of arms was on the left side and the Clark coat of arms on the right.

Caitlin was suspicious. "How do they know that I like fur?" she whispered to Henry.

He was as mystified as she was. "It's a coincidence," he assured her.

Prior to their wedding, the Australian government had requested an audience with the king when he was in New Zealand. On June eleventh, a delegation from Australia arrived to meet Henry. Walter and the foreign minister were present as were Caitlin and Carl when they were ushered into the king's office.

After the greetings were over, the conversation began. "Your Majesty, we have come to admire your government in a most profound manner. Our people view the prosperity and happiness of our New Zealand neighbors with a great deal of envy. As the result of a national referendum, we are directed by our people to begin negotiations with Your Majesty's government with the aim of incorporating our country into your kingdoms."

Emma called Caitlin on Tuesday. "It's true, Your Highness. They want to get married."

"Both of them?"

"Both of them. Wilma is more excited than he is. Not to say that he's not excited too but Wilma is beside herself."

"For heaven's sake, what does she see in him?"

"Your Highness, she likes his forthright ways. When he was in Kansas City for the wedding, he spent every minute they were alone trying to seduce her. He threatened to complain to the king if she didn't comply with his wishes."

"That scoundrel!"

"My sentiments exactly but Wilma sees it differently. Apparently nobody has ever been attracted to her with such intensity and she was touched by his ardor."

Caitlin was quiet, "What about him?"

"He's excited too."

"Did you tell him that he's got to behave? That he can't have his way all the time?"

"He reminded me that he knew how to act around 'purty wimmin'."

"He was a hit with the ladies at the wedding. Even Rachel liked him."

"He must have been something when he was a young man," Emma observed.

"I bet he didn't even take off his spurs," Caitlin laughed.

267

"I suspect that there are women with fond memories of him. Milady, as improbable as this sounds, I think they'll get along."

"In spite of the age difference?"

"He is remarkably vigorous for a man his age."

"He is at that."

"She wants to go through with it."

"What does she see in him?"

"He's different. She is too. She doesn't fit in very well with the palace staff. She told me that it troubled her sometimes."

"He wouldn't fit in either."

"That's for sure."

"Two oddballs on that Montana mountain."

"Sounds quaint, doesn't it, Your Highness."

"Henry said that she could stay on the palace payroll."

"That's very generous of him. She thinks she'll lose her income when she marries Slim."

"He doesn't have any money. She must love him if she thought she'd have to give that up."

"She does, Milady."

"So you think its okay?"

"I wouldn't say that, but I wouldn't deny them the opportunity."

"I'll tell Henry."

"It's going to upset some people."

"I know Henry's mom is going to be mad."

"She was beside herself when she found out that I was investigating it."

"What will she do?"

"She'll tell Henry that she doesn't like it. That's all."

"I'm sure that Henry will approve it."

"Tell him that Slim expects His Majesty to be his best man. He wants you to be there too."

"I wouldn't miss that for anything in the world but I hope he's not expecting a big wedding."

"You, His Majesty and the priest."

"That's good," Caitlin sighed.

"This ought not to be a public event."

"You're right. We'd be a laughing stock."

"It's pretty funny now."

"Thanks for your help. You can finish your vacation."

"Stewart and I enjoyed the lodge very much."

"Henry and I like to visit there too."

"When do you want me back in Kansas City?"

"We're meeting with the U. N. after we visit King William and Queen Anne. You probably ought to be there with me in case I have to say something important."

"Then, I'll see you in Brussels in August, Milady."

"Enjoy the rest of your vacation."

"You too."

Caitlin told Henry of the conversation that afternoon. He approved the marriage the next morning and ordered it for mid-October when the leaves in Montana were at their height.

On the seventeenth of June the Royal party left New Zealand, arriving in South Africa very early on the eighteenth. The early hour did not diminish the crowds as Henry and Caitlin rode from the airport to the palace. Although they were tired, they had the balcony exchange where Caitlin captivated yet another people.

On the twenty-sixth it was announced that the queen was pregnant with an expected due date of mid January. They also announced that if it was a boy, he would be named Edward Alexander. The Mexicans did their calculations and determined that conception occurred on their soil and immediately adopted the new prince as their own, calling him "Prince Eduardo". The High Governor called the king to request that he be named godfather to the "Mexican" prince. The Pope announced that God had given America and its Empire an heir and called a special holiday of prayers thanking God for his magnificent gifts to mankind. Henry and Caitlin thought all this rejoicing was a little premature. Henry dropped a characteristically firm suggestion that public comment be less extravagant.

During a concert in the spectacular hall in Durban, Caitlin was presented a magnificent diamond necklace. When making the presentation, the High Governor commented that a fair jewel was made more beautiful by South African diamonds.

On July first, they left for Namibia.

When they arrived in Namibia the crowds were big but subdued. Some waved flags and smiled broadly when the Royal party passed by but the raucous celebrations they had been accustomed to were absent. This was the shabbiest country in the Empire. The king's palace was still under construction and workmen were busy making it ready for them even as they arrived in the motorcade. They had to use a temporary stage because the balconies had not been built.

Caitlin noticed that the mood of the people was different from the other countries they had visited. Early on she realized that there would be no give and take from this crowd. They had gathered to see their savior and his new Queen. Henry was the star this time and she was his consort.

When Henry stepped onto the stage the crowd bowed on some prearranged signal and remained quiet. Then they parted to provide a path for a young girl in traditional garb as she moved shyly towards the stage, mounted the steps and approached the Queen. She curtsied. Then she presented Caitlin with a fine leopard robe. The girl was so shy and so serious that Caitlin was touched. She took the child into her arms, kissed her cheek and held the robe up for all to see. Then Caitlin put it over her shoulders. The crowd applauded and cheered for the first time and started the familiar chant. Then as if by a signal, all became quiet as they waited for their king to speak.

Henry thanked them for the honor they bestowed upon himself and his queen and for all the work they had done on the task of rebuilding their country. He reminded them that both he and their queen loved all of their subjects and did everything in their power to provide an environment where they could be productive and happy citizens. Caitlin observed the rapt expressions on their faces as they listened to this good man who'd been sent by God to rescue them from a hellish and brutal tyranny. Things were already better than any of them could remember. There was enough to eat, everybody had a job and they were safe.

After Henry finished his speech, Caitlin thanked them for their gift and for accepting her as their Queen. Then a local band played the national anthem followed by a young people's chorus singing "God Save the King" and "God Save the Queen". After that there was a picnic prepared for all present. Henry and Caitlin mingled and ate alongside ordinary people. The Namibians treated Henry and Caitlin as if they were a god and goddess. After the picnic there were other singing groups, each trying to outdo the others in entertaining their king and queen. It was late when they got to bed that night.

Kathy and Rebecca were beside themselves over the primitive accommodations available to their charges and Lance and Chrysie struggled to find ways to keep Caitlin presentable in the tropical heat and humidity.

The king and queen took it all in good humor which was a blessing to all. Rebecca commented later, recalling how upset the CIA spy had been one evening when the air conditioner failed at the

Montana retreat. "Her Highness is a Lady," she observed in making the comparison.

Actually, Caitlin and Henry enjoyed the primitive conditions and considered it a welcome break from the stifling protocol in more developed courts. Henry certainly didn't allow it to interfere with romancing his bride. He liked it when it was so warm that wearing pajamas and nightgowns were out of the question.

Caitlin commented that her being sweaty had not diminished his ardor.

"Is it supposed to?" he mumbled into her ear while his hand moved over her sweaty thigh.

"No dear. It is not," she replied as she shifted her position to accommodate his explorations.

Everywhere they went, they saw evidence of generations of horrors inflicted upon these poor people. Only the oldest could remember a time when life was endurable. But they remembered enough to pass on to eager ears that the changes their king was making would bear wonderful fruit. Most of the time people lined the roads along their route as if it was an honor to see their king and queen pass by. Occasionally a child would smile and wave.

Caitlin remembered the comments that Pamela had made about how despicable their former ruler had been and how downtrodden the people were. When she looked at those adoring, hopeful faces she admired this good Christian King that she had married and was reminded how proud she was to be his Queen. She admired Henry too, because no matter how squalid the environment, or how unclean the person to which he spoke happened to be, Henry never gave the slightest hint that he was uneasy. He moved among these, his newest people, in the same relaxed and easy manner that he moved among his subjects in Baltimore. Kathy was right. Her beloved was every inch a king.

She commented on it one evening, while they were lying in bed unable to sleep because of the heat. "Its good the way you mingle with the common people."

"I am king to all my subjects. Everybody deserves my respect, not just the aristocrats in Kansas City."

"I admire your attitude, Henry."

"I admire yours. Others who aspired to your position were appalled when I waded through mud to shake hands with a workman."

"It makes your people love you."

"Every person in my all my kingdoms and empire is important. God put them under my rule and I must always treat them with respect and protect them from harm. It is God's will that I do these things."

"That child in the hut will never forget your praise. Years from now his grandchildren will tell of the time their king spoke to him."

"He seemed to be a very intelligent child. I think he will go far."

They stopped talking and lay listening to the night sounds of the jungle outside their room.

"Your Majesty?"

"Yes."

"Your sweaty queen desires the romantic attention of her monarch."

He touched her and saw that it was so, "Then the King must accede to the wishes of his Queen."

"I do so love you, Henry," she giggled.

"And I so love you, my dear Caitlin."

He moved closer to her and soon the sounds of their love mingled with the sounds of the jungle.

On the day Henry and Caitlin left there were visible tears among the crowds that lined their route to the airport. These simple people were sad to see their King and Queen go as they waved their little flags.

"They adore you, Henry," Caitlin observed.

Saudi Arabia was a glittering contrast. They traveled in three hours from austere poverty to ostentatious wealth - glittering, garish wealth constantly on display. Even the relatively poor wore expensive jewelry. The poorest citizens of Saudi Arabia were far richer in every respect than the relatively well-to-do in Namibia. They turned out by the thousands to see their queen in person. The King and Queen rode to the palace in the High Governor's open car. It was painted with gold paint and it was so shiny that it hurt one's eyes to look at it in bright sun. The crowds were quiet but respectful as the cavalcade wound through the streets of Riyadh.

Henry and Caitlin didn't have an informal exchange from the balcony either because, while the crowd was excited, it wasn't rowdy. The people were so respectful that nobody would dare to address informal questions to the royal couple. They didn't want to converse with their King and Queen. They wanted to look at them. All Henry and Caitlin had to do was smile and wave at the crowd.

It was hot and even though the balcony had an awning they were sweating profusely by the time they went inside. There would be a formal reception and dinner that first evening attended by all government and civil officials. Caitlin wore the new diamond necklace she had received from the South Africans. Still, there were ladies in attendance that night wearing more elaborate and expensive jewelry than hers.

Caitlin noted that the Saudi Arabians had a different attitude towards them from what they had experienced in countries with western heritage. There was obsequiousness prevalent even among high-ranking people. They seemed to go out of their way to demonstrate their inferior position to their King and Queen and to demonstrate to their inferiors that they were superior. Caitlin did not find this appealing. For one thing, it forced her to always act like a queen. Only in the privacy of their quarters could she relax.

For the reception and dinner, Caitlin and Henry were decked out in traditional Arabian garb, except that Caitlin, like the Saudi aristocratic women, did not wear a veil. Caitlin was one of the very few ladies in attendance with dark hair. Aristocratic women in Saudi Arabia were either natural blondes or dyed their hair.

Monday was a free day for them. On Tuesday they began the series of public events associated with their visit. There was a public reception, a dinner or a ball every other evening for the duration of their stay, sometimes all three occurred in one evening. On those evenings, Henry and Caitlin didn't get to bed until the wee hours. The big public celebration was to occur on Saturday night at the arena in the desert outside the city. Everywhere they went people prostrated themselves on the street or sidewalk as they passed by.

The big night finally arrived. The Royal couple were dressed in white flowing robes and seated in the lowest box at the center of the southern end of the arena. The High Governor and his wife sat to Caitlin's right. This was not normal protocol as the governor usually sat to the king's left. But tonight positions were rearranged for some unstated purpose.

The evening began with Bedouin horsemen giving a precision horsemanship demonstration. They rode magnificent Arabian stallions elaborately festooned in colorful trappings and ornamental silver plates. Next came a chorus singing the national anthem and "God Save the

King" and "God Save the Queen" followed by a musical program by the Saudi Arabian Army Band. After this a group of veiled women in white robes performed a traditional Arab dance. Twelve Arab boys doing a vigorous gymnastics demonstration followed them. The last item on the program was another show of horsemanship by the Royal Saudi Arabian Calvary displaying flashing sabers and silver tipped-spears riding identical black Arabians. The last part of the demonstration was a cavalry charge directly at the royal box, coming to an abrupt halt twenty feet away with the horses stopping and kneeling before their King and Queen. Then they stood, the men saluted and marched off the field in single file.

Caitlin and Henry thoroughly enjoyed the show. They started to get up when the High Governor told Caitlin that there was one more event.

An expectant hush came over the crowd. They heard a gate creak open on the far right of the arena and a beautiful milk-white Arabian mare trotted onto the field. She was riderless and wore no halter or any kind of adornment. She received commands from her trainer through a small radio receiver in her right ear. After she was a few feet inside the arena, she stopped, tossed her mane a few times while she looked over the audience. Then she started to trot, then she moved to an easy, graceful canter as she crossed the arena circling the field until she came to a halt directly in front of Caitlin. The mare stood before her for a moment. Then she bowed three times to the Queen, reared up pawing the air, turned about and did three complete circles of the arena demonstrating her paces. She was magnificent in every respect. After the third circle, she turned towards the center of the field and came at Caitlin in a hard gallop, coming to a sliding stop six feet from Caitlin's seat. Then she walked close enough for Caitlin to touch her muzzle, stopped, bowed again and stood at attention before her.

"Your Highness," the High Governor announced, "Her name in English is "White Wind" and she is your gift from the Saudi Arabian people."

Caitlin was overcome. "She is so beautiful!" she exclaimed and clapped her hands.

"A beautiful Arabian mare to compliment our beautiful Queen and Empress. Tomorrow she along with her saddle and adornments, her trainer and two grooms will fly to America where they will be at your beck and call."

Caitlin stood beaming at the mare. The horse came closer and extended her muzzle into the Royal box where Caitlin could touch it. After petting the mare, Caitlin presented her cheek. The horse nuzzled Caitlin's cheek.

"She kissed me!" Caitlin cried out in delight.

The horse took two steps back, bowed to her new mistress, turned and trotted proudly to the gate and out of the arena. The crowd cheered wildly.

A microphone was handed to Caitlin and she thanked everyone for her gift. Then she bowed to all four sections of the arena. The crowd started cheering and applauding again and soon the familiar chant began, "Kate-Lin, Kate-Lin".

That night Caitlin snuggled up to Henry and said, "All this is fun but I was thinking how good it will be to get home."

"I'm a little homesick myself."

"Me too."

"For Baltimore or Kansas City?"

"For our home. I'm ready to stop being a bride and be your wife."

"I've been enjoying the honeymoon part."

"You mean the honeymoon lovemaking?"

"Yeah."

She smiled at him. "I expect you to keep that up."

"I'll try," he said as he began caressing her.

"Yes," she sighed. "I know that you will. I can't wait to put that fur blanket on our bed."

He grinned, "Remember what happened the last time you were on fur?"

"Yes," she said quietly. "It was a wonderful beginning for us. I loved you so very much."

"And I loved you too."

"It was touching how upset you got over our rushing things."

"Yeah, I was."

"You were so worried about a royal bastard."

"I had a hard time over that."

She laughed, "You weren't having such a hard time that you stopped loving me."

"I was mad for you in spite of the problems it could have brought us."

"My darling, I was no less mad for you."

"God has blessed us."

"He has. It was so wonderful. I get the sweetest feelings when I think about it." She took his face in her hands, "Henry, I still have those sweet feelings every time I look at you and remember how lucky I am."

275

"I'm the lucky one," he whispered. "I'd be lost and alone without you."

He kissed her and she began to respond to his touch.

"Oh, Henry!" she whispered, "I love you so much."

They left glittering Saudi Arabia on Sunday afternoon. Their next stop was Algeria, the first jewel in the Empire crown.

Algeria sparkled too. The Royal Algerian Army's magnificent marching band was drawn up in glittering array playing the National Anthem as they emerged from the plane. The three-hundred-voice Algerian Boy's Choir sang "God Save the King" and after that, the three-hundred-voice Algerian Girl's Choir sang "God Save the Queen." Caitlin was touched and had to wipe a tear when the girls finished singing. The crowd saw that she was touched and cheered even louder knowing that their new queen loved them. Crowds lined the route to the palace as the motorcade wound through Algiers. The now standard balcony appearance was more like the Saudi Arabian experience and proved to be another opportunity for the populace to get a glimpse of the royal couple. Henry made a short speech followed by Caitlin thanking them for their acceptance of her as queen and for the touching display of affection at the airport.

The Algerian stay involved many trips into the countryside because there was more to see in Algeria than in Saudi Arabia. There were trips into the Ahaggar Mountains where Caitlin took a hover platform ride to stand on the peak of Mount Tahat. They visited places like Tamenghest, Ideles, Adrar and a seemingly endless list of cities spread throughout Algeria. They toured the magnificent Haus Plateau region of the eastern section of the Atlas Mountain range.

When they weren't touring, they were partying. The residual French influence was by now almost non-existent except for the evident enjoyment of lavish parties and fancy balls. By the end of their stay, they were pretty much partied out.

On the second Saturday, the High Governor had planned a beach outing at Cap de Fer. It was held under a group of tents near an empty cottage set back a short distance off the Mediterranean beach. After a lavish lunch, he called the party together to make an announcement and asked Henry and Caitlin to stand beside him.

"Your Majesty and Your Highness," he said. "It is with the greatest pride, I offer you your wedding gift from the Algerian people." He pointed to the beach house.

They marched to the cottage and everybody took a tour. It was built in the Mediterranean style of white masonry with a flat roof and it had bright and airy rooms. The Governor mentioned that it was big enough for the royal family and the minimum staff but not big enough for any official functions.

He looked at Caitlin. "This will give you and His Majesty a small, quiet retreat from the cares of life. We hope that you like it and visit it often."

Caitlin was overcome, "It is perfect!" she exclaimed.

"We have left it unfurnished so that you may chose furnishings that suit you best," the Governor informed her.

Then Henry thanked the Governor and his Algerian people.

On August twelfth they departed for London. It was overcast when they landed at Heathrow. King William and Queen Anne met them as they exited the plane. This was the first time an American King had stepped onto English soil. William mentioned that historical fact in his long and elaborate greeting. Crowds lined their route to Windsor Castle and there were occasional chants of "Kate Lin, Kate Lin" as the motorcade passed by.

"Your Highness," William remarked to Caitlin. "I believe that you are as famous in our country as you are in yours."

"I've been surprised by all this attention."

"You have an appealing public personality. And your behavior when your life was threatened showed the world that you are worthy of their admiration."

"It is strange how things turn out sometimes."

"Yes, it is," William agreed, "Strange indeed."

They continued the rest of the way in silence, waving and smiling at the adoring crowds. It felt odd to Caitlin. Here she was, an ordinary girl from Baltimore, Maryland riding in an open car with two kings, one of which was from a line of kings going back hundreds of years and the other her husband. She was sitting beside the Queen of England and she was a queen herself, in possession of all the honors, benefits and burdens that such a high office could bestow.

Two years ago she had been a United States citizen working as a real estate appraiser in Baltimore, Maryland. Today she was second in command of the most powerful military force that the world had ever seen and first in succession as head of the most efficient autocratic government on earth. It was mind boggling to say the least. Tonight she would sleep beside her husband in the palace where two queen Elizabeth's and Queen Victoria had slept.

Caitlin was twenty-five years old and she was carrying her first child. Two days earlier they found out it was a boy and Mexico had declared a national holiday in honor of "Prince Eduardo", their Mexican prince-to-be.

Henry and Caitlin liked the English and the English liked them. William and Henry got along very well and William joked about "Henry IX" being on British soil. Crowds greeted them everywhere they went, even to the Shakespearean theatre where Henry got to see his two favorite plays, "Macbeth" and "King Lear."

Caitlin enjoyed the formal dinners, especially the conversations where her witty repartee gained her quite a following among the English nobility. Both she and Henry were fascinated by the historical tours that were scheduled for them every day. It was an arduous schedule, a private museum visit every morning, an art gallery tour after lunch and a formal dinner at an old English castle each evening. By the time Monday morning rolled around, the chance for a little rest during the flight to Brussels was welcome indeed.

The English King and his Queen rode with Henry and Caitlin to the airport, escorted them to their plane and sent them off in grand style. It was a memorable visit from everyone's point of view.

They did not expect such favorable treatment in Brussels, Belgium where the U.N. headquarters had relocated after the war between the United States and America.

Protesters lined their route to U.N. headquarters. Most carried signs suggesting that all religions were equal in the sight of God. There were a few people smiling and holding welcome signs and waving. This was to be a one day affair with the Royal couple leaving for America after a formal dinner with the Secretary General and delegates from the major European countries.

Emma met them at the airport along with Walter and the chairmen of the foreign and empire offices. They huddled in a conference room prior to meeting with the U.N. Secretary and his delegation. Walter whispered to Henry that the mission was complete.

This was the first meeting of this kind that Caitlin had attended and she was a little nervous.

The meeting began with an officious greeting by the Secretary General. His tone gave the impression that he was addressing a subordinate government. Caitlin thought it pretentious since he had no military forces at his disposal. Then he launched into a bureaucratic tirade taking Henry to task for his country's ignoring the U.N. and conducting its international affairs unilaterally.

After an hour the Secretary General finally got to the subject of the meeting. Caitlin watched Henry during the Secretary's tirade and saw how disciplined he was. Nothing the Secretary said produced any visible reaction on Henry's part or any of the American delegation. They appeared to be listening attentively and neutrally to everything the Secretary said.

Finally, the Secretary General finished what he had to say and invited Henry to respond.

Henry was prepared. First, he chided the Secretary General for not using the prestige of the U.N. to encourage government and religious groups to reduce violence like had occurred in Mecca. Then he reminded the Secretary General that America was not and had never been a member of the U.N. General Assembly, therefore they were not bound in any way to accept direction from that body. Then Henry deliberately angered the Secretary General by calling the General Assembly an ineffectual group of bureaucratic busybodies whose sole purpose was to stick their noses into everybody else's business. He challenged the Secretary General to identify a single international problem that the U.N. had addressed and resolved during its entire history.

These were as undiplomatic as any remarks Caitlin had ever heard and she was surprised that Henry spoke that way to anybody. Knowing him as she did, she knew that he was not upset or reacting to what the Secretary General had said. He was saying what he, and Walter, intended him to say. Why was Henry deliberately provoking the U.N. body?

In his closing statement, Henry reminded everyone that America and its empire were the safest, most prosperous countries on earth and it was his constitutional duty and obligation to his people to insure that they stayed that way. He also reminded them that he would take whatever steps he thought necessary to see that his citizens had freedom, justice, safety and economic prosperity wherever he ruled.

The Secretary General was stung to say the least. He sputtered a few words in rebuttal before he finally addressed what was really on his mind, "We are aware of the possibility that Australia may join your empire and we do not view it favorably. We know that your agents, some of whom are highly placed in the Australian government, have been guiding the Australian people to this conclusion for a generation." He paused to gather his thoughts, "But the burning issue is the likelihood that within the year, Argentina will be annexed to your empire. You must not do that, Your Majesty. It will inflame the world."

"Will it inflame the world, or will it inflame France, Germany and Russia?"

"They are in discussions with the object of forming a military alliance against you."

"They have been discussing that for years, along with the United States."

"The United States was invited but refused to participate. They have no stomach for further confrontation with your government."

"Why are you taking their side?"

"Your Majesty, I wish to prevent a world war and I believe that action would provoke one. I wish to prevent the deaths of millions of people, including many innocent civilians."

"Argentina is on the brink of chaos. Tens of thousands of Argentines are without food every day in a country rich in every resource needed for prosperity. My government has used every arrow in our diplomatic and economic quiver to aid them to no avail. I do not wish to alienate anybody or any country. But we cannot continue to stand by while Christians suffer under the most corrupt government on the planet."

"Your Majesty, I beg of you, do not annex Argentina."

"I understand your concern and I will consider it as we make our decisions over the coming weeks. I pray every day, and millions of my people also pray for a miracle. But if the miracle does not soon occur, my government will be forced to take action."

"That is terrible news, Your Majesty, because I do not believe in miracles. The situation in Argentina is beyond rational belief."

"Then you believe as I do that the situation will not be corrected internally."

"I do not believe it will."

"Then you understand that we cannot stand by and do nothing."

"Your Majesty, the peaceful nations of the world do not want a world war."

"Then tell France, Germany and Russia that Argentina is in the Western Hemisphere and it is not their responsibility. It is my responsibility. I will guarantee that French, German and Russian interests in Argentina are protected."

"That is not the issue, Your Majesty."

"What is the issue?"

"National jealousy. Your government's tremendous success and strength is galling to them in a most profound manner. They think its time to trim your sails and they are looking for an excuse to do so.

They fear that if they wait any longer it will be too late because the combined populations of your possessions will make yours the biggest country in the world. They fear that with the addition of Argentina to your domains, you will have an unassailable military capability."

"I must do God's will, no matter what the consequences are."

The Secretary General paused before he answered, "Then please pray for all of us, Your Majesty," he said quietly.

The room became quiet. Nobody said anything for a full five minutes. Then the Secretary General stood, bowed and thanked the king for meeting with them and for his honesty.

"If only such honesty and clarity of purpose existed elsewhere," he remarked to himself as he began to shake hands with the American delegation.

He paused before Caitlin, "Your Highness, I have followed your rise with considerable interest. I find that in addition to your great beauty, you are a most appealing personality. The king is very fortunate to have you as his mate and his Queen, and I rejoice with the world in the happiness that must be yours in your firstborn son."

"Thank you, Mr. Secretary General."

Then the meeting adjourned to prepare for the formal banquet to be held that evening.

The public statement prepared for the press said that the Secretary General and the King had a very frank discussion addressing a wide range of subjects and that both sincerely wished for peaceful solutions to problems facing the world.

Representatives from all the western European countries attended the dinner. Each one made a speech and every speech was couched in vague diplomatic language. Caitlin caught Henry doodling on his notepad and writing sarcastic notes about each speaker. The meeting lasted until nearly twenty-three o'clock. Both were squirming knowing that their plane was waiting to take them back to America as soon as the meeting was over. Finally, the Secretary General made his farewell speech and everybody shook hands. Emma succinctly described the meeting as, "Boring."

The French representative made it a point to invite Caitlin to Paris on their next trip to Europe. Then they rushed to the airport, boarded the king's plane and were on their way.

Caitlin was ready to go home. They had been away from Kansas City for eighteen weeks and she was homesick for familiar surroundings.

It seemed like ages since they left for their honeymoon. She was a new bride then and now she was sixteen weeks pregnant with her first son. She was beginning to show and Henry patted and kissed her belly every night before he went to sleep.

Henry was ready to get back home too so he could deal with pressing issues waiting for him when he returned. Both were eager to get out of the public spotlight.

Chapter Twenty Two

Home at last! They landed in Kansas City at midnight and were met by crowds of well-wishers welcoming the Royal couple home. They got to bed at one-thirty.

Henry was up at seven. He tried not to wake Caitlin but she woke up anyway. "We've had a busy week," he told her, "You ought to sleep in."

"I'm so excited about being home I'm ready to get up."

He sat on the bed beside her, "Remember that our prince needs rest too."

"He's starting to move a little."

"He is?"

"Yes, he woke me up once last night."

"Next time he does, let me feel him."

She smiled at her husband, "Yes, dear." He was king, yet so much a typical man and, in his case, so much a boy too. But then she was only a girl a few weeks ago. Not any more. She was a woman now and a mother-to-be. And she was the queen. When she thought about the staggering enormity of it all, she was humbled and whispered a prayer of thanks to God for allowing her so much happiness.

Henry was gone all day and she missed him terribly. They had been together constantly for nineteen weeks and suddenly they were separated during the day. She was beautifully dressed when she met him at the main entrance to the palace.

He kissed her. "I have missed you all day," he whispered in her ear as he held her.

"I have missed you too. I liked us being together all the time."

"They're fixing up an office for you next to mine."

"They are?"

"It will have a connecting door to my office and your office has a big fold-out couch in it."

"And the couch was whose idea?"

"Mine."

"Henry! Would you interrupt your work day for that?"

He grinned, "Absolutely. Wouldn't you?"

She pressed her body to him, "Maybe," she whispered demurely, "If the right man came along."

As they started up the elevator to their suite, Henry asked, "Would you like dinner in the suite instead of the dining room?"

She took his hand, "I was thinking that same thing. I have been lonely with you gone all day."

"I need a little more privacy than we've had these last few weeks. Being out in public all the time is wearing." He looked at her and smiled, "Besides, my wife is too beautiful to share with anybody this evening. I want her all to myself."

She put her arm around his waist and pulled him close, "Your wife agrees. I wish I could have a glass of wine to celebrate."

He grinned, "We'll celebrate in another, sweeter way."

"Is that all you think about?"

"No."

Normalcy meant problems. Henry's far-flung empire took a lot of governing. Plus there were American investments in foreign countries to protect and all the details associated with admitting Australia into the kingdom.

It was a very busy time but Henry had an efficient and loyal staff to manage his affairs. Henry, like his predecessors, was predictable enough for his staff to know the direction he would likely take and they managed his kingdoms and empire to that end. Henry's personal involvement was required only for unusual or dangerous circumstances, such as the current situation with Argentina. He abhorred its present state of near anarchy. But for some reason he had never been keen on annexing Argentina even though it was potentially a rich country. The conversation he had at the U. N. warning him of possible conflict with France, Germany and Russia if he annexed Argentina was troubling but it would not deter him from what he considered the proper course. The Clark attitude towards war had always been, be prepared and the sooner the better. The longer you waited the better your opponents were prepared. Walter kept reminding him that Russia was too big to swallow at this time.

Henry's days were spent reviewing strategies and options. In mid-September, it was decided to annex Argentina the following month. The Pentagon was ordered to finalize plans for invasion and annexation of Argentina and defense of Algeria in case the Alliance made good their threat.

They were also ordered to plan for defense of other strategic locations. Henry didn't want to leave anything to chance. The secret service apparatus was put on full alert to discover what actions the Alliance was contemplating.

Unfriendly foreign agents were fed information through supposed double agents, downplaying American preparedness for an outside attack. They spread the notion that Henry's government was confident that no one would dare attack American territory and that no defensive preparations would be made.

Henry wanted to damage the Alliance's confidence by overwhelmingly defeating and destroying their attacking force. It was a gamble that he and his staff thought worthwhile. In the end Argentina would get honest and efficient government and his enemies would pay a high price if they chose to make war.

It was a bold strategy. If it worked, Henry could cripple the Alliance's war making capability when he repulsed their attack.

Lord Blake came the eighth of October for briefing. He was to be appointed High Governor of Argentina. Wilma and Slim would be married October fourteenth and the invasion of Argentina would begin at one o'clock on the nineteenth. It was a very tight schedule.

Caitlin was looking pregnant now and every night Henry put his hand on her belly to feel his son moving.

She hadn't seen her parents since the wedding, so they decided to visit Baltimore on the twenty-sixth and she would stay over a few days to visit.

Debbie had told her that Eleanor was in New Zealand visiting Garrett Morris at his parent's home. He was stationed at Fort Bragg and had flown up to Baltimore several times to see her.

"She's crazy about him," Debbie told her.

"What about Matthew?" Caitlin asked.

The line was quiet before Debbie replied. Caitlin was beginning to wish she hadn't asked.

"He'll be here this weekend."

Caitlin laughed, "Is this a regular thing?"

"Pretty regular. When he can't come here, I go there."

"It sounds serious."

Debbie laughed, "It does, doesn't it?"

"You can tell me all about it next week. Henry won't be staying. He'll come back here on Monday."

"So we can have a nice visit?"

"Yes."

"How's married life?"

"It's wonderful."

"Are you showing yet?"

"A little. I can still wear regular clothes as long as they're loose."

"How about being queen? You were concerned about that."

285

"It's okay. Sort of like a job. I like being a wife much better than I like being queen."

"Everything I've heard is how you wow the hell out of people everywhere you go."

"People seem to like me."

"You're looking better that you ever have. Marriage seems to agree with you."

"I love being married to Henry."

"Every time I see you on television you look like a movie star."

"Three people are assigned to make me look beautiful."

"They are doing a very good job."

Henry came into the room.

"Henry's here. I've got to go."

"See you next week."

When she hung up, Henry was standing behind her, brushing her cheek with his fingers.

"Who was that?" he asked.

"Debbie."

"Walter tells me that she's swept Matthew off his feet."

"She didn't say much about it but I could tell it was pretty serious for her."

"I guess us Kansans can't resist Baltimore women."

By now, he was caressing her more seriously, "I guess not," she whispered, "But we can't seem to resist you Kansas men either."

He kissed her, lifted her up and led her to their bed. Dinner was a whole hour away.

Baltimore turned out en masse for the new queen. "Their Queen" as the signs professed. Many simply said, "Welcome Home, Caitlin" and "We're so proud of you."

Her office on Pratt Street had been enlarged to provide living quarters for the Royal couple and their staff and an office for Henry when he was in Baltimore. Emma, Kathy, Lance, Chrysie, Tia and Rebecca flew in on Caitlin's plane while Henry, Caitlin and Carl flew in his. Henry and Caitlin stayed with her parents over the weekend. Ashley and Brent came over for Sunday dinner. Caitlin decided to stay with her parents the remainder of the week, so Kathy moved into Ashley's room again. Lance, Chrysie and Tia came over as needed. It was nice to be home again and in familiar surroundings.

Caitlin and Ashley were helping her mother in the kitchen before Sunday dinner.

Ashley commented on it. "I'm glad to see you're helping mom again."

"What do you mean? I've always help mom."

"You didn't while you and Henry were dating."

"Yes, I did."

"I mean when he was here." Ashley laughed, "You never helped mama when he was in the house."

"You know, I guess you're right. I never thought about it then."

"I told mama that first night when we were here that you were in love."

"I was. I loved Henry from the start."

"Did he love you from the start too?"

"Yes. We were both in love."

"Henry seems very nice when he's around me. It's easy to forget that he's king."

"That's the way he wants it to be."

"He certainly looks the part in public."

"He always tries to give the right impression."

"He seems to think things through," their mother interjected.

"Henry is a very methodical man, Mama. I was surprised at how thoughtful and careful he is to always do the right thing."

"With the responsibilities that he has on his shoulders, he has to be."

"Are you excited about the baby, Caitlin?" her sister asked.

"Very."

"I hear that the Mexicans are more excited than anybody else."

"Yes, they are. They've already fixed up his nursery in the palace and assigned servants for his first visit."

"I heard that Governor and Lady Cardenas demanded that they be named god-parents," her mother said.

"Insisted is a better word, Mom. Nobody demands anything of Henry."

"Well, insisted then. Why?"

"They're claiming him as their prince because I got pregnant in Mexico."

"NBC had a special on the Mexican palace after the wedding. It is huge and the most lavish place I've ever seen. The royal bedroom is as big as my house," Ashley said.

"When we were there we had a great time. It is quite lavish."

"Didn't you ask to go there on your honeymoon?"

"Yes. And I enjoyed our honeymoon there but it is embarrassingly fancy."

"I bet you did," Ashley said with a smile. "And you've got proof of it too," she said as she patted Caitlin's belly.

"Caitlin," her mother asked, "Are you happy being married?"

"Certainly, Mom. Why would you ask a thing like that?"

"You were always so strong-minded, independent and carefree. You weren't interested in settling down. Before you met Henry you kept all of the men who were interested in you at arms length. You never brought a boy home to meet us until Henry came along."

"None of them appealed to me like Henry did, Mama."

"Another thing, I didn't expect to see you settle down so quickly. You're acting like a housewife and mother already. The change in you is startling."

"Mama, I love Henry and I like being his wife a lot."

"I also thought you'd wait a while to have a child."

"Mama!" Caitlin laughed, "I've wanted to have Henry's baby since we went to Clifton Park last June."

Now her mother smiled, "Well, I'm glad you waited until after you were married."

Caitlin laughed again, "You and the king's cabinet can stop worrying about having to deal with royal bastards now."

"Caitlin that is not funny!" her mother admonished her.

"It is, Mama. The very idea of the king's cabinet meeting in emergency session because of me is hilarious."

"Caitlin, they were right. You are queen now. Suppose they hadn't convinced Henry to tell you who he was?"

The question changed Caitlin's mood, "If he had continued his deception, I wouldn't be queen would I?"

"No, you wouldn't. You would be a real estate appraiser in Baltimore and you'd be bitter over the experience and even more suspicious of men."

"I guess you're right, Mama," Caitlin admitted.

"When they convinced the king that he was wrong and he forthrightly corrected his mistake, I knew why the Americans are so successful. It's because they are honest from the top down and they try to do what is right. Think about it, Caitlin. The absolute ruler of one of the largest empires in history humbly apologized for misleading you about what his job was. How many U.S. politicians would have done that?"

She reflected a moment, looked at her mother and replied, "None."

Dinner that evening was the most relaxed of any meal at the York's home when Henry was present. Even Caitlin's father relaxed enough to tell a joke in front of the king. Henry helped by behaving like a son-in-law around her parents. Henry and Brent got to know each other better and Henry invited him and Ashley to the lodge at Lake Louise between the holidays.

Henry returned to Kansas City early Monday morning. Caitlin wanted to visit her parents and friends but she also wanted to be with Henry.

"This will be our first separation since we got married," she commented sadly as she rode with him to the airport.

"I know. But you ought to spend some time with your family and friends. I'll be okay."

"I'll miss you."

"I'll miss you too." He took her hand and held it for the remainder of the trip.

They had breakfast in the Officers Mess. Caitlin watched his plane until it was out of sight like she had when they first met.

Carl observed her, "Her Highness hates for you to leave, Your Majesty."

"It's our first separation since we got married."

"She watched like that when we left that first time."

"Yes. With everything that's happened, that seems like a hundred years ago."

"You made an excellent choice, Your Majesty. She will be a great queen."

"I didn't marry her for her queenly qualities. I married her because having her at my side pleases me."

"That becomes more evident every day, Your Majesty."

"But I do agree that she's going to be a great queen."

Carl smiled, "You did very well indeed, Your Majesty."

On Monday night Caitlin invited Debbie to dine with her in her office suite.

"That way we can talk without drawing everybody's attention," she told Debbie over the phone.

When Debbie arrived at eighteen o'clock, Lord Roger brought her to the private dining room.

"Lady McIntosh has arrived, Your Highness," Lord Roger said as he escorted Debbie into the Queen's presence.

"Should I bow, Your Highness?" Debbie asked.

Caitlin laughed, "No, it's only me. I'm not playing queen this evening."

"You need to tell me in advance how I ought to act around you. I don't want to make you look bad or get in trouble."

"I will. You look great!"

"Not as great as you. You look better in person than you do on television."

"I feel happy."

"Being married to Henry must be agreeing with you."

"Henry is good to me."

A servant informed them that dinner was ready and they took their seats.

"I'm dying to hear about you and Matthew. Walter told Henry that you had swept Matthew off his feet."

"My mom says he's swept me off mine."

"How are your parents?"

"They're okay. But they're worried about all the aristocratic society stuff if we get married."

"Matthew is highly placed. Have you two discussed marriage?"

"Matthew brought it up last week but we haven't decided."

"Whether, or when?"

Debbie laughed, "When. His dad wants us to wait at least a year."

"That is a good idea."

"I know. But, Caitlin, I want to be with him all the time."

"I know how you feel about that. About the time Henry and I started to enjoy being together, he had to go back."

"When Matt's not here, Kansas City seems a million miles away."

"It is wonderful to be with the man you love."

"I know it is. It's written all over you."

"I am happier than I've ever been."

"Are you excited about the baby?"

"Very. I can't wait."

"Eleanor and I were surprised that you got pregnant so soon."

"Why?"

"Caitlin, you didn't strike us as the motherly type."

"My mom said the same thing."

"You are different."

"Mom mentioned that too."

"You got pregnant the first week of your honeymoon. That is not the behavior we expected from the Caitlin that we knew," she said

290

laughing. "We expected the coldly efficient Caitlin to plan everything to the nth degree and have the perfect child after she had learned to be the perfect queen."

Caitlin laughed, "Instead I've acted like a giddy, love struck high school girl. Is that what you're saying?"

"Well, yes. That's exactly the way you're behaving."

"I have enjoyed myself more than I thought I would."

"I hope I can one day."

"You will. It is wonderful with the man you love."

"You mean the sex?"

"It's more than sex. There's no way that I can explain the joy I feel with Henry."

"You're making me want to be with Matthew now."

"I know exactly how you feel. I wanted Henry to love me so much I thought I'd die."

"Was Henry your first?"

"There was a boy when I was in high school but it was pretty bad. He wouldn't even look at me afterward."

"Is that why you were always aloof with other men?"

"I guess so. But when Henry looked at me in that special way of his, I knew it would be different with him."

"One thing that I don't like about being an American is all this emphasis on waiting until you're married. I'm ready now. I know Matthew wants to but he insists that we've got to wait."

"Henry was like that too."

"Even he thinks you ought to wait?"

"Believe me, Debbie; it is worth waiting for sex with the man you love."

"I hope so because I melt when he touches me."

"Tell me about Eleanor."

"That's a good idea. We need to change the subject. You know how quiet, controlled and reserved Eleanor used to be?"

"Used to be?"

"Yes, used to be. Remember how she lectured us all the time about cooling it when we talked about hot guys."

"She even told me that Henry was not all that special."

"Well, let me tell you, Eleanor has got religion. You'd think the sun rose and set on Garrett Morris."

"Didn't you say that she was in New Zealand this week?"

"He has already popped the question and they've gone to his home to ask his parents for their blessing."

"It's only been six months!"

"Comparing your reaction to Henry and her reaction to Garrett is like comparing the Chesapeake Bay to Niagara Falls."

"That bad, huh?"

"Yes, that bad. I bet they're married before Christmas."

"I have one better than that."

"Who?"

"Slim is getting married."

"That old man? To who?"

"Lady Wilma Blankenship."

"Who's she?"

"She's the servant who was assigned to him when he attended our wedding."

"Isn't she kind of young for him? I heard he was over ninety."

"She's thirty-six."

"Wow. What did Henry's mom call him?'

"That old coot."

"What does Wilma see in him?"

"A chance to get away from the palace."

"Do you think he can do it?"

"I believe he can. Men half his age would have trouble keeping up with him."

"Well, I guess the old adage is true, beauty is in the eye of the beholder. Suppose he gets her pregnant?"

"Then I suppose she'll have his baby."

"Now that will be something to see. That cranky old man holding his baby."

"You know, I bet he'd be the proudest papa in the world."

"I bet he would," Debbie mused.

They had a lot to catch up on. It was after twenty-two o'clock before they finished eating dinner. Then they retired to her office with the big window overlooking the harbor where they talked until after one.

As she was getting ready to leave, Debbie asked, "Could we go to the beach together, just you and me and Eleanor, before it gets cold?"

"How about the week after next?"

"I'll run it past Eleanor when she gets back."

"I'll pick you up in my plane and we'll go to the Royal Retreat at Myrtle Beach."

"I hope Eleanor can. I want to get together like we used to. I don't want us to drift apart."

"I agree, Debbie. You and Eleanor are my best friends."

"Same here. Are you busy the rest of the week?"

"Let's have lunch Thursday at the Crackpot."

"See you there."

It took Caitlin a long time to go to sleep that night, thinking about old times and old friends and what dramatic changes had occurred in their lives. And it all stemmed from an enticing look from Henry that gorgeous June evening in 2084.

Caitlin could tell by their conversations that Henry missed her. She missed him too. But it was easier for her because she was visiting friends and family while he was working.

The original plan was for her to arrive on Saturday morning but without telling him, she changed the schedule so that she arrived on Friday afternoon.

Henry had had a busy week and was glad the weekend had finally arrived. He was excited about seeing Caitlin. Before going to his suite, he had dinner with his mom. He arrived at his suite after nine. When he opened the door, he sensed that someone was in the room and switched on the light. The fur coverlet from New Zealand was on the bed and it looked like somebody was in his bed. He lifted the coverlet and saw Caitlin snuggled under it without a stitch of clothes on.

"I couldn't wait," she whispered. "And I remembered that we hadn't tried out the fur blanket."

They had three days to themselves because Monday was Labor Day.

Next came the holiday celebrating Queen Mother Rachel's birthday. Time was flying by.

Caitlin was getting bigger. By September she began wearing maternity clothes in public.

Both Henry and Caitlin dreaded October with the briefings, Slim's wedding and the occupation of Argentina looming on everybody's mind.

Emma had called Slim and invited herself to his wedding, telling Caitlin that she was not going to miss this for anything. Princess Rachel invited herself for the same reason.

Caitlin picked Debbie and Eleanor up on the sixteenth of September for their trip to the beach. They had a wonderful time visiting, sunning and going to plays and shows. On the way back to Baltimore, Eleanor remarked about how their lives were changing.

"None of us are girls anymore. You're married, pregnant and the queen," she told Caitlin. "And all at once you're the most mature of us three. I never would have predicted that. Debbie is madly in love with Lord Matthew Jones and I bet they'll be married before next September. And I'm getting married before Christmas. Then I'll be an Army wife. Who could have ever figured this would happen?"

"Certainly not me," Caitlin replied.

"Or me," Debbie echoed. "Let's do this again next September and compare notes."

"That's a good idea," Caitlin agreed.

"You know, in some ways I wish it was like it used to be, back when we were inseparable buddies, before the Americans came. But in other ways, it is much better. I don't want to turn the clock back," Eleanor said. Then she added, "I guess that we are finally growing up. Maybe that's it."

"I suppose so," Debbie agreed. "Our lives are just beginning."

Henry was waiting outside the palace door when Caitlin arrived on the hover craft.

Lord Blake, Princess Elizabeth and their baby arrived quietly on October seventh. Caitlin's office had been completed and she accompanied Henry to his office on days that she had official business to attend to. She attended the conference where they reviewed the plans to occupy Argentina and defend Algeria. Walter always presided over these meetings.

After the military presentations were complete, Lord Blake gave his assessment that the Argentine military would not put up a fight citing that the current president had slighted the military in every way possible including halving their budget. "Their morale is at rock bottom," he reported. "They have few resources to fight with and they despise their government."

He had a sense that the Argentine government knew about the planned attack. "High ranking politicians are moving assets out of the country and some are sending their families abroad. Either they fear a coup from the military, a rebellion among the population or they know that we are coming."

The head of the Secret Service exacerbated concern by reporting a suspected security leak in the Pentagon or the Empire office.

"If they know what's coming, my best guess is that the president and some of the high officials plan to set up a government in exile in a friendly country."

"Where?" Henry wanted to know.

"France most likely," Walter suggested.

"Where would they get funding?" Henry asked.

"They're probably counting on the bribes we paid the president. France is nearly bankrupt. They can't afford to put him up."

"Walter, we do have a secure hold on all that money, don't we?" Henry asked.

"He can't touch a dime without my approval."

Then they ticked off the countries that might be supportive, those who would be neutral, those that would be hostile and those who would be hostile enough to retaliate. The latter group contained France, Germany and Russia; the Alliance. Everything was as ready as they could make it.

The Royal party arrived at Slim's cabin mid-morning on the fourteenth of October. Wilma had come separately and she was staying with the Walsh's until the wedding. Princess Rachel and Emma and Stewart Hamilton had invited themselves to witness the spectacle. Slim's kitchen was too small for everybody so they ate lunch outside. To everyone's surprise Alma, and Wilma hit it off and were getting along famously by the time the guests arrived.

Slim was all smiles when he greeted the king. "I'm real glad you could come, Henry," he said when Henry alighted from the car. When he saw that Caitlin was expecting, he said, "You got started quick." Caitlin hugged Slim and told him that she hoped he'd be happy as a married man.

"It shore is agreeing with you," he replied. "You look a whole lot prettier than you did the last time I seen you."

"Why thank you, Slim."

Rachel hugged Slim too when she greeted him. Emma shook his hand. Slim was wearing a suit, a tie and dress shoes. He actually looked handsome. Wilma was pretty in her pink suit with heels and a frilly white blouse. The wedding was at eleven o'clock with a reception and dinner afterwards. Alma had prepared a fine meal for the bride, groom and their guests. Ted had set up a big tent over a table big enough for everyone to sit together. Slim had brought his horse up from the corral so he could view the proceedings.

The priest began the ceremony promptly at eleven. Twenty-two minutes later Slim kissed his bride. Then he let out a cowboy whoop that echoed off the surrounding mountains. Sylvester Walker and Lady Wilma Blankenship were man and wife. They stood together holding hands and smiling as the guests wished them well. Henry marveled at Slim's manners during the meal and guessed that Wilma had been coaching him. Wilma had affected more change in his behavior in one day than anybody else had in ninety years.

As they drove away after it was over, Slim and Wilma stood with arms about each other smiling and waving, Caitlin remarked that they looked happy. She was glad it had worked out for them. Emma guessed that they'd be in the sack before the royal party reached the highway.

Chapter Twenty Three

October 19, 2085, 0001 in the morning.

[*Latin*] "The 107th Commandos have secured the airport, Your Majesty."

[*Latin*] "Any resistance?"

[*Latin*] "None, Sir. The Argentine Military Chief of Staff, Hector Gonzales, met our commander and surrendered the entire Argentine military force to us."

[*Latin*] "So they decided not to resist."

[*Latin*] "They welcome us with open arms, Your Majesty."

[*Latin*] "What about the police and judiciary?"

[*Latin*] "General Gonzales assures us that they too welcome Your Majesty's government."

[*Latin*] "Being patient has paid off."

[*Latin*] "Yes, Sir, it has."

[*Latin*] "Will we need to deploy the remainder of the force?"

[*Latin*] "I think the 33rd Corps and the 139th Commando Regiment will be enough, Sir."

[*Latin*] "Then send the rest home."

[*Latin*] "At once, Your Majesty."

[*Latin*] "What about the government officials?"

[*Latin*] "They have left the county."

[*Latin*] "Where did they go?"

[*Latin*] "Paris."

[*Latin*] "What moves have the Alliance made?"

[*Latin*] "None yet. They were caught by surprise."

[*Latin*] "What about the leak?"

[*Latin*] "They didn't believe him. They thought he was a plant."

[*Latin*] "Have we identified him?"

[*Latin*] "He was a janitor in the Pentagon."

[*Latin*] "A janitor?"

[*Latin*] "He is a French immigrant who deliberately scored low on the classification test and was assigned to the Pentagon."

[*Latin*] "What is his status?"

[*Latin*] "He has been interrogated and executed. His contacts are being arrested now."

[*Latin*] "Has Lord Blake occupied the president's office?"

[*Latin*] "Not yet, Your Majesty. He's being held up by the crowds."

[*Latin*] "Crowds?"

[*Latin*] "He is being welcomed as a savior by the people. American flags are waving and photographs of you and the queen are being held aloft all over Argentina."

[*Latin*] "Maybe we ought to admit them instead of annexing them."

[*Latin*] "That would be good, Your Majesty."

[*Latin*] "When will the proclamation be read?"

[*Latin*] "One o'clock."

[*Latin*] "Revise the proclamation to read 'Admit' to my family of kingdoms instead of 'Annex'."

[*Latin*] "It will be done, Your Majesty."

[*Latin*] "I might as well go back to bed."

[*Latin*] "I believe it's all over, Sire."

[*Latin*] "If any problems arise come and get me."

[*Latin*] "Yes, Sir."

[*Latin*] "The Queen and I will address them on their national television at nine o'clock."

[*Latin*] "Everything will be ready, Your Majesty."

[*Latin*] "Good morning, General. Well done."

[*Latin*] "Thank you, your Majesty."

"That was about as smooth as anything I've ever seen," Walter observed at the staff meeting the next morning.

"What are the Europeans saying?"

"Our allies are saying, it's about time, and our enemies are threatening to use force to make us relinquish our gains. They stop short of suggesting how they will do it."

"What about France?"

"The French government has not taken a position. Interestingly, they have not announced publicly that they are hosting the Argentine government-in-exile either."

"I wonder if they know the funds are frozen."

"They're probably waiting to be sure the funds are available before they take a public position."

"With friends like the French, who needs enemies?"

"What's the U.N. doing?"

"The Secretary General has called an emergency session of the Security Council at eleven o'clock our time."

"They're waiting to hear the king's speech to the Argentines."

"This is going to be a long day," Walter observed.

"Did you know that the king changed the proclamation to say 'Admitted' instead of 'Annexed'?"

"Yes, I did. That will cut the legs off the crowd that wants to brand us as brutal aggressors."

At nine o'clock satellite connections were up for His Majesty, Henry I and Her Highness, Queen Caitlin to address the Argentine people over their national television. The camera panned the king, the Queen and members of the Royal Cabinet as they were seated in the Cabinet meeting room. Then it focused on Henry.

Henry was, as usual, all business,

"Citizens of Argentina, I welcome you into my family of kingdoms. We come, not as conquerors but as liberators and I am pleased that you welcomed us with the enthusiasm that has been reported to me. It is my solemn Christian duty to respond with the same enthusiasm towards you as we welcome you to be one with us. You and your country have suffered these many years. Far too many I am pained to admit, but my government tried with diligence to affect positive changes in your condition in every way possible, short of invasion. Now we have crossed the Rubicon and happily we find a people welcoming us with open arms. You will find that I, and my government, are pledged to bring you security, order, prosperity, opportunity and a chance for you to achieve happiness so far as is possible in this world."

Henry paused.

"You have earned my enduring respect because you have persevered and you have earned my affection by your warm embrace of the freedom that has come to you and your country.

"I have appointed Lord James Blake as your High Governor. He is a man known to many of you. He has been our ambassador to your country for four years and has come to love your country and admire its people. He will be a wise and capable leader of my newest subjects.

"We will begin immediately to bring the order that you so ardently crave and safety to all of you. We will be fair but firm. We will also begin immediately to repair your infrastructure and your institutions that have suffered from generations of neglect. We will introduce societal changes that have worked so well in ordering American society. These changes will give you opportunity to excel at a level most beneficial to everyone, regardless of status.

"I must also tell you that we bring responsibility. You will be required to honor your commitments to my government, to each other and to yourselves. It is my wish and it is your constitutional obligation to achieve your life's dream to the very best of your ability. And it is

also your responsibility to love and honor your God and His Church. And, lastly, you must be prepared to defend your country and your King and Queen, with your lives if necessary, as members of the most powerful military force the world has ever seen. My fellow Argentines, I am proud that God has willed me to be your monarch. You must be proud too. First you must be proud to be Argentines and second, you must be proud to be Americans. Welcome to America.

"*My Queen and I will visit you on the twenty-eighth so that we can personally meet some of you and personally give you our warmest regards.*"

He paused, "*Now, it gives me great pleasure to introduce your queen, Her Royal Highness, Queen Caitlin.*"

Caitlin's smile was quite a contrast to Henry, who was stiff and formal in his address. Even in her pregnancy, she was very photogenic and her mannerisms appealing on camera.

"*People of Argentina, my husband and our King spoke of your duties, your safety, of your well being and the great work to be done. I share that hope and wish you success in this world and salvation in the next. However, we must not forget that life is more than work. Life must also benefit the soul and in our quest of the practical we will not neglect the cultural. Today, the repressed cultural energies of generations will be unleashed in your fair country. And that great unleashing will uplift your society to a higher level of achievement and a fuller appreciation of life.*

Citizens of Argentina, I am proud, and grateful, that God has willed that I assume the title, 'Queen of Argentina.' May that same God be with you and may He bless our fair kingdom. I bid you good morning on this historic first day of your freedom. I look forward to being in your presence beside our King on the twenty-eighth."

It was reported that as soon as the Queen ended her speech, crowds in the streets all over Argentina began chanting, "Kate Lin, Kate Lin."

Emma was beaming when Caitlin rose to leave the room. She came over and whispered, "Your Highness, that was a wonderful speech. You have knocked 'em dead again. "

The emergency meeting of the U.N. Security Council turned out to be remarkably civil except for the Alliance countries. The Italian and Spanish delegates were vocal in their support of the American government. Walter was both surprised and pleased by the Spanish attitude. Television images of joyous throngs celebrating the change of government tipped the scale towards neutrality in most cases.

But the Alliance was adamant that the brutal, greedy aggressor must be contained. But it was hard to see why in Argentina's case.

After hearing the report on the U.N. session, Walter sat back in his chair in the cabinet room and grinned, "We sell good government," he gloated. "The rest of them sell snake oil."

Henry and Caitlin visited their newest possession the following Sunday, arriving in Buenos Aires in time for mass at the National Cathedral. They rode with Lord Blake and Princess Elizabeth in an open car. It was a beautiful, cloudless spring day in the southern hemisphere. Delirious crowds welcomed them along the route from the airport to the church.

"Our concerns about a sullen, resistant population were ill founded," Henry commented as they passed the sea of smiling faces.

"Not everybody is this happy about it, but the ordinary people are, by a very large majority."

"The ordinary people are the ones we wanted to help anyway. Who's resisting?"

"Former government officials mostly. The government was corrupt at the lowest levels."

"What are you doing about that?"

"We are replacing them as quickly as possible."

"What happens to them after you fire them?"

"A couple have been murdered."

"Were they despised that much?"

"Yes. If they have the money, they leave the country. We encourage them to leave if they can."

"Should we grant the others funds so they can leave too?"

"I don't see the need for that expense. The troublesome ones will probably commit a crime pretty quickly. Old habits die hard, you know. Then we'll execute them."

"What about violent criminals?"

"Our reputation has preceded us. They have either left the country or are behaving. There has been very little looting and robberies have dropped off sharply."

"What about those in prison?"

"They have been executed."

"The city is dirty."

"It's a lot cleaner today than it was last Friday."

"Do you like your new job?"

"I love it. I've wanted this job since the day I arrived. This is such a beautiful and rich country and they are a wonderful people."

"What about the Argentine military?"

"If they didn't need training in our tactics and in the use of our equipment, the occupation army could leave today."

"I guess I was too cautious. It is a big country and I was afraid to move early because I didn't want to get bogged down militarily. That would make us vulnerable to attack somewhere else."

"Being cautious was the right thing to do," Lord Blake agreed. "It gave the rest of the world time to adjust to the possibility."

"That's true. Do you think the Alliance will take action against us?" Lord Blake asked.

"Walter doesn't think so but I believe they will. They've painted themselves into a corner. They have to show the world that they will stand up against us. All the bold talk about containing the rabid aggressor must backed up now with some kind of action. If they don't, they'll be tagged as windbags."

"So they'll target Algeria."

"That's my guess. It's close to them. It's cheaper to attack. They're almost bankrupt. They can't afford to do anything expensive."

"What is our strategy?"

"We will destroy the invasion force after it lands."

"That will humiliate them."

"That is my intention."

"When do you think they'll attack?"

"My agents say sometime in November if they can get their plan together. Germany is moving troops to Toulon now. The French will embark from Nice. They'll threaten Italy and Spain with retaliation if they attempt to stop them."

"Are they afraid of interference?"

"They are quite angry over Italy and Spain's strong support of us in the U. N."

"Are we in communication with Italy and Spain?"

"We've been growing closer to Italy over the past ten years. My dad and the former president of Italy got along very well. I get along well with Carlo. Spain is a new friend and we are cultivating them too. Caitlin and I plan to visit both countries after the baby is born."

"What about Russia?"

"They'll support the attack by sending a small amphibious force out of Odessa."

"Couldn't you stop them en-route?"

"I don't want to. I want to trap all of them inside Algeria. There must be no doubt that they invaded a friendly country."

"So you'll allow them to land?"

"We'll give token defense at the shoreline and fall back so they'll think we were caught by surprise. After all of their forces have landed, we'll destroy them and everything they brought with them. I don't want the Alliance to have anything left to fight with."

Elizabeth was discomfited by this war talk, "Can't we talk about something else, Henry? I hate it when we kill people."

Caitlin changed the subject, "I bet Ginger has grown."

"She's growing so fast," Elizabeth replied. "She's smiling at everybody and everything now."

"I bet she's so cute. I can't wait to hold her."

"She has become quite a handful."

"When can I see her?"

"We'll go to the nursery after church."

The church was packed. It was the first time that an Argentine ruler had attended church in public in one hundred years. The Archbishop of Argentina conducted mass himself and welcomed their new king to his service. In his sermon, he extolled the virtues of the good Christian king saying that the Clark Dynasty had, by their firm devotion and clear sense of purpose, rejuvenated the Holy Church and now its glory shone brighter than ever.

When the King, the Queen and the Blakes left the church, crowds of ardent admirers thronged the streets, trying to catch a glimpse of their king and queen. Caitlin was touched.

"Henry," she said to him on the way to the Blake residence, "Seeing the hope and love in these poor people's eyes makes everything else seem trivial, doesn't it?"

"Their reaction makes me feel guilty for waiting so long."

She took his hand, "Henry, you tried to do God's will. Don't feel guilty."

The ambassador's residence didn't have a balcony so they stood on a freshly built stage. A hastily assembled Argentine military band played first the Argentine national anthem, then the American national anthem. Then a beautiful Argentine opera singer led the whole assembly in "God Save the King" and "God Save the Queen." It was a profoundly touching scene and when it was over, many in the crowd were in tears.

Henry made a short speech, thanked them for their devotion and encouraged them in the rebuilding of their beautiful country. He ended by saying he was proud of his Argentine citizens and now they had reason to be proud again.

Caitlin was surprised and pleased by the Argentine's enthusiastic acceptance of the American take-over of their country. She spoke again of the importance of love of family, of their unique heritage and of their beautiful country. She concluded by reminding them that she was proud to assume the title, "Queen of Argentina."

There were no informal exchanges this time. The Argentine people were emerging from the prolonged trauma of living under a rapacious, greedy and corrupt government. It was slowly dawning on them that they had been rescued and their rescuer stood before them. Today they were, above all else, grateful and they adored their new king and queen.

Henry, Caitlin and the Blakes spent a hectic four days touring as many cities and towns as their time and energy permitted. Lord Blake was like Henry and enjoyed mingling with the people. At the end of every day both were filthy from walking in mud, shaking workmen's greasy hands, kneeling to encourage children and praising mothers for their devotion to their families. Nowhere did they hear a negative comment or see a single negative incident.

Caitlin garnered her share of attention as women and young girls pressed to be close to her and if possible, touch her. She broke down once when a pretty child of eight or nine, dressed in dirty rags, was heard begging her mother to move closer so that she could see the queen. Caitlin pushed through the crowd, picked up the little girl, hugged and kissed her. Then she asked for her name.

"Isabella," the little girl whispered shyly.

"Isabella, when I next come to Argentina, I want you and your parents to visit me in Buenos Aires."

On the flight back home, Emma commented, "Your Highness, they think of you as a goddess."

"They are so desperately, pitifully poor."

"Their lot will improve quickly now that they are governed by honest men instead of thieving scoundrels."

"I am very impressed with Lord Blake. He will do well."

"I was too. He's a lot like Henry in that he's very good at mingling one on one with ordinary people."

"He enjoyed it a little too much for Elizabeth's liking. She complained every night about how dirty he was," Caitlin observed.

"She would. Isn't Ginger the prettiest little girl you've ever seen?"

"I can't decide if she favors her mother or her father."

"I see a lot of him in her expressions. Lord Blake is a very handsome man," Emma said.

"Lord Blake is also a very ambitious man."

"Yes, he is. I think he has his eye on Walter's job."

"That's third in line for succession."

"Yes, it is and it doesn't hurt that he's married to Princess Elizabeth."

"How old is Walter?" Caitlin asked.

"He's in his 70's. He's held that same job for three kings."

"He is very good at it."

"Yes, he is."

"I'm reluctant to mention it," Emma said, "But I've never seen any hint of affection between Lord Blake and Princess Elizabeth."

"I haven't either. His behavior around her in public is a little too proper."

"If there was real affection, you'd notice it in unguarded moments. Everybody sees that you and Henry have a lot of affection. It was the same with his mom and dad."

"Elizabeth is somewhat of a cold fish."

Emma laughed, "It's a pity that some of Princess Rachel's passionate nature didn't rub off on Elizabeth."

"I like Rachel."

"I do too. You'd never have gotten Elizabeth to Slim's wedding but Rachel wouldn't have missed it for the world."

"I wouldn't be surprised to hear that Lord Blake had a mistress."

"Milady, it is amazing how much we think alike."

Caitlin was at home in the palace and had grown to like the routine. It was her home, whether she liked it or not. Prince Edward was becoming more active every day. Henry would put his hand on her belly every night to feel his son kick and squirm in his confinement. Henry was a homebody and she appreciated him being that way.

Kathy told her that Wilma had sent word that she was happy and that Slim treated her like a queen.

If it hadn't been for the Alliance and their threats to topple the monarchy, the world would be at peace. Walter dismissed the threat as inconsequential, saying they didn't have the wherewithal to mount a serious attack. Henry and Carl disagreed. They believed that the Alliance countries were victims of their own propaganda, like the United States had been in 2084.

People outside of American society could not comprehend how militant and prepared the Americans were about the defense of their countries. The tradition that began with King Alexander had become the bedrock of American foreign policy. Threaten, injure or kill an American and revenge would be swift and brutal. Some countries had figured out that if you left the Americans alone and provided reasonable protection for their interests, they would leave you alone. They were even generous to their friends. But they never forgot or forgave an enemy. God help you if you made them mad. The Alliance was about to do exactly that.

Walter finally came around to Henry's way of thinking and they began serious preparation for the defense of Algeria. Plans were developed to mobilize the Saudi Arabian army for deployment to Algeria if needed. Namibian troops were alerted for possible deployment for the first time. As always, the South Africans were spoiling to join in. Transport was assembled and deployment plans completed.

Henry wanted the Algerians to defeat the Alliance without any outside help. Everybody on the American side agreed that it was reasonable to expect that they would. Their concern was that the Alliance would surprise them with a new weapon or strategy and the Russian particle beam weapons were more effective than their information had indicated. In an unprecedented move, the Russians provided a number of their new weapons to the German and French contingent. Henry's spies told him that the Alliance countries held the Algerian armed forces in contempt. This was partly because Algeria was a third world country before its conquest by America and now they were considered a vassal state. The Americans played up their unpreparedness to such a degree that Walter was afraid they were overdoing it and their enemies would see through the ruse.

The American policy of keeping information about their military activities secret paid off. The Alliance didn't know that the Algerian Army outnumbered their invasion forces two to one and was itself a proud and formidable force. The Algerians had been awarded more unit citations and Alexander Crosses than any component of the American military. In 2084 they led the attack on central Washington. They would be embarrassed if they were unable to defend their own country. In addition they possessed American weapons and equipment.

By the first of November, the Algerians were ready.

On November third, Alliance troops stood off the Algerian coast. On the fourth, they landed simultaneously in the vicinity of Annaba, Skkida and Bejala. Prior to the landings, the Algerians evacuated all non-combatants from the area. At daybreak on the fourth, the French obtained lodgment at Skkida, found it lightly defended and by noon they were two miles inshore. The Germans landed at Annaba

306

at noon and had advanced thirty miles by nightfall. The Algerian army appeared unable to give serious resistance to Alliance forces and fell back in seeming disarray before the onslaught. In a cheeky display, the Algerian soldiers would occasionally turn and fight vigorously to throw the invaders off their stride. After killing a few hundred enemy troops, they would continue their retreat.

The Germans and French deployed and used the Russian particle beam weapons which they found to be very destructive on hard targets. A smaller unit managed to bring down one hover platform. They fired at several Royal Algerian Air Force fighters but failed to hit any. They were surprised and pleased at how well the attack went and how disorganized the opposing forces were.

After they were sure their partners had gained lodgment the Russians landed early the next day. By noon they had advanced to Guelma. Government spokesmen in Paris, Berlin and Moscow were delirious in their joy at catching the Americans with their guard down. They openly bragged about how helpless the Algerian military was when pitted against a top-of-the line European army. In their delirium, they failed to heed the tidbit from the front that their Air Forces had penetrated no further than fifty miles inland. They had been unable to do so because of fierce resistance by the Algerian Air Force. But the Alliance ruled the skies over the battlefield.

On Monday, headlines in all countries unfriendly to the Americans were proclaiming victory over the American king, gloating about how the Americans had been overconfident, how they had been caught unprepared and how the superior military prowess of the European soldier would always prevail over any third world army. One item missing from all those glowing battlefield reports was mention of Algerian casualties or prisoners. They were mystified by the absence of civilians from the battle area because their spy satellites had not revealed any mass movement of people or equipment out of the area.

The French Commander posted his headquarters in the American Queen's retreat at Cape de Fer.

On November eighth, the Algerian hammer fell. First, Algerian commandoes fell upon rear areas with devastating attacks from the sea. The Royal Algerian Air Force wiped Alliance planes from the sky. Plasma weapon armed hover platforms approached at wave top height and destroyed the flotilla of transport and support ships off the beach. All of their new beam weapons were with forward units and were not available for use where they might have been effective. As the Alliance military commanders deployed to meet attacks from their rear, the bulk of the Algerian army rose up on their front. Devastating attacks sent Alliance forces reeling to the rear only to be crushed on the anvil of those fearsome commandos. Then, to their utter dismay, they learned the effect a plasma hit had on a charged capacitor in a particle beam weapon.

It was over by Saturday afternoon. Not a single Alliance soldier returned to their homeland and not a single aircraft, or ship returned to home base. The last transmission from the French commander indicated that they had offered to negotiate surrender, had been rebuffed and were under brutal attack from which none were expected to survive.

The Alliance had begun this conflict fueled by bravado and overconfidence. It had suffered its first defeat. Gloom and embarrassment pervaded the capitals of the Alliance countries and their friends. Was it that hopeless? Could any force on earth prevail against the American King? The answer to the first question was, "Yes." The answer to the second was, "no." Meanwhile the Alliance countries wept for their lost sons and daughters.

There were no celebratory signals from the American Capital. American headlines simply stated that the Algerian Army had defeated the invasion force. There was no mention of outside assistance from any American or Empire forces. They also mentioned that the king had been present during the battle and was very pleased with the performance of his Royal Algerian military forces.

The New York Times commented in a somber editorial that an "American Peace" had descended over the world and that no country in its right mind would consider initiating hostilities against the American government.

Henry quietly returned home. The humiliation of his enemies was complete. His Empire forces had proven their capability and their loyalty. He was well liked by his subjects and could move freely among them without personal concern for his safety. No other ruler could say that. He was either admired or feared everywhere and he basked in an aura of good will.

His queen was responsible for a lot of the good will. Everybody loved the queen. She was even popular in countries that were unfriendly to his government. At least once a week, major newspapers and television stations ran some story or little anecdote about Queen Caitlin. A woman in England compiled a volume of the queen's public quotes and it became an immediate best seller. She was, indeed, very quotable. And she was very photogenic. Numerous magazines had contacted her office about having her on their cover, but she refused.

Caitlin was a homebody at heart like Henry and he liked that. She was thrilling to be alone with, being clever, spontaneous and uninhibited in the privacy of their suite. In public, every head turned when she appeared and every ear listened to what she had to say.

It was hard to believe how casually Caitlin approached her regal duties. She was like a breath of fresh air, so unaffected by her high position, so candid in conversation and so genuine in every way. She could afford to be candid because all her life she had been honest and she had nothing to hide. She also had the total adoration of the king.

Chapter Twenty Four

The admission of Australia to Henry's family of kingdoms was set for January 1, 2086. New Year celebrations usually held in Kansas City were held this year in Canberra. Government officials from all of Henry's kingdoms and empire states attended the celebration. Caitlin planned to attend with Henry but with the baby due in four weeks, he was concerned about the long flight. They decided she would attend and her physician would accompany them on the trip.

With the addition of Australia, Henry had added over 170 million subjects to his kingdoms in the last twelve months. That was on top of normal population growth in his other domains. This made his populations slightly smaller than India's. India and China still had bigger populations but Henry's people were healthier, better fed and had a much higher standard of living. Best of all, Walter was able to report that the kingdom and empire treasury ran a surplus for the twenty-second straight year.

But all was not well. Militant Islamists were resurgent in spite of depredations by the Secret Service. A hard-core group had managed to keep below American radar and avoid infiltration by His Majesty's spies. They were plotting revenge for last year's massacre of the faithful at Mecca. Fawzi Kibur was their hero. Posters of him adorned walls inside their compounds. Even with this, they had to be very careful because the king's spies were everywhere.

In a reversal of last year's schedule of holiday visits with her parents, Henry and Caitlin spent Thanksgiving with them in Baltimore and her family would join Henry and Caitlin at the palace for Christmas. Ashley was beside herself at the prospect of spending Christmas week in Kansas City. She had begun to like being associated with royalty and had grown very fond of her brother-in-law. Caitlin invited Debbie and Matthew and Eleanor and Garrett to be with them.

Eleanor and Garrett had gotten married in a small private ceremony the Sunday after Thanksgiving in a military chapel at Fort Bragg. Henry, Caitlin, their parents, Debbie and Matthew attended.

It would be Caitlin's first holiday season as queen and it was a busy time indeed. She agreed to host an American National Network (ANN) program about the Royal Christmas that included a tour of the palace. She also sent Isabella a nice gift and had Lord Blake send a servant to take her and her parents shopping for clothes. The little girl wrote the Queen a very touching thank you note. Caitlin was in tears after she read it.

Christmas dinner at the palace was the largest ever, with the York family, Caitlin's friends, Lord Blake and Princess Elizabeth,

Ginger and Rachel and her new consort and, of course, William. Rachel's friend was a prominent U.S. financier named Christian Gustav. He seemed to be genuinely fond of Rachel without being in her thrall. The Queen Mother commented that Rachel had finally met her match.

"Its about time," she observed acidly.

Caitlin always sat to Henry's right at formal dinners and not at the place at the far end of the table traditionally reserved for the Queen. Caitlin assigned it instead to the Queen Mother.

"It's your place," Queen Virginia fumed when Caitlin suggested it.

"I'm going to sit beside Henry," Caitlin insisted. "We always hold hands during grace and I can't do it at the far end of the table."

Virginia reluctantly gave in, "Okay, if you insist. But it really is your place."

"Your Highness, you are the mother of the king and you deserve respect. It is appropriate for the king's mother to sit at the place of honor."

The Queen Mother was still un-persuaded but relented. "As you wish, my dear, I will do as you ask."

The day after Christmas, Rebecca informed the king that Wilma was expecting. He didn't react right away. Then he looked at Rebecca with a solemn expression. "It's my fault. I'll have to make sure their child is cared for after Slim dies."

"You are very generous, Your Majesty."

"How are they?"

"They are both very happy."

He smiled, "I'm glad. It would be troubling if Wilma was having second thoughts."

"You did the right thing, Your Majesty. Your generosity made two people happy. I wouldn't fret about it if I were you."

Henry looked at Rebecca. She had been caring for him since he was four years old.

"How old are you, Rebecca?"

"Forty-eight, Your Majesty."

"We have been together a long time."

"Yes, we have."

"Have you ever wanted to do anything else?"

"No, Your Majesty. I love my job. I've never wanted to do anything else and I love you, Sire."

"And I love you too, Rebecca."

"I've never said it plainly before, but you made an excellent choice when you selected Lady York to be queen."

"It was not a rational act, Rebecca."

"Nonetheless, she is an excellent queen."

"She has certainly become famous in a short while."

"Everybody in the kingdom and empire loves her."

He laughed, "I knew you approved by the way you behaved around her."

"Yes, I suppose so. I liked her from the start."

"I also knew you didn't like the CIA spy or the woman from Alabama."

"They were shallow social climbers, Your Majesty and it showed. The Queen is genuine through and through."

"She certainly didn't put on any airs to impress me."

Rebecca laughed, "She didn't need to use any artifice, Your Majesty. You were hooked from the start."

"Rebecca, you are a very observant person," he said with a smile. "I'll have to tell the Queen the news."

"I expect Kathy has already said something to her."

"Good. Then she'll be prepared for our discussion on the matter."

Rebecca laughed, "I'm sure she will have a few choice words to say about it."

"She'll be okay. She likes Slim."

Caitlin rode with Henry to their offices.

"Kathy told me Wilma is pregnant."

"Yeah, I know."

"What are you going to do about it?"

"I'll be responsible for the child after Slim dies. It is my fault."

"Yes, it is." Then she added thoughtfully, "But still, you did the right thing, Henry. They are happy together and thrilled about the child. I'm glad you approved their marriage." She paused, "Henry, it's never wrong to give those you love a chance to be happy. Like when you married me. I am happy being your wife and having your child. It's like God meant for me to be your wife and my life wouldn't have been complete any other way."

She took his hand. "I love you, Henry." She said seriously without smiling.

He squeezed her hand, "I love you too, Caitlin."

The holidays flew by and suddenly it was New Year's Eve and the trip to Australia was upon them. Caitlin was big by now and didn't move with her customary grace. They would travel on the big official plane. It had a full size bed so Caitlin could rest during the long flight. Besides the crew, Rebecca, Kathy, her physician, a nurse and Henry traveled on this plane. Emma, Stewart and the Yorks followed on Caitlin's plane while Walter and the cabinet traveled on the king's.

They landed without incident at Canberra mid-afternoon on New Year's Eve. Cheering crowds met them at the airport and lined their route to the old English Governor General's residence, which had been refurbished to be the king's palace in Australia. Signs everywhere welcomed the King and Queen to their newest possession. Lord Joseph and Lady Amelia Gibbs met them at the airport and escorted them to their lodgings. Lord Joseph Gibbs had been prime minister and, because of his efforts in bringing the union of Australia with His Majesty's kingdoms to fruition, he had been appointed high governor.

Admitting the Australians was routine. The Aussies were laid back about everything. Celebrations were subdued because the queen couldn't party late and the king retired when she did. It was the tamest admittance celebration in anybody's memory because of the queen's condition. The Australians knew how to party but the attendees took note of the Royal couple's preoccupation with their son's impending birth and behaved accordingly. Everybody went home well rested after it was over. With this addition to his kingdoms, Henry ruled over a greater landmass than any ruler in history.

They arrived back home on Friday. The next event on the horizon was the birth of their son and the future king. America and the world waited with baited breath for the announcement that Edward Alexander Clark had come into the world. His parents waited with greater anticipation than anybody, except the Mexicans. They waited in what was close to a state of delirium. In mid January, they began a daily countdown in their national media.

Caitlin was pretty laid back about Mexican enthusiasm. She told Henry she wouldn't keep him away from Mexico but she wouldn't let them control the baby, or her, either.

Henry was like a child about the baby. He was so solicitous towards Caitlin she complained about it.

"Henry," she said to him one night, "It's only a baby. Women have had babies for thousands of years and most did it without their husband hovering over them all the time."

"But this is our baby."

She laughed, took his face in her hands and kissed him, "Will you ever grow up?"

He grinned, "Maybe."

He lifted her gown and put his ear on her belly. "He's singing!" Henry exclaimed.

She pushed him away laughing, "You silly boy. What is he singing?"

"Get me out of here."

"I never heard of that song."

"He wrote it."

She laughed, pulled him to her and kissed him, "I love you, Henry."

He smiled, "And I love you, my mama to be."

She became serious, "Are you doing okay without us being able to make love?"

"Yeah, I'm okay."

"It's been a while now."

"I know. I'm pretty excited about the baby."

"It won't be much longer."

"I'll wait."

"It'll be harder to wait when I don't have this any more," she pointed to her big belly.

"Yeah, I've thought about that. Maybe I ought to take a trip to Australia and a few other places."

"But I want you with me."

"How long will we have to wait until you can?"

"It varies, usually six weeks."

"That long?"

"I hope I heal up fast."

"I do too."

"Your bosom has filled out."

"They're full."

"Already?"

"In a few more days I'll need all this milk."

"I can't wait."

"Me either. Kiss me goodnight, dear. We need to stop talking like this or I won't get a wink of sleep."

Other less touching conversations were going on half a world away.

Two men in traditional Arab garb knocked on the door of a second floor apartment in Beirut. A voice from within asked a

314

nonsensical question. The taller of the two men outside gave a nonsensical answer. The door opened and they were admitted into a dimly lit room. Several men were waiting inside the apartment. There were no greetings, only somber acknowledgements indicated by the nodding of heads.

The tall one spoke first, "May Allah curse the Evil One."

"May Allah curse the Evil One," the others intoned in response.

Their discussions extended well into the night. They left in groups of two's and three's with small intervals between their departures.

On the twenty-ninth of January, Walter and the head of the secret service came into Henry's office.

"Islamic fanatics are at it again," the Secret Service minister told the king.

Henry was exasperated, "What is it this time?"

"They're planning another demonstration at Mecca. Kibur is their hero."

"There's something terribly wrong with a people who count failed assassins as heroes to emulate."

"They have visceral hatred of western heritage and Christians. You are the most famous and powerful Christian." Then Walter added, "And you have done them the most damage."

"What are they up to this time?" Henry asked resignedly.

"They're attempting to get agents into this country."

"Are they? Have they succeeded?"

"They haven't been able to make much headway so far. We let a few in so we could watch them and try to find out what they were up to. The immigrant card with the locator chip allowed us to monitor their locations and quietly arrest them before they do any damage."

"Do their leaders know their agents have been arrested?"

"No."

"And you interrogated them?"

"Thoroughly."

"What are they up to?"

"We don't know exactly. The ones they sent in had no idea what they were to do after they arrived. They were told to wait for a signal."

"What kind of signal?" the king asked.

The minister laughed, "Nobody knew. I think they were sending in sacrificial goats to test the system to see if anybody could get in."

"Have they done any damage?"

"None that we know of."

"Do we have any idea when they plan to act?"

"All we know for certain is they are going to do something, possibly in the area around Mecca when the Queen goes to the hospital to give birth to the Prince."

"That won't do them any good."

"The tiniest pinprick would give them great joy, Your Majesty."

"There's no danger to the Queen is there?"

"None that we can see."

"What do you think they'll do?"

"Some kind of demonstration."

"So they want to generate more martyrs."

"Apparently."

"Like at Mecca before?"

"We think so."

"Are we prepared?" he asked Walter.

"We are, Your Majesty."

"Then, we'll provide them all the martyrs they want."

On the thirty-first of January at two o'clock Caitlin was admitted to the hospital. Henry went with her and planned to stay through the birth of their son. She was in good spirits and things got off to a promising start until Edward got turned around. The physician called for a surgeon. Henry was worried and was such a distraction he was asked to leave. While he paced nervously with Carl trying to calm him down, General Hastings came with a message that Muslim fanatics had surrounded Mecca, threatening to massacre all the Saudi Arabians in the city and calling them vassals of the Christian infidel. She also informed the king that two companies of Royal Saudi Arabian soldiers from the Serengii tribe in northern Saudi Arabia had gone over to the fanatics. For the first time an enemy possessed plasma weapons. All of a sudden American and Empire troops were in danger.

Henry was furious. "Kill every one of the scum. Defile their bodies with dead hogs and bury them. Make sure every cadaver comes in contact with hog flesh."

"What about the rebel troops?"

316

"Activate the automatic destruct feature on their weapons the moment they are turned on loyal troops. Try to leave one alive. Force him to watch what we do to the other fanatics and then send him back to his tribe. He is to remain in poverty for the rest of his life. See to it that he wears the clothes on his back until he dies. No medical care, no money. Put him on a prison diet but make him live among his people. Announce that anybody who tries to help him will be committing a capital crime and enforce it."

"Is that all, Your Majesty?"

"Evacuate Mecca and level it."

The General was taken aback by the severity of the order.

"Don't, Your Majesty!" General Hastings pleaded. "Millions of your loyal subjects revere Mecca."

"Those are my orders, General," Henry replied coldly. Then he dismissed her and resumed his pacing.

At six o'clock, the doctor came out. "Your Majesty," he announced with a smile, "Prince Edward has arrived and he is healthy."

Henry grinned from ear to ear, "What about the Queen?"

"The Queen is very tired but she is doing fine."

"Thank God. Can I see them now?"

"The nurse will come for you when the Queen is ready. Her Highness wanted to freshen up before you see them."

A few minutes later the nurse came for him and escorted Henry to the queen's bedside. Chrysie and Lance were leaving as he entered. He could see fatigue in her eyes.

She was sitting up in the bed holding Edward. She smiled, "We have a beautiful son, Henry."

Henry stood beside the bed looking at his wife and son. Now, there were two to love and he loved them both more than he ever thought he could love anything. First, God had sent Caitlin to be his companion and now this son, product of his flesh and his beloved's flesh. Henry broke down when he leaned over the bed to kiss his wife.

She stroked his face. "My dear sweet husband, you give me such joy."

Henry couldn't say anything.

"Why don't you sit?" she suggested, pointing to a chair beside the bed.

He sat down and continued to beam at her and the prince.

The nurse entered, "Your Majesty, Lord Jones and General Hastings wish to speak to you on an urgent matter."

Henry didn't want to leave the bedside of his loved ones, "Send them in," he responded.

Caitlin noticed that Walter was agitated when he came in. It was the first time she had ever seen him look upset. Pamela was upset too and had a very worried expression.

"Pardon us, Your Highness. We apologize for barging in at this time of joy, but we must speak to His Majesty."

"You may speak to him here. We wish to be together."

"I understand, Your Highness." Walter got right to the point, "You must not do this thing, Your Majesty."

"Why not? I am removing a cancer from the realm."

"Over two hundred million of your loyal subjects revere Mecca. It will blemish the monarchy's name if you allow this to occur."

"What is he talking about, Henry?" Caitlin asked.

"I ordered Mecca destroyed."

"Why?"

"Because those damned Islamic fanatics chose the moment of our son's birth to spread their venom!"

She became upset. "Don't do this, Henry," Caitlin pleaded.

Henry stared at her. Why was she opposing him? "I ordered it because the damned Moslem heathens chose this precious moment to bring violence to my realm. I will not tolerate an uprising in Mecca every year! I will not have it, Caitlin!" His voice rose until he was almost shouting.

"Leave us," Caitlin said to Walter and Pamela. Henry nodded agreement.

After Walter and Pamela had left the room, Caitlin took his hand, "God has blessed us, Henry. We have our love and now we have a beautiful son and heir," she paused and looked away, trying to think of the right thing to say. "It is not God's will that you do this, Henry. Walter is right. Millions of your loving and loyal subjects choose to worship in another way. You do them great dishonor if you destroy their sacred place. You must not commit this sacrilege because a few have angered you, Henry, and that's all they've done. We're not in any danger. Your kingdoms and empire are not threatened. Don't do this terrible thing because you are annoyed over the actions of a few hundred men."

He stared at his Queen. He looked at their baby sleeping quietly in her arms. Maybe she was right. If she was right and he destroyed Mecca now, he could never put it back. If she was wrong, he could always destroy it later.

"I will rescind the order."

"Thank you, Milord." It was the first time she had ever called him that.

318

He opened the door and motioned for Walter and Pamela to come back into the room.

"I rescind my order to destroy Mecca."

"Thank you, Your Majesty," Walter said with evident relief. "We appreciate your reconsideration of the issue."

"I wish to modify my order concerning the prisoner to be left alive."

"What will you have us do, Your Majesty?"

"Force feed raw pork to the traitorous soldier. In addition, spare one of the outsiders and give him the same treatment. Force them to watch as their companion's bodies are defiled. Then have the Secret Service deliver them to their ancestral homes."

When Walter and Pamela took their leave, they thanked Caitlin for interceding. On their way back to the government office building, they talked about how Caitlin had grown into the queen's job and how much more favorably the monarchy had come to be viewed since she had become queen.

"She instinctively knows exactly the right pose, the right expression and the perfect phrase for the occasion," Pamela observed.

"She outdoes Alexander in public relations skills."

Pamela laughed, "Suppose she had been Alexander's queen?"

"We would rule the world."

"Her greatest asset is her honesty and lack of ulterior motive."

"The first time I saw them together I was impressed at how relaxed she was around Henry," Walter observed. "She wasn't afraid of him. I knew then she'd make an excellent queen."

"Did you hear what she told him the night he revealed who he was to her family?"

"No, what did she tell him?" Walter wanted to know.

"If they didn't hit it off, he was history, no matter who he was."

Walter laughed, "Nobody else has ever said anything like that to him."

"Kathy told me she joked with him all the time about king stuff and all the formality."

"She certainly has a mischievous streak. I couldn't believe my ears when I saw the tape of her balcony exchange in New Zealand," he observed.

"You mean the one about ironing the king's shirts?"

"Yes. Imagine anybody else saying something like that and getting away with it. I haven't heard anybody say anything critical."

319

"She gets away with it because everybody knows she loves the king. She's not hiding anything."

"She certainly does things her own way," Walter observed, "And we are all better off because she is the queen."

"She has grown to be quite politically astute these last few months."

"Yes, she has. In some ways she's more astute than Henry," he agreed.

"I think Lady Hamilton was an inspired choice to be her aide."

"They make a formidable pair."

"The queen's influence on kingdom and empire affairs will be beneficial over time."

"There is no doubt about it. None of the other aspirants for the king's hand would have been able to change his mind this morning."

"Thank God for our Queen," Pamela said.

"Amen."

They rode the remainder of the way in silence.

It was done as the king had ordered. No further Moslem fanatic incidents occurred anywhere in American jurisdiction for the remainder of Henry's reign.

On February fourth, Prince Edward and the Queen went home from the hospital. His nursery was next to their bedroom. Caitlin refused to allow him to be fed commercial baby formula so a wet nurse was made available for his nighttime feeding. Governor and Lady Cardenas visited "Prince Eduardo" on Sunday so they could give the Mexican people a report on their handsome young prince. On the day he was born, the Mexican council bestowed the title, "Prince of Mexico" on the tiny baby and voted to provide a Mexican attendant to augment the king's spare allotment (in their opinion) of servants to care for their future ruler.

Henry had two reasons to rush home after work now; his beautiful queen and his son. Although Henry and Caitlin were loving parents, they agreed that their son would be raised in the Clark tradition to be a responsible monarch. He would not be spoiled and he would be taught self-control, truthfulness, responsibility and self-reliance, dignity and perseverance. There would be no silver spoon upbringing for the prince.

Many aristocratic women shunned the actual upbringing of their children, leaving it to servants and nannies. Caitlin set an example for motherhood by caring for her child herself. She took him to the pediatrician and closely supervised those who assisted her in his care. Even the Mexican addition to her staff was made to understand they were raising a child destined to be a responsible adult, not a spoiled royal brat.

Caitlin was also careful about her appearance and soon regained her beautiful slim figure. She and Henry spent several torturous nights apart until the day finally arrived when they could once more enjoy intimate relations. She was beautifully dressed that afternoon when she met the king at the palace entry. She had assigned childcare duties to her staff for the evening and ordered a private dinner for two in their suite, including their favorite wines.

When he met her at the door he took one look, grinned knowingly and kissed her. When he walked into their bedroom, the first thing he noticed was the fur cover on their bed. Things were back to normal in the palace.

At the pleading of Governor Cardenas, they traveled to Mexico the middle of March to allow the Mexicans to see their new prince. The crowds were tumultuous in their joy. Edward was beginning to smile and laugh and suffered all the attention without showing any bad temper.

In May, the King and Queen made a State visit to Italy and Spain which resulted in the signing of a mutual defense treaty between Italy and America. This made Italy bullet proof in their relations with the Alliance and other countries who were not friends of the Americans.

The Italians went wild about Caitlin and Prince Edward. There were parties every evening and tours of art galleries, historical museums and scenic locations every day. Caitlin was quick to learn foreign languages and had made it a point to learn Italian before they arrived. She surprised and pleased everybody when she conversed with the natives in their language.

America and Spain had grown closer during the Algerian crisis and they had preliminary discussions towards the two governments working more closely together. The Spanish went out of their way to be cordial to the royal couple and their son. Caitlin was already fluent in Spanish so she was a double hit in Spain.

Their schedule while they visited the Spaniards was daunting and by the time they returned to Kansas City everybody was worn out.

"Your Highness," Emma observed on the flight back, "A few more of these trips and I'll need a month off."

321

"I need one off now. With Edward and all the festivities, I've had my hands full."

"You ought to consider letting his attendants handle more of his care."

"No. He needs my love and affection during this formative time in his life and I will not sacrifice his proper upbringing to convenience. I'll delegate part of his care after his personality is more developed but now he needs a mother's nurturing. He will be king one day."

"Your Highness, you are the most disciplined person I've ever known."

"I have a lot of responsibility."

"Yes, Milady, you do," Emma agreed.

Reginald Parker had been Caitlin's personal guard since the day of the assassination attempt. He was awarded the Alexander Cross for bravery because of his gallant actions when she had been attacked. This assignment placed them in close proximity every day. Because she trusted him, she was relaxed when he was around. She was relaxed in the same way she was around Lance and Chrysie. Sometimes he was around when she was being dressed. Caitlin never thought of herself as especially beautiful and refused to let all the comment about her attractiveness affect her attitude. In a way this was unfortunate because she was, in fact, a very beautiful woman.

During her pregnancy, she noticed Reginald was especially solicitous and she was touched by his concern. One day she told him how sweet it was of him to be so attentive to her. What she didn't sense was that Reginald Parker had become enamored of her and went out of his way to be in the room when she was being dressed. Nobody thought anything about it because he was always around anyway and the change occurred slowly over time.

Chrysie and Lance were responsible for Caitlin's public appearance and in the course of performing their professional duties they saw her in various stages of undress. Parker unobtrusively became part of this circle.

Nobody noticed the change and nobody knew the walls of his apartment in the palace were adorned with pictures of the Queen. Reginald Parker was an extremely handsome young man and nobody noticed either that he didn't have any girlfriends. In fact he longed to have the queen in his arms. Every day he looked for the slightest hint from her that she felt the same towards him and misinterpreted the

322

slightest deference she made to him as affirmation of her affection. Reginald Parker was a ticking time bomb.

After Edward was born and Caitlin had regained her figure, Chrysie and Lance were getting her ready for a public appearance. Reginald was in the room as usual and Caitlin caught him staring at her. She was in a dressing gown but when she leaned over for Lance to do something to her hair, the gown fell slightly open in front and she caught Reginald looking at her breast. When he noticed she had seen him, he looked away and left the room. His expression made Caitlin uneasy and suspicious. She began to watch him when he was around. As time passed she realized that Reginald Parker had more than a professional interest in her. She had to do something.

On Reginald's next day off, Caitlin asked Emma to meet her in her office.

The minute Emma entered the room Caitlin closed the door and informed her secretary that they were not to be disturbed. Then she told Emma of her suspicions.

Emma was aghast, "Milady, he'll be executed if the king gets wind of this!"

"I know. We've got to keep it quiet. He holds the Alexander Cross. It would blemish the award if something like this got out."

"Yes, Milady, we must manage this in a way that nobody finds out the truth."

"That's what I think too, Emma."

"Have you said anything to Kathy?"

"No."

"We must tell her at once. And you, Milady, must not be alone with him, even for a moment."

"He can't suspect anything when I'm around him either. We must not give him any indication that anything has changed."

"You are right. He must not suspect anything. Where's Kathy?"

"She's in her office."

Emma called Kathy asking her to come to Her Highness's office right away. When Kathy came into the room, Emma told her of the queen's suspicions.

"I've thought for some time he's in Her Highness's dressing room too much. I had even thought about speaking to him about it," Kathy said.

"What should we do?" Caitlin asked.

"Have you considered speaking to him about it?" Kathy asked.

"No. I'm uncomfortable with him around me now."

"Confronting him would only make him aware that we know. The queen's life is in his hands. We cannot afford to take chances."

Kathy asked, "Do you think you're in any danger?"

"I don't know. He looks at me a lot but that's all he does. I don't think I'm in any physical danger. The danger is he might say something or touch me."

"Unwelcome touching of the Queen is treason. He would be executed," Emma observed. "The Alexander Cross would be defiled." Then she added, "Some might even suggest that the queen may have led him on."

Caitlin was visibly upset by that thought. "Then we must do something," she said with new urgency in her voice.

"That is correct, Your Highness." Emma continued. "The Queen must always be above reproach."

Caitlin asked, "What is the best solution, Emma? He hasn't done anything yet and I don't want to hurt him. But somehow we've got to get him off my guard detail."

"Milady, how about a transfer with a promotion?"

"Like out of the country," Kathy added.

"Argentina?" the Queen suggested.

"I'll speak to the head of the Royal Guards Battalion today. Then I'll speak to Lord Blake personally."

"You can use my plane."

"What will you give as a reason?" Kathy asked.

"I will make a personal request on the Queen's behalf that Sir Reginald Parker is long overdue a promotion and the Queen recommends that he be put on the immediate promotion list. Then I'll speak to Lord Blake about finding him a position in Argentina."

"Lord Blake is an astute man. He will see through this."

"Lord Blake understands these things and he will cooperate fully in whatever I suggest. He will not ask the wrong questions and he will not divulge anything regarding this to anyone."

And so it happened. Within the month, Agent Reginald Parker was promoted to Director of Security in the State of Chubut in Argentina. He vehemently protested his elevation both to his superiors and then to the Queen personally, reminding her of his personal devotion. The biggest job in the kingdom paled in comparison to service to her royal personage. But the Queen told him it was selfishness on her part to retain his services to the detriment of his career. His advancement was more important to her than wasting his talents in a low ranking assignment. Emma penned an eloquent letter of appreciation signed by the queen and presented it to Reginald the day he departed.

To the day of his retirement from service, the Queen's letter was prominently displayed on the wall of his office. Being the queen's personal bodyguard had been his proudest achievement. Eventually he married the daughter of an important Argentine aristocrat and they had nine children. His Alexander Cross was displayed inconspicuously on another wall.

In 2088, Princess Alexis, nicknamed "Lexi" by the family, was born to Henry and Caitlin.

Chapter Twenty Five

Reid was getting more irritable by the day and it puzzled Jonathan. In over four years they had never had a cross word. Reid had disagreed with him three times in one day. Jonathan was irritable too. What really got to him was the level of discourse among their co-workers. Everything they said was banal and stupid. He knew he was working with dummies but they seemed dumber than ever. It irritated him. He knew Reid was also irritated by it too because Reid had called them stupid jerks several times. The thought of lifting one more can of trash and pushing a broom one more inch filled him with revulsion.

The winter of '89 in Baltimore was the worst in memory. Every week there was snow or ice and clouds hid the sun every day for nine weeks. It was depressing. In February, Jonathan got another shock. He woke up in the middle of the night after dreaming about Katherine and the boys. He started to tremble when he remembered the lieutenant telling him they were dead. Why? What happened to them? He couldn't remember why they were dead. Then, with a start, he realized the medication was wearing off and he was gradually becoming Jonathan. He could think again! Maybe this was what was happening to Reid too. Immediately he realized he couldn't let them know the medication was wearing off. He hoped they hadn't noticed any change in his behavior. He would speak to Reid tomorrow when they were alone. He wondered what Reid had been before they had zombied him. What had he done to make them put him in the labor corps?

Reid complained about the food at breakfast. Jonathan quietly suggested he ought not to complain.

"Why not?" was Reid's uncharacteristically sharp retort.

"They'll notice the change."

Reid stopped chewing and stared at Jonathan. Jonathan watched Reid's expression as he began to understand what Jonathan already knew.

"You're right," he replied quietly. "Thanks for telling me."

Since Jonathan and Reid had been friends from the start it was not unusual for them to be seen together. They took advantage of that. Whenever they were alone, they would talk between themselves about what they could do. They tried to be careful not to break any behavioral pattern. It turned out Reid had been a prominent real estate tycoon in eastern Delaware. He too had deliberately scored low on the classification test and they had tried to persuade him to retake it. But he was mad at the U.S. government for giving them up and he had stubbornly determined he would not participate in any aristocratic role. That decision had cost him his fortune and his family.

Reid's family had easily integrated into American society. His wife had remarried, both of his sons were already in the military and his daughter was married to the son of the Governor of Western Pennsylvania.

Now the medication was wearing off and Reid could think. Thinking about it made him more embittered every day and he and Jonathan fed each other's bitterness until their anger was barely contained. One day while they were discussing their circumstance, Jonathan suggested there might be others like themselves.

"James has gotten irritable lately," Jonathan observed. "He hit that stupid idiot Ralph yesterday."

"Tom talked back to a supervisor last week."

They went down the list of laborers on their floor and identified three more that had become noticeably irritable. They decided they would talk to them. Both agreed they had to be very careful.

"What do you want to do?" Reid asked Jonathan.

"Get to the United States."

"How?"

"I don't know."

"We can't drive. We don't have any civilian clothes. We stand out like convicts in stripped suits."

"You got any money in the U.S."

"Yeah," Reid replied. "You?"

"Yeah. Quite a lot as a matter of fact."

"I've got about two million. Wonder what inflation has been."

"Mine ought to have appreciated," Jonathan guessed.

"How can we get civilian clothes?"

"I don't know. Let's talk to the others. Maybe one of them will know."

Over the next few days they made surreptitious contact with the three men who were in similar circumstances. Tom had been a judge in Cumberland, Maryland; James a high school principal in Wilmington, Delaware; and the third was Will who had been a police detective in Baltimore.

Will solved the civilian clothes problem. "Steal them from the supervisor's lockers," was his suggestion.

Will's assignment was to maintain and clean the locker room and the administrative offices. Barracks locker inspections were done every other Friday so whatever they did would have to be between inspections. They were anxious to get started so they set a target day of February twenty-sixth, the Saturday after the inspection. Will told them some of the Americans kept a lot of clothes in their lockers.

"They're scared they won't have the proper attire if an important visitor, like maybe the queen, drops in unexpectedly," he sneered. "They have tailored suits, ties and dress shoes.

The next problem was how to get to and across the border. None of them had any idea if the border was fenced and/or patrolled. Crossing into Virginia had been routine before the war.

They had to address the problem of getting there without having access to a vehicle. It was forty miles to the nearest U.S. border because Pennsylvania west of the Susquehanna was American territory. And they didn't have any money.

They also didn't have ID cards like those issued to all commoner and aristocratic Americans. If they could steal ID cards, they could ride out on public transportation; maybe even have a decent meal at a government cafeteria before they left. Some of the men in their unit worked at the cafeteria in their district. They said the food was excellent and free to anybody with an ID card.

The managers and supervisors of their unit worked twelve hour shifts; two shifts a day. They lived on site when they were on duty and worked three days and were off four days.

Tom suggested they take clothes from the lockers of men who were off duty the first night they were off. That would give the conspirators four days to slip away before the clothes would be missed. Nobody could suggest how to deal with the ID problem. They gave the policeman their sizes and he was to go through the lockers to find five sets of clothes that would fit the conspirators reasonably well. Americans were very appearance conscious, so anyone in ill-fitting, poorly coordinated clothes stood out in a crowd.

They were getting excited and had to try hard to act like they did before the medication wore off. It was difficult because the possibility of freedom was exhilarating. They began to congregate more than was prudent. They were ecstatic when Will informed them there was a spare ID badge in every locker. Problem solved. This was going to be easy. Those methodical sons of bitches were not perfect after all and they were going to escape from this hellhole of regimentation and subjugation. They were going to make history!

Jonathan didn't sleep the night of the twenty-fourth. He tossed and turned in his bunk all night. He feigned sleep whenever he thought the night supervisor would be making his rounds.

They bolted their breakfast that morning, fidgeted during the barracks inspection and waited impatiently for night to come. Tom and James had to work off site and didn't return until dinner. Will had noted the routines in the locker room and told them they were empty an hour after the new shift began. They would have time to change in the

328

locker room and slip out the street entrance as the Saturday morning walkers were beginning to fill the walkways. The thing they worried about most was the chance one of their dumb co-laborers might recognize them as they were leaving and say something. They were too dumb to raise the alarm but they might say something that somebody else would notice. Even though Americans were relaxed, they tried not to be careless and they were habitually alert.

The night shift ended at seven o'clock. After eight, the escapees slipped into the locker room singly, trying to avoid the appearance of suspicious activity. Will had done an excellent job of finding clothes that fit and matched. Even the shoes fit. He told them he took something out of almost every locker to assemble their wardrobes. They acted like teenagers when they tried on the clothes Will had selected. It felt good to wear nice, tailored clothes again.

One troublesome detail was there were no names on the ID cards, only a bar code. They didn't know who they were posing as. Suppose someone, like the person checking them at a cafeteria or the Lightrail terminal ran the code and someone else's photograph appeared? Or, what if someone asked them their name? There was only one way to test that.

They walked boldly out the street entrance as a group and noticed immediately that they were overdressed. It was Saturday and everybody on the street, except themselves, was in slacks and sweaters. They relaxed when they saw nobody paid them much attention. Since they were uniformly overdressed, they stood out so much they spread out so as to avoid looking like a group.

They planned to walk out of their district. James calculated they could be at the adjoining district's cafeteria by noon. They would eat lunch, board the Lightrail at the adjacent terminal and head for the U.S. border.

It was chilly that morning but the sun was out and it was a beautiful day in Baltimore. It occurred to Jonathan that he was probably seeing his beloved city for the last time. Since the medication had worn off, he had thought about his old life. It was painful to remember images of Katherine and his sons. She was so beautiful. Tears flowed every time he thought of them. Then anger replaced sorrow as he thought about the Americans; so goddamned confident, so goddamned proud, so goddamned efficient and so goddamned ruthless. If this plan worked and he managed to get to the U.S., he would dedicate his life, talent and fortune to work toward the destruction of the American empire and strangling the last aristocrat on the planet with the guts of the last Catholic priest.

They reveled at their new freedom as they walked briskly toward the other part of town. Reid stayed with Jonathan but they didn't say much. Both were thinking about their past lives and what they could do to put them back together.

The cafeteria was crowded when they arrived. Jonathan volunteered to be the ID guinea pig so he got in line first. When he entered, he glanced at the wall on the left of the entry foyer and saw a painting of a woman in royal regalia. It was a portrait of Caitlin in her coronation gown after she had been crowned. It was the first portrait of any member of the royal family Jonathan had ever seen. He remembered overhearing the supervisors at the labor unit talking about how private the American Royal family was. The woman in the portrait looked vaguely familiar. When he got close enough to read the plaque he saw the title; "Her Royal Highness, Queen Caitlin." Then he recognized her. She was Caitlin York, Richard and Francis York's daughter, his backyard neighbors! She had babysat for them when Matthew was little. All of a sudden he felt like Rip Van Winkle. How on earth had Caitlin York, an ordinary girl from Baltimore, become queen? He tried to read all of her titles but realized he was holding up the line so he moved on. He glimpsed at the note which stated that Baltimore was proud to have been the childhood home of the American Queen. Then he remembered the times they were assigned to work in the district which was responsible for his old home area because the King and Queen were visiting. The king had been visiting his in-laws!

He watched the patrons in the line ahead of him so he could learn the drill. Each patron swiped his or her card and a clerk observed the information provided on a screen which was not visible to anybody else. He held his breath, swiped the card and sweated bullets while she studied the screen for a few extra seconds before waving him on. In the old United States, a person in her position would have languidly ignored him while she did something else. This girl actually looked at the information. She was professional and businesslike about it; very American. Being a businessman, he appreciated diligent employees and despised goof-offs. He looked around the cafeteria and found it to be tastefully decorated, spotlessly clean and immaculately maintained; nothing like comparable U.S. government facilities. Servers were well groomed and bustled about their jobs as if it was important work. He didn't notice any slackers. He had an unsettling thought that maybe all the slackers had migrated to the United States.

Food selections were excellent and diners could have a gourmet lunch. They could even have Russian caviar. The escapees took a chance and sat together at a round table. Each thought briefly that if they had obeyed American rules, they could have dined like this at every meal. Reid and Jonathan would still have wives and children, a fine home and would, in all likelihood, have been richer. It was obvious the American economy was robust and even working class people were well off.

The table next to them was occupied by a commoner family. It looked like a scene from a 1950's movie with a perky, well groomed, modestly attractive wife and mother, the father, who was a confident technician of some kind, four well groomed and well behaved children who bowed their heads when the father said grace and did the sign of the cross before starting to eat. The father mentioned something he had read in today's newspaper about unrest in southern Russia and made the comment, if the Russians were free like Americans and had a competent government, nothing like that would happen.

Jonathan choked on his food. Free! Americans free? What kind of newspeak was this? American freedom? What a contradiction in terms!

He whispered to Reid, "What a goddamned travesty to use the word, 'freedom' in context with 'America'."

Reid stared at him. "Calm down, Jonathan," he advised. Then he added, "They are free in many important ways. Look around you. These Americans are happy and secure. They have been relieved of having to make difficult decisions, like who will govern them. They are allowed to go about their lives, working, raising their families, growing old, without the bullshit we had to deal with. You and I liked the bullshit because it made us rich. The politicians loved it because it made them famous. But the average person hated it."

Jonathan stared at Reid, not believing what he heard him say. Then Tom agreed with Reid. They sounded like Katherine. Remembering Katherine made him sad.

Jonathan didn't say anything else while they ate but his mind was in a whirl. One of his many thoughts was if he went back to the barracks and spoke to the unit manager, would they allow him to retake the test. Then he remembered how much he despised the aristocracy and everything it stood for and decided it was not worth it. He'd rather continue with their plan, even if the probability of success was one in a million.

They finished their meal and quietly left the cafeteria. Jonathan would be the guinea pig again at the Lightrail terminal. It was three blocks away and their excitement was palpable. In less than two hours, if their luck continued to hold, they would be at the border and maybe even in the U.S.

The ticket clerk waved Jonathan through the turnstile after he studied the screen for a few extra seconds. Jonathan noticed the small delay and wondered why. On both occasions, they seemed to hesitate before letting him go. He watched the others this time and noticed the same phenomenon when the others passed through check in. The clerk studied the screen for a few more seconds than with others in the line. He shrugged it off. They got through. That was the important thing.

The Lightrail was nice. They had good seats and it was quiet. One could go to the dining car and have coffee, a cocktail, or even lunch. The passengers were polite and considerate. There were a few U.S. passengers. You could pick them out by their dress and manner. They looked out of place and they weren't as relaxed as the Americans. Jonathan guessed they were returning from visiting or shopping since all of them were carrying full shopping bags. He also noticed the U.S. women looked threadbare and haggard. He wondered how they got on. He hadn't seen anybody buy tickets. Maybe an American friend or relative got them a pass.

The conductor announced that they would arrive at the U.S. border on time at fifteen-fifty one and this was the end of the line. All passengers were required to disembark unless they were returning to Baltimore on this train.

Then, suddenly, almost unexpectedly, they were there! He looked at the others and saw expressions of relief, anticipation and a tinge of nervousness. Within minutes, they would be on U.S. soil!

After the train stopped, they filed off the train along with the other passengers. Most were traveling somewhere in the U.S. They crossed the border through a turnstile into the part of the station which was U.S. territory where another train was taking on passengers. They suddenly realized the dilemma they were in. Jonathan and the rest didn't have any money or any kind of identification.

There were no border guards at the turnstile and only a couple of railway police on the U.S. side. Jonathan approached the closest one. "We are political refugees and request asylum in the United States," he told the man.

The man stared at him in alarm and took a step back, "What did you say?"

Jonathan repeated his speech.

"Are you crazy?" the railway policeman asked.

"No. I am in full possession of my senses. There are five of us. We are all former citizens of the United States and two of us have considerable assets in this country."

"You are crazy. Stay right here while I get my boss."

On the way to get his boss, he stopped to say something to the other railway policeman who then kept an eye on them while his partner got help.

"So much for the open arms of welcome," Tom observed dryly.

They were getting nervous by the time the first railway policeman showed up with his boss. Both trains had already left the terminal. They and a couple of passengers waiting for another train were the only people in the terminal who didn't work there.

The supervisor was incredulous, "Let me get this straight. All of you want to leave America and come to the United States?"

"Yes. We were citizens of Maryland and Delaware when it was part of the U.S. and we want to be United States citizens again," Reid explained.

"Now that's a goddamned switch," he replied.

"What do you mean?" James wanted to know.

"Everybody over here is trying to get over there and you kooks show up wanting to be in the U.S. You're crazy. Hell, I'll trade with any one of you. You can have my job."

Jonathan was getting impatient, "Sir, we are requesting political asylum because we were held against our will in America."

"You're crazy. You're all crazy lunatics."

He spoke to the policeman, "Take them to the conference room while I make a couple of calls."

The policeman led them to a shabby conference room with a table and a few uncomfortable looking chairs.

"Wait here," he told them and left. He locked the door on his way out. There were no windows and no lavatory.

"Welcome to the United States," Tom observed sardonically.

"I'd forgotten how fucked up things were here," Reid observed.

"And how nasty it was," James added.

"Wonder who he's calling?" Reid asked.

"His boss, I guess." Jonathan replied.

A few minutes later, the second policeman entered the room and took a seat in the chair closest to the door.

"The boss said I ought to keep an eye on you," he advised.

Time dragged by. There was no clock in the room. They wouldn't have known how much time had passed except that Will had taken a Rolex wristwatch from one of the lockers. Tom observed that the watch raised the total of what they stolen to an amount that allowed the Americans to bring felony charges.

"Do many like us come over?" James asked the policeman.

"You're the first ones that I know about."

"I have money in the United States," Jonathan informed him. "We are not penniless."

333

The policeman eyed him, "You're not offering me a bribe, are you?"

"No, I'm not," Jonathan replied cautiously.

"That's good, because if the Americans want you back, there ain't nothing anybody here can, or will do. And if I take your money, I'll get caught too."

"What happened to political asylum?"

"It's different with Americans."

"What do you mean?"

"Right after the war, three kooks from New York highjacked a plane to Dulles Airport. Highjacking is a capital crime in America and they execute violent criminals and their next of kin. Our government rounded up all the highjacker's kin people and turned them over to the Americans."

"And they executed them?" Tom asked.

"Nobody ever said but I guess they did."

"Were there children?" James wanted to know.

"I heard there was a four year old girl."

"Those ruthless, arrogant sons of bitches!" Jonathan exclaimed.

"What about due process?" Tom asked.

"If the Americans say 'shit', the president asks how much and what color."

They didn't ask any more questions. A few minutes later, a man in a suit entered the room. When they saw him their hearts sank. He was an American. They could tell by his attire, his manner and grooming.

His first words were, "So all of you want to leave America?"

Jonathan answered for the group, "Yes, we do."

"Then I must apologize for disappointing you but it is not possible."

"Why not?" Tom asked.

"Because you have broken American laws."

"You mean stealing these clothes and the ID cards?" Will asked.

"That in itself is not such a serious matter. Non-violent taking of property is not a capital crime."

"Then, what did we do?" James asked.

"You refused to do your duty and assume your proper place in our society."

"What's so bad about that?" Jonathan asked.

"In America, failure to do one's duty is treason."

"Treason?" Tom asked.

"Yes, the king has the right to expect every citizen to do his or her duty. Failure to do so is treason."

"And the penalty is execution." Tom observed.

"Normally it is, but in all of your cases, the penalty was reduced because at the time you weren't American citizens."

"And we were medicated and put in the labor battalion?" Jonathan said.

"Yes. It was hoped you would come to your senses when the medication wore off."

"I guess we failed that test," Jonathan observed sarcastically.

"Yes, you did."

"Is there anything we can do?" James asked.

"Your fate lies with the Chief Justice of Maryland."

"What about mitigating circumstances?" Tom asked.

"There are no mitigating circumstances. You broke the king's law."

"We have assets in the United States," Reid volunteered.

"Your assets were transferred to the Royal Bank after the war and have been held in trust for you when you assumed your proper role in our society."

"So all of my money is in an American bank," Jonathan said despondently.

"Yes, it is."

Three American MP's entered the room.

"Where are you taking us?" Will asked.

"You will be taken back to Baltimore. The Chief Justice will review your cases tomorrow morning."

"How did you find us so fast?" Will asked.

"You have been under observation since early January and each of you has a locator chip under your shoulder muscle."

"So you knew about our escape plan all along?" Reid asked.

"Yes."

"Why didn't you try to stop us?" Will asked.

"We hoped you would come to us."

"So you left us alone until we crossed the border?" Jonathan asked.

"Yes. I was a passenger in the train car with you. You could have redeemed your lives at any point before you crossed the U.S. border and asked for political asylum."

Reid uttered a loud sob and started to cry. The MP's motioned for them to follow and led them to a waiting American Army bus.

Chapter Twenty Six

In 2090, the King, Queen and their children went on another progress where they visited all of the American kingdoms and empire countries. Henry used the occasion to designate South Africa and Algeria kingdoms instead of empire states giving their citizens more access to the benefits of being Americans and eliminating travel restrictions. Now any citizen of these two states could travel or move to any other kingdom without restriction.

Caitlin was now an accomplished diplomat and her popularity continued to grow throughout the world. Henry enjoyed watching her as she mesmerized the crowds that assembled everywhere they traveled. She retained her openness and public candor and she was, if anything, wittier than when she had captivated the world on their honeymoon. Everything she said in public was dutifully recorded and commented upon for days after she made the remarks.

While in Mexico, Caitlin promised the Mexicans that "Prince Eduardo" could visit Mexico for a month when he was six. Without telling anybody, she taught him Spanish. The Mexicans were joyous over the news that their beloved Prince would be theirs for a whole month. Henry characteristically reminded Governor and Lady Cardenas that they expected the Prince to return to America as disciplined as he was when he left and they must not spoil him. Cardenas grinned his sly grin and assured the King that Prince Eduardo would be nobly treated during his visit.

As before, the royal couple visited King William and Queen Anne in England on their way back. This time they stayed with them for two weeks. Caitlin enjoyed the English customs and moved comfortably among the English nobility. They in turn adored the American Queen and flocked to the many dinner parties she attended. The English King and Queen were in their late seventies and there was an undercurrent of talk about naming Henry his successor. When it was mentioned to him, Henry discouraged the prospect but Caitlin rather liked the idea.

"King Henry the IX! I like the sound of it," she giggled the last night they slept in Windsor Castle.

Henry grunted.

On their way back to Kansas City they made a ceremonial visit to the United Nations.

With encouragement from Walter, Governor Blake began to infiltrate Brazilian politics and government. As with Argentina, Henry was not enthusiastic about annexing or admitting Brazil but he did not discourage them and their efforts bore fruit. On January first, 2093, Brazil was admitted to Henry's group of kingdoms. The Queen was not pregnant this time so the celebrations were considerably livelier in Brasilia than those in Canberra a few years back.

Nobody complained about this latest addition to the American empire. Even the *New York Times* was philosophical about it, remarking only, in this case, the Brazilians, like the Argentines before them, would benefit from sterner management of their country. The U. N. and the Alliance were also uncritical in public.

The Brazilians adored their new queen. Walter remarked that the Brazilians must have agreed to be admitted as a device to get the queen to visit Brazil.

By the time they were admitted, the Brazilians had built their monarchs a lavish and beautiful palace on a bluff overlooking the Amazon River. The Brazilians latched onto Alexis and the new Brazilian cabinet's first order of business was to award her the title, "Princess of the Amazon." She was four and she was petulant during her investment ceremony.

On October 28, 2094, Prince George was born.

In early 2095, Henry had minor surgery on his foot and would be put to sleep for the operation. By law, his backup was the queen who would become Commander-in Chief of the Armed Services the moment he went under. This would be the first time anything like this had ever occurred. Walter and the Chief Justice were concerned about succession and prepared a will for Henry which named Queen Caitlin heir to the throne. Succession law stated that Prince Edward was next in line and the Chief-Of-Staff would act as his Regent until the Prince was twenty-one years old. If something happened to the prince and he had no heir, the Chief–of–Staff became king. Walter was over seventy years old and did not aspire to be Regent or King. His private comment to the Chief Justice was the Queen was fully capable of ruling the country on the outside chance that anything happened. Caitlin thought all this was ridiculous and commented to Henry and Walter when it was presented to be signed, "It's only a minor operation."

"Your Highness," Walter observed solemnly, "There must never be any question about who is to succeed His Majesty. We are paramount in the world today but one moment of hesitation or confusion at the top will result in our falling prey to our enemies.

Succession is the most serious problem with a government such as ours."

Caitlin thought this was unduly pessimistic.

The operation went without a hitch and Henry was awake and back in charge with the Queen by his side one hour and forty-five minutes later. He recuperated at Lake Louise with the Queen, leaving the children in Kansas City. They celebrated Valentine's Day in the same way they had ten years before, except this time they slept together every night.

Kathy and Rebecca reminisced. "They are still in love," Rebecca observed after they had left for their morning walk.

"She has been so good for him."

"She's been good for the country too."

"Yes, she has. The monarchy is actually popular now. Before she became our Queen, it was grudgingly accepted because nobody was strong enough to do anything about it," Kathy replied.

"It's hard to realize how big the change has been. Even countries hostile to us admire her," Rebecca said.

"And she is still herself. She has matured and she has embraced her duties as queen but she is still uniquely Caitlin."

"Her honesty shows in everything she does and says."

"Walter said she has become the most astute politician in the realm," Kathy said.

"Coming from him, that is a big compliment. Henry does depend on her a lot," Rebecca agreed.

"Yes, he does. Henry makes quick decisions but sometimes he's harsher than he needs to be and the queen moderates that tendency."

They looked out the window, "Here they come," Rebecca observed. "Holding hands like they did the first Valentine's Day."

"And smiling," Kathy replied. "I'd better get moving. I haven't laid out her ski outfit yet."

"I've got to get his out too."

They left the room and a moment later Henry and Caitlin entered. As soon as they unbundled, he took her into his arms and kissed her.

338

Chapter Twenty Seven

Willie Johnson was on the way to see his father in Philadelphia. He'd put it off way too long and now he might not make it on time. His mother called him after twenty-two o'clock the night before to tell him the doctor had told her the family ought to be notified. His dad had a heart attack two days ago. Willie ought to have left then but everybody thought his dad was going to be all right. They had told him to come to visit when his father got out of the hospital. It was a long way from Fort Bliss, Texas to Philadelphia, Pennsylvania. If his dad had been in an American hospital he might have made it but the U.S. hospitals were not up to date and you had to have a lot of money to get the kind of care his father needed.

The United Sates had universal health care but the free care was shoddy and many patients died from simple procedures. Only the rich or politically connected could afford to bypass the system and obtain quality care. Many rich U.S. citizens used American medical facilities. They sent their children to private schools too, not the public schools like Willie and his brothers and sisters attended.

Willie had been lucky. On his eighteenth birthday he managed to immigrate to America. All commoners and aristocrats in America had to serve in the military. During his obligatory four years of active duty he found he liked it so much in the Royal Army that he made it his career.

The Americans were big on education and he discovered he was a better student than he had been led to believe by the public school counselors in the U.S. As soon as he obtained American citizenship, he brought his high school sweetheart to America and now they were married with three healthy, intelligent children, all of whom would become aristocrats upon their eighteenth birthday. Because of this, they would have the advantage of excellent educational and career opportunities. In America everybody went to school until they had achieved their appropriate level of education. Nobody thought about dropping out. If you even mentioned it, you were ridiculed. The people in the United Sates were looked down upon by the Americans as silly, sentimental, lazy, and lacking the stern self discipline the Americans were so proud of. His daughter and two sons never doubted that they were lucky to be Americans. It was reinforced every time they visited their grandparents and cousins. The contrast in their behavior and appearance compared to their U.S. family members was stark and they didn't get along with their cousins at all.

Willie had flown on a military transport to Baltimore, Maryland where he checked out a U.S. built vehicle to drive to

Philadelphia. When an American drove in the United States they couldn't drive an American vehicle because it attracted so much attention and some parts of the United States didn't have the facilities to refuel fuel-cell cars. There were a lot of old U.S. vehicles in Maryland left over from the time it was part of the United States They were kept and maintained purposely for occasions like this when an American needed to travel by car in the U.S. He had forgotten how it was to drive a gasoline powered Chevrolet. It was noisy and sluggish compared to his Ford Monarch LVF back in Texas. He stopped at the border to exchange American dollars for U.S. dollars.

At two o'clock Willie stopped at a nearly deserted rest stop on I-95 south of Philadelphia. When he came out of the restroom to return to his car, he noticed three men standing beside the Chevrolet.

"Nice car," the biggest one commented.

"It's okay," Willie replied cautiously. He had forgotten about the crime problem in the U.S. and realized he might have made a mistake stopping here. He'd been careless. He didn't have to worry about this kind of thing in America.

"Where you heading?"

"Philly."

"Nice Chevy," the second man commented.

Willie moved to the driver side door. The big man moved to block him. The third man moved behind him.

"You're American, ain't you?"

"Yeah."

"You ain't one of us no more. You're a fucking black honky."

Willie didn't respond.

"God damned Uncle Tom nigger is what you are! Gimme them keys," he ordered.

Willie pressed the spot behind his ear where the locator and communication chip was. This alerted American security that he was in trouble. He heard a voice inside his head.

[*Latin*]"What's the problem?"

[*Latin*] "I'm about to be robbed and the Chevrolet stolen."

"Who the fuck are you talking to?" the big man demanded to know.

[*Latin*] "Where is your weapon?"

[*Latin*] "It's disabled."

"Motherfucker, you better start talking English. What kind of fucking gibberish is that anyway?"

[*Latin*] "I can hear them. Don't say anything else in Latin."

340

The third man grabbed him from behind and pinned his arms. The big man started going through his pockets and found his keys and his weapon.

"Don't take that!"

"What is it?" the second man asked.

"Hey! Its one of them Captain Kirk guns these motherfuckers carry all the time."

[Latin] "They've got your weapon?"

"Yeah."

The big man pointed the weapon at Willie's chest, "Gimme your money!"

[Latin] "Don't do it. I've programmed it to reverse fire. Make him try to shoot you."

The big man pressed the fire button and nothing happened. "It don't work."

"Maybe it's switched off," the second man suggested.

The big man found the "on/off" button and pressed it. The button popped up indicating it was activated. He pressed it to Willie's chest.

"Gimme your fucking money!"

[Latin] "Struggle to escape."

Willie tried to escape from the third man's grasp. The big man pressed the fire button. A burst of blue plasma covered his chest and he collapsed to the ground. This frightened the other two and the one holding Willie released his grip.

[Latin] "Can you get your weapon?"

Willie reached down and pulled it from the dead man's fingers. [Latin] "I've got it."

[Latin] "It's programmed to fire normally now. Kill the other two."

The second man turned to run away. The one who had been holding Willie moved a few yards back and stood staring at the dead man. Willie killed the man running away first. When he turned to the man behind him, the man dropped to his knees and began pleading for his life. Willie was well trained. Without a trace of emotion, he pressed the fire button and the third robber was dead.

[Latin] "An agent is ten minutes away. Stay where you are until he arrives. Then you can go on to Philly to check up on your dad."

[Latin] "Won't I have to go to some kind of hearing?"

[Latin] "The agent will handle everything. They tried to kill you and steal crown property. It's recorded here in case they want to know what happened. I ordered you to kill them so you're in the clear."

[Latin] "Thanks."

[*Latin*] "You're welcome. Keep your weapon activated while you're in the U.S. Hope your dad pulls through."

Chapter Twenty Eight

In 2096, Spain entered into an alliance with America. This was followed the next year by Norway, Sweden and Finland who were concerned about Russian expansion motives. Henry and Caitlin made official visits to all three countries for the occasion and Caitlin's popularity continued unabated. Rebuilding Argentina and Brazil was consuming a lot of Empire resources and Walter was loath to expand further before they were paying their own way and giving a little back to the king's treasury. Henry resurrected his grandfather's dream of a space colony but didn't have the wherewithal to do more than study the proposition.

In 2096, the American government, in an unbelievably high handed move, dismantled spy satellites and space stations belonging to other countries. The pretext was that there was too much space junk in the heavens. Russia and China were livid and threatened to take action. But memories of the Algerian invasion were fresh enough to allow cooler heads to prevail.

The king allowed all countries access to the American system for peaceful purposes and monitored it stringently to prevent unauthorized access to American military secrets.

American domination was palpable now. Between Henry's kingdoms, his empire, alliances with England, Israel, Italy, Spain, Norway, Sweden and Finland, he had greater military capability at his command than a combination of two of the three biggest countries. Only a combination of Russia, China and India could threaten America militarily and still there was the technological advantage favoring the Americans.

China was no friend but they remembered what Alexander had done thirty years before. On top of that, Henry was viewed as more militant than any of his predecessors. In eleven years he had annexed Namibia, won a war with the United States giving him Maryland and Delaware by treaty. Australia, Argentina and Brazil had been admitted. This was quite a chunk of real estate and every parcel increased the economic and military potency of the American government.

He had handily destroyed the Alliance force that invaded Algeria. Still, Henry, Walter and all of his senior government officials knew the price of liberty was eternal vigilance and they kept the Royal military machine honed to perfection insuring that America was the most formidable military power the world had ever seen.

The man at the top had as his wife and Queen the most popular woman on earth.

Chapter Twenty Nine

In the summer of 2097, Henry started complaining about headaches. He wasn't a complainer and Caitlin worried about it to the point she insisted that he see a specialist. The medical examination revealed nothing and it was suggested that he make some minor changes in his diet. By October, the headaches were worse and he was taken to a famous neurosurgeon in Stockholm but the expert couldn't discover the cause of the King's headaches. Different medications were tried to no avail. Henry had days when he couldn't function.

On November twelfth, Henry woke up in the middle of the night with a pounding headache. He was rushed to the hospital. At four-forty-six an aneurism deep inside his brain ruptured. The King was dead!

The nation and the world were stunned. Caitlin was devastated and it took all of her strength to carry on. Every night she prayed for God to take her so she could be with the man she adored.

The funeral mass was said by the same Pope who had performed their marriage ceremony a short twelve years earlier. Millions of mourners passed Henry's casket while his body lay in state at the National Cathedral. The heads of state of every country in the world also paid homage to the fallen king.

It was a whirl for the Royal family. The Queen Mother was as devastated as Caitlin and Henry's sisters and brother were stunned and sorrowful. Caitlin was strong outside but inside her pain was unbearable and she longed to join her husband in death because he had been her life.

On the morning of the funeral, Pamela came to the queen's quarters with an urgent request. "You must meet with the council at once, Your Majesty." Caitlin didn't notice the change in address.

"I'll meet with them after I bury my husband," she replied in an anguished voice.

"This is an emergency, Your Majesty," Pamela insisted.

"Can't it wait?"

"Your Majesty, your Kingdoms and Empire are in grave danger. You must meet with the council."

She reluctantly followed Pamela to the waiting hover platform that whisked them to the government building. When they entered the chamber, the council rose to attention and with their right hands over their heart solemnly intoned, "The King is dead, long live the Queen." There were tears in their eyes and some were openly weeping.

Caitlin addressed Walter, "Why did you bring me here?"

"You are Commander-in-Chief. We have a national emergency."

"Why can't you handle it?"

"You are the King's heir to the throne."

"But that was for a foot operation."

"The King's will names you his successor, Your Majesty."

Caitlin sat down to take in the meaning of this as she looked quietly over the council. Then she wiped her tears and stood up.

"What is the emergency?"

"Your Majesty, the Russians are massing to attack Alaska and Northern Canada. What are your orders?"

"Defend our borders."

"It has been American policy to take territory from countries that attack our interests."

"Occupy Siberia to the 16th parallel."

The room became quiet for a few seconds. "There is one other matter, Your Majesty."

"What is it?"

"It is known that you objected to the treatment United States prisoners received after the war with the U.S. It has been American policy to destroy the enemy army. Do you wish to change that policy?"

"No, I do not."

"Thank you, Your Majesty. We apologize for disturbing you on this most unhappy occasion."

"The Kingdom and Empire must be defended."

"Your Majesty, we grieve with you in your loss."

The Queen stood before them, saddened, grieving, proud and beautiful, "My loss is the Kingdom's loss and all of our hearts weep for the King."

The council bowed. The Queen and Pamela left the room. Both of them were sobbing as they boarded the hover platform.

The world wept with the Queen as haunting images of her and Prince Edward, Princess Alexis and Prince George filled television screens all over the world. In Argentina, Isabella prayed into the wee hours for God to ease the burdens of her beloved queen and mentor.

It was February, 14, 2098. Caitlin had gone to Lake Louise without the children to mourn her loss. It was no comfort to her that she was absolute ruler of the largest kingdom and empire ever ruled by anybody. For some reason God had chosen her for this unpleasant task. Thirteen years ago she had been here with Henry and she was drawn to this place of such sweet memories. Tonight she felt his presence.

She had been very busy since the funeral. Walter had begged her to allow him to retire. He was eighty-one and he had served three kings.

"I love you most of all, Your Majesty," he said tearfully, "But I am old and tired. Please let me rest."

Walter and the council recommended Lord Blake as his replacement. Everybody had assumed for years he would replace Walter one day. Blake was eminently qualified but Caitlin held back. He was a little too overtly ambitious and too perfect. Besides, she had to protect Edward's interests. She appointed Pamela to be her chief-of-staff and as compensation, made Lord Blake Foreign Minister. Blake was disappointed but he was too professional to let it show, even to his wife. Princess Elizabeth was livid. Lord Matthew Jones was named High Governor of Argentina which made Walter and Debbie happy. Emma stayed on as her aide. Caitlin was now Empress of Eastern Russia.

Caitlin dined alone by candlelight on Valentine's night. She had a place set as if Henry would dine with her. She was in the dome room at midnight when she dismissed Kathy for the evening. After pacing around the room, she lay on the couch and wrapped herself in the fur robe. As she lay there looking at the sky, the northern lights flared in a spectacular display and to the east, a meteor shower appeared. She sat up and for a brief instant she saw Henry outlined by the window, looking over his shoulder at her like he did the night when he ordered her to join him and she had refused.

The End

346

Appendix One

The Clark Dynasty

William Clark m. Dorothy Campbell
William d. 2008 Dorothy d. 2012

Children
Elizabeth B. Clark (Married James Powell)
William M. Clark, Jr, (Married Diane Forsyth)
Graham C. Clark (Married Rachel Hunt)

Robert Atkinson and Jane Hunt

Children
Rachel Hunt

Graham Clark, First Lady: Rachel
NC Governor - 2020-2032
SC Governor – 2024-2032
GA Governor – 2028-2032
Graham d. 2032 Rachel d. 2040

Children
Graham Clark,Jr (Married Donna Johnson)
Thomas Clark
Melissa Clark (Married Timothy Clayton)
George Clark (Married Alexis Cole)

William Clark, Jr, First Lady: Diane
NC Governor - 2032-2040
SC Governor - 2032-2040
GA Governor – 2032-2040
VA Governor- 2034-2040
TN Governor – 2036-2040
KY Governor – 2036-2040
William d. 2040 Diane d. 2036

Children
Alexander Clark (Married Celeste Oppenheimer)
Stephanie Clark (Married Mark Hatcher)

Alexander Clark, First Lady: Celeste
NC Governor - 2040-2048
SC Governor - 2040-2048
GA Governor – 2040-2048
TN Governor – 2040-2048
KY Governor – 2040-2048
OH Governor – 2044-2048
IN Governor – 2044-2048
MI Governor – 2044-2048
IL Governor – 2044-2048
TX Governor – 2044-2048
AL Governor – 2044-2048
MS Governor – 2044-2048

Separated from the United States and Declared Kingdom of America
Alexander crowned King
NC, SC, GA, TN, KY, OH, IN, MI, IL, TX, AL MS
January 1, 2049
HM Government moved to Nashville, Tennessee in July 2049

HM King Alexander I
HM Queen Celeste
Western PA admitted 2051
Maine admitted 2051
Vermont admitted 2052
Algeria annexed in 2054
OK, LA, AR, MO, IA, MI, MS, KS, NE, SD, ND admitted in 2055
NM, AZ, UT, CO, WY, MT admitted 2057
UT admitted 2058
OR admitted 2059
Venezuela annexed 2060
Panama annexed 2061
Mexico admitted 2065
King Alexander abdicates in favor of George Clark January 1,
2066
Alexander died in 2072
Celeste died in 2074

George crowned King George I
January 1, 2066
Alexis crowned Queen

348

HRM George I, King of America and Mexico. Emperor of Algeria Panama and Venezuela.
HRM Queen Alexis
Royal Government moves to Kansas City in 2068.
New Hampshire admitted 2068
George I died in accident 2072
Eulogized as "George the Great"
Alexis died in 2080

Children
Prince Edward (Married to Princess Virginia Dare Harris)
Princess Grace (Married to Sir Richard Custis)
Prince John

Edward crowned King Edward I and
Virginia crowned Queen 2072

HRM Edward I, King of America and Mexico. Emperor of Algeria, Panama, and Venezuela.
HRM Queen Virginia
Alaska admitted 2072
British Columbia admitted 2073
New Zealand admitted 2075
Saskatchewan admitted 2075
Ontario, Newfoundland, New Brunswick and Yukon admitted 2078
South Africa annexed 2077
Saudi Arabia annexed 2080

Children
Princess Elizabeth
Prince Henry (Designated heir to the King)
Princess Rachel
Prince William

Henry crowned King Henry I
2084CE

HRM Henry I, King of America, Canada, Mexico and New Zealand. Emperor of Algeria, Panama, Saudi Arabia, South Africa, Venezuela.

Appendix Two

Admissions and Annexations

Admissions to the Group of States
1) North Carolina- 2021
2) South Carolina- 2024
3) Georgia- 2028
4) Virginia- 2034
5) Tennessee- 2036
6) Kentucky- 2036
7) Ohio- 2044
8) Indiana- 2044
9) Illinois- 2044
10) Michigan- 2044
11) Texas- 2044
12) Alabama- 2044
13) Mississippi- 2044

Kingdom Declared- 2049

14) Pennsylvania- 2051 (Western 2/3rds)
15) Maine- 2051
16) Vermont- 2052
17) Oklahoma- 2054
18) Louisiana- 2054
19) Arkansas- 2054
20) Missouri- 2054
21) Iowa- 2054
22) Kansas- 2054
23) Nebraska- 2055
24) South Dakota- 2055
25) North Dakota- 2055
26) New Mexico- 2057
27) Arizona- 2057
28) Utah- 2057
29) Colorado- 2057
30) Wyoming- 2057
31) Montana- 2057
32) Idaho- 2057
33) Mexico- 2065
34) Oregon- 2065
35) New Hampshire- 2068

36) Alaska- 2072
37) British Columbia- 2073
38) New Zealand- 2075
39) Saskatchewan- 2075
40) Northwest Territories- 2075
41) Alberta- 2076
42) Manitoba- 2076
43) Ontario- 2078
44) New Brunswick- 2078
45) Newfoundland- 2078
46) Yukon- 2078

Annexations into the Empire

1) Algeria- 2054
2) Venezuela- 2060
3) Panama- 2061
4) South Africa- 2077
5) Saudi Arabia- 2080
6) Namibia- 2084

Appendix Three

List of Characters

1. Alston, Sir Will N: General of the occupation forces over Washington, DC.
2. Anderson, Gerry: NBC talk show hostess, moderator on Caitlin's meet the press appearance.
3. Archer, Sir John: Jonathan Forbes' lawyer.
4. Archer, Lady Ellen: John's wife, Katherine Forbes' friend.
5. Atkins, Lord Jerome: Colonel Royal Army Civil Government Unit, advisor to Mayor Carver.
6. Blake, Lord James: Princess Elizabeth's husband, ambassador to Argentina.
7. Blake, Lady Virginia: "Ginger." daughter of Lord Blake and Princess Elizabeth.
8. Blankenship, Lady Wilma: Palace servant.
9. Butts, Rebecca: Duchess of Dallas, Henry's personal servant.
10. Cardenas, Lord Jorge: High Governor of Mexico.
11. Cardenas, Lady Christina: Wife of Jorge.
12. Carpenter, Roosevelt: US Mayor of Washington, DC.
13. Carver, Arthur: Appointed Mayor of Washington, DC by HM government
14. Chin, Lady Tia: Caitlin's wardrobe manager and dressmaker.
15. Clark, Alexander: Succeeded his father, William, becomes the first King.
16. Clark, Alexis: George's Queen.
17. Clark, Celeste: Alexander's wife and the first Queen.
18. Clark, Diane Forsyth: William's wife, Alexander's mother. Posthumously named Queen Mother by her nephew, King George.
19. Clark, Edward: Third King of America.
20. Clark, Prince Edward Alexander: Son of Henry and Caitlin
21. Clark, Princess Elizabeth: Edward's oldest daughter, Henry's sister, married to Lord Blake
22. Clark, Graham: Credited with initiating the changes which resulted in the monarchy.
23. Clark, Henry: Fourth King of America.
24. Clark, Rachel Hunt: Graham's wife. Posthumously named the first Queen Mother by her grandson, King Edward.
25. Clark, Princess Rachel: Edward's youngest daughter, Henry's younger sister.
26. Clark, William: Succeeded Graham after his death.

27. Clark, Prince William: Henry's younger brother.
28. Clark, Virginia: Edward's Queen, Henry's mother.
29. Clayton, Sir Stephen: Reporter for the *Baltimore Sun*.
30. Cole, Alexis: George I's wife and Queen.
31. Cox, James: Former U.S. high school principal who was in Jonathan's labor battalion.
32. Churchill, Lady Ashley York: Caitlin's sister.
33. Churchill, Sir Brent: Ashley's husband.
34. Creamer, Shonie: U.S. hijacker.
35. Crowell, Samuel: Editorialist for the *New York Times*.
36. Dickens, Lord Roger: Caitlin's secretary in the Pratt Street office.
37. Fitzgerald, Lady Abigail: President of the Baltimore Woman's Club.
38. Forbes, Jonathan: Former U.S. citizen who refused aristocratic status.
39. Forbes, Lady Katherine: Jonathan's wife.
40. Forbes, Matthew: Jonathan & Katherine's oldest son.
41. Forbes, Robert: Jonathan & Katherine's youngest son.
42. Forsyth, Diane: Maiden name of William's wife. First woman named Queen Mother.
43. Gates, General Horatio: Commanding General of the Maryland/Delaware occupation army.
44. Gibbs, Lady Amelia: Joseph's wife and the Duchess of Canberra.
45. Gibbs, Lord Joseph: High Governor of Australia and Duke of Canberra.
46. Gillespie, Lord Carl: Henry's aide.
47. Gonzales, Lord Hector: Appointed Lord by Henry, Commander-in-Chief of the Argentine military services.
48. Grant, Hugh B: Commanding General of the United States forces in 2084.
49. Griffin, Melanie: Reporter for the *Boston Globe.*
50. Hamilton. Lady Emma: Caitlin's aide.
51. Hamilton, Lord Stewart: Governor of Delaware. Emma's husband.
52. Harris, Queen Virginia Dare: Married Edward I, Henry's mother.
53. Hastings, General Pamela: Royal Air Force General and friend of Caitlin.
54. Hastings, Lord Zachary: Pamela's husband.
55. Hunt, Rachel: Maiden name of Graham's wife.
56. Hyde, Walter: Council member of Washington DC.

57. Ibrahim, Abdullah: President of Egypt
58. Jackson, Andrew: United States president who originated the attack on America in 2084.
59. Jackson, Lord Thomas J, ACOV: Duke of Atlanta, Commander of the American forces in 2084.
60. Johnson, Thomas: Former U.S. Judge who was in the labor battalion with Jonathan.
61. Johnson. Paul: Editor of the *Atlantic Monthly*.
62. Jones, Sir Matthew: Lord Walter's grandson.
63. Jones, Lord Walter: Earl of the Empire, Henry's chief-of-staff.
64. Kibir, Fawz:. Religious fanatic from Egypt.
65. Lee, Lady Elizabeth Ann: Society page editor for the *Richmond Times Dispatch*.
66. Le Penn, Lady Chrysie: Caitlin's cosmetologist.
67. Lewis, Lady Eleanor: Caitlin's friend.
68. Marisa, Isabella: Young Argentine child befriended by Caitlin.
69. McIntosh, Lady Deborah: Caitlin's best friend.
70. Morris, Lord Charles: High Governor of New Zealand.
71. Morris Lady Gwendolyn: Wife of the governor of New Zealand.
72. Morris, Sir Garrett: Oldest son of the governor of New Zealand.
73. O'Donnell, Lady Kathryn: Duchess of Memphis, Caitlin's personal servant.
74. Oppenhiemer, Celeste: Alexander's wife and the first Queen.
75. Parker, Sir Reginald, ACOV: Member of the Royal Guards Unit, becomes Caitlin's personal bodyguard.
76. Pickett, Lord Jeffery: Royal Governor of Virginia.
77. Pickett, Lady Denise: Wife of Jeffery, Duchess of Shenandoah.
78. Reid: Laborer who befriended Jonathan Forbes.
79. Rockefeller, Norman IV: Head of the U.S. State Department.
80. Rogers, Sir Lance: Caitlin's hairdresser
81. Salama, Sabri: Fawzi's cousin in Baltimore.
82. Short, Lord Edward: Henry's appointment secretary.
83. Simpson, Will: Former Baltimore police detective who was in Jonathan's labor battalion.
84. Speck, Arnold: Reporter for the *Philadelphia Inquirer*.
85. Spruill, David: Supervisor of the labor company where Jonathan Forbes was assigned.
86. Townsend, Lady Roslyn: Baltimore Channel 6 news anchor.
87. Tucker, Lord Guy: Governor of South Carolina.

88. Tucker, Lady Amanda: Lord Guy's wife, Duchess of Charleston.
89. Walker, Sylvester (Slim): Henry's cowboy friend.
90. Wallace, Sir George: Commander of the commando unit that killed the hijackers.
91. Walsh, Alma: Ted's wife and Slim's cook and housekeeper.
92. Walsh, Ted: Slim's caretaker.
93. Watson, Lady Madeline: Owner of Towson Realty, Caitlin's boss.
94. White, Father Jacob: Priest assigned as advisor to the Forbes family.
95. Whitehead, Pamela: Columnist for the *New York Times*.
96. Whitford, Lady Constance: Thomas' wife, Duchess of Baltimore.
97. Whitford, Lord Thomas: Royal Governor of Maryland.
98. Windsor, William: King of England.
99. Windsor, Anne: Queen of England.
100. Whittemeyer, Jason: Columnist for the *Baltimore Sun*.
101. York, Caitlin Rose: Henry's wife, Queen of America, Empress of the Empire.
102. York, Lady Francis: Caitlin's mother, Duchess of Cumberland.
103. York, Lord Richard: Caitlin's father, Duke of Cumberland.

The Author in his living room with his favorite books.

E. B. Alston is a retired executive. This is his fourth book to be published. He lives with his wife, Barbara, in Timberlake, North Carolina.

LaVergne, TN USA
03 January 2009
168769LV00007B/5/A